Savant
Prison Breaker
Book 1

Joseph Daniel

Text Copyright © 2022 Joseph Daniel

Publisher: Greenfield Press Ltd

The rights of Joseph Daniel to be identified as author of the Work has been asserted in accordance with the Copyright, Designs and Patents Act 1988

All rights reserved.

The book is copyright material and must not be copied, reproduced, transferred, distributed, leased, licensed or publicly performed or used in any way except as specifically permitted in writing by the publishers, as allowed under the terms and conditions under which it was purchased or as strictly permitted by applicable copyright law. Any unauthorised distribution or use of this text may be a direct infringement of the author's and publisher's rights and those responsible may be liable in law accordingly.

'Savant' is a work of fiction. Names, characters, businesses, organisations, places, events, and incidents either are the product of the author's imagination or are used fictitiously. Any resemblance to actual persons, living or dead, and events or locations is entirely coincidental.

To Y,
If anyone enjoys this story, I hope it's you.

Table of Contents

Chapter 1
Chapter 2
Chapter 3
Chapter 4
Chapter 5
Chapter 6
Chapter 7
Chapter 8
Chapter 9
Chapter 10
Chapter 11
Chapter 12
Chapter 13
Chapter 14
Chapter 15
Chapter 16
Chapter 17
Chapter 18
Chapter 19
Chapter 20
Chapter 21
Chapter 22
Chapter 23
Chapter 24
Chapter 25
Chapter 26
Chapter 27
Chapter 28
Chapter 29
Chapter 30
Chapter 31
Chapter 32
Chapter 33
Chapter 34
Chapter 35
Chapter 36
Chapter 37
Chapter 38
Chapter 39
Chapter 40
Chapter 41
Chapter 42
Chapter 43
Chapter 44

Chapter 45
Chapter 46
Chapter 47
Chapter 48
Chapter 49
Chapter 50
Chapter 51
Chapter 52
Chapter 53
Chapter 54
Chapter 55
Chapter 56
Chapter 57
The story continues with Book 2 – available now!
Other books by Joseph Daniel

Chapter 1

Two types of people know what I am: those who want to hire me and those who want to kill me. I was still determining the category of my newest customer.

I peered unblinking at where he stood in the doorway of my Class C, decade-old RV. My favorite newsboy cap angled low over my face, casting my eyes in shadow where I stood straight-backed in my velvet, Italian cut with notched lapels.

"Good morning," I said. "But no, thank you."

My new potential client hesitated, then spoke with a cautious English accent. "I drove two hours through the mountains to reach you." He glanced over his shoulder at the others queued outside my door, then back at me with a knowing tip of his head. "You can't say no until you hear what I have to tell you." He reached back and shut the door with a *click*. My eyes narrowed at the presumption.

My would-be customer was a clean-cut fellow with glasses and silver sideburns that always accompany the word "distinguished." Not the sort you'd expect to find in a fortune teller's studio, but all sorts are interested in the arcane and the archaic. He wore a tie and seamlessly stitched vicuna wool suit.

Now, though, alarm bells jangled in my head. The only people who dressed that well in a quaint little mountain village were divorce attorneys on lunch break or the sorts of people 'in the know' and trying to make an impression. And in these mountains, an impression came costly.

My RV window displayed a mountain pass cradling a lake in the Wenatchee forest preserve of Washington state. The two-million-acre preservation covered a greater space than Chicago, Los Angeles, New York City and Washington D.C. *Combined*. It served as the most recent stop for my employer—the Amazin' Bandini's Traveling Circus. Through the thin walls of the RV drifted the blare and buzz of circus barkers and milling patrons, accompanied by the scent of reheated caramel, salted dough, and matted animal fur laced with sweat.

I studied him a moment longer. "Remove your shoes. Then you may enter."

The man looked perplexed. But with cautious movements, he bent over, undid his suede penny loafers and set them next to the door. He straightened, clearing his throat expectantly.

I still felt a twinge of unease but then puffed a breath. I wasn't exactly in the financial position to turn away potential customers of *either* variety. Besides, thank heavens, he was actually *clean*—I could almost detect the hint of soap.

I beckoned him over, and we both settled at the circular table in my RV, all sidelong glances and rutted brows, like a couple of snuffling hounds interpreting the unspoken language of scent molecules and pheromones. I faced the window, which, like the rest of my mobile home, displayed the sort of cleanliness found only in the strictest of boot camps or prisons. My only friend, Preacher, suggests I have a phobia where dirt and germs are concerned, but I'd like to think I simply have a higher standard for hygiene than most. I guess it's like they say: you never quite leave your past behind you.

"Not exactly what I expected," said Sideburns, eyeing the place.

I began to shrug, but caught myself. An uncouth gesture; I supposed Preacher was rubbing off on me. Instead, I dipped my head slowly, and then settled straight-backed once more, folding my hands. "I get that a lot."

He looked at me. "You're not what I expected either."

"Oh?"

"Mhmm. You're the palm reader, then?"

"The sign says fortune teller."

"Ah, well, I didn't see the sign. Your bodyguard was blocking it. Scary looking gent, isn't he?"

I didn't like speaking ill of my friends, but I also knew better than to engage in needless correction. So I deflected, "Preacher is definitely a sight."

"His name's Preacher? Charming." He eyed me again and clicked his tongue. "As for you, I was picturing someone... a bit more imposing."

I examined him but didn't reply immediately.

It was the birthright of ex-royals to overlook an insult, which I chose to in that moment. I'm not midget short, but I wouldn't be playing center for any recreational teams either. I'm about 5'8 and built like a gymnast with steely muscles built for rapid and acrobatic motion. When I'm not wearing a disguise for a job, I've been told in the right light I look like an old school Italian gangster. Except for my eyes, which were a rare blue, like starlight suspended in winter frost, flecked with the telltale indigo of an eternity-toucher. My beard was prominent, as intended. It covered most the scars on my face and helped to disguise my features from the few who might recognize me. Though, the skeletal talisman hidden inside my shirt was telltale enough if anyone got too close. Removing the pendant wasn't an option.

I stroked said beard then murmured, "I don't appreciate your comments. You're overdressed and undermannered. What is it you want?"

Sideburns' eyes and nostrils flared as if oscillating between surprise and offense. He cleared his throat. "That's forthright of you. I appreciate honesty."

"No, you do not. You want something from me, so you're pretending not to be upset, but there is a line outside and you're wasting my time. What do you want?"

This time Sideburns' eyes narrowed. Most people aren't used to unapologetic honesty, but I can't afford the socially acceptable, everyday deceptions others participate in. My abilities, as they were, rely *heavily* on an uncluttered mind. I've found over the years that lying of any variety (which includes flattery, direct omission and half-truths) muddies the mind. In my father's courts, only those with my talent were ever able to slip by with such blunt conversation. Though we often had to work twice as hard to make up for it in other areas.

"Well, then," Sideburns said, flustered. "I mean to say..." He trailed off, examining me to see if I was serious.

I just watched him back, allowing him to gather himself. My intention wasn't to dishonor; I don't like offending people, but that's sometimes the cost of clarity.

Sideburns cleared his throat formally, mustering the residue of his dignity, then said, "My employer wishes to hire you."

"I don't do house calls." I jerked a thumb towards a sign on the wall behind me. I caught myself again and closed my hand. Preacher's blunt motions really *were* rubbing off on me. "Sixty for fifteen minutes, thirty for five. I'll have to charge you for the full quarter-hour if we don't hurry this along."

Sideburns shook his head primly. "I'm not talking about this," he spread his hands and a sneer crept into his voice as he mulled over his word choice, likely skirting past options like *charade* or *fool's errand*, but then he glanced at me and settled on, "er, sideshow. My employer wishes to hire you for a masterpiece."

He carried the terminology of the knowing. But the way he said it, with a tilt of his eyebrows, like some harlequin detective revealing a key piece of evidence far too dramatically, told me Sideburns was either new to the game or a small player. Given his reference to "his employer," I wouldn't have been surprised if both were true.

"I don't know if I'd call them masterpieces." I didn't fidget, nor did I blink. My hands rested still as ice on the wooden table. A deflection—not quite a lie, but close enough to put me on guard. I'd have to be careful here. "But our caricature artist is two tents past the caramel apple stand."

My customer's nose twitched as he adjusted his round-framed glasses. "I heard you never turned down a job."

"I don't know you."

"My employer is highly, ah, *motivated*. They're willing to pay twice your normal rate."

This caught my attention. "My normal rate is high."

"Like I said, they're motivated. You'd be doing it for double."

I steepled my fingers beneath my bearded chin, watching Sideburns. "Take off your sunglasses."

"Ah—" Sideburns hesitated. "You're not getting off on this are you?"

I glanced towards his penny loafers by the door and suppressed a smirk at the unbecoming humor. "No; glasses off, too."

"My employer mentioned I ought to keep them on."

"Did your employer say *why*?"

"No—sh—er, they just said to keep them on."

He'd been about to say "she." I filed the information away under "further use."

"I won't conduct business unless I can look someone in the eye." I didn't *need* eye contact to get what I wanted, but it made things much easier and harder to detect.

Sideburns made no move to comply.

"Return to your employer, then." I gestured dismissively at the door. "Tell them I'm not interested. That will be thirty dollars."

"Wait—no, here." He took them off, revealing dull gray eyes. His gaze flicked towards the crucifix on the wall behind me. It was the one ornament on Preacher's side of the RV. My friend's half of the mobile home looked like a Jackson Pollock painting, but I'd learned to live with the discarded clothing and empty food wrappers as long as it didn't encroach on my half, despite every instinct in me screaming for orderliness.

"Are you a praying man?" he said, sounding mildly surprised.

"Not as much as I could be. Cross isn't mine. That a problem?" I cleared my throat, frowning. "Pardon. I mean to say *the* cross isn't mine. *Is* that a problem?" No excuse for truncating sentences like some agent of chaos.

His lips curled, twisting up one side and curving down on the other in a grotesque sort of half smile. "No problem. Just figured... a savant like yourself, well..." He glanced back towards the crucifix. "Didn't think you'd be the sort is all. Do you really... *believe* it? Like resurrecting bodies. War in heaven? Celestial assassinations on earth?" He winced and gave a sort of disarming smile, as if to say, *"come on, you can tell me the truth."*

I suppressed a frown, but then felt this was too close to dishonesty and allowed it to curdle my lips. I'd personally tasted of the wars in the second heaven—they were no laughing matter. Watching a legion of the angels of death descend in chariots of lighting on the giant, golden dominions of the fallen host was enough to bring even the most courageous man to his knees.

Clearing my throat, I studied my customer for a moment, and then reached out.

I was starting to suspect Sideburns didn't know *everything* I was. Someone had told him I was a savant, but by the way he was acting, and confirmed by removing his glasses, I was nearly certain he didn't know I was also an eternal talent.

There are six eternal talents, found hidden throughout the bloodlines of some few, traceable back before the first penned letter in a history tome.

The talents have always existed. Some suggest they were created by the offspring of angels and men. Others say they were gifts from the gods to their champions, using humans as proxies in their unceasing wars. Others whisper of an age-old barter from the dryad queen of the Hidden Kingdoms or the genie lords of old.

Others simply embrace the mystery. The eternal talents are, have been, and will be.

That's enough as far as I'm concerned.

There was a time when the world respected the arcane, but then TV shows and movies came along with their superheroes and teen witches. The painful arts became a facade. Then again, those in the know prefer it that way. We'd rather the rest of the world—the rest of *you*—go through your lives sneering at the eternals as fairy tales and wishful thinking. We're a private folk.

Also, what you don't know, you can't defeat.

Regardless, mine was one of the rarer, more peculiar talents. Those in the know call it "the Wit." I kept my gaze fixed on Sideburns' and, gently as a wafting breeze across meadow lilies, I extended my consciousness towards his.

Our minds touched, but he didn't withdraw. His expression stayed the same: quizzical, with undertones of scorn and discomfit.

He wasn't trained, then.

Reading someone's *mind*—not brain—isn't at all like reading a book. Were I to play a slideshow of the things I saw, it would resemble gibberish, or some Rorschach test. Decades of training has taught me the language, however, so in my mind what I saw was as clear as writing on a wall.

A kaleidoscope of images and thoughts and impressions and inaudible words inundated me, playing across my mind's eye like shadow puppets. I don't mean "mind's eye" in the way charlatans use it. Most people, even the unknowing, have access to it. One must simply close their eyes and look for pictures. The ancient Roman lawyer Cicero called it the *mentis oculi.* Modern scientists refer to it as *hypnagogic imagery*.

I prodded gently at Sideburns' mind, questioning it, directing it, like a shepherd herding his flock. If Sideburns had fallen into the hands of an Imperial mind talent, he would have been putty in their hands. They could have mined him for any skills or talents he'd developed over years. Some of the more powerful Wits could have taken control completely, inhabiting his body for a few days before dispensing of it like a snake shedding its skin.

I wasn't interested in anything so dramatic. I probed further, feeling the images as foggy shadows flit across my own consciousness—I asked another few questions, found the memories and thoughts I needed, then, just as I was about to withdraw, I spotted something...

The rest of his mind lay open to my pillaging, but this one small portion was guarded as if by an Imperial talent themselves. After another few failed attempts to access the guarded memory cluster, I withdrew my reach, my frown deepening. Whoever had sent him here knew *what* I was and had gone to great lengths to conceal their own identity.

The hairs stood to attention on the back of my neck, and I felt like a deer in a hunter's sights right before the gunshot. Even in that moment, I felt a slow, chilling certainty that some unseen finger was tightening on a trigger.

Chapter 2

The mind-reading took less than a minute.

"Well?" said Sideburns, still staring at me with an expression of confusion. "My sunglasses are off. We're looking eye to eye—do we have a deal or were you just looking for a more intimate moment? Because if that's what you're interested in, I have to say, I'm happily married and—"

"No you're not, Dale." I leaned in, tipping the brim of my newsboy cap to get a better look. Dale instinctively leaned away. "You were married, six years ago," I said, tapping the table in rhythm. "But that ended poorly. I'm surprised you'd leave Emily. She seemed a great woman."

Sideburns a.k.a. Dale gaped. "My name's not—," he began weakly, but I cut him off, still leaning closer than manners might dictate. This, of course, was entirely intentional. I am no stranger to physical etiquette, but I needed Dale off his game.

"It is, Dale. You go by Antonio with your employers—you think it sounds more impressive. I quite like Dale, though. Dale Rodrick, born in Charlton, England, 1970. Parents: Ed and Cheryl. They never knew, by the way."

Sideburns a.k.a Dale Rodrick a.k.a Antonio Banerune looked like he'd not only seen a ghost but like he'd been given a big ghostly hug. Even the hair on his arms stood on end. "I don't—I don't understand—"

Either Dale Rodrick was the best actor I'd ever met, or he really didn't know what had just happened. Which meant whoever had safeguarded his memories had done so without his knowledge. His employer—must have been. Intriguing and more than a little worrying.

Dale stared incredulously, and I gave an absentminded wave and leaned back, the chair creaking with the motion. "They never knew you were the one who killed the cat. You were only ten, correct? I know it was an accident, but I quite like cats." I brushed a long strand of fur—*far* too long to have come from any house cat—off my sleeve absentmindedly. "I would have been displeased if you'd done it on purpose. Though, even at ten, you should have known better, shouldn't you have? I know it scratched you, but locking it in that cupboard with no air..." I shook my head sadly, "Schrodinger would have been disappointed."

"How are you—who have you been talking to?" Dale said. His face reddened and both his fists clenched. Contrary to popular belief, clenched fists aren't always an aggressive tell, rather they're often defensive; it's the enclosing of fingers over the vulnerable palm. Kind of like hugging your body or crossing your arms.

"No one," I said simply.

He pried one pointer finger from his fist to jab it trembling at me. "No one knows that—*no one*—how could you—Who are you?"

"I call myself Leonidas Rex," I said, without the usual apologetic inflection I give when introducing my name.

"You may call me Leon. I tell you all that so you know I'm no imposter. If you lie to me, I'll know."

This was completely true.

"So, tell me. Who is your employer, and what *exactly and precisely* do they want?"

Dale hesitated, finger still hovering. In his frightened state, his subconscious struggled to make sense of the flow of conversation. I had answered his question by giving my name; now social cues prompted him to answer mine. Of course, I'd glossed over the unspoken and stuttered queries entirely, but years of conversational conditioning are hard to undo.

Dale slowly lowered his finger and took his turn. "I—I can't tell you my employer's name."

"Why not?"

"Because—sh—they don't want me to."

"I know it's a she. Just say she. Why doesn't *she* want you to? I don't work with people who don't trust me."

Dale shook his head, mouth agape.

At first, I thought he was still reeling, but when I extended my consciousness for his surface level emotions, I found a surprising amount of calm. Dale was a more resilient bloke than I'd given him credit for. But I also found not dutifulness but forgetfulness. He didn't know his master's name. Had he at one point, and then had it been locked away? Perhaps the guarded memory cluster I'd failed to enter. I could have broken in, given enough effort, but I didn't want to risk injuring Dale—so far all he stood guilty of was lackluster manners.

"Alright then, what does she want?" I asked.

"I never said it was—"

"It's a she."

"But you—"

"Yes, I can possibly know."

"Stop—"

"Saying what you're thinking before you say it."

"Purple elephants!" we both shouted in unison.

Now that some of the initial shock had worn off, Dale was watching me like a caveman glimpsing fire for the first time. "You're really a fortune teller? Incredible."

"I'm not a prophet," I said. "I don't see the future. But tell me, what does your employer *want?* Surely, you at least know that, or are you here to waste my time?"

I put iron behind those last words and also reached out and pushed on Dale's fear receptors, doubling the intimidation effect.

Immediately, he cringed in his seat and clenched his fists tighter again—whitening the knuckles—and declared, "I do! Yes—of course I do; I'm not trying to waste anyone's time."

"What is it?" I said.

"She wants you to break someone out of prison."

I sighed, folding my hands. "Ah," I said. "So, you do *know*."

He jutted his chin, half defiant, half relieved to have at least this small concession. "Yes," he declared. "I told you. I'm here for a masterpiece."

I studied him with a frown, considering his words. It wasn't like I couldn't use the money. He'd promised double. Besides, by now I was more than a little intrigued. "Ah, but masterpiece doesn't really mean *masterpiece*, does it, Dale?"

Dale gulped, tensed in the posture of a man on the verge of motion. "No... Of course it doesn't. You're an escape *artist*. A prison breaker. A savant."

I exhaled. "And what do you know of savants?"

"It's not relevant. My employer wishes—"

"I wasn't asking about your employer," I said, some of my rough facade crumbling. I could tell I had him frightened, which hadn't been my intent. Gently, I murmured, "What do you know, Dale?"

"I... I know you're good at what you do."

I spread my arms slowly, facing the window as if to hug the scenic vista beyond. "Did you know there are more than *two million* continuous acres of thick forests, subterranean caves and treacherous mountain passes in Washington State alone?"

"I—what?"

"The prisons of our war. The wars of the knowing... Your employer must have told you of this, no?" I felt a jolt of sympathy and leaned across. "Dale... I realize you might have been brought into *some* of our world. But understand: this isn't a safe place, not for the likes of you. You had best simply leave. Leave your employer. Leave this place."

Now, though, it seemed as if I'd offended him. "Pshaw! I'm a part of this world!"

I shook my head gently. "For the last five years, yes? After a particularly interesting series of visits to an old haunt in the mountains. You stumbled upon *some* of the truth. I don't know how you met your employer—that part is guarded from me. But this is all new to you, Dale. You can't even tell me the source of these wretched prisons. Can you?"

Dale squeaked, but glanced off to the side, muttering darkly, but confirming my words with eventual silence. Most of humanity lived blissfully ignorant of the things that go bump in the night. Our wars, our empires were fought and built in the hidden places—the distant forests and mountains and deserts, untouched and unnoticed by mortalkind. Most folk contentedly go about their 9 to 5, come home, observe a game on TV, or consume some Netflix, then retire for the evening. The worlds of the knowing and the unknowing live parallel, but rarely collide.

When the worlds do meet, mortalkind's skepticism and blunt disbelief always covers the gaps of secrecy. Area-51 was the single greatest failure on the part of my kind to keep things hidden, safe. But even then, mortalkind's government officials—those very, very few who knew *anything*—helped to hide what actually transpired.

Most of humanity enjoys being lied to. As long as it keeps them safe.

And so the world of the knowing and the unknowing lives in a symbiotic relationship. Parallel, but not quite touching each other.

At least, not yet.

I leaned back again, folding my hands. "You're certain you want to know? To truly be part of this? It isn't safe. It isn't pretty."

Now, though, it was like offering a glass of brandy towards one with wavering sobriety. He swallowed and leaned forward, nodding, his eyes wide. "Tell me," he said. "I know parts and I know pieces. But… but I don't know everything. You really are a prison breaker, then? I've heard of the prisons. I've heard of—"

"Have you heard of the wars, though, Dale?" I spoke quietly at first, my voice low, careful, like wisps of fog curling over a moonlit forest floor. "These two million acres of thick forest give ample room for the hundreds… yes, *hundreds* of hidden, concealed, camouflaged and veiled prisons of war dotted throughout the region. Hidden in mountains, beneath lakes, amidst unassailable forests. Hidden from most the world, but not all. They're not the sorts of prisons you might imagine."

Dale let out a leaking sound. "What sort of prisons are they?"

"You really are new to this, then, aren't you?" I frowned even more deeply, put off by his seeming hunger at my words. Most the knowing, most of mortal kind were wise enough, shrewd enough to guard themselves from such thoughts, to refuse, refute, doubt and go their merry way.

Dale, though, seemed only more intrigued.

"Only some of the prisons are occupied by humans, Dale. Understand, this isn't a safe world. Nor is it a comforting one. For the last hundred years," I said, through gritted teeth, my tone rising as if in an effort to communicate the seriousness of my words, "sparked by the start of the American Revolutionary War, known by my great, great, et cetera... grandfather as the Colonist's Treachery, a bitter war has been waged in the secret places of the world; the knowing call it the Eternal Wars. The unknowing, like most my clientèle, and most of *you*, don't know anything about it."

"I'm *not* unknowing!"

"No? Can you tell me about the wars, then? Tell me how the war churns out both casualties *and* captives. The captives of the Eternal Wars are not your harmless, run of the mill serial killers you hear about from some blond damsel narrating a teleprompter on the evening news. The sorts of captives I'm speaking of are always of the magical variety with a dose of immortality often thrown in: eternal talents, sphinxes, stump trolls, famishes, angels, demons—you know the sorts."

Dale shuddered as if embraced by a ghost, a twisted sort of giddy delight crossing his countenance. He licked his lips like a parched man in desert heat. "The Accords of Preservation. What are those?"

I blinked. "Who told you of the Accords?"

"A friend. What *are* they, though?"

I glanced out the window again, my tone no longer pressing. Dale seemed decided in his direction. But perhaps... perhaps if he knew... *really knew,* he might change his mind, and his life might be spared. For the sake of a single life, my words were worth it. Dale didn't know what he'd stumbled on. "The Accords of Preservation," I said slowly, "were signed by both the Imperium and the Endeavor at the start of the war—it created a deeply binding agreement to refrain from killing the prisoners on either side. Even still, the agreement is often ignored."

"So prisoners of war are taken to these places? And you break them out?"

I nodded a single time. "It isn't without reason. Already, the magical sorts have dwindled to near extinction in the world. Wars have a way of exacerbating this. The Imperium—a magistocracy—is all for maintaining the lives and the pure blood line of those touched with eternal talents—even the non-human variety, regardless of political affiliation. In their mind, a couple hundred years under lock and key will show the rebels the error of their allegiance and help assimilate them nicely back into the utopia they are creating. The Endeavor—the rebel faction—"

"I've heard of them!"

"Yes, well, they made their name on promise of a new rule—though they preach more than practice. Really, it was politics, pursuit of *power,* that brought both sides to the table to sign the accords. Wars continued and POWs abounded."

"That's where you come in?"

I shook my head. "Not yet. See, the capturing side has a heavy interest in keeping their prisoners out of the fight. The greatest magical inventors, the cruelest captors, the cleverest tacticians create the sorts of prisons that make Alcatraz look like a daycare. Do you understand? Only the most specialized prison breakers even stand a *chance* of entry. *That's* where I come in."

"Well..." Dale nodded, his eyes hooded, his features still. "My employer wishes to hire you."

"You should leave, Dale."

"I won't."

I sighed, wondering if I should say more, but he seemed decided. At least I'd tried... His fate was his own then.

Still, Dale's choices aside, the job intrigued me. "Which prison?"

Dale hesitated, and for a moment I thought that piece of information was also locked away. I hadn't spotted it when I'd looked. But then, as if the question itself unlocked the memory, Dale's eyes brightened and he said. "She wants you to break someone out of the Hollow. It's a prison for—"

But Dale was no longer speaking.

He was still trying, but the words wouldn't come on account of my fingers wrapped around his windpipe.

Chapter 3

The moment Dale had named the prison "The Hollow," I'd leapt across the table and grabbed his throat. For the briefest moment, the *cold* took me. All the instincts honed in me over the course of my childhood, all the training—the breaking—told me to squeeze. My father's courtiers hadn't just taught table manners or ballroom dance—I'd learned other, *darker* things in those palatial halls.

Dale's windpipe pulsed beneath my thumb. Just a quick clench.

How dare he come in here and mention that place?

I half thought to kill him there, to execute him for such a—no, no... Not my thoughts, those were my father's thoughts—my family's thoughts... Not mine.

I loosened my grip with more effort than it had taken to clench.

Dale yanked his head back and tumbled over his chair, sending it, and himself, clattering to the pristine, polished, faux floorboards. I glanced sharply at the window across from us. In the reflection, I vaguely spotted the blue eyes of a child in the glass. I stiffened, my tongue stuck to the roof of my mouth. A blink. Then, the reflection of the child vanished.

"I'm sorry," I said immediately. And I meant it.

I placed my hand, which had gripped his throat, back on the table. Unlike Dale's, my hands were still as stone. I half glanced towards the window again, a frigid chill along my spine. But the image was gone; I felt a flutter of relief—just a trick of the light, had to be—and I returned my attention to my customer.

Dale looked up, caught between outrage and terror, more nostril and eye oscillating.

"Leave, please," I said coolly. "*Now.*"

Trembling, he approached the door and pulled on his discarded penny loafers. He glanced back at me, eyes wide. I pressed on his fight-or-flight impulse, but Dale stayed put. I frowned and pressed harder, but Dale didn't move.

"I said get out!" I shouted, failing to control my temper.

But Dale just stared at me vacantly, as in *truly* vacantly. That isn't a description of his emotional state, rather it was one regarding the location of his soul. Wherever it was, it had been temporarily put on time out. Whatever was staring out at me *now* wasn't Dale.

A new mind had entered my RV.

"So," said a feminine voice, emitting from Dale's mouth. "You won't take the job?"

I stared at Dale, then realized. His employer had taken control. I knew, almost instantly, she wasn't one of the Wit—the control was too weak. But there were rituals, artifacts and creatures that could create a similar effect, especially in willing subjects.

"Get out," I snarled, my chest rising and falling rapidly. It took an effort, but I caught myself, slowly forcing my emotions to quiet. It wasn't suiting to display histrionics before a stranger. Quieter, in an ominous tone, I said, "Don't think to impress me with your tricks. Leave before I make you."

Dale tilted his head, his eyes wide and bright, his lips twitching in a mischievous sort of smile. His employer didn't seem the least bit concerned by my soured mood.

Chipper now, the voice said, "It's why I came to you, Leon. I need the best and you're that, aren't you? That's what everyone says. *Everyone*," she prattled. "Oh Jeez Louise, you look so angry. It's going to be okay! I promise!" Then, to my awe, she skipped forward and gave me a quick hug, pressing Dale's cheek against mine. "It's going to be fine," she said, gently in my ear, patting me on the back. I tensed—I wasn't used to physical contact. She seemed to sense my discomfort and skipped away again, a look of hurt in her eyes. She studied me, sad. "It's going to be okay. Really. I promise. Look—don't hurt me. Listen first."

I stood stunned in the face of the cheerful prattling and the complete demolition of my personal boundaries, but I swallowed my pride and murmured, "I request you don't touch me again. And I won't hurt you. Not yet. But only if you leave. My answer is no."

"Hmm. Alriiiight," the voice said, stretching the vowel as if stalling. "But... but *why?*" There was something almost childish about the inquisitive tone. The voice had a soothing effect communicated in strangely jaunty notes, clashing with my dark mood, like the twittering of some sparrow in a graveyard. I checked to make sure it wasn't toying with my emotions, but my defenses and barriers were still in place, completely untouched.

I said, "You don't know what you're asking. You *can't* breech the Hollow."

"No—of course. That's why I need you!" I noted again how conspicuously devoid of *fear* the tone seemed. Normally, even the most stoic sorts spike with terror when placing their thoughts within the reach of an Imperially trained Wit. But *this* mind offered no amount of fear whatsoever. I frowned, checking again for the emotion, certain I'd missed it. Even my own fears often flared, though I could suppress or numb them because of my talent.

This mind, though, held no fear.

It almost seemed...

My frown deepened.

It almost seemed as if it *couldn't* feel fear.

I glared. "The Hollow is only accessible *once* per year. I suppose you know this."

The puppetting voice coming from Dale Rodrick continued. Still energetic, still gushing words, "Oh yah, for sure. I know. Once day every annum—that's what I was told. Annum. Such a funny word. But one day a year the Hollow can be found."

"And if you miss that single day's window of time..." I snapped my fingers. "Gone for another year. But it isn't just the Unlocator you have to worry about!"

"Unlocator? Huh—interesting."

She didn't seem at all perturbed by my warning. Of course, this made sense. She wasn't uninformed. I doubted it was a coincidence she'd come to speak with me about the Hollow exactly *three days* before it was accessible. Four days from now, though? She'd have to wait another year. No. She knew it was opening in three days. She'd chosen to approach me now on purpose. Who was this person?

I scowled. "Let me put it this way—you could send a million search parties throughout the Northwest, searching for the Hollow for the next three days. You wouldn't find a thing. No matter who you hired."

"Right. *Un*-locator. I get it—cute name." She reached out to pat me on the shoulder, but then seemed to think better of it and withdrew her hand.

"It can't be done."

"Well... what if we look for it at the end of the third day?" she said, glancing up at me with Dale's face.

She was informed. Even this information, the day on which the Hollow became locatable, would have cost her a fortune.

"In four days... perhaps," I said. "But only if you know where to look."

"And do you?"

I shook my head. "Only a confidant can tell you the exact location."

She shrugged as if this wasn't a big deal. "So who's the confidant?"

"I don't know." This was true.

"But can you find them?"

I sighed. "Yes. But they won't just *give* the information. That's the whole point. The Hollow isn't meant to be found or entered."

"So we just wait the three days," she said. "Find this confidant. Find the Hollow."

"You say it like it's so easy. Do you know who's kept prisoner there—not to mention who's *in charge?*"

"Mhmm, oh boy—I *know* the warden," said the voice eagerly. "I don't mean to get you swirling, but you—well, no real nice way to say it, so I'll say it." Dale bit his lip, tucking his tongue in his cheek in thought, his eyes still wide and bright. "Yeah," he nodded quickly, as if on some sort of sugar high. "Yeah, yeah. I'll just say it: you kinda messed up the last time you went, right? Hmm? Like, as in, you failed the job. Only one!" the voice added quickly as if to spare my pride. "It's the only job you failed. Isn't that right? You've been there before."

I was taken aback by the strange combination of good cheer, deadly circumstance, and fearless ease. Part of me admired the person behind the voice. In our world, to keep one's humor took a herculean feat.

"Yes, I failed and it cost me," I snapped. "The lieutenant of the saboteurs has taken residence in the Hollow, did you know that? February herself. Have you ever faced a saboteur—stood across from one of those wereblade wielding death machines, staring into those dead-eyed helmets? Not again. And not—not the Hollow..."

Dale's cheeks maintained the smile that hadn't been there when the true occupant had been in charge. "We'll see. I'm not done with you yet, Leon."

Then, Dale got up and wandered across the RV. The puppet-master opened the fridge in the small kitchen cubicle and began rummaging around.

I stared, dumbfounded.

She withdrew an apple, which she polished on Dale's sleeve.

I watched, unblinking.

She took a bite out of the apple, causing juice to slosh down Dale's chin, and she gave a shuddering sigh bordering on delight. "Can't eat those in my body," she said, in manner of explanation.

Then, she began rooting through one of my cupboards. The invasion of privacy, speaking with her mouth full, stealing my food—such things simply weren't done!

"Excuse me!" I snapped.

"Certainly," she replied. She pulled out a box of cereal, Preacher's favorite fruit puffs, and reached in, grabbing a handful and shoveling the fruity, sugary feast into her mouth.

I could feel my temper rising, but she seemed entirely unaware of my mounting anger. Some people pushed personal boundaries out of contempt or disrespect.

I sensed neither of these motives in her.

It was almost as if she didn't realize—whoever *she* was—that she was doing something socially untoward. In between bites of her apple and handfuls of cereal, she tried to speak, but spluttered food and crumbs onto my polished and vacuumed floor.

My eyes narrowed. She reclined against the cupboard and tipped the cereal box back, pouring its contents into her mouth.

"You know, Leon," she said, through a mouthful of food, chewing with her mouth open, "I could get used to this." Half the words came out mumbled, and half her mouthful tumbled down Dale's shirt and scattered across my floor.

She gestured with the cereal box to the air. "Living on the road, with no one for company but your silent gunman."

"Preacher's my *friend*," I said tersely. "Could you put that down? You're making a mess."

She blinked in surprise, but quickly lowered the cereal. "Oh, sorry. Just," she trailed off, staring at me now. "Once in a palace, surrounded by people, now on the road, living sooo *free*, is that right?"

I felt a cold prickle. "Who said anything about a palace?" I whispered.

She didn't seem to realize she'd touched a nerve. She gestured at me with Dale's sticky fingers. "It's not my place to say it, but I'll say it..." She bit her lip, but nodded. "Yeah, I'll say it: you can't hide forever, Leon."

"It's worked so far," I replied, tight-lipped.

"Has it?" she said, studying me. "Okay. If you say so." She giggled and spread her hands in front of her face as if framing a billboard. "Leonidas Rex, the lone ranger with a heart of cold iron. Beware all who draw near! Bound by none, bound *to* none." She smiled again and waggled a finger at me.

My irritation was mounting. I was done talking. I had told her—whoever she was—to leave. She hadn't. But in entering her employee's mind, she had also entered my domain.

I couldn't lie, however. I'd told her earlier, when she'd queried, that I wouldn't hurt her. I'd said "yet." To lie is to muddy the mind.

So I said, "I'm going to hurt you now."

Then I reached out, the full force of my mind bearing down—a tsunami of consciousness against a sandcastle of thought.

But even as I latched onto Dale's mind, hunting down the foreign, invading presence of his employer, I could feel her retreating. Cereal fell limply from Dale's hand and the apple dropped to the ground, rolling across the once-pristine floor, leaving a trail of juice.

She may have dabbled with the mind—but she knew better than to duel a Wit devoted to his eternal talent.

"I *really* hope you'll change your mind," she said, her words fuzzy and faded. Dale blinked now, regaining control. But his lips were still hostage. "I'm not going to betray you. This won't be like last time you went to the

Hollow."

"I don't believe you," I snarled. I sent fragments of my mind scouting through Dale's thoughts, like hounds with the scent of blood. I found a murky presence somewhere near his capacity for speech. I surged forward, seeking to snare it.

But the presence was quick—I had to give it that. Faster than I could reach it, the presence fled. Unable to resist a parting shot, Dale said, in slurred, disjointed speech. "Believe this: The Endeavor has found you. They're sneaking up on your RV as we speak. I—"

But whatever she'd wanted to say, she didn't manage before I'd completely chased her out.

Her presence vanished, her thoughts whisking away.

Her words, though, left their impact. I felt a prickle across my spine, and my eyes darted to the window, staring out into the small village.

The Endeavor had found me?

A trick. Had to be.

It was one thing for her to know my name... But to know my past? Many, many people carried the name "Leonidas Rex." It was an inside joke among those in my business. The *real* Leonidas—the son of Maximus and brother of Augustus was the heir, and emperor-to-be, of the Dwindling Imperium... He was wanted by both Imperium *and* Endeavor.

The Imperium wished to restore him to the throne, to rally around him and reclaim their lands. The Endeavor wished to assassinate him before he could.

The name itself was a joke among the fringes of the magical world. Leonidas Rex was little more than "John Doe," to us. It just so happened to also be the case, I was *actually* named that, and my father *had* been Maximus. To call Augustus a brother might have been a stretch, but that giant, psychotic pyromaniac and I did share blood. The Endeavor has in mind for me a coffin, the Imperium a crown. I don't want either.

I shivered before turning to my customer.

Dale sat on the floor, dazed, struggling to regain control of his thoughts. The strange, mischievous smile had vanished. I left his mind, careful not to break anything on exit. As I did, I pressed on his fear receptors, but this time muffling them, allowing Dale to relax.

Then, I hurried to the window and peered into the streets.

The Endeavor wasn't usually one for subtlety. Once upon a time they had been, but no longer. But I didn't see anything out of the ordinary. Well, I did see a bearded lady making eyes at the strongman, but nothing out of the ordinary for a carnival. Certainly no teams of arcane assassins sneaking up the streets.

I went to the other window and peered along the side of the caramel stand. Again, nothing unusual. My unsettlingly gregarious would-be employer had been trying to spook me; that was all. Then again, not only did she know I'd lived in a palace, she knew about the Endeavor's interest in me.

It was time to move on. One of the benefits of living in a home on wheels: moving is never a problem.

Before I could plot a course of action, though, I was interrupted from my thoughts by someone else's thoughts. Someone standing directly behind me.

I only knew one person capable of moving so quietly I sensed their mind before I heard their footsteps. And his presence heralded danger.

Chapter 4

I turned to find Preacher standing in the doorway, hunched so his giant girth could fit through, one of his six-shooters drawn, his cattleman crease hat, with its two red feathers, cutting an ominous silhouette.

My friend crossed his wrists over each other, holding fists, then spread his fingers. The sign for "safe." He raised an eyebrow beneath the shadowed brim of his hat, inflecting a question.

I shook my head. "His employer knows who I am," I said, making no effort to speak slowly. Preacher could hear just fine. He'd taken a vow of silence long before I'd met him; I still didn't know why, and I'd never heard him break it.

While Preacher wasn't technically my bodyguard, I'd never been able to tell him that. He was, perhaps, the single best shot with those revolvers of his I'd ever met.

Though, perhaps I risk dishonesty by exaggeration...

...no.

He is the best shot I've ever met, that includes the saboteurs. I've seen him single-handedly take down *two* eternal talents, both of them trained in the Element. But their blasts of lightning and jets of fire were an insufficient match for Preacher's trigger fingers.

Preacher frowned at Dale, and the gray-eyed messenger quailed beneath my friend's stare.

It was an intimidating stare. While I was on the shorter side and built like a gymnast—the ideal physique for sneaking into tight spaces—Preacher was built more like a sturdy brick wall. He was at least six-foot-nine and towered over nearly everyone. Even the herds of minotaur, when we passed through the hidden Kingdoms of Pilfery, gave Preacher his due respect based on physique alone. His shoulders were twice as broad as mine and his head was buzzed.

Also, he had cauliflower ears. Preacher had grown up fighting in backwoods boxing matches under his father's training. His lumpy ears and crooked nose were testament to his number of bouts. Preacher had darker skin and wore sloppily applied make up—it really was an art form to behold. Currently, his eyes peered out from rings of blue eyeshadow which did little to soften his fierce glare.

I suspect Preacher has his own reasons for wearing the makeup; he always applied it sloppily, as if done by a child's hand. On occasion, I'd walked in on him weeping as he did it, his tears streaking through the blush.

"Wh—what happened?" Dale said, glancing nervously from Preacher's imposing form to me.

"Your employer took your mind. I chased her out but not for your sake."

Dale stared as if expecting me to continue, rubbing apple flecks from his lips, but I'd said what I'd wanted to.

I glanced out the window again. Fewer people now milled in the streets. The carnival sounds seemed *less* somehow. Frowning, I glanced up at the sky. Storm clouds pulled over the horizon.

"Was it supposed to rain today?" I murmured.

A couple of critters moved on the ceiling, prompting a yelp from Dale. "What's that?" He started to panic again, scanning the ceiling and the walls now for the fuzzy, eight-legged critters who sat unnaturally still against the aluminum surface.

"Tarantulas," I said. "Better surveillance than cameras. Plus, built-in biters."

My mind reading wasn't limited to humans. Spider brains were so small I could maintain the connection at a very long distance. So, if I was out on a job, I could tap into the minds of the tarantulas in my RV; If they saw intruders, so would I.

Rain began drumming against the top of my RV now, and I heard the distant crash of thunder as the inside of my mobile home illuminated with a flare of lightning.

I frowned further. "I could have sworn we weren't expecting rain today." I turned sharply to Dale, my eyes hooded. "Did you tell anyone the name of that prison? Anyone besides me?"

Dale froze as if pinned to the floor. He swallowed a lump in his throat and shifted uncomfortably, shrugging with one shoulder. The image he was going for, sleek, professional, stylized all faded to a petulant jutting lip. "No," he said in a tone communicating something like, *I didn't steal the cookies.*

My spine tingled now, and I stared directly at Dale. "The Hollow," I said softly. "Is not a safe word to go tossing about like loose change. Who else did you tell, Dale?"

"No one!" More jutting lip. Crossed arms followed.

"The Endeavor is keeping a close eye on people who speak of that prison, Dale. They didn't set up an Unlocator and a confidant for nothing. Do you know why? Hmm?"

He just winced and glanced off, breaking eye contact now. I didn't have the patience to do this the slow way anymore. I didn't want to go rooting around though, so I went fishing with my next words.

"Dale, look at me. No, look. Whatever you do, *don't* think of anyone else you mentioned the Hollow to."

Dale blinked, and then he did the exact opposite. I spotted the memory suddenly surfacing, and I reached out, trapping it.

My own vision swam, shadows narrowed in and then took over my gaze. I watched a memory, wincing a second to pick up the noise as well, fishing it from Dale's auditory capacity.

A pretty brunette with a pierced ear... A waitress... Dale sitting at a small table in the Sleeping Dwarf Inn. He a room upstairs. He was back in the dining hall just to see the waitress again.

She sauntered over to his table, her nose-ring flashing in the dim fireplace. She smiled at him, leaning in and pressing her arms to accentuate her chest.

In the memory, Dale was spluttering. I could track his thought processes. Could track the way he looked for something, anything to say. He settled on, *"How's it going?"*

In the memory, the waitress just smirked, poured his water and begun to turn.

"You have nice eyes!" Dale called after her.

She paused by another empty table, placing one hand on the wooden backrest and twisting at the waist, causing the ice to slosh in the pitcher.

"You're not my type, honey," she said.

Dale stared forlorn. *"You don't even know me."*

"But that's just it," she said, still smiling in that charming way. *"To know. And you don't. I'm not an unknowing type of girl. Don't trouble your little head. You're not supposed to know what that means."* She'd turned again.

Dale, now, caught somewhere between rampant hormones and burgeoning indifference called out. *"I'm not an unknowing!"* he yelled. I winced, still watching the memory, feeling my heart hammer. *Don't say it.* I thought to myself, even though I knew the end. *Don't you say it.*

"I'm here to hire a savant!" he continued.

She'd turned now, her eyes narrowed, fixated on him. "Where'd you hear that term?" she demanded.

Dale had taken his time, now, enjoying the impact of his words while sloshing the ice around his glass and listening to the pleasant *clink*. "Oh, I don't know..." he'd said, taking a sip. *"It's a dangerous job too, you know. Not some second-rate prison."*

The woman had leaned in now, interest painted across her features. Too much interest. *"Where's the job?"* she said.

Dale coughed and glanced towards the fire. For a moment, he almost seemed dazed. Then, as if the question itself unlocked the memory, his eyes widened and he said, *"Oh—I... I don't think I can tell you that. I mean, no one actually knows where!"* A nervous chuckle. *"It's Unlocatable. At least, not for a few more days."*

I could feel the memory slipping again, dipping quickly back beneath the surface of his subconscious.

The pretty waitress was turning to move away again, grunting in disgust. *"Well, you enjoy playing pretend! My shift is almost up."*

Dale, watching the lady saunter away, panicked. He didn't think she believed him. *"I'm not lying!"* He called.

"Whatever!" she called back, waving.

"It's the Hollow!" Dale blurted out at last.

The woman turned, finally, her eyebrows high on her forehead. A soft, coy little smile played across her lips. *"I see,"* she murmured. *"You really are knowing, aren't you?"*

Dale, in the memory, felt a slow flicker of satisfaction as she was once more paying him undivided attention. He smirked, leaning back in his chair, one hand still resting against the cold glass, beads of moisture forming around his fingers.

"I can tell you about it, if you like," he'd said.

"I'd love to hear more," she replied but then paused, hesitant, glancing over her shoulder. *"Actually, one second. Can I talk to you after work? I have to clock out."*

Dale had nodded, and he'd watch her leave, *feeling a sense of slow, smug satisfaction...*

I blinked a few times, allowing the memories to clear, and then I fixed my gaze on the side of Dale's face.

"Dale," I growled. "Did she ever end up coming back?"

He shifted. "Huh?"

"The waitress."

"What waitress?" he said reflexively, his eyes unblinking now.

"Dale—I read minds. I know. You opened your big mouth. Did she ever come back? The pretty waitress with the dark hair? The one you told."

"I didn't—"

"No time, Dale!"

"Fine," he huffed, wincing. "No, she didn't. Are you happy? I got stood up! I don't have bowling balls in my sleeves like that friend of yours. Not all of us are so—?"

"Dale, the point isn't your love life. The girl, you told her about the Hollow, and you told her it could be found in a few days' time. People aren't supposed to know that!"

He blinked, still struggling to keep up. "But... *you* know it."

"I'm a savant! I have my sources and that's why I live on the move. I also don't go blabbing to waitresses about my jobs!"

"Er... so?"

"So," I snapped, "Endeavor has informants all over these mountains, embedded in the towns, among unknowing and knowing alike."

"Embedded in..." he trailed off, frowning.

I resisted the urge to slap him.

His eyebrows shot up, as late to the party as his sense of realization. "Wait—you think... No, not Diana! No—no, she was just a waitress. She couldn't be—she isn't—"

Preacher brushed knuckles against his palm, signing *danger.*

I mouthed the words, *"Check the window."* My own fear arose like a creeping tide, threatening to spill over, but I reached out, pressing on my fear receptors, dampening all sense of terror. Slow at first then more quickly, I pushed the fear from my mind until only an echo remained.

I inhaled deeply, calm as a cadaver.

Preacher suddenly rapped his knuckles against the glass. He pointed sharply and stepped quickly to the side, away from the window. He flicked his eyebrows up to one of the scars on my cheek then glanced at the tattoo on my wrist.

"Endeavor? Here? You're sure?" I darted to the window and peered out. Dale's employer had been right. She'd known they were coming.

It's amazing how a little rain can clear a carnival. All signs of the residents of the Cascade Mountains had vanished. Raindrops thrummed against the ground and tarps of the scattered tents, joining the staccato tap against my aluminum ceiling. A few of the tarantulas shifted restlessly, but I reached out, muffling their senses.

Then, I peered through the rain-slicked glass. "Where?" I snapped. "I don't see them."

Preacher could pick out a target in a blizzard at a mile away. I was so used to creeping in dark, enclosed spaces, while avoiding monsters and demons that my attention was better served in more proximate scenarios.

Preacher tapped my shoulder roughly—his were not gentle hands—then directed my gaze, pointing towards the low roof of the main office building for the Sleeping Dwarf Inn.

A large shadow moved on top of the rectangular building. Golden eyes flecked with indigo peered out at me.

Then, the aluminum door to the office clattered open and six figures stepped into the deluge. Five of the figures carried guns; one of them, with their shirt slick against them in the rain, looked like a skeleton. He was little more than skin and bones, his face gaunt like a ghoul's, his eyes pulsing indigo.

"Elementalist," I said sharply. "Vyle's teeth," I hissed, trying not to think what my old head instructor would've thought if he heard me curse. I jerked back out of sight as well. "Looks like a Kindred too, on top of the roof."

Preacher gave me a questioning look.

"Oh, Corker's breath, I hope not. It can't be."

Preacher tilted his head slightly.

I cursed. "Why assume the worst? Maybe it's just a normal Kindred. It doesn't have to be—"

Preacher signed at me.

"I am *not* in denial. Grendel hasn't found us for months." I shuddered as the name threaded the air, piercing and pointed. Endeavor, I could deal with. But Grendel and his friend Caliban? Those two had been hunting us for nearly a year now. In the past, the hunters and trackers sent after us rarely came close. But Grendel... there was something off about him; he was an eternal talent like myself, except a Kindred instead of a Wit.

"Wh—what's that?" Dale whispered, staring up at me. "What's a Kindred?"

I looked at him, hard, breathing slowly. "You need to get out of all of this. When you can—leave."

"What *are* they though?"

I scowled, but then rapidly spoke, "Kindred are one of the six eternal talents. Humans in form at times, but melded with something deeper and darker. I'm sure you've heard of werewolves or lycanthropes? Yes? Flesh and mind affected by an aberration. Kindred, though, are affected deeper than flesh, deeper than mind—their souls are shaped by their birthright. Monsters in DNA *and* thought *and* spirit. Demons in sheep's clothing. Stay clear if you can."

I shivered at the memories of Grendel and his offspring.

Preacher had nearly died the last time we'd crossed paths; he'd taken a bullet to the cheek. And then Grendel had ripped a chunk out of my chest, eating the bloody flesh while I'd watched.

Sometimes, Grendel appeared as a human.

But not always.

My gaze returned to the golden-eyed shadow on the roof, but it had vanished. I leaned against the aluminum wall, peering cautiously towards the edge of the window.

The six figures, led by the emaciated, ghoulish Elementalist, another one of the six eternal talents, were charging my RV, their weapons glinting in their hands, lightning flashing behind them.

Chapter 5

I grew up as the heir to a tyrant. As such, the first cycle of solutions to cross my mind were usually wrong.

"Do we kill them?" I said, glancing over at Preacher. Sometimes, especially in moments of danger, my conscience goes on sabbatical and I resort back to the impulses from my youth. It isn't that I *can't* empathize, but that portion of me was trained to shut down, replaced by cold calculation when confronted by immediate threats.

Funnily, my family was unable to stamp out my conscience entirely. One of the drawbacks, in their assessment, of someone with the Wit was their ability to empathize with anyone. Spend enough time rooting around someone's head and you *really* get to know them. Not just the putrid dross, but the childhood memories, the hopes, dreams, loves, hates—all of it.

"Wait, hang on," I said, shaking my head. "No—if you can help it, don't—"

Before I'd finished the thought, there was a loud blast from next to me. Preacher stood in the RV doorway, his six-shooter poking out into the rain.

The Endeavor agents were still hundreds of yards away, but one of them had collapsed in a heap by a car. I noticed him writhing, clutching his leg.

I whistled softly. I'd already suppressed my fear—and now all that remained was calculation. Sometimes, waiting was the best policy; letting the enemy over-commit often yielded interesting options.

Preacher crossed himself once—thumb moving from forehead to sternum to heart. He closed his eyes in silent prayer, opened them again, and took aim once more, watching as the five remaining agents left their fallen companion and raced forward, this time zigging and zagging. Preacher squeezed the trigger again. Another figure fell, clutching his leg and squealing in pain.

"What—what are you doing!" Dale screamed.

I turned back, examining our trembling companion, and said, in an even tone, "Preacher just shot two men in the legs."

"Wh-what? Are you insane!"

I shook my head. "They're Endeavor—they'll have healers. The pain won't last, and we can't have them after us. If you don't calm down, you're going to wet yourself, and your voice is shrill."

I inhaled shakily, relieved to have that last part off my chest. Nimue, my adopted sphinx mother, had told me once, "Being honest isn't about saying *everything* that's true. It's about saying *only* things that are true." I was still working on the proper balance.

The Endeavor agents had taken up behind a row of cars across the street, now returning fire, but at this distance their aim was suspect. Preacher fired again, eliciting a third shout of pain.

For a moment, I couldn't see a third body, then I noticed the first wounded agent was now clutching *both* his legs, rolling side to side and screaming bloody murder.

"Really?" I said, glancing at Preacher. "The other leg, too?"

Preacher's eyes widened and he quickly shoved me to the side. A jet of lightning flashed through the doorway, obliterating my table in an explosion of splinters. I smelled ash and smoke as I tumbled then rolled to my feet in the same motion. I wasn't just *built* like a gymnast.

"The Elementalist," I snapped through gritted teeth where I pressed against the aluminum wall beneath my window. "We have to lead them away from the RV."

Preacher gestured at his revolver then nodded towards me.

"Yes, probably," I whispered. I watched my dining room table smolder, broken pieces and shards of wood littering my entryway. The *cold* pawed at me, infiltrating my mind. I wanted to rip them to pieces, to cut them to ribbons and—*No. Not my thoughts.* With herculean effort I shrugged off the liquid hatred seeping through my veins.

I reached out, but then winced, shaking my head.

"They're too far," I said. "I need to get closer." I glanced towards the second window next to the crucifix. "Ready, Dale?"

Would-be Antonio Banerune stared at me, spluttering and whimpering.

"I can't understand you," I said patiently. "Apologies, but you're annoying me."

He began to whimper some more.

I sighed. "Dale, I do not care about you enough to allow this inconvenience. I hope you understand. Preacher?"

The big man reached down and lifted Dale like a toddler, hefting him over one shoulder. The man in the suit kicked and squirmed. One of his expensive loafers fell off again, thumping to the ground, revealing a green, silk sock with ease-linked toe seams.

"Out the window?" I said.

Preacher rolled his muscular shoulders. His enormous bulk would hardly fit through the frame.

I sighed. "Out the front it is, then. Ready?"

Preacher didn't bother to reply. He fired three more times, emptying his first revolver, providing covering fire, then bolted out the front door, sprinting around the RV and towards the tree line behind the inn. I followed but paced myself. At a sprint, I was faster than Preacher, but I didn't want to leave him too far behind.

The chatter of automatic weapons ripped the air, competing with the sound of thrumming rain for dominance. More lightning jetted towards us from the ghoulish-faced Elementalist. All Elementalists shared the same look—small, bony, thin as a rail. Their powers taxed them in ways I didn't fully understand.

This particular Elementalist was screaming at the three Endeavor agents, gesturing wildly at us and demanding they break cover. His bony arm circled like a windmill behind one of the cars. Every so often, his fingers glowed blue and another pulse of electricity arced towards us.

Thankfully, he didn't have Preacher's aim, but if not for the rain, the forest likely would have burned.

Most Elementalists practiced a *single* force. Sometimes fire, sometimes ice, sometimes lightning or acid... Variety was the spice of creativity, and Elementalists *hated* creativity. They were a hammer and every problem a perceived nail. I'd encountered my share of these eternals before, and without fail, they all reacted the same way in combat: pound your enemy into dust, and keep blasting until it worked.

This emaciated eternal was no different. Plus, by the looks of things, he was also a coward.

The chatter of machine guns and zaps of lightning faded somewhat as we ducked around the RV, dipping beneath the jutting terrace of one of the log guest cabins and using the structure to shield our retreat towards the woods.

Just as we neared the forest fringe, I pulled up sharply.

Preacher froze as well. He moved like someone half his size in the forest—a gift from growing up in the countryside on his father's farm—but he took cue from my motions.

"Four more," I whispered fiercely, pointing to the trees. "They're waiting behind the bramble clumps by that rusted tanker."

I double-checked, extending my consciousness to graze our ambushers'. Preacher drew his second six-shooter; that's how you knew things were serious.

Four goons behind us, one of them an Elementalist, and four crouched ahead. We were trapped. Shouts and thudding feet betrayed the Endeavor now circling the RV, searching for us, their weapons raised.

In all haste, I reached out, sifting through the minds ahead. Two had defenses. Given a minute or two, I could have broken through, but time was a dwindling commodity. So, I settled on the two other unguarded minds.

I hunted their thoughts for secret phobias in commonality. Then, in my own thoughts, I conjured an image of a giant, fanged, hairy spider. At the same time, I placed the image as a *glimpsing* in the open minds of our would-be ambushers.

Then, the screaming started.

Gunfire followed.

Two men came sprinting from behind the tanker, sub-machine guns dusting the trees where I made them imagine the grotesque arachnid. I held the image in their minds a moment longer, causing its mandibles to pinch and its legs to wiggle. I added a headless corpse for good measure, dangling it from a web behind the spider.

Two other voices behind the rusted tanker and brambles were shouting after their bullet-spraying companions.

"What is it?" someone cried. "What do you see?"

"That big bloody spider, you idiot!" screamed one of the men waving his gun and trampling through the underbrush. He tumbled over a log and regained his feet just as quickly. He slammed another magazine into his gun and continued to pepper the air and the trees with lead.

"Where? I don't see a spider!" shouted another voice. "Do you see the targets?"

Mimicking the voice of the Elementalist, I created *resounding* in their minds, plucking the words I'd heard by the cars from my memory. *"Get after them!"* the voice screamed inaudibly in their heads. *"They're getting away!"*

Resounding is a weak enough effect it's doable even against defenses and blockades. Those experienced with Wits usually know to wear close-circuit comms. Static is difficult to mimic, even for the best of us. These men, however, hadn't come prepared. That's Endeavor for you.

I doubled-down on the effect and two more men emerged from behind the tanker, blinking owlishly and looking one way then the other.

Fear flooded their senses; I could sniff it like a bloodhound. Fear was the single worst corrosive for mental defense. Now, all four of our would-be ambushers had lowered defenses. The Elementalist and his underlings had paused at the sound of gunfire, fearful to stick their heads out from behind the RV lest Preacher take them out.

For a moment, two of these new soldiers began turning towards me, but I reached into their minds, found optics and reversed *glimpsing*.

We didn't turn invisible, but to the men, we might as well have been.

They stared at us but couldn't see us. They peered past us but still couldn't see. I nodded quietly at

Preacher, gesturing around the other side of the bramble-covered rusty tanker.

As we hurried away, I placed the *glimpsing* of the enormous spider next to the RV.

More shouting, more cries of panic. The ambushers started shooting at the RV, blowing my home to bits. The other Endeavor and the Elementalist fired back, screaming in horror.

I continued to race after Preacher into the woods, following his loping gait. As I ran, I connected with the minds of the tarantulas back in my RV. The spiders' beady eyes peered through the windows. The Elementalist and the remaining Endeavor agents huddled behind the metal hull, popping shots off around the RV whenever the chatter of submachine guns faded. The Elementalist cursed. I watched him through the open door as he ducked inside the RV, setting foot next to the table he'd incinerated.

I frowned at this intrusion.

"That's my home," I muttered. I flooded the tarantulas with aggression then watched through their eyes as six of the hairy creatures dropped from my ceiling, landing on the Elementalist.

He screamed in blood-curdling horror as the tarantulas started to bite.

Still staring through the tarantula's eyes, I didn't watch where I was going until I rounded a tree and came to a sudden, painful halt.

A rifle butt met my cheek, sending me reeling.

My gaze snapped to the present. A shout of pain fell mute in a gusting breath as a knee landed in my stomach.

I collapsed to the forest floor, gasping. I looked up through blinking eyes to find an Endeavor agent with a large black rifle and full tactical gear glaring at me. He stumbled a little, struggling to maintain his balance.

I realized then why I hadn't sensed him: he was drunk. Not just sort of, but completely, knock-out wasted. It took everything in him to retain his feet.

One thing the Wit struggled to track, beyond the normal mode of mental defenses, willpower and self-control: drunks. I wasn't sure why, but alcohol had a directly proportional effect on how easily I could sense someone's mind. This particular agent had either knowingly or unknowingly protected his mind from detection.

His bloodshot gaze stared at me from behind a visor and he glared, pointing his weapon at my head.

"Don't do it," I said quietly. "No killing unknowings or untalenteds, remember?"

The man tried to speak, took a moment to remember how, then, in a slurred voice, he spat. "Death to tyrants—*Leonidas Rex!*"

I shook my head. "I wasn't speaking to you."

Preacher stepped from behind a tree and fired once—but not to kill. Preacher's conscience was far stronger than mine. The drunk Endeavor spun like a top, clutching his shooting arm, howling. The sound was cut short, however, as Preacher stepped in, hard, spinning his six-shooter into a pommel grip and slamming the weapon deftly into the side of the agent's head, dropping him like a marionette with snipped strings. Preacher didn't even seem out of breath where he stood over the fallen man. For a moment, he murmured a silent blessing of protection for the man on the ground. Then he eyed me and gestured I should follow.

"Vyle's teeth," I said, staring at Preacher, then dropping my gaze to the still twitching body. "Close one."

"Ah, don't partner so with surprise, *kardish*," said an accented voice from above. "Found folded in the chest of soldiers and men, their loyalty breeds predictability."

I froze, as did Preacher. The voice came soft and lilting, a pleasant, sunny tone completely out of place in the rain-slicked forest. Slowly, with dread in my heart, I glanced up at this newest threat.

Grendel leered back at us, grinning from one of the lowest branches.

Chapter 6

My back shuddered, prickling with goosebumps brought on by the gelid breeze and freezing rain. Preacher and I both stood still, cautious in the forest, each of us fixated on the man reclining on the lowest branch of the giant oak.

There should have been no way to scale such a tall, wide tree and reach the dangling, ancient branch. It was nearly twenty feet off the ground, for one, with no visible handholds leading up to it. Yet, still, there the bounty hunter sat.

Grendel.

Like an echo seeking its point of origin, Grendel's presence always heralded a *second* arrival.

My gaze whipped down, scanning the forest for his pet, but I spotted no trace of the giant beast. This, perhaps more than anything, stayed Preacher's hand; he kept his pistol raised without firing. The bullets would be needed for Caliban.

The bounty hunter sat with a dirt-streaked face, a dusty top hat tilted over his head. His eyes gleamed gold, tinged with the eternal indigo. He wore what looked to be a Sunday suit, indicating the appearance of a rascal who'd been dressed by his mother for church, but who had played in the mud just before the service. Silk and lace and intricate weave ornamented his ensemble, but so did rips, tears and mud stains. Hardly a presentable spectacle.

Grendel smiled down at us, a lazy, cat-like smile. Currently, Grendel was taking a bite from something brown; he ripped off a piece of the indeterminable item and munched it, flashing teeth filed to points. Grendel made a strange gurgling sound of pleasure in his throat, and then he dropped from the branch, falling twenty feet and landing nimbly on his toes. He made no sound of exertion or pain. His glowing eyes peered from his dirt-streaked face.

"Salutations, Leonidas," said Grendel, still speaking in that soft accent of his. "A wee mammal informed mine ears of one savant in likeness of the lost heir. Eyeing the Hollow, no less." He tutted softly. "Imagine my heartfelt surprise when I found it was *you*."

I shivered both at the smile and his soft accent. I could never quite place the region. I'd even asked Nimue, and she'd seemed troubled. Her exact response had been, *"Sometimes, if you're not certain where something comes from, perhaps it comes from nowhere at all. At least, not anymore."* The more I thought about it, I'd realized what she'd meant. Whatever Grendel's nation of origin, it had long since faded into the footnotes of history.

"We're not going with you quietly," I said, keeping my tone even. I stood still in the forest. Any movement—any at all, could be perceived as a threat. The Kindred bounty hunter was unpredictable in these things.

"I request your presence, but expect not compliance," said Grendel, still speaking in that calm, musical way of his.

"Suppose we make a deal?"

"Raise admonishment to your associate—require the submission of his weapons, and then, perhaps, we may bargain."

I coughed. "Er, Preacher, would you mind lowering the gun?"

Preacher shook his head.

I resisted the urge to shrug back at Grendel, and simply said, "He doesn't want to."

"The terms, I'm afraid, are unflinchingly rigid," Grendel said, his tone hardening.

"Preacher, please?"

Another shake.

I winced at Grendel. "It seems like a hard no."

His face became brittle, but before he could react, I reached out slowly, inquiring towards Grendel's mind. As in the past, it felt like assailing a castle wall with a water pistol. Grendel's mental defenses had been honed over millennia.

For a moment, I thought Grendel might choose this moment to lunge. But instead, he glanced up at the trees, and a couple of sparrows dropped out of a nearby branch and flitted towards the Kindred through the tapping rain. He lifted a finger, allowing them to land and stroking their feathers. He reached into one of his many mud-stained suit pockets and withdrew a small handful of seed which he offered, and the birds accepted then flitted away. One of them didn't go far, however, and simply circled his top hat, halting, at last, on the brim.

Dale was now kicking against Preacher, demanding he be lowered to the ground. The rain had streaked the mixture of makeup along Preacher's face, creating a mangled mess of brown, not quite unlike the dirt streaking Grendel's cheeks and forehead. Preacher shrugged once and allowed Dale to collapse like a bag of potatoes, landing on the ground in a hissing fit, spitting leaves and wiping rapidly at his expensive suit as he regained his feet.

"I have nothing to do with these men," Dale declared in a warbling cry. "I don't even know who they are. All those guns, that lightning guy—none of it, just, I.... Just, just don't hurt me, please..." A sob stretched his words, filling the space between him and the bounty hunter. "I'll tell you anything you want to know."

Grendel cast an amused looked towards me, and I resisted the urge to roll my eyes. Instead, I scanned the trees, watchful, waiting. Where was Caliban? My gaze flicked towards Preacher's. Nearly imperceptibly, he nodded towards a distant copse by a darkened hill with a small, metal, fenced-in portion—some sort of private graveyard.

For the faintest moments, I thought I saw a shadow shift in the trees.

Then nothing. A shiver crept up my spine. I nodded, also faintly, showing Preacher I'd seen.

Grendel dusted off his shirt and extended a piece of the brown substance he'd been chewing towards Dale. "Would you like some? It's very nutritious."

Dale looked caught, indecisive. I didn't have to read his mind to know he was calculating if this was a trap. In the end, he decided to accept the extended piece of what looked like beef jerky.

"Well," said Grendel, nodding insistently, but politely. "What do you think?"

Dale held the brown substance up to his mouth and took a bite. Immediately, he began to retch and spit. Grendel barked laughter, clapping a hand against his leg and dancing a little jig, skipping where he stood and clicking his heels together.

"What was that?" Dale demanded, still spitting and hacking.

"Human liver," I said blandly. It wasn't obvious at first glance, but I could see, among the mud-stains of Grendel's Sunday best, there were dried streaks of a rusty hue. A dark substance had buried in the swirls of his fingertips and there were flecks of black beneath his long, untrimmed fingernails which caused physical pain to the germaphobe in me. "He dries it himself."

Grendel tapped his nose and pointed towards me, nodding feverishly. "You recollect; of course you do. I deign to season it with only the finest wyvern dung. I have some fresh if you'd prefer. Liver, I mean—not the dung. I parceled it from a mewling child... Again, the liver, not the dung." He smiled, jovially. "A pitiable sound that child's cries. He missed his parents—of course, I hadn't intended for him to watch Cal eat them. Their intestines were split at the poor child's feet. He could smell their innards."

Grendel shrugged, still speaking in a tone as if he were commenting on the weather. "Cal can be a bit impetuous at times. Though, the young boy's crying ceased soon enough. The liver was some of the best, you know. Like veal, young flesh tastes best. Human hunters taught me that with the screams of my friends. Here, try some more." Grendel began to reach for his pocket a second time, but Dale quickly shook his head, his cheeks taking on a greenish tinge.

The entire while, I stayed on tenterhooks. If I bolted, Grendel would be faster. If we attacked him, without spotting Caliban, we'd be ambushed. Grendel often played with his food, but, as a representative of said food, the enjoyment wasn't mutual.

Grendel kept his tone pleasant, polite, and he glanced over at me, murmuring, "Our game has granted me immeasurable enjoyment. I promised my friend I wouldn't kill you without him." As an afterthought, he quickly added, "I don't normally ask permission... Right of conquest and all that, but as a show of respect—and, might I add, admiration—would you mind if I ate your eyes? After I killed you, of course. Fresh eyes from a living body taste nice, but they tear and rip if you haven't sedated the livestock, believe me."

My hands felt cold and my eyes watered and itched all of a sudden. I didn't want to blink. I knew I couldn't show fear—I quickly reached out, suppressing both disgust and outrage in a flickering instant.

Grendel's gaze flicked impatiently towards the gated copse of darkened trees. He sighed and called out, shouting. "Leave the graveyard alone—old corpses won't taste as fine as fresh ones!" The bounty hunter shook his head once. He reached up, patting the bird affectionately that was still nestled against the brim of his hat. By the looks of things it had relieved itself but judging by a few of the other stains on his clothing, this wasn't the first time a bird had taken a potshot at the Kindred.

More movement from the trees by the graveyard, a dark, growling sound. Out of the corner of my eye, I spotted Preacher twitch. I stiffened, sensing what was about to happen.

"Careful—" I began to say.

But too late.

Preacher squeezed the trigger, twice. The aim was true. I could tell, even from where I was standing, that if Grendel had stayed still, the bullets would have buried into the back of his head.

But, as fast as thought, Grendel formed into something else. He was a blur of color and movement, and, as I watched, a giant, blackened shape burst around a tree, disappearing from sight, and then emerged again, this time in a swirl of claws and stained, matted fur. The scent of decaying meat and sweaty muscle lingered on the air as the blurring creature moved from tree to tree, the ground pattering with the sound of wild movement.

Then, Grendel reappeared, the fur fading, the shadowy form disappearing like ice melting from a statue. Indigo flecked eyes flashed beneath the tilted top hat at Preacher. A soft growling emitted from Grendel's throat and then, strangely, he began to whistle.

The sound sent goosebumps spreading across my back. Icy pulses trembled my skin like sweat glazing my body. Frantically, I scanned the forest for a way out. But the forest was Grendel's domain. As good of a tracker and survivalist as Preacher was, as comfortable as I was moving through rough tract in dangerous places, this was the terrain of woodland creatures. Grendel's friends.

The whistling grew louder, and I heard the crunch of leaves and sticks and could see trees shaking from the direction of the small copse. A giant form now tore through the woods, answering its master's call. I heard thumping footsteps, a rumbling growl like a crashing river, a deep, huffing breath like a storming gale...

It was coming straight at us.

Chapter 7

As the trees shuddered, splintered, moved, parting as Grendel's friend approached...

Dale stepped forward, no longer spluttering, no longer gagging or coughing. He held up a halting hand, and in a stern, commanding voice, he called out, "Son of the Shard Prince, Hound of the Carpenter's Sister, Grendel ap Evelon—I forbid you! Not this one."

It wasn't Dale's voice. It was the same, feminine voice I'd heard back in the RV.

This time, though, the voice no longer held gentle cheer. Now, it rang out like steel, a hammer smashing an anvil, resonating the air with the teaching of iron certainty. Grendel immediately ceased whistling.

He stepped forward as fluidly as water leaving a riverbank and swirling onto shore. He stopped in front of Dale, peering closely into the messenger's eyes. He sniffed a few times, and Grendel's own eyes widened. He whistled beneath his breath, and the sound of rustling leaves and crunching twigs faded.

Caliban remained hidden midst leafy shadows and sodden bark, watching, waiting. I let out a slow breath of sheer relief...

"Mistress," said Grendel, polite once more, "I did not know it was you."

On a lark, I reached out, testing Grendel's barriers. To my astonishment, there were cracks in the wall. *Fear.* Just as quickly as the cracks had appeared, though, they faded, and once more, the wall was complete. Who was this would-be employer of mine? I looked sharply at puppet Dale, but before I could reach out, the female voice spoke again, still cold and hard, "I'm afraid I need this one for a job. I can't have you kill him."

Grendel actually bowed at the waist, tipping his top hat. As he did, he revealed a mass of bluish-gray hair, and a couple of field mice peaked out from the tangle. "A job? The savant? Dangerous job if one as tempered as you requires aid." He paused, tilting his head.

"Sometimes we all need help. But, as you know, anyone in my employ is also under my protection. And—"

"—of course, course, I wouldn't dream of harming one under the evening lady's watchful eye. Though... my children may be harder to convince. They're a day's travel from here..." Grendel's eyes narrowed and he tilted his ear, listening to the breeze, then shook his head once. "The mortals I came with are busied with each other. The clever one made them see phantoms. The big one pierced their limbs."

Now, some of the eager energy returned to my would-be employer and it was as if she went through a physical change. She shifted from foot to foot, flashing a look back at me; Dale's face split in a sudden grin beneath the damp skies. "I'm so, so glad to hear he's good at what he does. Oh boy, imagine if he wasn't—what a disaster that would be." She giggled, and reached out, patting Grendel affectionately on the arm. The cold words were gone, the iron certainty vanished. Grendel stared at her hand, and looked up, his eyes

36

predatory. Normally, a look like that from a monster like Grendel would've cowed even the heartiest warriors. This person, though, just smiled and, half-yawning, said, "Sorry—late night. Anyway, what was I saying? Oh—right. Hmm, dear me. You can't hurt Preacher, either."

"Why ever not?" said Grendel. The Kindred paused a moment, then shook his head, as if trying to figure out a difficult problem. Then, he clicked his fingers, "Oh, of course. I understand. If the savant serves you, and I harm his lackey, it might upset him—harming his work output, yes?"

The whole train of thought seemed to stretch Grendel's capacity for reason. My hand reached towards my hip, grasping the hilt of the dagger I kept strapped to my thigh, through my pocket-slit. If he made a move for my friend, I would act. Preacher also kept his gun leveled, frowning. My tall friend was not accustomed to missing or being called anyone's "lackey."

"But as I said, only my employees are under my protection." Here, Dale turned sharply towards me, his eyes swirling with a strange, black energy. His mouth bunched up on the side of his face, and he gave a little shimmy-shrug of his shoulders. "Not to be *too* demanding or anything—just, you know…"

I couldn't help but notice Dale's shadow was behaving oddly, like blackwater trying to seep out of a bowl. It wavered and shimmered with the substance of a heat mirage on a sunny day.

The woman's words, through Dale's lips, sent chills up my spine. Her eyes glimmered with mirth. "So, lost heir, will you accept my contract? Say yes, and Grendel won't hurt you."

"You're frightened by her," I murmured, glancing towards Grendel.

I thought Grendel would be offended by this, or defensive, instead, however, the bounty hunter shrugged once. "The mistress is dangerous."

"Who are you?" I demanded of Dale's puppet master.

"That's not important—not really. What *is* important, if you don't mind me saying, is your answer. Will you take the contract?"

I shuffled uncomfortably, glancing at Grendel. "Isn't it your job to prevent the breach of Endeavor prisons?"

Grendel, though, just smiled at me. "My job is to find and kill lost heirs."

I frowned, collecting my thoughts, standing beneath creaking tree boughs in a rain-streaked forest, the scent of petrichor dallying on the air. "You want me to find the confidant, locate the prison, then break into the Hollow in three days' time," I said, raising one finger. Then I raised a second. "After that, you want me to contend with a deep prison, protected by a saboteur and filled with a clan of crazed genies. If you knew what lay in there, you wouldn't ask me to return."

Dale's form shrugged, turning his back towards Grendel, seemingly without a care in the world. The simple gesture caused prickles across my own spine. What sort of person presented their back to a thousand-year-old Kindred?

"I trust you can find it again. And it's because you know what's in there that I need you. I'm still more than delighted to pay you double. I heard you're the best, Leon. Well?"

It wasn't much of a decision. Grendel respected this employer enough to leave us unscathed while in her employ. She had the upper hand, and she knew it too.

I fought back my own fear, my own dreaded memories from my first visit to the Hollow. Of course, I was telling her the truth; if she knew what was in there, regardless of who she was, she'd stay a thousand miles away, then flee ten thousand more. She didn't know. She seemed confident I could find the location. But with only three days before it became Unlocatable again? Last time I'd had six months to find the confidant. The location-secreter changed every year. I didn't even know who the new one would be.

If she could have read my thoughts, I felt certain she'd change her mind then and there.

But, for now, I needed to survive, and I needed to make sure Preacher did too. So, I nodded once. "Alright, we'll take the job. But only if I speak with you in person."

Dale's eyes flickered. Then he nibbled on his lip. "Fair enough, Leon. But if we only have three days to find—"

"I'll set a rendezvous on the way to my black-marketer contact. It won't cost us any time. Besides, I have to grab something first."

"Okay... if you think we'll have enough time..."

"We *already* don't," I said. "But we either do this my way or not at all. It's worth the sacrifice. We need to meet, and I need to retrieve something."

"So where do you want to meet?"

I coughed delicately, glancing over my shoulder towards Grendel, and shooting him a look as if to say *do you mind?*

Grendel was an odd fellow, bound by a strange sense of duty. I knew he'd hunt me to the ends of the earth and back if he had to. A hunter's purpose thrummed in his heart. But also, he seemed to respect my would-be employer enough to give a brief hiatus. Little more than a stay of execution. Grendel didn't care about prisons, or the Hollow, or any of it.

He cared about hunting.

And I was his prey.

Still, a stay of execution brought me a bit more time to figure a way out of this mess.

The bounty hunter watched us, eyes narrowed as I put an arm over Dale's shoulders, grateful again for his apparent sense of hygiene, despite his brief tumble in the mud.

I led him away from Grendel, across the clearing, well out of earshot. Grendel didn't follow, didn't chase. He just watched.

I glanced again towards the mercenary, grateful Preacher was now walking up and down, his heavy steps crunching leaves and twigs, creating more of a distraction from where the top-hat wearing predator stood. Caliban was still somewhere on the other side of Grendel, far enough away he couldn't hear either—not that I thought he could understand words.

Grendel gave me one last long look, staring at my eyes and licking his lips. Then he turned without another word and moved back through the trees, melting amidst the bark and leaves.

Once I was sure he was gone, and well out of earshot, I whispered, "Do you know the Librarian's mansions?"

Dale still spoke in his employer's voice, matching my volume. "I'm afraid not. You want to meet there, hmm? I don't mind. Not really. Well—unless I'm wrong. Is that where you want to meet?" The prattling tone seemed familiar all of a sudden. But I didn't have time to chase the lead of memory.

I lowered my voice even further, to barely a whisper, so faint even Dale had to lean in to hear. My lips practically tickled his ears as I said, "The left mansion," I whispered. "Top floor."

"Oh, goody—*secrets*! I love secrets. Why there, though?" the voice returned. I thought she'd be suspicious, but the woman didn't seem to possess a suspicious bone in her body.

"There's something we need."

"What something?"

"You were right. I have been to the prison before."

"The time you failed, right?"

I frowned but didn't let the emotion show for long. "There's a key. I keep it at the mansion."

"Oh, alright then. If you say so. This will help us enter the Hollow?"

I began to nod, pressing a hand to keep my newsboy cap from slipping beneath the low, dangling branches above. I shot another look past Preacher. Grendel was gone, though I could still hear the faint sound of footsteps in the trees, still heading in the opposite direction. "If we do, by some miracle, manage to locate the Hollow on the proper day, the key accesses the sewers." I whispered. "Though it won't be enough to survive once we're inside."

"Tell me where the mansion is. I'll meet you."

I paused, sucking air softly and wincing, picturing what would need to come next. "You don't have any gold dust, do you? Either on Dale or on your actual person." I coughed. "My lady," I added.

"Gold dust? Why?"

I sighed, dropping to my haunches and drawing a circle in the mud. I winced at the dirt on my finger, and, keeping the digit away from my body, I pointed at the circle of mud. "The Hollow isn't easy to access," I murmured. "One," I held up my muddy finger, "we have to contend with the saboteur lieutenant. That's going to come down to maneuverability."

"I see."

"Which means," I stressed, "we need teleporting stones... I can get those from my black market contact."

"Alright," the woman said, distractedly fiddling with a leaf she'd plucked from a low branch.

"Are you listening?"

"Yeah—listening. *If* we find the Hollow, big if, you then need a teleporting stone from the magical black market."

I nodded once. "Stones. Plural. It won't be easy meeting up with my dealer, given," I swallowed, "Some past issues. But I'll figure that out. Second," I said, pointing at the circle, "the walls surround the mountain crater itself. To enter at all, we need this key. Lucky for you, I still have it from the last time."

"Got it." She said, allowing the leaf to flutter from Dale's fingers. "We need teleporting stones and a key." Dale's nose wrinkled. "What's the gold dust for?"

"The genie guardians," I murmured. "They eat the stuff. Or they'll eat us."

The woman shivered. "Ah, wow. Yuck. Okay, so we need gold dust. Is that it?"

I hesitated, breathing shallowly, but swallowed once and nodded. "That should do it," I murmured. "Gold dust for the genies. Teleporting stones to escape the saboteur and my key to the sewers for entry and exit."

"Sooo... where do we get all that?" my would-be employer said, watching me again, raindrops flicking from Dale's bangs.

"Well," I said, rising back to my feet, and wiping my muddy finger off on my handkerchief. "Same place I'm going to find the confidant. The gold dust and teleporting stones are *both* sold by my black market dealer." I hesitated. "Though... if I remember correctly, we might actually have some gold dust left with the key from our last trip. I'm not sure it'll be enough, but it's worth checking."

My would-be employer rubbed at the side of Dale's head. "I—well, I can't actually keep up this connection for long. So I'm going to have to meet you there."

I nodded. Mental links, especially for non-Wits, even in willing minds, were hard to maintain. "Just remember, we'll meet in the leftmost mansion, top floor. And don't... don't touch anything until I arrive."

"Because of this key?"

I nodded. "And the corpse."

Now, Dale's head actually rotated, fixating on me. "Wait, a corpse? Oooh—spooky! You didn't say anything about a corpse."

"If you want to enter the Hollow, it's the only way I know of." I shrugged. "Well?"

She nibbled one of Dale's lips, and then she wagged her head excitedly. "Can't *wait* to meet you! Yay—it's like a party! But you haven't said *where* exactly are these mansions."

Before I could answer, though, I heard a soft *crack*. I frowned, whirling around.

The noise had come from the opposite direction of Grendel, from the opposite portion of the woods where Caliban had been skulking. I paused for a moment, eyes on the shadows, darting about, looking through the trees, the underbrush and the tangle of low-hanging branches.

"Hello?" I called out.

Another *crack* followed another faint sound I couldn't quite make out. I reached out, frowning, and thought—very briefly—I felt a faint, retreating level of surface thoughts. But they were wild, woodsy thoughts.

An animal?

I shivered.

Something else?

Grendel had mentioned something about his children closing in. He'd said they were a day out...

What if he'd been lying and they were closer? I continued staring through the dark, watching. Did Grendel have backup hiding in the woods? Had they heard what I'd said to my would-be employer?

I went rigid, staring, but seeing nothing. At last, I glanced back, my voice low, carrying an edge now. Prickles continued up my spine and every second or so, between words, I shot another glance in the direction of the trees.

"We need to hurry," I said.

"Uh-oh. What's the matter, Leon?"

My eyes narrowed, and I turned, moving back towards Preacher. "Just meet me in Picker's Lake!" I called, stalking through the woods, rejoining Preacher where he stood. Grendel was gone now. Caliban gone too. Even Preacher seemed to have relaxed.

But for myself, I could feel my anxiety mounting. To enter the Hollow, we first had to find the key and the corpse. It would be our only way in or out. Next, the confidant could be found in the same place I'd purchase supplies. Ear to the ground, with some clever maneuvering, I *might* be able to locate the Hollow in the short timespan available.

But had someone overheard me mentioning the Librarian's mansion? I winced. I'd been distracted by Grendel, by my own troving fear.

We needed to hurry... I could feel the sense of urgency rising in my chest. We'd waste a day to reach the key, but it couldn't be avoided. Besides, it was on the way. That would only leave us two days to find the Hollow. Time was not on our side.

Preacher quirked an eyebrow at me as I moved rapidly to join him.

I answered his unspoken question. "I don't think we're the only ones going after our old key," I murmured. "We better hurry."

Chapter 8

Raindrops stippled celestial patterns against the aluminum RV; the wind protested our flight down the interstate further into the bleak green mountains. Columns of mist and patches of fog rolled along the concrete barriers, peeking through the trees lining the empty road.

The quiet whistle of wind tempted its way through the various bullet holes in the side of my mobile home. It irked me to leave the bloodstains on the ground after disposing my charred table, but we hadn't had time to clean in our hurry to flee The Sleeping Dwarf Inn.

No more fortune-telling for a while, it would seem. The Endeavor's assassin team had disappeared by the time I'd returned, whether on Grendel's orders or for some other reason, only the breeze and the birds would know. Now a sense of urgency filled the RV, with Preacher at the wheel, both of us watching the winding mountain roads.

Had someone overheard my words? I'd been so stupid—so careless. Grendel and Caliban had taken all my attention. I hadn't thought they might have backup hiding nearby.

What if someone was following us? Or worse—ahead of us, loping through the trees in an effort to reach the Librarian's mansions before us.

I grit my teeth. "Faster," I said. Preacher floored the pedal, taking us tearing through the night-time highways.

I leaned back in the leather chair, listening to the whining hum of the engine and the whirring of wind through punctured metal. Preacher had agreed to take first shift at the wheel. To reach the designated location in the mountains, that we set for our client, we'd have to drive through the night. To reach it first? We'd have to go fast. Of course, entering the mansions at *night* was folly—given what came out to play in the dark. But we had to at least reach Picker's Lake just after sunrise.

Briefly, I caressed my neck, running my hand through my hair and pushing back the newsboy cap angled over my eyes. It had been a long day. Even flooring it, the RV didn't manage much over seventy, and despite the excitement of the day, my mind began to wander. My hand followed suit, roaming down to my forearm... A finger circled the tattoo there. The blue crown tattoo had been given to me as a child, but over the last ten years, I'd tried to remove it. A couple of times, in fits of frustration, I'd resorted to acid and fire and even a knife. But while I added to my mural of scars, the tattoo would always reappear somewhere on my body.

Imagine the most hated symbols of dead dictators in the unknowing world, the blue crown was that to the arcane realms. My father had treated the unknowing and untalented as little more than livestock. Even farmers didn't do to their animals the things my father enjoyed inflicting on mortalkind. The things he encouraged his soldiers to do.

I shivered at the memories. The tattoo stood as the ominous emblem of the Dwindling Imperium—once called the Grand Empire.

Once an imperial, always an imperial. At least, that's what they would have you believe. Until most the leadership, including the Grandest Imperial Maximus himself, daddy dearest, were assassinated by the Endeavor during the night now known as the Grimmest Jest. I was eighteen when my father was killed.

Just then, I was distracted by a flash of blue in the window, and I looked sharply over.

A familiar chill probed up my spine. But the streak of color vanished as quickly as it had come. Another car heading the other direction, perhaps? The mountain roads during this time of year, this late at night, were usually abandoned.

I blinked, and *again* another glimpse of blue reflected out of the mirror to my left. I whirled just as sharply, no longer sitting. But once more, all that met me was my own reflection.

Fear welled in me, and I pushed from the chair, maneuvering nimbly across the floor which buzzed from the engine. I stepped over Preacher's discarded jacket outside his door and a pile of Sunday comics which had toppled from an overhead shelf. I sighed and picked up the comics, placing them neatly back in the compartment, organizing them by page length. I draped Preacher's jacket over his door handle. Then, I returned to the front of the vehicle and plopped back in the passenger seat next to my large friend.

He glanced over and gave a small nod.

I sighed, releasing a weight of unease with the exhalation. No more signs of blue in the window or the mirrors. My mind was simply playing tricks. I glanced at Preacher, forcing my attention to divert. Through numb lips, I mumbled, "Thanks. Back there..."

Preacher gave me a long look, his one hand gripping the steering wheel, the other squeezing an economy-sized stress ball meant to build up his forearm. The flash of safety lights through fog illuminated his face in a continuous strobe. A small family photo dangled beneath the mirror, attached by a thin green ribbon. The photo displayed a woman with dimpled cheeks and smiling eyes. In front of her stood two young girls leaning back in familiarity.

Preacher's family—his mother and two sisters. His father was notably devoid from the photo, though still very much alive.

I'd met Preacher's father before, a good man who always offered to pray for me when I visited. I glanced back at the crucifix on our wall and breathed slowly. The symbol had never provided me the same peace it did Preacher or his father. I'd seen too much of the world to trust unseen intent. I settled back in my passenger seat, ignoring the buckle dangling over my right shoulder. Even so, I'd never refused his father's offers.

I needed all the prayers I could get.

For a moment, I thought to retrieve some of the incense and pilfered pastry I kept in the chest beneath my bed. It had cost dearly to learn the sealing words, but I could summon Hermes' raven. I frowned and thought better of it. Last time I'd spoken with the trickster god, he'd turned Preacher invisible for the day and then taken my RV for a joyride—didn't even fill up the tank and left two of my wheels flat. Cost nearly a grand to fix all the damage he'd done, which saw us eating rice and beans for two weeks until our next contract. Though much had changed in the last ten years, the one thing I still hadn't yet grown accustomed to was *microwaved* meals. Even now, I shiver at the thought. Seven course feasts prepared by the best chefs in the land compared to thin, flimsy plastic containers of suspect material with odd flavoring.

I sighed, closing my eyes. The gods were jealous sorts anyhow...

If not a God or a god, perhaps I could look for aid from one of the chiefs in the Hidden Kingdoms of Pilfery. But entrance at the best of times was tricky, and I'd already upset the genies.

"Guardian angel, then?" I murmured out loud, flicking an eye up and over my shoulder.

For the faintest moment, I felt a surge of regret. I missed Annie—my old friend would have been able to *see* my guardian. According to her, everyone had one. But it was forbidden to set your eyes on your own.

I slouched even further, mulling over more options. Of course, if ever I needed help, Augustus was always offering. But I'd rather die than return to my family, especially not that seven-foot, psychotic pyromaniac.

"Just you and me, this time," I said, my gaze flicking along the dashboard to Preacher.

He raised an eyebrow beneath his cattleman hat. He signed: *mother?*

I hesitated, glancing at the long strands of fur that still laced my sleeping sweater no matter how many times I set-to with a lint-roller or handheld vacuum. I shook my head. "Nimue is gone for a couple of weeks—Gnash business. Her pack called her up for the fortnight."

Preacher winced, a look of concern crossing his features.

"I know," I said, mirroring his expression. "But Nimue can take care of herself. And so can we—no help this time, my old friend."

Preacher gave the stress toy an extra squeeze, his eyes fixated on the road once more. He then dropped the ball beneath the seat and tapped his forehead.

I raised a questioning eyebrow, but reached out, slowly, my mind grazing his.

Think someone's racing us to the key?

I sighed, shrugging. "I was stupid," I muttered. "I knew Grendel couldn't hear but didn't think someone else was nearby."

Were they?

I shrugged again. "Hard to say. The only minds I sensed were... Wild."

Animal?

I winced. "I hope so."

Preacher frowned, his fingers curling over the wheel now. *Think Grendel will come after us? He seemed scared of our new employer.*

"Not Grendel—no. He's bloodthirsty, but seemed genuinely scared of her. Whoever she is." I trailed off, frowning at this but then shaking my head and sighing. "I don't think he'll come... But if he has allies." I swallowed. "His children, for instance... They might come instead. He's not above riling his offspring to do his own dirty work." I cleared my throat. "He's clever, Grendel. Keeping tabs." I shook my head. "I got sloppy. The mere mention of the Hollow, plus rumors of a savant in the area brought him to our doorstep. We're going to have to be more careful from now on."

Possible on this job?

I breathed a shaky sigh. The Hollow—the Endeavor guarded it fiercely. Grendel used it like cheese in a mouse trap. And I was the unwitting whisker-twitcher. Inevitably, I knew it would all end in the Hollow.

Still. I needed that key from the Librarian's mansion. Also, if I'd remembered correctly, we might have left some gold dust there as well.

Finding the Hollow while enticing the confidant to locate it, however, would be a more difficult ask entirely. And that didn't even mention actually breaking into the place.

Preacher scowled through the window, his dark brow lowering, his attentive gaze fixed on the road ahead. One hand drifted from the steering wheel, though, as he maintained our rapid pace through the night. He signed the word for *sleep.*

I paused for a moment, but then decided perhaps he was right.

Meeting this strange new client of ours now seemed an inevitability. We were going as fast as we could to reach the key first. Besides, if someone else beat us there and went snooping... they'd have the corpse to deal with.

The deeper parts of the mountains, the hidden roads and trails that sliced the forest preserves would come, but for now, I needed my rest.

I patted Preacher on the shoulder in gratitude, then turned again, moving across the RV, daintily stepping past the blood stain by the door. Tomorrow, I'd attack with maximum strength cleaning detergents and buckets of soap. I shivered in delight at the thought. For now, though—rest. I checked my connection with the tarantulas remaining on the ceiling. A few of my furry, eight-legged friends had been blasted by the

Elementalist, but six still remained.

Once I was sure my connection still stood, I approached my door and flopped on the bed.

I flicked the generator lights with my toe then collapsed into my pillows, laying still, but then, muttering to myself, I got back up, hurried over to the mirror facing my bed, pulled my sweater off then threw it over the mirror, blocking it from sight.

I glanced around at the windows once more; no more flashes of blue staring at me.

Good, I thought. That score I'd settled long ago.

I lay back on the bed and calmed my mind, humming quietly. In one corner of my room, a well-used twelve-string acoustic guitar rested on a stand. I was too tired to pick it up, though, and settled my soul with quiet murmurings of half-written songs and memorized lyrics from folk artists and country jams.

I'd grown up on Beethoven, Schumann, Wagner, Mendelssohn and the like... Lyrics were frowned on by the courtiers and nobles in my father's palace. Lyrics could be political—lyrics could spread propaganda, in their mind. Now, though, my tastes had shifted.

All sorts of people have strong opinions about country music, but frankly, I find it soothing. Whispering the refrain to *Country Road,* I drifted off to...

***

A thump.

My heart introduced itself to my throat, and I jerked into a sitting position, whirling around, my eyes wide.

The bedroom lights were still off, but due to the highway lights, flashing through the slats, I glimpsed my sweater lying on the floor, crumpled at the foot of the mirror like a woman's discarded dress.

I felt a flicker of fear in my chest and reached out, trying to suppress the emotion, but before I could, I glimpsed a flash of blue. My eyes zeroed in, narrowed, fixated on the figure in the mirror.

A boy stared back. A boy with blue eyes.

Terror gripped me, introduced as cold spasms along my spine. I ventured a shout but found my voice strained and weak, I attempted to rise from my bed but found my limbs weak.

The boy in the mirror raised a hand and waved.

My voice returned all of a sudden, too loud, rushing in like a sudden tide.

"No... Not again!" I screamed, reaching out with a groping hand as if to fend off a blow, but nothing struck me, and so my hand twisted into a talon, clenched as if in anguish, straining towards blue eyes. "Leave! Not again. I fixed this... I fixed this, you can't be back, you can't—"

The child stepped through the mirror.

He had dark hair cut neat and tidy against his pale forehead. A fresh bruise settled on his right cheekbone and a couple of scars traced his chin. The child looked to be no more than six years old, and he wore orderly, black clothing with blue trim in the fashion of a uniform. It was an old uniform—rarely seen nowadays, but it had once been the official garb of the Imperium.

The child stared back at me, a slight shimmer around his outline. The room felt cold all of a sudden, a swirling, glacial air twisted through the window—which I'd been certain I'd closed—fluttering the shades and brushing the calendar on the wall. The guitar strings began to strum in clashing, grating patterns, filling the air with a jangled mess of noise.

"Go away," I murmured softly, staring wide-eyed at the child. "Leave... You're not welcome here!"

"Help me," the child said softly. "Please. Help me."

I snarled and grabbed a book from the nightstand and flung it at the boy. He flickered like a sputtering light bulb, then reappeared a foot to the left, the book passing harmlessly over his shoulder.

"Help me," he repeated.

"I beat you," I cried. "I'm done with you!"

The boy stepped forward, his eyes swirling with darkness, his hair ruffled as if by the breeze, though he didn't face the window. He bumped into the table and it shifted slightly with a scraping sound.

The boy stopped a few feet from me, arms relaxed at his sides, feet at shoulder width, adopting the posture of a child brought up in the Imperium. He acknowledged my fear, noting the horror etched across every furrowed line of my face.

Then, he smiled, a small pink tongue wetting his lips in delight.

My brothers and I had been trained at a very young age to enjoy the scent of fear—to delight in it. We had been taught with many painful lessons to *use* fear in others, to weaponize it.

The boy was only doing what he'd been trained to.

What *we'd* been trained to.

I knew the boy's thoughts, because they were my thoughts. Or, at least, had been once upon a time. The boy was me from nearly two decades ago.

Nimue had found me with him, both of us huddled together years ago. At the time, I had thought him a hallucination—it isn't common, not even for someone with the Wit to see their six-year-old self, wandering about and bumping into things.

The Sphinx, however, had known better.

This was a poltergeist. A malevolent spirit birthed from my fractured soul and tethered to my memories.

We still didn't know quite *why* the poltergeist kept appearing. Sometimes, interacting with the world, other times simply watching. An omen, I'd thought. But more than an omen... Something else lurked beneath those cold blue eyes, something watching and malevolent. Just another gift of my father's. My brother Augustus had been cursed by daddy-dearest. Sometimes, I wonder, if perhaps the poltergeist was a curse of my own. Growing slowly in power, feeding off me until it would eventually lash out and fulfill its hidden designs— whatever those might be.

I shivered even at the consideration.

One thing was certain, this particular poltergeist always heralded my past. Something unavoidable crested the horizon even in that moment.

"Go," I yelled, glaring at the child. "Get out of here!"

The blue-eyed boy smirked, reached out and snapped one of my guitar strings. He winked at me, then snapped another. Music brought me peace—so of course, he'd try to ruin it. He snapped a third string then turned, stepping back through the mirror. The glass shattered, scattering about the ground; the wind immediately died, the clashing notes from the guitar faded, and I was left trembling, covered in sweat beneath my blankets.

It had been years since I'd seen the poltergeist.

What did it mean?

I wished Nimue was here; I desperately wished I could consult my adopted sphinx mother, but I knew she was indisposed at the moment. As I'd told Preacher earlier, we were on our own.

Every time the poltergeist showed up, though, it meant something from my past was on its way to meet me.

The Hollow? Not Augustus, surely? Something worse?

I kicked the mirror over, covering it now with a spare blanket. Then I rolled back over, pulling my covers tight around my head and curling up with my knees to my elbows, trembling beneath my blankets. It took me another two hours to finally fall asleep. As I did, images of the blue-eyed child flashed through my mind. Caught somewhere between dreaming and waking, I sifted through my own thoughts, searching—*hunting*. For what? A clue? Why was the poltergeist back?

I swallowed, pulling the covers tighter, starting to feel a chill in the room, though the windows were shut. I never much liked contemplating my childhood. The poltergeist looked to be no older than six or seven. That had to mean something.

I cast my thoughts even further back, sifting through my memories...

One memory in particular stood out...

I frowned into my pillow and rolled over, staring at the ceiling now. The chill now seeped into my muscles, and my arms began to tremble as the memories flooded back.

I never knew my mother. Maximus wanted it that way.

Mother would give birth to one of us, and before the labor pains and infant screams had fully subsided, we were taken to some nursery in the palace, and our mother was shipped back off to whatever hellhole my dear old father kept her in when he wasn't making use of her womb.

I'd heard stories of my mother's pregnancy. One of her handmaids, a round, dimpled girl had also become pregnant near the same time. My mother, I was told, kept the girl close—for company most likely. The palace was a scary place for those so unfortunate as to have caught the attention of Grand Imperial Maximus Rex. It is no small thing to carry the son of an emperor—to bear the burden of iron legacy in one's womb. I was to be Maximus' first son, his heir. And thus, I was protected with greater greed than all the treasure hordes of the genies combined.

Guards were stationed around my mother's room day and night. The only person allowed to see her had been her pregnant handmaiden. Together, the children—*we*—had grown in them.

It was said, around the palace, the young girl and the new heir would kick and twist in their mothers' bellies when they were in the same room, almost as if they could sense each other, though blind and enshrouded in darkness.

The other child's name was Annie; we were friends before either of us were born.

We were born on the same day—within minutes of each other. Tragically, Annie's mother died in the birthing room. My own mother wept bitterly, even while holding her newborn boy, baptizing my entry into the world in matron's tears.

Eventually, I'd been stripped from my mother's arms and Annie had been raised by one of the palace nutritionists.

...Annie. The name felt important for some reason.

At the time, Annie had been my only friend. She had also been the reason I first attempted murder. I was five years old at the time.

Chapter 9
Then...

A day destined to end in violence started in sunlight. There I stood, in the cobblestone courtyard beneath the cherry blossom trees blooming white on the spring morning next to a newly ripe apple tree. An unusual sight in the palace grounds to have two separate fruits planted so close together. Five-year-old Leonidas Rex waited for Annie to finish her chores.

I never waited long, however. And this day pulled from memory was no different.

I reached up, plucking an apple and munching on the sweet, green fruit while waiting patiently. I could feel the apple tree's rough bark at my back as I watched the curling stairs to the bakery's second level and spotted an olive complexion covered with a dusting of flour in the window.

A moment passed, and then I heard a series of urgent shouts. "Out there, now!" a voice screeched from the first floor. "Don't make the prince wait; are you mad? Go! Go! I'll finish the biscuits."

Not long after, the wooden door swung open, and a small girl traipsed down the stairs into the orchard. Annie didn't like her hair long, so she wore it sheared. She was a pleasant-faced girl with large green eyes in an olive complexion; she had a gently sloped nose crooked on the end—a gift from the cook's errant fist and a badly set break.

Her eyes weren't green in the way one might think of green. She had a precious tint to her soul-searching gaze, and she received a good number of beatings from the palace's private security for how her attention discomforted them.

Her eyes weren't always green, though. Sometimes they turned gray—when she was *seeing*. Annie claimed she could see ghosts. At that age, I always watched closely, excited to catch the flicker of color, and then bombard her with questions about what she saw.

Now, though, instead of using her *sight*, Annie was also munching an apple as she exited the kitchens. I glanced absentmindedly at her fruit and took a bite from my own. I'd long grown accustomed to us behaving similarly even when apart. Sometimes, we would have the same song stuck in our heads even though we hadn't seen each other for a week. Other times, we would think of the same word and blurt it out simultaneously.

At first, I thought this strange psychic link a result of my burgeoning abilities with my eternal talent. But the nature of the connection wasn't something intentional on my part...

Looking back, I suppose it made sense. Annie and I had grown in the same locked and guarded room as offspring in our mothers' bellies, with no one for company except for each other and the ones who carried us. Some people were just meant to be close, I suppose. Of course, if my father ever discovered this connection with a servant girl, it would be disastrous.

"Hi!" said Annie, giving a small wave with her tiny hand holding the apple.

In between munching the fruit, she would balance the mixing bowl with one hand, and, with the apple still clamped in her teeth, she would use her free hand to whisk the spatula a few times.

"I have an idea," I said, meeting my friend's green eyes. I felt a flash of disappointment they weren't gray today.

"Oh, nice. What is it?"

"Could I use the batter?"

Annie frowned, her mouth bunching on one side of her small face. "Ummm. No, thanks. I'm making biscuits."

"Yes, but could I use some of it?"

"No," she said, her voice still patient but firm. "I'm making biscuits."

I frowned. People didn't usually say no to me, not even my brother Augustus. She reached up and scratched at her temple with the spatula, leaving some dough stuck against the prickles of her shaved head.

I decided I would have to convince her to play with me. I had learned all sorts of interesting lessons involving trickery and manipulation. I puffed out my chest, thinking for a moment. But just then, Annie frowned in my direction.

"No you don't, either," she said sternly.

Her eyes were now tinged gray as she stared off over my shoulder. I turned quickly, looking the same direction but saw nothing. I never did.

"What is it?" I demanded, still twisting and trying in vain to see what she had spotted.

"It's a nasty one," Annie said, shaking her head. "It's sitting on your shoulder with hooks in your neck. Gray, with no eyes and a long, long nose like a mosquito. But the size of a bat—it has wings." Annie didn't use to describe the things she saw, but over time, she'd learned I would bombard her with questions until she did.

Alarmed at her words, I reached up, wiping a hand through the air next to my ear.

"Is it gone?"

"No, it's waiting."

I tried to peer at my shoulder again, and still didn't see anything. "Why is it there?"

Her eyes still filmed with gray, she addressed my shoulder. "Excuse me, spook, why are you on my friend's shoulder?" Annie paused for a moment. "They don't always like it when I speak to them," she added for my benefit.

"Did this one reply?"

She cocked her head, as if listening. "Would you please leave? I don't think he wants you there. No—I mean it." Annie raised her spatula threateningly.

I felt nothing, saw nothing, heard nothing, but a second later Annie smiled, placing the spatula back in the mixing bowl. For a moment, I felt strange. I no longer *wanted* to trick Annie into playing with me.

"Did the gray creature say what it wanted?" I asked, crossing my arms beneath the apple tree.

"Yes," she said. "It said you were planning on tricking me."

I paused, feeling the urge to lie. But then I remembered my father's painful punishments for untruth. "I wonder how that ghost knew."

Annie shrugged and turned back to her mixing bowl, her eyes green once more. "There are a lot of ghosts around the palace. Way more than when we drive into Seattle for more unbleached flour."

"Well," I said hesitantly, "while you mix your biscuits do you want to go watch shooting practice?"

I turned and started walking, knowing Annie would fall into step like she always did. Eventually, as she came after me, carefully, lest she spill her bowl, I began to hum beneath my breath. Music had always fascinated me, even at such a young age. It was one of the few things that brought peace to my mind.

The song was an odd one about unfamiliar words—*harleets* and *hores*. I'd heard it late at night through the window in the barracks.

Annie often laughed at my songs, and we would spend hours making up definitions for the words we didn't know. Last week, we'd decided "engorged" was a type of cave in the mountains, and "lubricant" was a different word for a white lie. Granted, Annie had been cuffed twice for confessing she'd told a "lubricant" to her fellow serving girls, so we'd retired that definition rather quickly.

"You have such a nice voice," Annie said, smiling as she mixed the biscuits.

I sang a bit that rhymed all sorts of interesting words with "song," and Annie joined in humming along. We chortled each time we finished before starting again.

The sounds of gunshots faded for a moment, and I glanced across the courtyard in the direction of the indoor shooting range—little more than a cement building jostled against the wall. For a moment, I thought I might have heard shouting. But then it faded as well.

Later, of course, I'd learn the security in my father's palace were encouraged by daddy dearest to practice on locals—any of the unknowing, the untalented. He had them brought in trucks, like livestock, used for sport... For practice. For worse things, too.

I hadn't known at that age.

A couple of the security officers stood in front of the shooting range. They frowned in our direction and began to head over, likely preparing to send us off, but then they noticed me; instantly, they paled and retreated to their posts, examining the grass or their fingernails with utmost interest.

"Why do people do that?" said Annie, her lips bunching up one side in a curious expression. "They don't do that when I'm around."

"Do what?"

"Run away when they see you. See that one? He has a big ugly ghost sitting on his shoulders—it wasn't there until you showed up."

I frowned towards the indicated guard. "What's the ghost doing?"

"Rattling chains," Annie said after a moment. "Two thick, rusty chains in each hand; he's rattling them next to the man's ears...See? I mean, I suppose you can't see—but that's alright. I'm not sure who else can see. Sometimes, I wonder if anyone can. But, well, it is interesting when—" She paused, catching herself mid-sentence. "Oh, sorry," she said quickly. "Corporal Viddagost says I'm not supposed to prattle on so..."

I looked at my friend. "It's okay. I like it when you talk." I turned back to the guard. "A spook with rattling chains, you say? Really?"

I couldn't see, but I did notice the man wince as I caught his eye and he looked away again, moving his head to avoid eye contact.

"But why do they run from you?" Annie reiterated, glancing back at me.

"Do they? I don't know. We should ask them."

Annie scratched her flour covered ear but then seemed to see the sense in this. The distant sound of gunshots renewed with heightened intensity. "Alright. Here, hold this."

She handed her apple core to me. I glanced at it, frowning in disgust. Daintily, so as to not touch the moist, fleshy, eaten part, I held the apple on either end, and then tossed it behind a tree when Annie wasn't looking. I tossed my own apple as well. Eventually, years later, a twisting apple tree had started to grow there, intertwined, I'd heard, with another. Both had been cut, only a year after, but it had meant something to me at the time, and had seen me through some rough months...

"Hello," Annie called, waving a hand towards the retreating guards. "Hello," she called. Her words, though, only seemed to fuel the guards, and they rounded the door into the gun range.

From within the shooting range, I glimpsed flashes of blue light through the dim windows. The soldiers of the Imperium would often train with unique ammunition. Sometimes, normal bullets didn't work on the hidden kingdoms. Nor would they work on angels or genies or the gods. But there were chemists and eternals who came up with all sorts of interesting devices for killing non-humans.

"Do you see that?" said Annie, watching the retreating guards. "They can't hear me."

"They can hear you," I replied, bored again. "They're just ignoring you." Then, I leaned over and grabbed a handful of dough from Annie's bowl.

Before she could protest, I launched the chunk of dough at the guards, aiming through the doorway. "Score!" I cried in delight as I pegged one of them in the back of the head; the man whirled around, glaring daggers. When he spotted me, though, his expression morphed into a forced smile, and he reached up to wipe dough from his head. It dropped in gooey clumps to the ground, and he saluted with his offhand, then, stiff, he continued to turn through the door into the concrete building.

I nodded towards the guard as if to prove a point. "The guards don't like talking to me."

"And I don't blame them!" Annie shouted, one hand on her hip, her body sheltering her biscuit bowl from further invasion.

I weighed my options for a moment. On one hand, Annie was angry with me. But on the other, I was still bored. I didn't think she could get much angrier, but I certainly could become less bored. So I reached into the bowl and grabbed another clump of dough. This time, I threw it at Annie, pegging her in the face.

The thing about boundaries—they're usually established by peers. As I had no peers, I was a bit underdeveloped in areas of tact and compassion. I'm not a very good man, nor was I a good child.

I burst into laughter, clutching my stomach as dough dripped down Annie's nose and plopped onto the back of her hand. She glared at me and then hit me with her spatula.

The guards looked sharply over at this, both of them indicating Annie and her implement. Their countenances darkened as they hurried over, their boots stomping against the ground, their rifles slung over their shoulders. They wore the uniforms of the Imperium: navy blue, streaked with golden numerals on their lapels. They also had the twisting tattoo of the Imperium's blue crown on their cheeks.

Judging by their scowls, I realized they were about to hurt my friend. My father often got a similar look before beating me or Augustus.

Both guards came to an immediate halt. "Young master, are you alright? Did the little skint hurt you?"

"What does *skint* mean?" I asked, certain I'd heard the word before in one of the barracks' songs.

"Well," the guards exchanged a strange look. The one on the left scratched his chin, and then, cautiously, said, "it means disgusting and vile." He glared at Annie. "How dare you hit Prince Leonidas!"

"Oh," I said. "No, she isn't *skint*. She's my friend. She hit me because I ruined her biscuits." I frowned, lost in thought for a moment, but then nodded reluctantly. "Yes, I deserved it I think."

"She *hit* you, sir," said one of the guards, insistently. When I didn't react, he rounded on Annie, thunderstruck, and slapped her hard across the face.

Annie yelped.

"Stupid, ugly rat!" the guard snapped. He whacked her again, harder, this time with his other hand. Tears welled up in her eyes, dripping past her nose and intermingling with the dough residue still stuck to cheeks.

"What are you doing?" The *cold* curdled my veins, rising in my chest. At the time, I didn't know how to suppress it.

Annie was staring at me now, fear in her tearful eyes. She gaped just over my shoulder though, her green eyes filmed with gray like clouds heralding a storm. "Leon," she yelped. But it sounded, instead of being scared *of* me, like she was scared *for* me. She took a step forward in a protective move, but one of the guards grabbed her wrist, holding her still. The cold arose even more, and Annie whimpered, still staring over my shoulder, her eyes bugging in her head.

I could feel a slight chill against my neck and vaguely, I glanced back. But I saw nothing.

I rounded on the guards once more. "I don't want you to hurt her," I said, my teeth gritted now. "Let go of her!"

The guard hesitated at first, but then, with a final squeeze which elicited a squeak of pain from my friend, he stepped back. The cold was on me now, an armor of rage shielding even the most poignant of my gentler sensibilities; Annie's gray eyes were transfixed by whatever she could see over my shoulder.

"Eat that," I said, pointing towards the spatula in Annie's hand. The guard who'd slapped Annie stared at me. "Eat it!" I screamed.

The guards shifted, wincing towards other soldiers now looking our way. Men with rifles were starting to approach from the direction of the gates, frowning. Both the nearby guards trembled, shaking their heads. "Please, Prince Leonidas, we were just trying to help!"

I knew that forcing them to consume the rough splinters of the wood might damage them, perhaps irreparably. But I didn't care, in fact the prospect delighted me in ways that scared me even then. "I said, eat it. Or I will *tell my father!*"

The magic words worked like they always did. Without further hesitation, both guards scrambled for the spatula in Annie's hands; they yanked it from her, and she jerked her fingers back, sucking at her thumb. Then the men gripped the spatula and snapped it in half. Helplessly, their eyes bugging in their skulls, they jammed the wooden halves into their mouths and began chomping as hard as they could. I heard the crunch and wasn't sure if it was their teeth breaking or wood snapping. Blood poured from their lips where splinters gouged into their mouths and tongues. Both men cried from the pain but glanced frantically towards the approaching guards with the big weapons and kept chewing.

These men were royal security officers, but one of those approaching had the gold numeral "X" of a lieutenant

"Leon, please, don't. You'll kill them!" Annie was crying now. I could feel the cold swirling inside me, but something in Annie's gaze seemed to calm it. As I watched her, the feeling of murderous rage and indifference and apathy and loathing began to subside. The feeling of snapping small animals in my hands—my father's first training—began to flit away.

"They hurt you," I said adamantly. "So they must be punished."

The guards were now looking at Annie with pleading glances.

She swallowed. "But-but, please, Leon, they're in pain."

I frowned. Couldn't she understand? "They *hurt* you," I said slowly, trying to explain. "So they must be punished."

Annie hesitated, and then almost seemed to glance over her own shoulder. She listened, it seemed, for a moment to the wind. Or, perhaps, to one of her spook friends. And then Annie grabbed a handful of biscuit dough and flung it at the guards.

"See," she said. "We can throw the dough at them. Just don't make them eat the spatula. It will hurt them."

I considered this for a moment, but then concluded it was fitting for Annie to decide the punishment. "Alright, you don't have to eat it."

The guards spat out the splinters; blood and spit and wood pulp spewed from their mouths, landing on the cobblestones outside the gun range.

"Now run," I said.

Both guards turned and began sprinting away, rushing as fast as they could to distance themselves from us. Giggling, I grabbed handful after handful of dough, launching it at the fleeing guards. I glanced over at Annie, wondering if she was having as much fun as I was.

But she wasn't throwing any dough. She had a sad look in her eyes, and, as she watched me, she slowly lowered the bowl, allowing it to dangle next to her side.

I paused, my sticky fingers still raised. Looking at Annie's expression, I knew I'd done something I ought not have.

"I'm sorry," I said reflexively. Annie often talked about thinking of others and trying to imagine what they would feel. It wasn't easy. But, slowly, as I mulled it over, I clicked my fingers. "I'm sorry they hit you."

"It's okay," she said.

"I'm sorry I ruined your biscuits. I'll have someone make some for you."

Annie shook her head, though. "I don't want someone else's biscuits. I'll make my own when I get back."

"Okay. Well, I'm sorry." I had seen Annie cry on more than one occasion but had never been able to muster up the emotion myself.

For a moment, remembering the look of fear in her eyes as she'd looked past me as the cold came on, I thought she might flee.

"What—what did you see?" I asked carefully.

Annie swallowed, then said, "Nothing." Instead of recoiling or running away, though, she began to cry again. Annie reached out and wrapped her small, girlish arms around me in an embrace.

No one in the palace was allowed to touch me, so it was a strange sensation to feel another body pressed against mine. To feel hands on my shoulders and a soft cheek flecked with flour pressed against my own. I could feel her fuzzy head rubbing the side of my forehead. She was a bit taller than me.

"It's going to be okay," she said. "You're okay. It's going to be okay." She kept repeating the words, again and again, cooing softly in my ear like one of my father's monster hunters trying to wrangle a particularly unruly predator. She held me close, and I could feel the *cold* had completely faded now.

I miss those days.

Annie disappeared from the palace two days later. I never saw her again.

Chapter 10
Now...

I jolted awake to the sound of sirens, growling in frustration as I flipped the covers from my body and slid off the edge of my bed. The echoing memories sifted through my thoughts like sand between clutching fingers, drifting away into my subconscious once more.

"Tomb's trove, Preacher—what is it?" I called in the dark.

My mute friend didn't reply from the front of the RV. However, through the windows over my bed, I glimpsed the flashing blue-red of dancing lights. For a moment, the blue startled me, but I suppressed thoughts of my poltergeist and, instead, pushed to my feet.

I found my body glazed with sweat, and I pressed my forehead against the window, feeling the cold against my warm skin as a puff of breath fogged the glass.

The RV rolled to a halt on the side of the mountain road. Night had long since dominated the sky. Darkness rolled in waves over treetops and mountains beneath moonlight. Behind us, illuminated by the single working brake-light of my RV, mixed with the flashing sirens, I spotted two figures step out from a police cruiser.

One of them *clicked* something cylindrical in their hand, and a beam of pale light streamed towards me, blinding me for a second before the flashlight moved towards the front of the vehicle.

Police in these parts of the mountains? Rare.

Police pulling us over? Not so rare. I grabbed my flat cap from the hook behind the door, where it dangled perfectly centered against the clean, painted wood—and pulled the hat over my eyes. Good first impressions wouldn't have been *everyone's* first instinct in such situations, but I'd grown up knowing the value of presentation.

Then, growling, still in my sleeping sweater and slacks, I stepped out into the main compartment.

A female voice drifted through the driver side open window. "Well, hello there, big fella," the voice was saying. "Pleasant evening, ain't it?"

The voice spoke in a quiet southern drawl, as out of the place in the Northwest Washington mountains as wings on a bullfrog. Frowning to myself, I approached the front of the RV, sidling past the scorch marks. My eyes darted towards the bullet holes peppering the walls and I felt a flicker of unease. Had the patrolmen spotted the perforation? Whatever the case, we were wasting valuable time. If someone else was gunning for that key...

I shivered. We needed to hurry.

Preacher sat with his hands gripping the steering wheel, his head turned at an angle to acknowledge the officer through the window. A click. Then, the beam from the flashlight faded. Illuminated now by the glow of headlights alone, two figures stood out against the night.

Both of them wore police uniforms. Both of them had black radios attached to wired battery packs. Both of them had their hands on their hips—not quite resting on their firearms—but close enough to alarm.

"Ah—I see our silent driver has a friend. Howdy," said the female officer.

I sat in the passenger seat, unbuckled, looking across Preacher's muscled chest at the two faces peering up and into the RV.

The woman had curly, uncombed hair pulled back by a simple band. She wore no makeup, and her features did little to betray her age. Perhaps as young as twenty or as mature as forty. Her upper lip had the thinnest film of fuzz on it, and her large chest protruded towards the window. She stood with one hand on her hip, with her body postured in a way that best displayed the natural curvature of her form.

She smiled through the window at Preacher, eyeing him up and down. My spine tingled and the hair on the back of my neck stood on end. Preacher said nothing but gave me a sidelong glance, elevating one eyebrow.

"Couldn't help but notice your taillight is out," she said, tapping long, manicured fingers against the door frame and examining Preacher hungrily. "Noticed a thing or two about your tail."

I folded my hangs gingerly. "Can we help you?"

"I don't know, darling," she drawled. "I certainly hope so."

She didn't have the look of Endeavor. They tended to travel in teams. Besides, we'd left Endeavor territory miles ago; these portions of the mountain were still under the control of the Dwindling Imperium or, in parts, under no one's control at all.

But these folk didn't strike me as members of a magistocracy either. For one, the woman seemed to have a sense of humor. She commanded attention in the way few could manage, and yet, at last, I pried my gaze away and glanced over her shoulder at her partner. I did a double take.

The man, if possible, was even larger than Preacher. He had a short-cropped, buzzed head, and an enormous beak of a nose, resembling, if anything, an ex-NFL linebacker. His eyes were like granite, both in color and compassion.

He noticed my attention and gave me a flat stare, curling his fingers against his chest into a massive fist.

Preacher gave me another quick glance.

"What seems to be the problem, officers?" I said quietly.

The woman was now leaning completely through the window. Her elbows rested on the sill; her head poked towards me, across Preacher's chest. "So you're the fella with a tongue?" She cocked her eyebrows, which were even more bushy than her upper lip. "I have a tongue, too, my bearded pal. Wanna see?" She licked her lips, but instead of sensuous the gesture bordered on ravenous.

At this point, I was fairly certain we weren't dealing with regular highway patrol. Then again, I'd encountered stranger things in the mountains of Washington State.

"Were we breaking the law?" I said coolly.

"I'm not sure... Have you been a bad boy?"

I cleared my throat. "Were we speeding?" I knew we weren't as Preacher was a stickler for the rules. Sometimes, I thought he went out of his way to *find* rules just so he could have the delight of obeying them.

"No," she said, her tongue still half-hanging. "I don't *believe* so. Leonidas, Preacher," she nodded to both of us in turn. "My brother and I are here on behalf of our father."

My back prickled again, but I kept my gaze impassive. She knew our names. It was starting to feel like my efforts to protect my anonymity had completely imploded in the last few days. "Your father?"

"Yes," she said. "He... has grown more compliant with age."

At this, the giant behind her grunted and cleared his throat.

"Oh, no, silly, I don't mean disrespect to Papa. However, my family... you must understand... needs to eat. We can't allow every little field mouse to escape in a spurt of compassion."

I felt the prickle now extend down my spine. "Your father?" I said. "Pardon me, but who might that be?"

"Oh, you two just spoke. Apologies. Where are my manners? My name is Euryale. This is my brother Gog."

The cold chill drifting through the window now seemed to probe at my neck. "Ah, of course," I said carefully. "Grendel's children. How could I forget?" I remembered Grendel mentioning how his brood were a day's travels away. Clearly, they'd covered ground. Or the eavesdropper I'd heard had been one of these two. Which meant they knew about the key, and they knew about the Librarian's mansion. Were they here to distract me? Or worse?

"Last time, we were in different forms, I imagine. You were quick. I'll give you that." She smiled sweetly back at me, her large bosom pressing against the windowsill, where she still leaned into the vehicle. I felt my cheeks flush a bit from the way my eyes wandered. It wasn't seemly for a gentleman to stare. For the first time, her eyes flashed gold and indigo but then flickered back to a vibrant hazel. It took mild effort, but eternals could disguise the coloring of their eyes if they suppressed their gift for long enough.

Preacher's hands had now drifted from the steering wheel and were resting on his lap, within reach of the six shooters beneath his trench coat. I'd encountered Grendel's children before. They were, if possible, even more bloodthirsty than their father, though far more asinine. A trait that made them even more rash and unpredictable.

The fact they'd hunted me down and pulled me over in the mountains, away from the rest of the world, didn't bode well.

"I'm not sure if you're aware," I said, delicately folding my hands and keeping my eyes fixed on hers, resisting the urge to glance down. "But your father has made a deal with, ah, my employer. He won't harm us while we work for her."

Gog grunted again behind his sister. Euryale waved a hand. "We heard—we weren't delighted, though. We've been savoring a chance to meet again. Especially after last time."

I winced at the recollection. "Ah, yes. And how is Mago doing? Still limping?"

Euryale shook her head. "You can ask him yourself soon enough."

I definitely didn't like the sound of that. Delicately, I said, "With all due respect, you creep me out."

She flashed a sharp-toothed grin in my direction. At the same time, I tentatively reached out with my mind. Grendel's children didn't have the same defenses as their father. As I placed myself in their surface thoughts, though, it felt like inundating myself in a river of freezing blood—shocking and vile at once. A worming, gnawing sensation of hunger settled on me and filled my chest. I felt a shock of adrenaline, of bloodlust. My mouth began to water, and just as quickly, I pulled back, releasing my probe.

These two wanted only one thing.

Kindred often traveled in packs. And a Kindred as old as Grendel had many children.

"My father may have made a deal with you, human," she said, soft now, a seductive quality to her voice. "However, his oaths aren't ours to keep."

I wet my lips. "You are frightening me and giving me reason to anticipate imminent violence."

She quirked her head. "How very... transparent of you."

"What will your father think?"

"I look forward to finding out."

And with that, she lunged with feral strength *through* my window, hands groping towards my neck—her manicured nails seeming more like talons all of a sudden.

I wasn't waiting, though. While I'd left her mind, I'd sensed the imminent attack. The moment she flinched, I flung myself back and kicked out, sending her rebounding back through the window.

"Preacher! Go!"

My friend needed no further invitation. He shifted into gear and floored the pedal. My eyes flicked to the rearview mirrors.

"Dumb and dumber are letting their hair down," I muttered beneath my breath.

Preacher's eyes narrowed and he pointed to the buckle next to me. Quickly, I yanked the seat belt across my chest and clicked it into place. For his part, Preacher pushed the RV as fast as it would go, tearing up the desolate highway beneath sputtering safety lights and through swirling mist introduced by prickling leaves.

My heart hammered against the seat belt crossing my chest. I glanced towards the mirror again, watching the silhouettes of Grendel's two oldest children reform. Golden eyes blinked from the darkness, tinged with telltale indigo. The Kindred were on the move.

Chapter 11

Though we were traveling at least seventy miles an hour—as fast as my poor RV could manage, the golden eyes were closing the distance. I heard a howling sound and a snarling response. I heard the thumping noise of heavy feet against asphalt. A bellow and then—

THUD.

The RV shook and nearly toppled. Something had rammed us from the side. For a moment, the vehicle angled as we flew across the highway on two wheels. Preacher flung himself against the window, trying to readjust the momentum. We hung suspended, half toppled, and then, with a *crash,* the vehicle landed on all four wheels again.

We twisted around, nearly slamming into the barricade on the side of the road. We'd spun out—coming to a full stop, our windshield glinting beneath the bluish safety light glaring down at us. Preacher moved fast, despite the collision. He pulled a revolver from his hip holster, rotated in his seat, sighted through the open window and squeezed off two shots in rapid succession.

A snarl, a squeal of pain. But the golden eyes and large, furry shapes kept coming. Whatever had struck us from the side was circling for another collision.

"Mago too," I said quickly. "A third!"

Preacher nodded and grabbed his second six shooter. Instead of raising it, though, he tossed it to me, and inclined an eyebrow. He tapped his forehead with a finger.

"You're sure?"

He nodded once, tapping his temple again, and then put us in reverse, and the RV squealed away from where we'd smashed the barrier. I swallowed, steadying myself. Normally, I wouldn't invade the minds of my friends, but Preacher had given permission. Desperate times...

I reached out, revolver clutched in my fist. Instantly, I was surrounded by shifting shadows as Preacher's thoughts were played around me like a three-hundred-and-sixty-degree projector screen of shadow puppets. I sifted through his mind, touching as little as possible to reach my goal.

Muscle memory.

And then I delved in—feeling a tingle along my fingers, a pulsing throb along my knuckles and hands. Fire flooded my tendons for a second, and I drank deep of Preacher's training, flooding myself with the same—a copy. Some imperial talents engaged in *ripping* whatever skills they would find, leaving their subjects empty, talentless. I made sure to damage nothing. It took me longer this way, but it left Preacher unharmed.

Eventually, I fully extricated what I needed, feeling it meld with my own mind. By leaving Preacher his skill, it meant I only had an impression of it. Temporary access. It would fade within an hour or so.

Plenty of time. My arm responded to my intention far faster than usual. I raised my revolver, aiming through the right window. I fired once, shattering the glass as my eyes narrowed, my attention drawn by the faintest of movements between the trees. I tried to aim, but then my new instincts, Preacher's instincts, took over and I aimed ahead and far higher than I thought made sense.

I squeezed the trigger twice, a smooth, pulling motion.

The dark form speeding through the trees next to us loosed a terrible yelp. To my left, I heard Preacher fire his own weapon again. I could feel the RV straining to keep up pace. We were still speeding in reverse, racing *backwards* down the highway at an angle towards the opposite shoulder. If anyone was coming from behind, it'd be disastrous. For now, though, our luck held out.

Preacher slammed the brakes, spinning the nose of our vehicle towards the road again.

For a moment, a *thing* was illuminated in the headlights. A massive, armored beast of a creature with golden eyes flecked with indigo.

"Hello, Gog," I muttered beneath my breath.

He had the appearance of an armored rhinoceros, except twice as large with two horns protruding from his nose—this was the thing that had knocked us off the road. Patches of blood twisted down his thick, gray hide. *Bullet wounds,* my borrowed instincts told me, but nothing significantly damaging. The creature charged, barreling straight at us, tearing up fragments of asphalt from the sheer weight and power of its thundering steps. Legs the size of tree trunks moved like logs in an avalanche; feet like stumps slammed into the road, cracking it. The thing's horns lowered, glinting, thick—more dull and protruding than sharp. A battering ram of muscle and stupid headed straight for us.

"His skin is too thick," I said, quietly.

Preacher nodded to me and then flicked his eyes towards the window. We were still moving forward, but slowly now, giving us time. Gog's form continued to rush, tearing up the ground.

Shoot first, Preacher mouthed.

I blinked. "You're joking."

He kept his eyes on the road, pistol raised. *You first,* he mouthed.

The thing was nearly on us now, thundering down the open highway. I glimpsed other shadowy shapes off in the trees, hungry, watching, howling at the stars.

Muttering darkly, I poked my head out of the shattered window, aimed—allowing foreign instincts to take over my arm. This never would have worked anywhere else. Preacher was the best shooter I knew. But, for a brief instant, for a few moments, there were *two* Preachers, both sharing the *exact* same instinct, the *exact* same muscle memory.

My weapon raised. Out of the corner of my eye, I noticed his did too.

I sighted, fired.

A split second later, Preacher's weapon discharged a final shot—empty now. The enormous, charging form of the horned beast pulled up short. Its skin was too thick. So why was it stumbling?

I stared, stunned. Gog took a drunken step, then another. It was now directly in our headlights, Preacher swerved around it, speeding back up the highway, away from Grendel's children. As we passed, I glimpsed a bug-eyed, monstrous face. Between the two horns, a single bullet hole.

I blinked. No—my instincts told me. Not *one* bullet hole. Too wide.

Preacher had hit the thing *exactly* where I had hit it a split second before. Same muscle memory, same instincts.

He'd driven my bullet deeper with his own.

I stared, stunned, mouth agape as we sped past the wounded creature. Gog was thick-skulled. It would take more than a couple bullets to kill that beast. But, for now, he was out of the fight.

My hand trembled and I lowered the revolver, placing it on the tray behind the gear shift. "Nice shot," I said, my voice shaky.

In the rearview mirror, I spotted silhouettes reforming—dark, beastly shapes turning human again. Five of them now. More of Grendel's children than I'd first seen. They gathered around their fallen brethren.

I watched in my rearview mirror as they paused, sniffing at Gog's form. And then, like a pack of hyenas, they descended on him, ripping flesh, tearing chunks of meat and howling beneath the blue safety lights of the mountain highway.

I shivered, looking away, clasping my hands together in my lap and breathing heavily as we sped down the road, leaving the nightmarish scene behind us and heading towards Picker's Lake and towards my new employer.

"They know about the key," I murmured, glancing at my friend.

He nodded once.

"Should we get to the mansion at night? Should we risk it?"

Preacher winced but then glanced towards my wrist.

I swallowed. He was right. Imperium still patrolled these mansions. Even in a race against Grendel's brood, messing with Imperium at night would be a mistake.

"Get an hour or two of sleep, then?" I asked. I glanced in the mirror. "They seem occupied enough for now."

Preacher signed at me.

"I guess," I murmured. "I mean, it's not like they know *how* to get to the key. We could slow down—a bit. Just to wait for sunlight. To avoid... well, you know."

Preacher didn't even hesitate. He nodded once, flashing a thumbs up.

After all our haste through the mountains, we'd made good time. *Too* good. We'd be arriving at Picker's Lake under the cover of night. Never a good choice in contested territory.

It was a risk.

On one hand, if they reached the key first, and managed to find it, we'd lose our sewer entrance strategy for the Hollow.

On the other, we'd slowed them down a good deal by dropping Gog. Plus, if we waited for sunlight, it would clear additional and, in some cases, *worse* obstacles from the mansions. Not to mention, we'd have to access the Hollow in less than three days in order to make it in time before the Unlocator spell hid it for another year.

"An hour of sleep when we get there," I said firmly. "Park outside the tent. No one from either side goes there."

Preacher's lips tightened a bit, but he nodded again and I returned to looking out the window, frowning to myself.

An hour to wait for sunlight. Had we bought ourselves an hour by taking out Gog, by allowing the Kindred to feast on their brother? Was an hour going to cost us our window of opportunity? Perhaps... Surely even Grendel's children wouldn't make good pace on full stomachs.

Grendel had backed off, but clearly his offspring had other ideas. Perhaps they didn't care what their father thought. Or perhaps they just didn't know enough to fear my employer.

The Hollow—she wanted us to find and breech the Hollow. Another chill of dread filled me, eclipsing the first.

"Preacher," I said, quiet now, still awed by his marksmanship, but troubled by what lay ahead.

He grunted. His eyes lowered from the rearview mirror, and he inhaled a steadying breath. One hand scratched at a cauliflower ear.

I closed my own eyes. My nerves settled and I washed the fear from my system with a flood of courage pulled from discardable memories. We were no longer being followed—I double and triple checked just to make sure, but the roads were clear behind us once more. Then, settled, my mind switched track. "If... If I can't do it. You have to."

Preacher frowned.

"No—I mean it. If that's who she wants us to rescue—if that's who we're supposed to break out... You know what we have to do."

Preacher stayed silent as ever.

A small sob escaped my lips. "I—I don't think I'll be able to." I pictured my hand squeezing Dale's throat.

Preacher kept one hand on the steering wheel, but the other reached out, patting me on the shoulder. Then it retrieved his revolver and placed it back in his holster.

"If she wants us to rescue Napoleon... I know he's my baby brother but..." I said, finding some amount of strength in another deep breath. "Then you have to do it, okay? If I can't. If she found out. If she wants him to escape... You have to put a bullet in his head."

Preacher crossed himself, murmured a quiet prayer and we lingered in silence for a second, still driving up the highway, observing the speed limit under Preacher's watchful eye. He was the sort to use turn signals even at midnight on an empty, abandoned road. We moved through the mountains and beneath gusting wisps of fog. The wind ushered through the shattered window across my tense body. Before confronting my brother, or locating the Hollow at all, we still had to snag our sewer key and meet up with our employer.

And not just any employer, but the sort of person who could cheerfully puppet a willing mind, demand the respect of a killer like Grendel and, also, thought it wise to blackmail a savant into taking a suicide mission.

Chapter 12

Found in forgotten forests beneath bashful skies, one might stumble upon a village such as Picker's Lake. Once a mining town, now, the water sluiced through dredges and wash plants, all that remained of the lake was a dried crater used for fertile soil. A place born of gold lust now served as the graveyard for ambition. The two diners—not quite restaurants—and one dance hall passably entertained the some five hundred occupants of the small forest village.

For others, though, it was an oasis hidden in the woods and mist of the Cascade Mountains. Most the residents of Picker's Lake had lived there for generations, and yet, were you to ask the IRS, UPS, or any other alphabet soup government agency, the town itself is an unknown quantity. Most the residents have no social security cards, nor passports. To some, the community resembled that of the Amish—an insular, familial town, built on archaic notions of reputation, legacy and family bond. But like the lineages of the small village, the secrets are also old and long buried.

My RV sat parked on the outskirts of town in a forest clearing. Through my window, I heard the loud bark of pistol fire. Groaning, I rolled out of my bed, glancing blearily towards the light glimpsing through my window. Our hour of respite, waiting prison.

More gunshots retorted outside my RV. For most, a matter of concern. For me, though, as good as any alarm. Preacher, without fail, woke up at four A.M. every morning. He would get in a five-mile jog, a hundred push-ups and a hundred sit-ups by five. Then, he'd spend the next two hours practicing his marksmanship. Judging by the light through the window, we were only at the start of the practice, suggesting he also knew we needed to get going.

I heard another series of loud blasts, followed by the dull thunk of—what I assumed—were bullets hitting their marks. Sighing at the inevitability of the wake-up call, I slid out of bed, approaching my small bachelor's chest and, delicately, looked through the neatly folded shirts in the top drawer. It took me a few moments to finally decide, but then, with care, I removed a crew-neck with breathable fabric. Today, I would need mobility.

By the time I dressed, showered in the small C-class bathroom, grabbed a granola bar—the extent of my cooking abilities—and then exited the RV, Preacher was already waiting, peering up at me from beneath the brim of his cattleman crease, red-feathered hat.

"Morning," I murmured.

He eyed my damp hair.

I stared back at him. "It was a *quick* shower," I said.

Preacher glanced at the sun, then back at me.

I frowned. "I know, I know. Don't you think I know?"

Preacher glanced over his shoulder towards a large, white tent centering the clearing where we'd parked. Other vehicles, closer to the tent, were stationed in a sort of semi-circle around the shelter. From within, Preacher and I could both hear the sounds of someone speaking and a murmur of response. This was an early morning meeting—I'd seen evenings where the entire field was covered with vehicles as people from all around spilled out the front of the tent, clogging the space between the cars, all desperately hoping for a chance to see Preacher's father.

Our meeting place with our new boss would take place on home turf. We needed every advantage we could get.

"Do you want to go to see him after?" I asked, quietly.

Preacher gave a shake of his head, then, hands jammed into his trench coat, he strode away from the enormous white tent, and our parked RV.

We followed the dusty trails, leaving the large, white revival tent behind us and maneuvering beneath low boughs of prickling firs. Preacher had to duck a couple of times as we moved, but he did so with a practiced ease—Picker's Lake was his hometown after all. He'd grown up in these woods.

We reached the main hub of the small town, and I spotted *Catherine's* diner across from *Rizzo's*. The only two businesses in the area that weren't operated from someone's backyard, save the General Store, about a mile's walk to the north.

The buildings in the town were of wood and concrete. Modest in structure, but displaying carvings around the trims and beneath the shingled roofs. On closer inspection, the carvings depicted strange creatures, beings seen neither in story nor imagination of most mortals. Personally, I knew them as creatures from the Kingdoms of Pilfery. The streets were dusty—cobblestone, an older era. Concrete and asphalt had invaded portions of the town center but avoided the outskirts.

"The sun only just came up. Don't worry. We have time," I muttered to Preacher. "Do you think Imperium is still watching the roads?"

He shrugged once, but one hand meandered to his belt as we moved along the sidewalk outside *Catherine's*, ducking beneath a sputtering pink sign that read *Welcome!* Beneath it, there was another sign which read, *We don't call the Sheriff.* This second one had a picture of a rifle on it and a pointing finger silhouetted above the words.

"The militia meets here, yes?" I said, glancing towards my friend.

He seemed to be studying his reflection in the glass, his eyes fixed on his own face. My six-foot-nine companion with his cauliflower ears and handsome features streaked in makeup struck an odd figure where the pink lights reflected off his dark skin, pulsed in his auburn eyes and filled both our ears with an itching buzz.

I tugged the edge of my newsboy cap just a bit lower. Picker's Lake was a sleepy town, and it didn't take well to strangers. Preacher, though, was no stranger—as long as I was with him, I had nothing to fear from the locals.

Then again, more than just the locals visited this area and lurked in the surrounding woods.

"Let's hurry," I muttered. "Taking down Gog might not have been enough to deter Grendel's brats."

I paused in front of a small hedge gate, delicately extracting a silk handkerchief from my pocket. Carefully, I reached out, lifting the fork latch, making sure not to contact the metal with my skin.

I pushed through, hastily folding my handkerchief and stowing it back in my pocket. The gate moaned like the tentative cry of a waking child as Preacher swung it shut and latched it for me. He met my gaze, rolling his eyes as I tucked my handkerchief back in my pocket. I sniffed in response. "If you catch gangrene, don't come crying to me."

Preacher snorted laughter, patted me with a meaty palm on the back, then resumed his trek.

I also moved with quickening steps along the trail, uphill in the direction of the old, abandoned mansions. "Grendel fears her," I murmured as I walked. "That much is clear. She knows a spell, or has a ritual to possess willing minds—though a weak connection. She also knows who I am." My eyes flicked towards my friend. "That perhaps is most troubling. Not just my name, but that I belong to it."

Preacher hesitated then signed, *Trap?*

It wasn't a comforting thought, but I peered along the dirt path behind the diner. My eyes flicked back towards the sealed gate on rusted hinges. For a moment, I felt a chill which had nothing to do with the weather.

"Let's hope not," I muttered. "Grendel's children know we're here. Endeavor might have figured it out, too. Not to mention the Dwindling Imperium still controls these mountains... We have enough enemies around. If our employer is leading us into a trap... might not be a way out this time." I frowned, wrinkling my nose at the truncated word. "Pardon. *There* might not be a way out this time."

Preacher reached beneath his jacket to his seemed leather holster and pulled out a revolver. He handed it towards me and inclined an eyebrow above a deep, auburn eye. But I patted his hand, pushing the weapon back.

"A kind gesture, but in this situation, I feel as if two in your hands will prove better than ten in mine. I'll keep my eyes peeled. If you think anything is awry up at the mansions, we'll run to the RV and drive across the country down into Argentina, or something—I hear they're always on the lookout for a savant. Plus, I know a place that serves commendable pecan waffles."

Preacher's cheeks stretched with a quietly amused smile, and he holstered his weapon again. Then, the two of us made our way along the dirt path, up the trail and towards the abandoned mansions where we'd arranged to meet our new employer.

***

Two mansions, both of them looming hunched buildings, reclined in the skirt of the mountains with the ease and comfort of long familiarity. Deep arches and stone turrets outlined against a backdrop off a postcard: green peaks with trailing rivers shedding from naked slopes. The idyllic scene beyond was marred, however, by the dark and ash-stained portions of the mansions.

Half of one structure bristled with charred beams and burnt siding. Another was in ill-repair, though I did spot a well-maintained sliding cover for a swimming pool just within a black, metal fence.

I gestured towards the pool cover. "Not as dusty as I remember it. Do you think someone's been living up there?" There was no further sign of intruders.

Preacher and I paused at the edge of the dirt path which spilled between two flanking hemlocks. Around us, the fragrance of rhododendrons and other mountain flowers intermingled with the sodden dirt from an incessant sprinkler spritzing the ground. Lilac had overgrown, crowding against cracked windows and dusty walls, though I noted a couple of portions trimmed back.

"It looks like gardeners have come through," I said quietly.

Preacher was frowning towards the pool, seemingly disconcerted by my comment. The mansions were supposed to be abandoned—they had once belonged to the Librarian, a reclusive millionaire who had made her wealth, it was rumored, fencing stolen goods for the Jester, a notorious thief who robbed treasures from Endeavor and Imperium alike.

Rumor had it, the Imperium tracked down the fence, and burned her out of one of the homes. One mansion, it was said, she kept for herself. The other, the rumors held, was full of secret passages and hidden items. The remainders of the Jester's treasures.

Of course, Preacher and I had been up and down both mansions many times. We'd found no treasure, but ample evidence of burnings and vandalism. I little doubted the Imperium had been through; likely they'd burnt half the western mansion. But as for fenced items stolen by the Jester—I hadn't found any.

Still, the two of us had lived in the eastern mansion's basement for the better part of a year after we'd first met, locking ourselves in at night and giving ourselves ample opportunity to explore the large houses.

Home turf advantage. Our new employer wouldn't be able to lay a trap for us too easily.

Preacher led the way up the creaking wooden steps of the eastern mansion, taking them two at a time. One hand hovered over the weather-eaten rail, his fingers trailing splintered wood. The air smelled of must, sodden lumber and wild lilac.

The scents were soon replaced, however, by the overpowering odor of mold assailing my nostrils as I followed Preacher into the heart of the mansion. Water damage wreathed the walls in crowns of dappled black against peeling wallpaper speckled by sketches of chrysanthemums. I stood beneath a chandelier missing the glass baubles which had once dangled from the conspicuous ornament.

Preacher glanced back at me, his features touched by the dark of the still mansion. He raised one pointer finger, spinning it in a small circle. He signed, *are we alone?*

I hesitated, but instead of glancing down the long halls, or up the stairs, I closed my eyes. I sent out my consciousness *seeking,* searching the rooms, the chambers, the halls, the three floors and the basement.

I frowned, closing my eyes to focus. My arms rested stiff against my side, lest I accidentally rub against the mold and muck. I emitted a shallow, exhaling breath. The closer I got to the threat of imminent action, the shorter my sentences came, "Upstairs, third floor, observatory. One mind."

Preacher kept his auburn eyes fixed on me.

"Could be our employer... could be someone else."

My dark proclamation was met by the sound of metal sliding against cloth and the dull snick of a hammer being pulled back as Preacher prepared his weapon. I allowed my enormous companion to take the lead, in part for the protection, but also, this way, I could step in his footfalls, avoiding dust and dirt as much as possible. My mesh and leather hiking shoes weren't nearly as expensive as Dale's penny-loafers, but despite the abuse I put them through in my job, I tried to keep them as clean as possible.

We circled the banisters, up towards the second floor. The entire stairwell was nearly collapsed. Only a thin sliver of the steps allowed passage. I winced, rubbing against the wall, and clinging to the wooden rail as I pulled myself after Preacher. My movements were surefooted, graceful, like the choreographed steps of a dancer. After all, I'd trained in ballroom dance through my childhood.

Preacher wasn't so graceful, but he covered the gap with one mighty surging step and a hefty yank of the rail.

A splintering sound followed and Preacher was left holding a shattered section of banister. He eyed it for a moment and then tossed it off into a gray, dusty corner filled with stained rags and a small sleeping bag.

I examined the bag for a moment, but then shook my head towards Preacher. "Old—no one's used it in a while. I'm still only sensing the single presence above us."

Even as I spoke, though, I felt a sudden jolt in my extended consciousness. I frowned, and suddenly held up a halting, quieting hand towards my cauliflower-eared friend. He stared back at me, an eyebrow crooked.

I clenched my eyes now, and strained as if seeking a word on the tip of my tongue. But then, like blips on a radar, I detected another presence step into my range of *seeking*.

Then another. And another. And another.

I glanced sharply down the shattered stairs. No movement below just yet. I gestured frantically at Preacher and together we moved in silent synchronization across the dusty floor towards a smashed window above floorboards rotten with rain damage. I eased against the soggy ground, careful, lest I fall through.

Then I pointed through the window, through tangled hemlock branches, down at the lilac-padded ground between the dilapidated mansions.

Preacher leaned in as well.

We both went still at the same time, poised, like deer perked at the sudden sound of a nearing wolf pack.

Endeavor had found us again. But this time, they weren't alone. Eight gunmen, in black body armor and helmets, carrying AR-15s moved quietly along the trail, weapons raised, eyes peeled. In the lead ventured a large-chested woman with a hairy upper lip. Euryale, from the night before—Grendel's daughter. Apparently they'd been smart enough to avoid this area at night.

Behind the group, a stooped, hunched figure in a thick gray cloak limped along on a bum leg. "Mago?" I said softly, glancing to Preacher.

My eagle-eyed companion nodded once, confirming that another one of Grendel's offspring had brought himself center-stage. Clearly, their father's oath hadn't suppressed their hunger.

Eight gunmen, two bloodthirsty Kindred. Had our employer led us into a trap? If not, would she think we'd led her into one?

I hissed quietly, snapping my consciousness back to the present and angling off with Preacher in tow. This last flight of stairs was completely gone. We stood on the bottom step, my ears echoing with the sound of groaning wood, protesting our weight.

"One at a time," I murmured. "You first."

As I watched my friend, Preacher grunted, flung himself towards the top landing, gripped at the ground, and heaved his body up with muscles the size of small bowling balls. As he did, though, I heard a creak then a desperate groan.

I cursed and scampered back a couple of steps.

A chunk of the floor above, the width of a king-sized bed, came crashing down in a flurry of powder and debris, slamming into the ground where I'd been moments before.

Preacher, with a wild lunge, managed to roll to safety on the third floor, out of sight. For my part, I stood coughing, choking dust. The sound of the commotion would certainly have alerted our hunters; if not the Endeavor, then at least the Kindred with their heightened physical senses.

I waved a hand, feeling some of the offensive powder settle on my sleek silk shirt and the brim of my newsboy cap. I scraped my fingers through my beard and then eyed the path up to the top floor. Preacher extended a hand over the edge, gesturing.

But instead, I took two quick steps, shoving with one foot off a banister; I snared an electrical box dangling from the fallen floor, pulled myself up the gap between the floors and rolled to my feet at the top.

Once settled, I dusted off my shirt, straightened my sleeves, and huffed an impatient breath, which also served to clear the dust from my sinuses.

Preacher rolled his eyes, but then his expression froze and he raised a hand to his battered ear. I paused too, listening, holding my breath.

Movement from below, the sound of voices, quick footsteps.

"Better move," I murmured, tracing the surface level thoughts below. "They don't know we're here yet. Let's find our employer, get that key, then get out quick."

Together, Preacher and I hurried along the hall, in the direction of the observatory on the top floor—a room we'd visited before, years ago. And one, I knew, had no exit whatsoever.

If our employer was leading us into a trap, we were like a couple of mice just waiting to hear the click of a spring.

Preacher and I hastened along the hall towards the sizeable oak door at the far end. My six-foot-nine, muscular companion glanced down at my spry, five-eight form. I reached into my pocket, slid my hand through a slit and withdrew the knife in my thigh strap. Preacher raised his pistol. I spun my knife with a practiced flick, allowing it to rotate between my fingers, the opalescent handle glinting dully in the light poking through smashed windows, cracked walls and fractured shingles across the worn ceiling. Etched into the paper of the wall, I spotted a spray-painted symbol of a circle within a circle. Someone had come along after, and with slashing red paint had crossed out the first symbol. Corkers and Palmers at it again—but these were symbols from another life. No longer my business. My eyes flicked up, back towards the mealy oak door.

Preacher shoved into the door *hard,* and we both entered with rapid footfalls.

This room was larger and more illuminated than the halls had been.

I blinked, adjusting, following the sense in my mind until my eyes sprang directly towards the form standing beneath the window.

A familiar mind—I'd sensed it in Dale, back in the RV.

Our employer reclined in a window alcove, beneath an open skylight, her silhouette illuminated by streams of sunlight casting shade across the floorboards. In one hand, she was spinning a large splinter, rotating it around and around. Only after a moment did I realize the pattern seemed to match the same motion I was making with my knife.

I stopped spinning. Nearly instantly, so did she, though she wasn't looking in my direction.

I frowned, reaching out, but sensed no mental connection; the woman wasn't reading my mind.

She was tall, perhaps an inch taller than me, and her hair was sheared close to her head, little more than a prickle against her scalp. As she turned, she tossed the splinter off to the side, and the sunshine through the skylight illuminated her features.

The woman had a gently crooked nose, as if from a poorly set break. Her eyes tasted every hue of green, stippling droplets of the vibrant color across her pupils. She stared at both of us and I stared back. With one hand, she reached towards a small, silver flask, pulling it from a hidden pocket inside her peacoat. She lifted the flask, took a drink, and exhaled softly, before returning the silver container back into her hidden pocket.

Then, her eyes flashed gray, the green swallowed by a shadowy veneer. She stared at me, her gaze searching, seeing.

In a ghost of a voice, a voice that carried the same care, the same compassion I remembered from all those years ago, a voice that echoed in my memories, vibrating from my deepest dreams, the woman said, "Oh my. It's really true. You're alive."

She was older now. More than two decades older than the last time I'd seen her. But my chest seemed to burst, as if my heart were trying to flee its restraints. I knew that I knew that I knew...

"Annie?" I said, my mouth suddenly very parched.

Chapter 13

Blood rushed in my ears and, for a moment, I forgot to breathe. It didn't make sense. It didn't... make sense. *It didn't make sense.* And yet, I was seeing her with my own eyes. Seeing the resurrection of a decades old corpse. "Dear God, you're... you're... I thought my father had you killed."

Her watchful eyes pulsed gray. She then smiled—the same mischievous, dimpled smile from back in my RV. It suited her face far better than it had Dale's. She didn't speak at first, and I noticed, cradled in one hand, a small, whiskered mouse.

The little creature squeaked, and Annie scratched absentmindedly at the creature's ears before lowering it and placing it gently on the floor. "I found him here," she said, in manner of explanation. "He's so, so cute, don't you think?" she giggled as the small mouse nudged her foot and then scampered off into a bolt hole beneath the window. As the mouse left, Annie's expression flashed with momentary sadness. She sighed, though, turned once more and watched me. She extended a hand slowly, bracing herself against the wooden window frame. Then, all at once, she broke into motion, dancing across the room in three long, skipping steps before coming to a stop right in front of me. She exhaled deeply, her breath smelling of whatever had been in that silver flask—a tinny, sweet odor. Her smiled faded somewhat now, her expression solemn, but her eyes vibrant with excitement.

She leaned so close, her nose nearly pressed into my cheek, as if she were studying every pore in my face. I cleared my throat, uncomfortably.

"I thought," she said, in a breathy voice full of anticipation. "I thought the Endeavor had killed you. The night of the Grimmest Jest..." She trailed off and skirted around my other side. She looked me up and down from this new angle, her eyebrows flicking up.

Annie... Here and now... She's back... I shook my head, stunned, trickles of sheer awe swarming through me. "I escaped," I said, losing a trembling breath as if somehow I thought this might calm me. My skin buzzed.

I heard a shuffling sound and then quiet giggling. A second later, a faded, nearly transparent version of my poltergeist dangled his blue-eyed head through the open skylight, indifferent to the glass, upside down, his normally combed hair splaying towards the floor. He grinned from me to Annie and back again. Now, I knew what he'd heralded. Why he'd returned. He seemed to be enjoying my shock, my longing, my pain, my yearning. The others didn't notice him. Just as quickly the spirit vanished.

I felt an icy whisper of fear, but took a hurried step back, spinning now to face my old friend again. Somehow, watching Annie, thoughts of my poltergeist slipped. I felt a stupid grin paint across my face, my chest heaving as my breath came in hyperventilating gasps. I felt flummoxed, stunned, but also... a niggling in the back of my mind... *suspicious.* Why was Annie here? Where had she been for twenty years?

A second later, I heard a loud scraping and I turned to watch Preacher drag an old, rotten bookcase across the oak door, barricading it.

I blinked in the shadow-cast room. "Good call," I murmured.

He straightened up then glanced towards Annie.

"Of course," I said, "Where are my manners. Preacher... this... this is an old friend of mine. I—I didn't know she still lived." I turned back to Annie again, shaking my head in disbelief. "Apologies, I'm stuttering like some loon. But I'm," I swallowed, "pleasantly surprised is all."

Then, cautiously, I extended my consciousness, reaching out. My mind grazed hers, and I felt awash in warmth, in excitement... She seemed truly glad to see me. But also... other things... Things beneath the surface. Pain. Mostly pain. Torment of a kind. I reached out, like dipping my fingers in a river, and probed towards a cluster of dark memories flitting by.

I went stiff, suddenly, and gasped as if I'd been doused in ice. I spotted Annie, no older than six, trembling in a dark room, with little more than a shirt for warmth. She tucked her small arms around her ankles, shaking and shivering, no light to be seen. Deep voices echoed from the walls; I heard a sudden howl of pain. The sound of chains rattling on the ground, a slithering noise, like a snake. And then the figure in the memory screamed, the child's voice screeching helplessly at the sky.

I yanked out of the memory, blinking, gasping, feeling a tingle along my arms. I took a step back, pausing beneath the skylight, but then stepped forward again, tentative, one hand half-extended towards my friend. She raised a hand at the same time, unprompted by my motion, and covered the rest of the distance between us, her fingers nearly touching mine.

"Why didn't you tell me?" I said softly.

She stood solemn, still unsmiling but with an eager energy in every movement. Her eyes held joy as she regarded me, but for a brief moment, the emotion seemed trapped in an otherwise stony countenance. She had the look of soldiers I'd seen in my father's palace—not the young, untrained sort. But the old veterans, the ones who'd seen battle, seen death, seen the worst humanity had to offer. She peered down her gently sloped nose. "I had to be sure it was you."

"Where have you been?"

She shivered, turning away towards the barricaded door, her eyes flicking to Preacher. She swallowed and looked back at me. "Nowhere nice."

"I'm—I'm so sorry. I have so many questions—"

"Questions probably should wait," Annie replied. She smoothed her peacoat, self-consciously, and glanced at me, as if wondering what I was thinking. The pain in her eyes drifted away once more, replaced again by the mischievous smile, hidden once more by a cheerful grin. "It's so, so, so nice to see you again!" She let out a little squeak of delight, clapping her hands. "I could scream—though, don't worry, I won't. But really, I'm as happy as a clam!" Her cheeks dimpled again.

I grazed her surface emotions and felt a flicker of confusion. She seemed a mass of contradictions: she'd struck fear into the likes of Grendel, carried the pain of a wounded soldier in her eyes, but now she behaved like her five-year-old self, fearful I might not like her, flustered by Preacher's silence, and excited like a child on Christmas morning.

My hand still gripped my knife. "Annie," I said hoarsely.

"Yes, Leon?"

"What were you making the last day we spent together?"

Her brow wrinkled, but then her expression brightened above her gently bent nose. "Oh, I remember! Jeez Louise, what a day that was, huh? Biscuits."

I forgot to breathe for a second, as if I'd been punched. It really was her... It truly was Annie. I knew it—no trick. This was my friend, my long-lost childhood friend. If I'd ever learned how to cry, I'm sure I would have in that moment.

Annie's fingers brushed mine, and I was brought back to memories of apple trees, singing barracks songs, playing marbles in old, forgotten hallways at the top of a palace. My old friend returned to me after all these years. Now, she seemed to prattle on without cutting herself off. She'd changed, of course. Twenty-three years could do that to someone. But I could see familiar glimpses.

I gestured towards Preacher now, waving him over. "Annie and I grew up together."

Preacher, though, remained where he was, back against the bookcase, partially barricading the door with his sheer girth. For a moment, I'd even forgotten the hunters searching the mansion for us.

Annie stepped past me now, her fingers lightly grazing my shoulder, her shadow shifting across me in the light as she moved. She extended a hand towards Preacher in greeting. He simply looked at it then back at her.

Her eyes flickered gray. Then her mouth formed a small circle as she stared at Preacher. "Wow," she said. "Your guardian angel—he's scary looking."

Preacher raised an eyebrow at me.

I shook my head. "She's not crazy. She's always been able to do that. She sees spooks and ghosts and things unseen. It's not one of the eternal talents—it's something else."

Preacher crossed himself and murmured a silent prayer as if to ward off evil. He then lodged his large arms over his inflated chest, peering suspiciously towards Annie. I reached out with my mind, giving Preacher the psychic equivalent of a poke to the ribs.

You're acting like an ass, I said, projecting the words in his mind.

Preacher replied, also in his mind. *I don't trust her. There's something off about this girl, Leon.*

She's an old friend.

She's a new threat.

I huffed an impatient breath at the same time as Preacher, and we held each other's gaze, glaring for a moment.

But then Annie stepped even closer to Preacher, her eyes still gray, now peering just off over his shoulder. Suddenly, a film of tears swam across her vision. She blinked, and a couple of tears escaped her eye, trickling down the inside of her cheek. She murmured, shaking her head. "Oh dear... Dear... You've been through a lot, haven't you?" she asked, staring at Preacher now, openly crying in the dusty sun beam stretching through the skylight.

Preacher again gave no response. He looked at me patiently but then gave a firm nod towards my old friend.

The surprise wasn't near wearing off, nor my delight mixed with a hefty dose of confusion and fear. But some of it I managed to push aside at Preacher's gesture.

"You thought I was dead... and yet you found me?" I said.

She turned back to me, her eyes green once more as she nodded. "Oh, yes. Mhmm. That's true for sure. I'd heard of a prison breaker—a mind reader. Which, good for you by the way. I always knew you could do anything you wanted. I was so sad when I'd thought you'd died the same night as your father." She winced apologetically, but then shifted back and forth, moving on her heel as if she didn't much like staying in place for too long. Absentmindedly, she reached out and picked another splinter from a busted section of the wall, peeling slivers and tossing them onto the ground. She watched the curls of wood land at her feet and then nodded in simple pleasure.

"What are you thinking?" she said, looking at me.

I hesitated then replied. "You still shave your head."

Preacher rolled his eyes.

She giggled though. "Ah—lies muddy the mind. I remember that!"

"It's not the only thing I'm thinking. I'm also wondering why you didn't think to call? Write?"

She wrinkled her nose. "I only just tracked you down. You weren't even on my radar until..." she swallowed. "Is it actually true you tried to break into the Hollow but failed?"

I blinked for a moment, threatened by a sudden memory attempting to rise to the surface. I swallowed, shoving the recollection down and dodging the question with one of my own. "Where were you all this time?"

For a moment, she looked hurt. Her voice, which had been chipper, drifted somewhere closer to hesitant. "I—I get it, no, like, really I do, if you don't trust me. We haven't, you know, *seen* each other in almost two *whole* decades! Wowsers," she muttered. "That's a *looong* time. But... But I still need your help."

"Helping someone without trust is a tall order. And you didn't answer my question."

"And see, once more, I ignore it again," she said with a laugh. "Leon, I heard you were the best. Which I totally believe by the way. And I knew for this job I needed someone *I* could trust." Annie wagged her head, her fingers drumming against one of her peacoat pockets which held the silver flask.

"Two decades is a long time to retain a flame of trust."

"Maybe we can start with kindling, then, hmm? Would that be okay?" She paused, hesitantly, her expression taking on the same sort it had when reaching down to pet the mouse she'd found in the abandoned mansion. Most people were scared of mice. It made sense Annie would befriend it. Now, though, cautiously, she said, "You—you haven't entirely forgotten me, have you?" There was a vulnerability to that question, a willingness to invite pain. And I knew, even after all these years, if I answered the wrong way, I'd wound my old friend. I didn't speak, though, still watching her, wishing I didn't distrust so thoroughly, but I'd seen too much of the world to rush headlong into anything like affection. "Have you forgotten our hours spent hiding beneath the stairs, singing songs overheard from the palace security? *Run, flee, sneak,*" she sang softly, *"can't catch me..."*

"Hiding where you cannot see," I murmured back, finishing the lyric with a ghost of a smile. "I remember you, Annie. I remember your hand in mine, your fingers soft and stained in beet juice, as we snuck off into the water gardens to toss breadcrumbs to my brother's koi."

She beamed. "I had hoped you hadn't forgotten."

"I remember. Some people were just born to be friends. That's what we used to say, isn't it?"

"It's still true to me."

"Two decades—"

"—Is a long time. But it's still true to me," she said, her voice hardening all at once. "The knowledge that I'd had a friend... That I'd had you even if only for a few years... got me through..." She grit her teeth. "Through hell and back." The ire didn't seem directed at me, though. Rather, she stared off, facing down some unseen demon—whether literal or metaphorical, I didn't know.

"You ask me of my trust," I said gingerly. "Well, after two decades, why do you trust me?"

Annie paused, meeting my eyes. She glanced towards my hip then towards the splinter she'd been twirling, the same way I'd been spinning my knife. I remembered the same songs playing in our heads, even when apart. I remembered the whispered conversations, where half the words would go unheard, and yet we'd know the other's intent. I remembered the stories of our birth, kicking in our mother's bellies whenever we were close, as if reacting, as if—even then—before born, blind, deaf, dumb, helpless, we *knew*. Like drowning victims swiping wildly, droplets frothing as they lashed out for a thread-thin lifeline on gray waters. We found a lifeline in each other. Two links in a chain. Me, a tarnished, copper thing, destined for brokenness. And Annie... a pristine golden band. The only warmth in a frigid home. And yet, we'd found each other. We'd drawn near.

And then she'd died.

Or so I'd thought.

And yet there she stood, looking me dead in the eyes.

Chapter 14

I could feel the *cold* rising in me now. I didn't know how to cry—I wished I could. But anger was more expedient for my father's designs, for the kingdom. To blame my father fully is farce. Anger protected me. Guarded me. Befriended me.

But now my only other childhood friend was back.

I swallowed the cold, storing the anger, pushing it deep and holding it like a rubber ball beneath the same gray waters. The exertion was taxing, but I'd learned to keep such things submerged through white-knuckles and gritted teeth.

"I don't know if I trust you, Annie," I said softly. "I can't lie. But for the sake of our mothers. For the sake of our past. In exchange for *your story,* I'll help you."

"Oh dear, hmm... My story is kinda long. And now isn't the time." Her fingers felt very cold where they trailed against my cheek. "Leon, as glad as I am to see you—which is so, so much—I do have a proposition."

I went stiff. "Right," I said, my emotions a complete mess. "Yes. The job." Preacher kept his stony gaze fixed on Annie. "What for? Who's the target?"

Annie puffed a breath, her worry written between the cheerful smile lines. She gnawed on a lip, and then, softly, she said. "It's why I wanted you, Leon." I could feel a cold shiver creeping up my spine. "I know your brother—not Augustus—your youngest brother, little Napoleon, is trapped in that horrible prison. I need you to break him out."

She spoke further, but I wasn't listening; my mind was reeling. It felt like my stomach had fallen like a lead weight through the floor. I resisted an urge to gasp but still found myself breathing heavily.

My old friend, my old dead friend knew about Napoleon, knew about the Hollow, knew about it all.

I looked to Preacher again, and he was staring straight at me. I blinked a few times, trying to gather my thoughts. Rescuing my brother was an impossibility. I would have to put a bullet in his head to avoid unleashing what he carried back on the world.

I turned to Annie again, suppressing some of my emotions now, realizing how foolishly I'd left my mind open for pillaging. Annie was no mind-reader, but she'd proven with Dale she had a ritual or two, or spell, or creature aid that gave her some level of influence.

"That's impossible," I said, croaking out the word.

She shook her head, and moved over to Preacher now, seemingly unaware of his open hostility. She poked at his face before he could react and then removed her finger, studying the makeup on the end with an open interest. She then wiped the makeup off on her own shirt, before turning back to me. Again, I was struck at the childish curiosity, recalling how she'd acted back in the RV when inhabiting Dale's form, rummaging through my kitchen as if unaware of the social norms. She'd said she couldn't eat food in this current form of hers. What a curious claim... She'd disappeared at the age of five. Where had she been since then?

"That's the job, Leon. It's the only way I'm able to extend my protection."

I breathed. Annie couldn't possibly know what was at stake. No one did, not even Preacher—not fully. Napoleon couldn't be allowed to escape. Only a fourteen-year-old boy, and yet the greatest threat of them all. Strong, an eternal like all of us, but not unusually powerful, not overly strong. Dangerous for another reason entirely.

But I couldn't tell her—not even Annie. I didn't know if I could still trust my old friend. Some secrets were best left unexhumed, guarded only by corpses.

"And Preacher and I," I said, "If we refuse, what then?"

Annie fidgeted, twisting one foot back and forth. "Grendel will keep hunting you, I imagine. I'll try talking to him—to get him to leave you alone. But he might not listen."

Mistress. That's what Grendel had called her. Fear. He'd been afraid of Annie. I looked her up and down. She wore a simple black shirt beneath her thin peacoat and scruffy black sweatpants. Nothing to fear here, was there? I spotted an old gray backpack in the corner of the room. Why had Grendel been scared of Annie? Why was she back, why now?

"And you—will you look for another prison breaker?"

Annie wiped her hands across her pants again, leaving a streak of Preacher's blush over her thigh. "Yes, I have to. There's a lot depending on this—and as you know, I don't have a lot of time. I can't wait another year."

"Why get involved at all?"

Her expression twitched in a frown, her gently crooked nose tilting with her head as she studied me. "Huh... Weird. I kinda thought you'd leap at the chance to free Napoleon. Of all your brothers, from the stories I heard, he was the sweetest, the kindest. The least like your father."

I nodded at each word. "He was, and still is. He is a gentle boy. But that doesn't matter..." I trailed off, struggling to think. Annie knew about my brother. Knew he was in the Hollow. Napoleon was the target.

I could no longer sit idly by. I'd tried, two years before... And I'd failed.

But if anyone released him... if anyone freed my brother...

I shivered. "Why do you want him?"

Annie looked away now, sheepish. "Oh, well, I dunno... Just, he has something I want—something important." She looked back at me, half-wincing, half-smiling. "I need your help, Leon."

My gaze flicked down to her old backpack and then at the back of my own fingers. If she hired another savant, I might not be able to stop her. I might not be able to intervene. No—this was too close for comfort. She knew too much. Annie or not, Napoleon couldn't be allowed to escape.

So I tipped my head.

"I don't mean to be rude, but I need your word, Leon," she said. Suddenly, she spoke with an authority, an iron tone that sent prickles along my skin. Her shadow flared around her feet. "Give me your oath!"

I loosed a sharp breath at the whiplash change in mood. I could feel Preacher staring at me, willing me to say no. But not even Preacher understood what was at stake. No choices... when did I ever have choices? I could feel my frustration conceding to dread.

So, I said, "You have my oath as a Wit—I will help you locate and break into the Hollow." What I didn't say, I thought, *But I'll do everything in my power to stop you from freeing Napoleon.* "You have my tethered word as an eternal." At the words, I felt a slight twist in my belly and a mild headache that, after a couple of pulses, flitted away. No small words, those... To lie is to clutter the mind. To hinge one's powers on a lie? A far greater damnation for dishonesty. And I wasn't lying—not really. I would help her break into the Hollow. This all had to end. Napoleon had to die. The thought alone sent my chest prickling with grief and guilt. But what other choice did I have?

Annie's expression broke into another smile; her shadow was motionless once more. "Super-duper! Now where is this key you mentioned, hmm? I can help get it, if you want." The smile became rather fixed. "Also, you mentioned something about a corpse?" She inflected the phrase as a question.

"Yes. And gold dust," I said. "Hopefully it's still there. Very important that."

Already, I was gathering myself, steadying my pounding heart and moving across the room towards the exact window well she'd been standing in front of.

This was the moment of truth.

Now, more than ever, it seemed crucial I found a way in and out of the prison.

Instead of reaching towards the window, though, I dropped to my knee, bathed in sunlight streaming through the glass. My fingers probed at the molded floorboards, my eyes fixed on the grooves and imperfections in the rotted wood beneath the mouse hole. I glanced at my friend and winced. "Stand back." Then, I loosed a shuddering little sigh.

The key would have to be there. And *it* would hopefully be asleep.

Chapter 15

"Well?" Annie said, leaning so close I felt her breath on my ear.

In response, I found the floorboard wedged against the wall beneath the window and pulled it. The thing was thicker, more maintained, perhaps, than the rest of the boards.

It had been two years since I'd placed the Hollow key in hiding. Two years since I'd dropped it off at the Librarian's mansion.

Then, a *clicking* sound.

The floorboard slid along with my hand. I pulled it, lifting the wooden plank in a cascade of sawdust particles swirling beneath the light.

Coughing and waving a hand in front of my face, I delicately placed the board to the side. Annie's shadow fell over me, and I glanced up to find her watching me closely.

"Don't follow," I said softly. "It won't like it."

I reached into the slot beneath the floor, my hand pressing a metallic rim. My fingers scrabbled against the cold, dusty surface, looking for purchase. And there, a twisting lever, like the type one might find on the side of a jack-in-the-box.

I winced in anticipation, fingers against the handle.

Then I began to rotate it, slowly.

A quiet little musical noise, a tinkling sound, filled the room for a moment.

"What is that?" Annie said. "What is—"

Then she yelped as there came a grating sound from the most shadowed portion of the room, near the least molded section of the floor.

I turned too, no longer cranking the handle, my eyes fixed on the human sized opening in the back of the upper room. It looked no wider than the entry into a walk-in fridge.

In fact, like a fridge, wafting gusts of chill air now fluttered from within the dark entry, circulating the room. I shivered in response, staring towards the hidden room.

"I—what is that sound?" Annie murmured.

There, coming from the open door, along with the frigid air, I could hear it too: a low, moaning sound. A soft, whimpering, whispering mewl.

I flinched, glancing at Preacher then pointing at him.

He frowned and pointed back at me.

I pointed at him.

He raised a fist and I sighed.

Together, silently, we played rock paper scissors.

I lost, both times.

Preacher crossed his arms now, leaning back against the moldered bookcase, wearing a self-satisfied expression.

For my part, I shivered, rising to my feet and glancing towards the blockaded door behind my tall friend. The sounds of our pursuers had faded, suggesting perhaps they were searching the lower portions of the mansion.

My attention returned to the moaning sound coming from the pitch-black room. The darkness seemed unnatural, the cold air like the breeze over a graveyard on a winter's night. My stomach twisted in anxiety.

I glanced at Preacher, wincing, but he wasn't having it. He shook his head, pointing at my chest and towards the door.

I sighed. Ever a respecter of the outcome of rock-paper-scissors, I moved towards the hidden room, swallowing as I did.

"Smiley!" I called, wincing. "Greetings! Are you in there, dear fellow?"

The moaning, groaning sound increased in volume. A small tinkling accompanied it.

I winced, stepping towards the cold door. The darkness grew as I neared, almost blotting out the sunlight behind me. The emanating cold made my teeth chatter.

I paused for a moment, glancing to the left side of the door, then the right of the frame.

"Which side?"

Preacher pointed to the right.

I hesitated, keeping my voice low. "Are you sure? I thought it was left."

He pointed more insistently to the right.

I frowned, holding up a finger, closing my eyes and *sifting,* I sorted through my memories. A kaleidoscope of rapid images flashed across my mind, rewinding until I paused, staring at the old memory. I watched the recollection play out, watching as, years ago, I stepped into the same, dusty cabinet.

Another gift of the Wit; I could replay any memory, as far back as I wished to venture. Though, the emotional ramifications could be taxing.

I watched, in the faint pictures of my mind, as my old form pressed against the *right* side of the door.

I snapped back to the present, blinking once like the shutter on a camera lens.

Once again faced with the present, I pressed my back *hard* against the frame on the right side of the door, practically sucking my stomach in as I did.

"Hello, friend," I said, my voice drifting into the cold, dark room. "It's me, remember? I'm just going to be quick. Don't do anything..." I swallowed, "Overhasty."

"Spooky," Annie whispered. "Oh boy—what's *in* there?" Again, I noted how entirely devoid of fear her voice was, as if she were watching a scary movie, rather than standing in the midst of an actual horror show.

I didn't glance at her this time, fixing my eyes on the darkness within, my shoulder blades pressed to the rough grain of the right-side of the wooden frame. "This used to be a hidden room for the Jester's treasure," I murmured. "We found it by accident a few years ago, while hiding out in the mansions. Also, keep it down; we have guests downstairs."

She seemed entirely unconcerned with the mention of *guests* and instead, intrigued, asked, "Treasures?"

I shook my head. "A hiding place for treasures. They were gone when we got here. Only an empty chest and a couple of bottles, also empty. But," I swallowed, "whatever was *guarding* the treasures was left behind. Don't follow me. It doesn't like crowds."

And then, I side-stepped into the room, wincing and breathing heavily, my shoulder blades scraping against the wall at my back. I remained pressed against the rightmost side of the room, my eyes unblinking in the dark.

I shivered, hearing the faint clink of a chain now, rattling from within.

"Hello, old friend," I said, wincing. "I'll be in and out, right quick." I spoke with a soft, cajoling voice, like a frightened trainer wrangling a ferocious hound. The same sort of tone my second brother, Augustus' tutors often used when he got in one of his moods.

I winced as a splinter wedged through my shirt, but even then refused to push off the rough wall at my back.

Chains clinked even louder now. Then a soft moan resounded from directly in front of me.

I smelled it before I saw it. The darkness of the room was nearly complete. I couldn't sense a mind at all— nothing whatsoever. Though it moved, Smiley had been dead for a long time.

I continued to side-step, hugging the right side of the wall, wincing now against the odor of rotting meat and fresh maggots.

I wrinkled my nose in disgust, desperately trying to breathe from my mouth alone.

My eyes were now adjusting to the blackness. I spotted the chest on the opposite side of the hidden room, the bottles strewn on the ground where we'd left them. And there, on top of the chest...

My heart skipped a beat.

My old leather satchel. It still bulged, suggesting, perhaps, the gold dust pouches and the key remained within. The outlines of the chest and satchel were faint in the dark.

The moaning began to change now, turning from a soft, desperate, wretched sound, into an accusing growl.

"Just another second, Smiley," I said desperately. "I'm not here to hurt you!"

Directly across from me, I spotted Smiley shift.

A hunched, emaciated shape with gaping eye sockets in a shriveled face. The thing wore a jester's cap, complete with little bells, the source of the tinkling sounds I'd heard up until now. The head was rotten, missing its nose, its ears, most of its teeth and much of the skin from its cheeks and neck. Rotten muscle exposed beneath old, worn clothing. A single phrase was written in red paint across the wall above the zombie: *Smiley says hi!*

A thick black chain dangled from Smiley's neck, bolted to the wall opposite me.

On the left.

The thing eyed me for a second, its shriveled arms limp in front of it, dangling to the ground, its cap-wearing head tilted, the many bells tinkling as it watched me with ghoulish, empty eye sockets.

I swallowed, glancing towards the satchel on the chest, then back to Smiley again. "Good zombie," I murmured. "Stay. Staaay."

I heard Annie's voice behind me. "Aww, it's adorable!" she exclaimed. "Look at his itsy-bitsy bells!"

I couldn't say I shared the sentiment.

Smiley suddenly lurched at me, withered fingers snapping forward with demonic speed, scrambling for my neck.

I yelped, but remained wedged against the wall, chin high, trying not to move a muscle.

Smiley's fingertips just *barely* missed my face. I could feel the wind as they swept past my chin. The chain went taut and snapped, and Smiley clotheslined itself, going flat with a horrible, sickening grunt and then toppling backwards like a dog on a yanked leash. Annie made a sympathetic sound from behind me, but I called back. "Stay away—stay back!"

As the zombie tumbled in a pile on the ground, I made my move, bolting towards the satchel, shivering as I did, snagging it from the top of the chest.

I glanced in, wincing, but couldn't see much, even with my vision now adjusted to the cold, dark room.

"Sorry, Smiley," I muttered, taking a running start, then jumping over the fallen guardian of the Jester's treasures.

Whoever had left the zombie here probably hadn't expected their guardian to ever watch over someone else's stash, but in the age-old parlance of treasure hunters everywhere: finders keepers, losers weepers.

I landed nimbly on the other side of the thrashing zombie and then took two skipping steps out of the hidden compartment, back into the main room, breathing heavily and clutching my satchel.

As I stepped out, Preacher moved in and slammed the door shut with a deft motion, causing it to *click*. The moment the hidden compartment in the wall sealed, it camouflaged once more in the cracks and dust of the rest of the room, hidden again from sight.

The chill air faded somewhat, and the moaning sound vanished entirely.

Annie watched where I stood breathing heavily and gripping the satchel. "That was incredible!" she said, delightedly. "I'm so impressed! Did you get what you needed?"

In response, I lowered the bag gently to the ground and opened it, practically wincing in anticipation. When I spotted the contents, my stomach jolted.

Memories came spilling back, and I closed my eyes against the dark, swishing images in my mind.

I waited for the prickle to leave my skin, then reached in, pulling out the key on the end of the leather thong. I held it up to the light. The crude, iron key dangled in front of my nose, catching beams of sunlight through the window over Annie's shoulder.

She stared at the thing. "Oooh—cool. So, hmm—that will get us into the Hollow?"

"Yes," I murmured. "But we still have to find the place." Hastily, I placed the leather strap around my neck and tucked the key into my shirt, resting it against my chest along with my skeletal pendant.

With careful fingers, I probed into the rest of the satchel and pulled out three small leather bags.

"That's the gold dust?" Annie murmured.

I nodded, opening one, then revealing the glinting, glistening contents within the bags. I smiled softly then laced the small satchel and placed all three back in the larger bag.

"The key is for getting through the sewers," I murmured. "The gold will help us survive the genie guardians."

Annie crossed her arms. "How so?" Unlike most humans, she seemed entirely indifferent to the glister of the yellow metal.

"These genies love the color," I said. "The Bane clan, specifically." I glanced at Preacher, and he winced back at me, likely also remembering our last encounter with the crazed djinn. "They guard the Hollow."

"Wow, okay. And the gold will help bribe them?"

"Er, not exactly. They..." I glanced at Preacher again and he mimed eating something.

Annie's eyebrows flicked up towards her short-cropped hairline. "They eat the gold? I've never eaten gold before. Is it tasty?"

"To the Banes, yes," I murmured, getting to my feet and hefting the satchel over my shoulder. "And they share Grendel's palate for eyeballs," I added beneath my breath.

"Sorry, what was that?" Annie said, leaning in.

"The Hollow is deadly," I said. "We still need those teleporting stones." I looked at her. "The black market should be our next stop. That's also where the confidant will likely be—they're always Union-connected. Those boys get their fingers in every money-making pie."

Annie began to nod, but stiffened at a sudden sound of barking, then thumping steps, far too fast to be from a human. Then something large, something powerful, slammed into the barricaded door on the other side.

The bookcase slipped, groaning as it scraped across the floor.

Voices now echoed, harsh and demanding from the other side. Another loud *Thump*. Something crashed into the door again.

Annie hastened back over to her discarded backpack, threw it over one shoulder, and fixed an eye on Preacher and myself. Her eyes flashed gray and she glanced towards the door. If anything, she almost looked amused as she said, conversationally, "We probably should leave."

Chapter 16

I have often considered Preacher an unstoppable force. And when he's in the proper frame of mind, there is no such thing as an immovable object. Shouts vibrated from beyond the barricaded door, and the bookcase shuddered as something slammed against the other side. Preacher's full attention, however, fixated on the floor.

My pulse raced as I spared two words for Annie. "Follow Preacher."

My old friend's expression flickered. "Off on your own again?"

"No time," I snapped as the bookcase trembled. "They're here for me. We'll meet up."

Before Annie could protest, Preacher grabbed her hand, pulled her close—his faithfulness to me outweighed his suspicion of her. He looked me dead in the eyes, and I knew what he was thinking even without reaching out.

I gave a faint shake of my head.

His eyes narrowed in frustration.

But I shook again. "Trust me," I said. I knew for Preacher, abandoning me to save a stranger went against the grain of his character.

He gave me one last look of frustration and pointed a thick finger at my chest.

"I'll be fine," I insisted.

Preacher huffed a resigned breath. He knew better than to argue with me in situations like these. Then he slammed a foot into the most molded section of floor. The floorboards creaked and groaned. Preacher picked Annie up, and she didn't protest, her backpack wedged against his chin. With the added weight, Preacher jumped, bringing his full force down, *hard* against the floor.

At the same time, the door blockaded by the bookshelf slammed open, and a furry shoulder beneath golden-flecked indigo eyes came barreling through. The monster seemed a cross between a wolf and a stray cat—though the size of a small horse, with long mangy arms and claws that ripped chunks of wood wherever they hit the floor. Men with guns stood just beyond the fuzzy brute, their weapons raised.

Before they could fire, though, Preacher and Annie fell straight through the floor in a shower of splinters and cracked floorboards; Preacher even managed to get off a shot.

The Kindred howled in pain, knocked off course and sent stumbling over the collapsed bookcase. My companions landed with a *thud* in the room below and then, with a flurry of tapping footsteps, hotfooted away.

Which left me standing over the cratered floor, facing eight Endeavor carrying assault weapons, and a wounded Kindred snarling and reforming, fur fading to flesh, and muscles shrinking back into a tensed, sweat-slicked body. Euryale howled, her eyes wild in her raging expression.

"Bring me the savant!" she screeched, trying to push up with an arm wounded by Preacher's bullet. "And bring me that key!"

Tomb's breath. They were here for me. Which meant, if I couldn't go *down,* endangering my friends, there was only one direction left. One must improvise in situations such as these. I reached out, *glimpsing,* sending images into the minds of the gunmen.

Three of them had defenses, a fourth managed to ignore my influence. But half spotted me standing in four different places in the room, where I'd mimicked a mirror of myself.

Gunfire erupted, wood chips exploded, holes punched through drywall.

I was already on the move, racing towards the window leading to the roof. Bullets skipped past me, and a hot flash seared my shoulders where one nearly found its mark. The skeletal pendant over my chest, next to the dangling key, thumped against my body, smooth and weighty where it met the beat of my heart.

The *glimpsing* had created chaos. Enough for me to reach the window but no more. If I hesitated, I'd die—I was already living on borrowed time.

No time to unlatch the thing. I flung myself *through* the glass.

A shatter—shards fell around me, pierced me. A slick pain across my cheek, more along my braced elbow as if I'd been stabbed. The satchel over my shoulder ripped and one of the gold dust pouches fell, tumbling from the roof. I tried to snag it, but missed, watching in despair as it plummeted out of sight. As I surged through the glass, though, I screeched as a bullet finally found its mark.

Hot lead tore through my lower back, puncturing meat and muscle.

For a moment, I stood on the window ledge, in agony, bright lights dancing across my vision. My precarious foothold scraped glass and blood as I tested my legs and found I could still move—the bullet hadn't hit anything too vital, then. But now, with blood pouring, I had to escape.

Wit though I might be, I couldn't heal, couldn't turn my flesh to stone, couldn't do anything to stop a bullet once it had found its mark. If I took another gunshot, I'd die.

Already, the Endeavor had shaken off the *glimpsing* and now obeyed the shouted and snarled commands of pursuit from Euryale's injured form. Eight soldiers in the room. Euryale on the ground, kicking away from the hooded, limping form of Mago, who'd entered the room last. Injured Kindred—judging by what had happened to Gog the night before—didn't trust each other.

Euryale even gestured at one of the Endeavor. "Stay!" she screamed. "Guard me!"

I slipped along the lip of the roof, ignoring the glass scattered beneath me. Shards scraped and crunched as I scrabbled up the shingles, growling against the pain in my back.

Reaching the top of the first mansion's angled roof, I noted the caved, burnt-out portion of ceiling at my feet. *Vyle's teeth.* I paused, trying to plot a less precarious route.

Now, my seven pursuers also reached the roof, crawling up with their hands and knees. At least, momentarily, this meant their weapons were stowed on straps over their backs. Shingles scraped, and a few of the gray-black tiles skittered off the roof into a free fall.

"He's heading towards the second mansion!" someone shouted, a helmeted head peering after me, over the lip of the window well as the agent groped for his weapon.

But I was already moving, leaping the burnt portion of ceiling and lunging towards the other side. I raced across the shingles. Bullets started spraying, but I veered down the slant of the roof, blocking the view of my pursuers, at least for a moment. Before I'd gone far, though, another burst of gunfire tore through the roof to my left. The agent who'd remained *inside* the room below was taking pot shots through the ceiling.

Voices barked on the opposite side of the triangular roof; tottering, uncertain footsteps announced more Endeavor regrouping on the shingles before coming after me again. I glanced towards the covered swimming pool below, then across towards the second mansion—even more burnt than this one.

The gap between the two mansions was large. Too large to jump... Unless I was lucky. But the pool below was covered with a thick, plastic seal. I'd break every bone against the cover.

Helmeted heads now appeared over the top of the roof. No time to wait. Another burst of gunfire from the room below slammed through the ceiling, spewing out at the sky.

I raced across the shingles, not bothering to dodge left or right. I cast my thoughts back, invading the minds of the soldiers who'd reached the edge first. I wasn't going for anything fancy, so I slammed through the mental defenses.

I couldn't control them—not with such a ham-fisted approach. But I could use *beholding*. As I fled, my vision swam and, in my mind's eye, I brought up the sight of the men behind me. I stared through their eyes. I could see them aiming, I could see the way their red dots lined up with my spine. I watched them prepare to fire.

Then jerked left.

Bullets whistled past, slamming into the shingles, knocking them free and flying. A burst of gunfire struck a chimney, exploding the bricks in a powder of red dust.

I maneuvered until the chimney was behind me, cutting off their line of sight, at least for the moment.

I dropped *beholding*. For what came next, I'd need my wits about me. I also needed full range of motion. With a growl of frustration, I tossed the satchel with the remaining gold dust pouches off to the side. It struck a window protrusion and tumbled down the slope of the roof. No more gold dust. We'd have to find a way to get more.

If I managed to escape, that was. They were still coming after the key, and—more importantly—coming after me.

A twenty-foot gap stretched between the first mansion's roof and the second. No way I could make it. But... maybe if I aimed for something besides the roof. No time to think—no time to hesitate. Nothing like the threat of imminent gunfire to provide temporary courage.

I flung myself from the roof, screaming as I did. Both from the fear of the moment and the agony in my lower back from the still-lodged bullet. Another chatter of gunfire accompanied my jump, and I felt another hot bite of lead, this time through my extended hand.

Of course, twenty feet was too far. The roof was an impossibility. If I fell all three flights, I'd crush my skull and snap my neck against the ground.

So, I'd aimed lower. Not at the roof, but at the third floor window opposite, about six feet lower than the roof itself. If I missed, I was dead. If I hit it and the glass didn't break, I was dead.

My limbs flailed, one of them still pulsing agony from the gunshot.

A moment of helpless momentum, rushing wind and...

Then...

My shoulder slammed into the fire-weakened glass in a calamitous shatter.

Pain was my fate. I tried to brace myself before I plummeted though a burnt crater in the first room, but I screamed as I leveraged my weight on my gunshot hand, skidding across splintered wood and glass shards. More slices and cuts, like knife wounds, up and down my chest and just below my neck.

For a moment, I lay gasping, in agony. I wanted to close my eyes. To sleep, to let it go.

But I couldn't. Annie was back. I couldn't. Napoleon couldn't be free. I thought of Nimue and all she'd sacrificed to keep me alive. To keep me from despair... even, at times, despair to the point of death.

There's nothing like unwarranted, unearned kindness to trick someone into valuing their own life. And so I pushed up, despite the pain, despite the desire to close my eyes. I screamed from the agony in my everything.

Limping, I turned to face the windowsill.

The eighth gunman, who'd stayed to protect injured Euryale from her brother Mago was aiming through his own window, pointing his gun at me. I ducked as bullets tore through the open window. Lead slammed into wood, but missed me. I breathed sharply through my teeth until they hurt and glanced around the room. The only exit lay in perfect view of the shooter.

I couldn't make a break for it. Not without getting pelted. I needed a gun. But Preacher was already on the move—I could sense him disappearing through the trees, protecting Annie as I'd asked.

Two truths remained. I was on my own. And I needed a gun.

I was pinned down, ducked behind the shattered window, as another burst of gunfire slammed into the wood and flecked the doorway with shavings of floorboard. The eighth gunman seemed to realize he had me stuck. All he had to do now was wait for his allies to reach me.

I heard more shouting, more screaming. I reached out, desperately, finding the least guarded mind and *beholding*. The seven soldiers on the roof were all hesitantly staring at the window I'd jumped through.

Even without my gift, I would have heard one of the Endeavor shouting, "If he can make it so can you! Go! Go!"

I watched through enemy eyes as two soldiers backed up, preparing to follow across the gap between the mansions.

If I bolted now, the eighth gunman would pepper me with bullets. If I didn't move, though, two more heavily armed soldiers would careen through my window.

I needed a gun to take out the man in the opposite window. He remained the only shooter with my escape route covered.

I reached with my mind, but felt erected defenses. I couldn't puppet or control. This was one of the Endeavor who'd avoided my *glimpsing*. If I had the time, and wasn't so distracted by pain, perhaps I'd manage something. But now, the gunman was calm, focused. His defenses were up. He had no fear.

Too late for me to move. The two indicated soldiers who'd been chosen to leap after me had tossed their helmets aside. I heard the clatter of the metal against shingle, the shouts, like incoherent battle-cries, then they jumped.

Only one plan came to me.

It would have to work.

I waited for the vaulters to reach *halfway* through the air. A matter of split-seconds. And yet timing was key. It was at this zenith their fear was greatest.

Fear weakens minds.

Still crouched behind the window, pinned by their eighth gunman, I grasped the fearful minds and caught them. Immediately, I used *glimpsing*.

I moved the image of the window three feet to the left in their minds. Not a big illusion, but enough. I heard sudden screams of horror as the two soldiers mid-air supposed they'd miscalculated.

As they arched down and tried to readjust to the fake window, I emerged from cover. Their bodies would shield me, for a precious moment from the other gunman. One of the leaping agents, mid-air, missed the real window completely. He'd tried to readjust and slammed body-armor first into the wall and ricocheted off.

The second agent was smarter. He kept the course, but without seeing the true window, he nearly missed. His hands scrambled at the windowsill where his body slammed with a *wumpf*. The breath knocked from his body; dazed, he gripped the windowsill with scrambling, gloved fingers.

The eighth gunman in the lower room couldn't find an angle where he didn't risk his companion.

I stood up, glaring *over* the head of the scrambling agent on my windowsill. I reached along his body and unhooked the sidearm from his holster. The desperate agent tried to grab me, but then nearly fell and returned to gripping the windowsill, gasping.

I raised my newly acquired firearm, sighted and shot twice. Two loud retorts.

I caught the gunman in the lower room of the opposite mansion in the chest. Two slugs to the body armor. The path to the door was now clear. I shoved the firearm into my waistband and, leaving the agent behind me, desperately screaming where he tried not to fall, I limped away, hurrying quickly towards the open door. My wounded hand throbbed and my lower back felt like fire.

I could hear the soldiers on top of the roof shouting. "Get down! Down!"

Three more soldiers jumped from the roof. They'd discarded their AR-15s for better maneuverability. But bullets from pistols killed just as well. And now the soldiers hurtled through the air towards the open window. Three left. Still far too many.

This wasn't over yet.

Chapter 17

I broke into a stumbling, pain-laden surge through the door, pausing at the top of the stairs for only a moment to look over my shoulder. The soldier whose sidearm I'd stolen managed to scramble into the room, gasping but pushing to his feet. Two more hurtled through the open window, rolling along the floor and jolting to their feet. A fourth, by the sound of a crunch and a horrified shout, missed completely.

The remaining soldiers on the opposite roof desperately stumbled along the shingles to get back inside their mansion and rejoin Euryale. If I knew Preacher, he'd be watching the exit to their mansion, covering my escape. By the time they reached the ground floor, though, I'd be long gone. Which meant only three agents remained in pursuit. One of them unarmed, two of them down to their sidearms.

But I was shot twice and covered in cuts from glass. In addition, my *glimpsing* and *beholding* had cost me. I could feel my mind heavy with exhaustion.

Now wasn't the time to give up though.

I stumbled down the stairs, listening to the sounds of pursuit. I raised the gun with my good hand and fired aimlessly, buying time as I bounced off a wall, leaving a streak of red against the molding paint, then continued my rapid descent down the stairs.

"Stop!" an agent screamed.

Small caliber bullets struck the wall above, powdering me with dust. I stumbled. The floors in this second mansion were nearly entirely burned. Everything creaked where I ran. Half the stairs were little more than jagged shards of ashen wood.

I had to reach the ground floor. But my abilities were worn. Like with any muscle, overuse brings exhaustion. If I pushed further, I might pass out in front of them.

As I raced down the final flight of the burnt mansion, scattering old dust and gray ash beneath me in a cloud, I heard more gunfire above—tentative, probing bullets. None of them hit their mark. My hand felt like fire, my lower back was killing me. The glass shards embedded in my chest and lower stomach nearly made me vomit with pain.

Outrunning the enemy wasn't an option. I was bleeding too much.

Vaguely, I remembered what I'd seen on the way in.

Would it work? It would have to. If it didn't, the heir to the house of Rex would meet an untimely demise.

More bullets behind me, then a sudden shout of frustration, followed by the empty *click* of a spent sidearm.

Two of my attackers were unarmed now. I had a couple bullets left in my own handgun by my count, but I was no Preacher, and *mining* his skill would take far, far more time and energy than I had remaining.

I didn't even have enough juice to suppress the rising tide of terror. So, I embraced it, allowing the exhilarating sense of fear to course through me. I broke through the burnt doors of the second mansion and lurched down the steps out among the trees again. I moved with limping, stumbling steps towards the swimming pool.

Not a good plan. Not even great. But I couldn't outrun them. Too much blood loss. Too much pain. Already, dark spots danced across my vision.

I glanced back where three Endeavor burst through the burnt doorway of the mansion. They spotted me, shouting. Two of them had their handguns stowed—likely the ones on empty. One of them aimed. Fired. Another jolt of heat across my forearm. Just a scrape.

I sighted my own weapon, fired twice, but in my broken state I missed completely.

Gasping, I reached the metal black privacy gate near the pool and flung it open. I limped towards the covered swimming pool. Branches from an enormous tree angled over the encircling black fence.

"Stop, Leonidas!" one of the agents shouted from the gate. "There's nowhere left to go!"

I aimed my empty weapon towards them, and they instinctively ducked behind the metal fence, giving me a moment, gasping, to hit the electronic button to the pool cover Preacher and I had seen on the way in. The cover opened, rather quickly, sliding to reveal the cool, blue water beneath.

Someone still used the pool. The cleaners had been by. Jester? The Librarian?

It didn't matter. What mattered was escaping.

"He's empty!" someone shouted.

"You sure?" another retorted.

Tentatively, my three pursuers emerged from behind their cover, waiting to see if I'd shoot, but when I didn't, they pushed through the creaking gate as well. Their eyes fixed unblinking on me. One kept his gun raised, pointed at my head. I waited, droplets of red tapping to the tiled ground from my hand and back and chest; I watched the pool cover slide back.

"Can't swim away," the remaining armed man growled. "Nowhere left to run, Leonidas. Give us the key."

"What key?" I said, swallowing, feeling where the leather strap shifted around my neck. Then, feeling I'd risked dishonesty, I amended. "I know what key you're referring to. But I'd rather keep hold of it." I didn't have the *time* for this. Only two days left before the Hollow closed but, then again, dead men can't break into prisons.

The man's eyes narrowed. "Hands up—Euryale wants you alive. For a bit."

I tried not to think of all the lovely torments Grendel's eldest daughter might inflict on my already agonized flesh. From behind the agents, I heard distant gunfire.

Preacher most likely, keeping the rest of the attackers pinned down. His final attempt at helping. As for these three, I was on my own.

I stared at the glossy water, exhaling slowly. The man with the remaining handgun kept it pointed at me.

"You're nearly out too," I murmured.

The gunman frowned across the pool, his expression flickering. I exhaled, trying my best to look defeated. It wasn't difficult—I nearly was. Only one trick left up my sleeve.

"Lower the gun. Let's fight like gentlemen," I said.

The man snorted, nearly a laugh. "Corker's breath, do you think I'm an idiot?"

How many bullets did he have left? One? Two? More? Did he have another clip?

The two other, unarmed Endeavor were glancing uneasily from me to the water. "Shoot him," one said. "He's going to try to make us drown ourselves. Kill him!"

The one with the gun though, snarled, trying to hide his voice with his shoulder and whispering fiercely. "Don't be stupid. Euryale promised triple pay for alive. Look at him—he's practically dead."

"You don't be stupid," the unarmed agent retorted. "Drop him."

The gunman hesitated, his eyes shimmering with greed.

"If you want me," I spat, "you have to catch me."

Then, I flung my spent pistol at them and spun around. The gunman fired. But his companions' words had affected him. He seemed to think I wanted something from the pool. And so he aimed just a bit ahead of me, anticipating me diving into the water.

Except I didn't. I went up.

His shots missed, and I snared the lowest branches dangling over the black fence, beginning to climb, rapidly, ignoring the agony in my hand. I could feel sap and splinters and rough bark mingling with my blood, prodding like hot irons against my palm. Pain and I were familiar though. Pain and I had befriended long ago.

And so I scaled the massive tree, climbing, desperately climbing.

The agents below cursed one last time but circled the pool now, with thumping steps of booted feet. They flung themselves at the lowest boughs and began to climb too.

They could tell I was exhausted. Could tell I was on my last legs.

I glimpsed below my feet, through the prickling branches, down to where they were rapidly ascending. One of them still had bullets, judging by the way he kept his gun drawn while still climbing after me with grunts and curses.

In near silence, for a moment, the skies witnessed us. No gunshots from the distant mansion. No gunshots from below. Eventually, no cursing either. Just winded breaths and pain as three black-garbed soldiers clambered after my bloodied form.

After nearly three minutes of climbing, we were even higher than the mansions. I no longer could see Euryale or the other soldiers, but I did glimpse Preacher, behind a straggle of rocks, his gun aimed towards the doorway of the first mansion. His small form crossed itself, thumb over heart, to forehead and back as he offered up a silent prayer. Then he fired and I heard a shout of pain from within the other mansion. Ever reliable, my friend.

But the three figures behind me were still following. I might climb faster, even in my injured, broken state, but eventually, I'd run out of tree. And even Wits couldn't conjure wings. Perhaps another *glimpsing?*

I tried. Thinking of flames, making it look like the tree was blazing. I reached out, placing the image in the minds of the two agents closest to me. As I did, though, I felt a swirl in my gut of exhaustion and nausea. I spat, the stray strand of bloodied saliva darkening the bough beneath my good hand. For a moment, I thought I might fall from exhaustion. *No more talent,* I thought desperately, clinging to consciousness.

The men below shook their heads, staving off the *glimpsing.* Their fear was diminishing, fading. They knew they had me cornered. The one with the gun looked up, aimed. I ducked behind the thickest branch I could. But I'd nearly reached the top of the tree and the cover was sparse.

The bullet slammed through the branches, ripping small boughs, and sending some twirling to the ground. The shot ended as a white indentation in the dark wood, an inch from my thigh.

We were higher than the mansions. But nowhere near other trees. I couldn't move from one to the other—an escape I'd performed once before while being chased by a grave ogre after breaking into one of the minor lake prisons.

"Nowhere left to go, Leonidas!" snapped the man with the gun. "Come down *now.*" He aimed again, pointing at my chest. No missing this time. I couldn't dodge. I couldn't *glimpse,* as I was already spent. I was a sitting duck.

I looked back, breathed a shallow sigh, tipped my cap.

Then jumped.

"Vyle's teeth!" one of them screamed.

Another swiped at me, but missed, nearly falling himself. A gunshot echoed, but even this close, it's nearly impossible to hit a plummeting target. Especially if caught by surprise.

I dove past them, head first, angled down.

The Endeavor shouting again, but the words were lost in the fluttering breeze and the echo of the wind. Of course, I'd aimed towards the pool I'd opened.

I slammed into the water, swallowed by the blue. Water in my ears, chlorine in my nose. Pain from impact, but cushioned by the liquid.

For a moment, suspended in the water, my head beneath the glaze of blue, I felt weightless, relieved. My wounds stung. My chest cuts and scrapes and gunshots in my hand and lower back pulsed. But I felt swaddled, safe for a crystal moment.

Then my head broke the surface.

Voices shouted above, nearly lost on a rising wind. "Jump!" one of the agents was screaming. "Go!"

"Are you insane?"

"If he can, you can!"

I scrabbled with the last vestiges of my strength to the edge of the pool and pulled desperately from the water, gasping. Chlorine stung my nostrils, stung my aching wounds. The agents above were tentatively stepping to the edges of the branches, preparing to follow. They had courage, I had to give them that.

I pulled out of the pool, rolling onto the tile with a gasp and reached up, slapping my hand against the electronic button. There was a whir and the pool cover began to close.

The agents above didn't seem to notice at first. One was still shouting, "Jump! Go! Go!"

I heard a gunshot. Tiles exploded at my feet. But then, from above, *Click! Click!*

No more bullets. I gasped in relief. One of the agents jumped. And only then did he seem to realize what I'd done.

I heard the scream as he plummeted.

The pool cover closed nearly completely by the time he hit. If he'd been unlucky, he might have struck the water, but then been trapped *beneath* the cover.

Instead, the man shattered against the plastic, having swan-dived from nearly seventy feet in the air, straight into the hard pool cover.

The remaining agents both shouted in horror, witnessing the fate of the bravest among them. I watched, through narrowed eyes, breathing heavily from where I stood next to the now covered pool, dripping water speckled with blood.

The remaining Endeavor slowly began to shimmy back down their branches cautiously, returning the way they'd come.

I didn't even bother to run this time. I listened to their grunts, their desperate breaths as they tentatively lowered themselves. Full of fear now, neither wanted to end up like their intrepid friend turned crimson stain.

Gasping, one hand clutched against my ribs, I winced against the pain in my lower back and limped off into the trees, heading in the direction I'd spotted Preacher.

I'd made it. Survived. At least another day. But Grendel's children wouldn't be happy. The Endeavor wouldn't be happy. The Endeavor would want my blood even more.

Not only that, but I had Annie to think about now. My old friend wanted to break into one of the most well-guarded prisons of the Eternal Wars. To face off against a lieutenant of the saboteurs—the deadliest assassins magical or otherwise in the world.

She wanted to unleash my brother. I couldn't allow that to happen, but I had promised her, given an oath on my powers, that I'd help her break into the Hollow. I would. I had to. But only so I could stop her from rescuing Napoleon. Either this year, or the next, she could always hire a new savant. No, I had to cut the risk off at the source.

First, though, I needed to heal. I also needed to find the confidant so they could *lead* us to the Hollow. The price would be steep, but we'd have to pay it. Additionally, we would need supplies to stand a chance of breaching the prison. I'd lost all my gold pouches, to begin with. And crazed genies weren't the only guardians. Which meant our next step was clear: we'd have to visit my old black marketing friend, Kay Kelly.

And while Kay was an ally, the mobsters, assassins, and gangsters he hung out with were less than chummy. It didn't help that I owed some unsavory sorts a fair amount of treasure. I could only hope they wouldn't be at the Loophole when we arrived, otherwise, things could get even bloodier.

Chapter 18

I knew I was asleep because the pain had dulled. But I couldn't linger. Things to do, black-marketers to haggle, magical trade laws to break. Endeavor were on our trail, Grendel and his children at their helm. Annie, my long-lost friend had hired us to free my fourteen-year-old brother from a horrific magical prison. If my injuries were anything to attest to, we needed to resupply. Magical contraband, inventions, and defenses required cash; something in severely short supply. Even though I could feel the pain threatening to return with my waking mind, I knew I couldn't sleep forever. The allure of laze and sloth were unbecoming to those of any station.

And so, with every air of half-stupor reluctance, I pressed towards consciousness, rousing.

But I didn't make it.

As my subconscious began to move towards *awake,* it was mugged on the way by a rizzle. Two in fact.

Perhaps I should explain.

Rizzles are dream imps—a creation of Gildquail Lockwood, genie inventor extraordinaire. They also, for most in the magical world, are the single most used postal and courier service even, I'm told, among the magical creatures and beings of the Hidden Kingdoms. In addition, rizzles provide—*in dreams*—the news of the day (or night as often the case.)

Currently, I found my subconscious self sprawled on the ground from where a tripwire had been pulled across my dream state between a make-believe door and an imaginary wall textured like substantive smoke.

Two of the ugliest creatures one might ever set eyes on were now sitting on my back where I lay.

"Unhand my person!" I snapped, aware that I was still trapped half in a dream. Sometimes, my old speech patterns came nipping back when I was annoyed.

The rizzles scattered as I began to rise. The diminutive creatures were only a foot tall and looked like a fuzzy cross between chipmunks—complete with oversized buck teeth and puffy cheeks—and vampires due to sharpened fangs and their odd penchant for wearing crimson or black capes over their onesies. The sketches printed on the onesies were tailor made to the dreamer. In this case, both of them had exaggerated, cartoon sketches of me falling from the Librarian's roof with a stomach like a beach ball as I belly-flopped into the pool. It also showed me clutching my injured hand, cartoon Leonidas complete with newsboy cap bawling thick, dewdrop tears in two arches. This last tasteful sketch on their onesies was situated near their rumps and the flicking trident tails that protruded from the fabric.

"What?" I snapped. I wasn't in the mood for this.

The little cretins aren't dangerous, just annoying. Their creator, Mr. Lockwood himself, had maxed out all levels of mischievous and minimized any sense of *decorum*. Just another middle finger from the genie folk to humankind. Why we put up with their nonsense might be hard to understand. Sometimes, tradition is hard to break; on this front, I'm well versed. But also, rizzles are magically bound from revealing their messages to anyone unpermitted. It's hard to intercept a magical message sent only through dreams. Such secure communication appealed to most involved in a centuries long magical war.

As my subconscious shifted and moved, sitting up, the rizzles began to play hopscotch with the tripwire they'd set up, humming and singing to themselves.

I huffed, got to my feet, tried to take a threatening step, then fell again, realizing they'd tied my (still imaginary) shoelaces. I faceplanted and the rizzles cackled.

Somewhere, I could feel my physical self trying to wake. Distant voices echoed as if down a well—Annie and someone else. Not Preacher, obviously. Who, then? And why had they been invited into my RV? I could feel the buzz of the RV wheels even through my unconscious form, plus the faint, ghostly sensation of a cushion against my back, suggesting I'd been placed in my bed.

Mercifully, the pain had yet to return.

This time, I didn't bother to sit up and instead propped my chin against an enclosed fist. "You have a message?" I said, my frustration mounting.

One of the rizzles tried to approach and sit on my head, his little onesie—depicting cartoon Leonidas bawling like a baby—pointed towards my face, his tail swishing. I reached out and shoved the thing, sending him tumbling.

The other rizzle stared out at me from his wide, deep purple eyes, his chipmunk cheeks puffing and then, in a bellow—far louder than was necessary—he screamed. "Breaking news!"

The second rizzle swung a bat, which had appeared in his hand, and slammed it into a glass window which emerged in the wall next to the make-believe door.

I didn't try to make sense of it. Rizzles had more power in the Dream-Plane than I did. But such abilities had little effect on the waking world... at least, so goes the theory.

"What news?" I snapped.

Even rizzles have protocol. I usually find them quite funny. But something about being shot twice and meeting a friend once thought dead has a way of emotionally draining a man.

"Saboteur July has been murdered!" the rizzle continued screaming. "Saboteur July has been murdered!"

At this, I went suddenly very still, staring at the dream imps. They seemed to realize the effect their words had and were grinning now, their vampire teeth flashing, their Dracula capes swirling around their onesies.

My imaginary mouth felt very dry. "Dead? A saboteur?" I shook my head, frowning. "Impossible."

But the rizzles just leered.

"Well?" I demanded. "Tell me more."

In a message like this, dream imps would carry news through all the empire, to everyone with a willing mind. They didn't choose a side between Endeavor or Imperium. And rizzles couldn't lie to a direct question. Ever.

Which left me entirely confused. Because what they were shouting was impossible. No one could kill a saboteur. I'd seen them in action, seen them in war. I'd once had the misfortune of witnessing a saboteur face off in the First Battle of Cragged Hill against a herd of centaur. Their demonic masks had shifted and quivered, their wereblades—a glistening magical item built by the genies—had reformed into any manner of weapon. Imagine a Sith Lord (from unknowing picture shows) on steroids. And I'd witnessed as a single saboteur massacred a battalion of Hidden Kingdoms' soldiers, a veritable blur of shadow and violence, fury and storm. The saboteur had fallen on the centaurs and within *minutes* the battlefield itself had fallen silent.

Some said even the archangels and minor gods faced difficulty when destroying a properly motivated saboteur.

So the rizzles had to be lying.

The rizzle who'd spoken first, though, was now unfurling a formal looking scroll; he cleared his throat, putting on an offensive attempt at an Indian accent, and began to narrate:

"Three days ago, near an Unlocated Endeavor prison, Saboteur July was ambushed in the night. Stop."

The other rizzle chorused. "Stop!" like a telegram. They didn't have to do this, but seemed to enjoy the look of frustration it elicited from me.

"Saboteur July was traveling alone, according to the Twilight Citadel. Stop!"

"Stop!" came the echo.

"January herself has visited the scene of the murder and vows retribution on the guilty party. Stop!"

"Stop!"

"Stop," I said. "Do they know who did it?"

The rizzle's eyes flicked down the scroll, bound to answer a direct question honestly. Then, faking a Texan accent, equally offensive, it said, *"Speculation abounds to the identity of the killer,* y'all*! Reporters with the Ardent Gazette interviewed both leaders of the Hidden Kingdoms and lieutenants of human divisions. As well as the wardens of the prison Saboteur July had been traveling to."*

"And who do they think did it?" I said, feeling an itch now down my spine.

"Auditor Cornelius Affer, believes—"

"Summarize for me!" I said. Then I caught myself and rephrased in the form of a question, prompting an honest reply. "What is the summary? Who do they think did it?"

The rizzle's eyes darted around a bit, as if trying to find a way to further waste my time, but then it huffed a small little breath, flashed me a fuzzy middle finger from a three-fingered hand and said. "Archangels, demon kings, old gods, dominions..."

I felt a flutter of fear at the words. Of course, the speculation was only that. Nothing concrete. But reporters at the Ardent Gazette weren't fools. Like me, they knew the sheer potency of a saboteur.

But if an old god had woken and decided to murder a saboteur, or the demon kings and archangels ongoing war in the second heaven had spilled to earth, then humankind was on a collision course with history. Such events always ended in calamity. The last time Zeus and Hades had taken up arms against each other, World War II had resulted. And when an angel of death had fallen on the world, loosed to its own designs, over half the planet had been wiped out in the bubonic plague.

Someone was killing saboteurs. I couldn't shake the sudden pulse of fear spreading down my spine and robbing my breath even in this in-between land of dreams.

I exhaled, slowly and paused before I looked the rizzle directly in the eyes and said, "The Unlocated prison. The one Saboteur July was going to visit. Which one?"

The rizzle's eyes scanned the document, its puffy cheeks finally twisting up into a mischievous leer and droplets of spittle scattered before its mouth as it said, "Only days before she could enter, the saboteur was murdered outside The Hollow."

Chapter 19

I jerked awake in my RV's bed, groaning in chorus with my mattress springs. I glanced slowly down, wincing as I did. Someone had managed to bandage my chest with thick gauze and cloth strips, careful to avoid the ashen black skeletal pendant dangling from the chain around my neck where the cursed pendant now rested against the pale bandages along with the blunt, iron key. I shifted and aroused a spasm of pain in my abdomen.

My gaze flicked past the twelve-string guitar next to the floor-to-ceiling mirror. For a moment, I expected to see my poltergeist, gloating at my pain, but only my reflection stared back from the few remaining shards of reflective material.

The bandage had a couple of minor red leaks near the portions where glass had gouged the deepest, but, for the most part, they appeared clean. I shifted and winced again, checking my gunshot hand. A similar mummy-wrap of gauze and cloth entombed my palm and fingers. The pain in my palm was worse than my chest. I could feel sharp jabs of agony in my lower back as well.

I groaned as I sat up, gritting my teeth against the effort and leaned against the headboard for a momentary breather.

"You alright?"

I looked sharply up and spotted a figure standing in my door. The second voice I'd heard through my subconscious. Not Annie, but her intern.

"Dale," I said, with a short half-nod, sparing my body too much motion.

Dale scratched one of his sideburns, his dull, gray eyes fixed on me from behind his round glasses. By the look of things, he'd managed to find a new pair of shoes. Equally polished and expensive as his loafers. I felt a flash of faint approval.

"You look like you've been through a cheese grater," Dale Rodrick said.

"Amusing. Why are you in my RV?"

Dale shrugged. "The boss needs me."

"You are useless in fights and scared by your own shadow. Why does she need you?"

Dale tapped his nose, pointing it at me. "That honesty thing. The boss told me. You're a Witty." He said this last part with a self-satisfied little smile.

"Wit—just called a Wit." I groaned.

Dale took a half step into my room, offering a helping hand.

"Don't," I said sharply, glancing towards the smashed mirror, then back again. "Stay out."

He held up his hands and retreated to the doorway. It wasn't suiting to appear weak in front of an unknown quantity nor did I appreciate having him in my RV at all. I closed my eyes for a moment, checking the tarantulas on the ceiling in the main compartment of our vehicle.

I blinked and then, through images of black and gray, I spotted Preacher in the chauffeur's seat with Annie sitting passenger-side, her legs tucked up on the seat, her arms wrapped around her knees as she stared out the window. She seemed to be motor-mouthing breezily about something, while Preacher pretended to listen. She didn't seem at all perturbed by his lack of response, launching into an enthusiastic anecdote I couldn't quite hear.

I blinked again, snapping back to my own gaze and looking Dale dead in the eyes, a question now roused at the images of black and gray. I felt the question press against my lips, and then I released it at once. "Where has Annie been for all these years?"

"Umm. The boss? I—I don't know. She hired me a few months ago. Mostly a messenger, sometimes courier. Pay is good. Plus, she's really easy-going. I like her."

"Tell me the truth. What is she hiding?"

Dale gave a helpless little shake of his head. "I don't know."

"Don't lie to me!"

"Check. For real. Look in my mind. You've already done it. See if I'm lying." He jutted out his chin.

Of course, I'd already been in the middle of checking. And, much to my frustration, I detected no dishonesty. Perhaps I was too distracted by the pain, or, *more likely,* Annie was playing her cards closer to the chest than I'd first assumed.

I scratched at my chin. "Vyle's teeth. Fine."

"Hang on," Dale said, his eyes narrowed again. "You ask me something, now it's my turn." He puffed his chest in the manner of someone finding hidden courage.

I stared at him. "You have a question?"

"I have a lot."

"I'll probably ignore you and avoid most of them."

"Noted. Look, I was just curious. What's with the big guy's makeup?"

I paused, half-wincing, one eye near squinting in anticipation but as the question registered, I blinked. "That's your question? About Preacher's makeup?"

Dale bobbed his head once.

For a moment, still in pain, I just leaned back, allowing my bed to support me. A soft, weak little sigh left my mouth, fleeing to less painful pastures. At last, though, I shrugged. "I don't know."

Dale frowned. "I thought you couldn't lie."

"It's not a lie. I genuinely don't know. I've never really asked him."

Dale stared at me, but I stared back now.

"You... what, like never?"

I shrugged but then stopped the motion mid-gesture. It hurt too much. "It never came up. Over the last ten years, it just... hasn't really mattered, what with all the fleeing for our lives, and trying to survive." I grunted. "I've seen weirder from stranger."

Dale tapped his nose, pointing it at me. "That's how he's such a good shooter, isn't he? His make-up somehow gives him power."

I wanted to shake my head but didn't want to risk another painful movement. So I kept my head as still as possible. "Don't know. Ask him if you want." Of course, I knew Preacher wouldn't answer him. I didn't pry into my friend's past, because he didn't pry into mine. Questioning someone else always, inevitably, opened the door to return fire.

And whatever secrets my friend had, they wouldn't be nearly as horrible as my own. No, far better to allow the time we'd known each other to suffice. Anything before could remain buried as far as I was concerned. Besides... the make-up was a painful subject. I knew that much. I'd seen him cry more than once while applying it. I sighed softly, closing my eyes, feeling a lance of grief at the thought of Preacher's tears.

Glancing out the window, studying the hills and misty trees flashing by in a blur of greens and gray, I forced a change of subject. Our rapidly dwindling time-frame for the mission was starting to rise above my sense of pain. "Where are we going?"

The expression of curiosity faded from Dale's face now, to be replaced by a giddy grin, which he tried to hide. "The Loophole," Dale said, an eager edge to his voice. "I've never been before, but have heard about it. Is it true that the Hillbilly Godfather operates from there?" His gaze gleamed hungrily as he looked at me, further implying his lack of experience with the knowing world.

"Hillbilly Godfather? Don't let him hear you call him that," I said with a snort. "The last person who did ended up eaten by a shark. On land. Over the course of days. One piece at a time. And I don't know," I winced. "He owns many establishments. The Loophole isn't even the most profitable, it's just the most popular."

"The boss says they sell contraband behind the fighting aquariums."

"They don't call Baron O'Shea a godfather for nothing. Anything mob and magic related can usually be found in his businesses for the right price. *Anything,*" I added with a grimace. Inwardly, I was glad Preacher had made the right call. I felt a flicker of unease, considering the Loophole... I still owed money to some unsavory sorts. But we'd have to take the risk. We already had the sewer key for entrance, but we needed the gold for the genies, and the teleporting stones for mobility against the other guardians. Not to mention, the Union often frequented the Loophole. The confidant would be a Union boy. For us to find the Hollow, we'd have to start greasing palms. We already were running out of time—less than two days left before the Hollow opened for twenty-four hours.

After all, I'd given my word to break us in. The thought alone left a sour taste in my mouth. But it had to be done—to destroy my brother so no one could attempt to free him ever again. If I sabotaged the mission this time, Annie might just find another savant, or wait until next year... or the year after that. Eventually, the skeletons in my closet had to be dealt with. I couldn't live with it hanging over my head for another year. No—the problem had to be solved *now*.

Kay Kelly, my contact, usually had something for wounds. I groaned again, pressing my good hand against my lower back and gingerly prodding towards the bandages found there.

"Preacher gave you some pain-killers," said Dale, helpfully. "I can get more if you like."

He really was trying. "I appreciate the offer, but no." I massaged my forehead and took a wobbly step up. My body protested with aches and spasms and I collapsed onto the bed.

If I entered the Loophole looking like this, sharks would be the least of my worries. I couldn't heal myself. Wits had no control over flesh. But... pain? Pain existed mostly in the mind.

Numbing pain had a cost, though. For one, it required an incredible amount of focus. Focus that once used *couldn't* be used elsewhere until I released the *numbing*. Which meant I could either wander into a wretched hive of scum and villainy disarmed or in agony. Neither prospect much appealed to me.

So I settled on a compromise. I closed my eyes, extending my mind, reaching internally. I exhaled, watching pictures and shadows dance across my vision. I extended my thoughts like a surgeon's scalpel, but instead of cutting, I muffled my pain receptors. Not all of it. I left the pain in my chest from the glass and most of the pain in my hand. But I lifted the agony in my lower back, swaddling it in fantastical thoughts and make-believe.

Nothing numbs pain nearly so much as pretend.

Of course, I also knew that once I ripped the *numbing* off, it would return in double agony. Wounds left untended always festered, even those of the mind.

But I couldn't enter the Loophole in this much discomfort. I pressed, swaddling my thoughts in ripped chunks of imagination, pulling on old movies I'd seen, or books I'd read, using them like gauze against my mind.

I felt a prickle along my body and loosed a slow, steady sigh of relief, like someone slipping into a warm bath. Immediately, my lower back stopped pulsing. I reached around, pushing at the bandage, but felt nothing.

The pain in my chest was irritating, but not crippling. The jabbing feeling in my hand would simply have to be managed. I stood up now, feeling nothing in my back and releasing another sigh. This time I didn't collapse and started striding with confident steps towards the door.

Dale blinked in surprise, his mouth opening just a bit.

I'd only numbed in part, which meant I still had some of my gift left in case I needed it later. And when wandering into a place like the Loophole, even with coin for contraband, the more weapons at one's disposal, the better.

Chapter 20

Mountains encircled us, wreathed in looming cedars, larger even than redwoods. The trees themselves were as wide as skyscrapers, with root stems like whale humps in the ocean. The cedars were ancient and *alive* in the truest sense of the word, hidden in the heart of untainted, unknown land, adorned by thousands of miles of forests and uncivilized wilderness.

Preacher parked the RV outside the entrance to the Loophole and I braced myself against the back of the passenger seat as the vehicle jarred on the dust, scattering leaves and pine needles. It wasn't so much a parking lot as a clearing—a section of forest hacked back, allowing the many vehicles parked in haphazard directions and angles with no apparent rhyme or reason. Preacher, currently, had the nose of the RV facing the side of a long, pink limousine. The limousine nearly bumped up against the wheels of a monster truck which in turn, due to its sheer size, had been parked *over* a small, rusted green Beetle.

Dale leaned past me, desperately scanning the area with eyes as wide as a child on Christmas morning. "Where is it?" he said, practically panting. His gaze flicked to the enormous trees, the shadow of one cedar stretching over the entire collection of nearly two hundred vehicles both visible, and, likely, invisible.

"Look at that!" Dale said suddenly, staring through the windshield at a rusty old minivan loop-de-looping the roots of one of the tremendous cedars. "No driver!"

I grunted. "It's a flying car pet. Don't go near it. Djinn are territorial about their family vehicles."

As we watched, the minivan in question spun its wheels, kicking dirt up against the trunk of the nearest tree.

"What... what is it doing?"

"Car pets don't like trees," Annie replied, as if the answer was obvious. "Too many airborne collisions. It's an old feud. Leon, are you sure you're alright?"

I nodded and pushed open the door, stepping out onto the dusty ground. The pain was mostly suppressed, but I could still worsen my injuries if I wasn't careful. "Fine," I said, tugging the brim of my flat cap and wincing. "The confidant will be here. The Union has nothing better to do. Look for someone wearing a jade bracelet."

"A bracelet," Annie said. "Got it."

"We go in, buy what we need, then skedaddle. No sight-seeing, no participating in the gladiatorial aquariums," I said, turning gingerly to glance at Preacher. "And no accepting anything for free from the dryads," I finished, looking at Dale.

He scoffed. "Of course not."

"I mean it. You strike me as somewhat rash. Don't accept anything for free."

But Dale was already out the door, his expensive loafers hitting the dusty forest clearing with gusto. Wearily, I followed with Preacher and Annie close behind. "Tab is on you," I added, glancing at Annie.

She nodded once, a slight bounce to her step. "I'm happy to cover expenses for the job," she said. She paused though, glancing at me with a look of concern. "You look troubled. Are you okay?"

I grimaced, running a hand through my hair, and tipping my newsboy cap. I could feel the weight of the key around my neck, but gave a quick shake of my head. "I—I have some unpaid debts in the Loophole," I muttered. "Debts to people that aren't very nice."

I shared a look with Preacher and his jaw clenched ever so slightly.

"Debts?" Annie said. "Darn... Sounds scary. It won't mess with the job, will it?"

I coughed delicately, considering the question. "I—probably not." *Unless the confidant is who I think it might be...* I thought, but didn't voice this part aloud. "We should be fine."

Annie held out a hand though, placing it gently on my wrist, and looking me in the eyes. She didn't speak, but she watched me, curiously, her bright eyes studying mine the way they often had back when we were young, seeing far more than I would have been comfortable with if watched by anyone besides Annie.

"It should be fine," I insisted, wincing. "Right now, we have our entrance strategy." I tapped the key around my neck. "But we need to first locate the blasted prison."

"What if this... this confidant isn't here?"

I snorted. "They will be. Or someone who knows them will be."

"How can you be sure?"

"Because the Union runs contracts for Endeavor. They set up the Unlocator spell on the Hollow. So one of their goons will be keeping confidant. Like I said, just keep an eye out for a jade bracelet—that'll be the marker."

"So we find this person then we bribe them?"

I shrugged. "More or less. That's on your dime, too, by the way."

Her mouth bunched to one side, and she placed a hand on her hip, her nose wrinkling. "I'm sure you know, but—just, you know, so I can think about it, if the entrance is guarded—and its guarded, right, you said guarded? Then even with a key and a location, how do we get in without being noticed?"

I tapped my nose and pointed at her. "That's where tiger's eye comes in."

"Ooh, okay... Hmm, what's that?"

"Tiger's eye," I said. "Teleporting stones. You'll see. Come."

I grit my teeth from my injured hand, but increased the focus suppressing the pain in my lower back. My steps quickened, and I breathed easier as I modified my pain levels, but at the same time, I felt a flicker of unease. The more pain I suppressed, the more concentration required, the less talent I'd have available in case of trouble. In case the people I owed money decided to pay the Loophole an ill-timed visit. Plus, I was counting on the Wit to locate the location-keeper.

We emerged into the coolness of the mid-afternoon, and yet the area fell to shadow from the sheer weight of the foliage above. The cedars were so tall, the branches so high, the leaves and highest boughs mingled with cloud cover, a strange marriage of greens and cottony white.

Hovering lights in the form of oversized lightning bugs danced through the trees. When Dale spotted these, he stared in awe.

I rolled my eyes. "Don't touch them!" I called. "They have stingers."

Dale retracted his fingers from where he'd been prodding one of the glowing bugs.

With Preacher supporting my weak arm, the four of us moved around the parked and scattered vehicles. The largest means of transportation settled in the clearing resembled an eighteenth-century frigate, complete with cannon ports, weather-stained prow and thick, red sails.

Dale kept staring at the frigate, shaking his head. "How," he murmured. "How did it get here?"

"It," I said, "flew," Annie and I replied in unison.

Preacher snorted.

"Dale," I began.

He waved dismissively. "I know, I know, I'm starting to annoy you."

I blinked and he looked back, flashing a grin. "See, mind-reader, I'm catching on." Then he turned to examine what looked like a tank from the second world war parked on *top* of a low-rider motorcycle which had been crushed like a tin can.

"Where is it?" Dale kept repeating, glancing to the trees and frowning as he spun about, his eyes flitting one way then the other.

I marched to the largest tree of them all. An enormous knot, the size of a manhole cover, faced me, glossy and shiny with words scraped into the surface reading, "*What do you offer?*"

I gestured at Annie. "Ladies first."

"How chivalrous," she said, chuckling and skipping past. As she did, I noticed her shadow *behind* her.

Nothing to suggest anything awry, save one thing.

The little beams of sunlight managing to claw through the trees, and the majority of the glowing bugs, were also behind us.

I stared at her shadow and noticed Preacher doing the same thing. Before either of us could comment, though, Annie stood, raising both her hands in the air as if to embrace tumultuous applause. "Do I have a cool one for you! I once supplied the ammunition to throw clumps of dough at palace security. Have you ever done that? I mean, do you even like biscuits?"

As Annie continued to chatter, the letters inside the tree knot teetered back and forth, like a scale, as if weighing her response.

Then the words shifted and read, "Suitable *Malfeasance*."

The knothole spun, twisting now like a top, or like the ripples on a pond from a tossed stone. A second later a doorway appeared in the heart of the massive tree. A sudden gust of wind emanated from inside the Loophole, carrying the scent of cave water tinged with alcohol and herbs. I detected the shouts which broke into a sudden force of laughter.

Annie caught herself mid-sentence and let out a squeak of excitement. "So awesome!" she declared, and then stepped through, wiggling her fingers in temporary farewell at the rest of us. "I'll miss you," she snickered, winking. "See ya in a sec."

Dale made to follow, but Preacher grabbed his arm, yanking him back before he was swallowed by the sudden closing doorway. The wood swam in like quicksand pouring into a well and then went solid once more. Again, etched as if carved by a knife, the words gouged into the tree read *"What do you offer?"*

Dale blinked, his nose inches from the tree. He glanced, trembling back at Preacher. "Th-thanks."

"Would be a pity to be cut in half on your first visit here," I said dryly. "Normally that delight is saved until *after* you enter."

"I... What do I do?"

"Tell the tree one time when you broke the law," I said. "Try not to lie. If you lie, it might suspect it and open just enough to bait you in before closing again."

Dale shivered. "If that happens?"

I made a chopping motion with my uninjured hand.

Dale swallowed, leaning in a bit closer now to study the words. Carved into the wood, what might first be taken for sap seeping through, the letters carried a far more reddish tinge. Annie's intern grit his teeth, then declared in a powerful, commanding voice, "I once stole a Mars bar from a gas station back in Cheshire!" He waited, expectantly.

The tree seemed to take a long time on this one, the words once more shifting up and down like scales, weighing his claim. Then, the letters shifted and this time read, "Pathetic *Malfeasance.*"

The knot in the tree opened, but glacially slow this time and began to close before Dale had even stepped forward. Even the trees above the Loophole had mastered the art of contempt. Luckily for Dale, he dove, headfirst, unwilling to risk decapitation, tumbling safely to the other side. I glimpsed Annie catch him, steadying him and dusting him off before patting him affectionately on the head. Then, the wooden doorway closed completely.

At last, Preacher glanced at me, and I shrugged. "He shot Endeavor agents this week," I said, on Preacher's behalf.

The words gouged in wood shifted to "Spectacular *Malfeasance.*" The tree took no time in opening and Preacher stepped through before the knothole spun shut again.

I stood at the entrance to the Loophole, frowning at the wood as the letters swirled then settled. "Hello, Leonidas," the letters said.

I rolled my eyes. "I don't have time to talk, Contrua."

The tree above shifted and swayed, branches stretching like someone waking from a nap. The letters moved again. "Offer me something *new* this time."

I glared at the wood. "Tomb's trove, did Percy put you up to this?"

The tree shook now, bark creaking, bits of wood and twig falling around me.

"Meddling git. Fine," I said, my stomach twisting with a sudden spurt of guilt. "I broke the illegitimate son of a gorgon out of the Glade."

I waited. But the tree didn't shift.

"Are you serious?" I demanded, crossing my arms and then gasping sharply as my injured hand contacted my elbow. "Come on, Contrua. Percy isn't your boss."

The letters shifted again. "Something *new.*"

I'd been here so many times, I didn't know what I'd offered the tree-spirit before. I wracked my brain but then shook my head. I felt a cold chill down my spine and my thoughts were drawn like water swirling in a bathtub, inevitably swallowed by the drain. In a quiet, careful voice, I said, "In a few days' time, if I can't figure a way out of this mess, I'm going to have to betray my childhood friend and put a bullet in my youngest brother's head."

The tree shuddered in an off-putting sort of way. I could hear the boughs above creaking and shifting. The letters gouged in the wood swirled and now read, "Demonic *Malfeasance.*" The letters shifted again. "The Union sends its regards."

"That skint, Percy," I muttered to myself. The knothole opened, revealing the entrance to the Loophole once more, and I strode into the establishment.

If the Italians had magic during prohibition, I'm convinced the crime families never would have lost power. At least, so was the case with the patrons of the Loophole. In a land of division, with two major players vying for power, often things in the dark went overlooked or slipped through the cracks. The criminal element of the magical world found solace in the hiding places of the forests and mountains, keeping well to themselves.

The Loophole was filled with all sorts—savants like myself, black marketers like the man we were here to purchase from, Union boys like the confidant we wanted to find, but also more nefarious types: thieves, harvesters, murderers and the like.

And yet for me, The Loophole was a place of rest. Politics were expressly forbidden on the premises. It was one of the few remaining places in the world where my past didn't nip at my heels.

Inside the knobby tree, the Loophole itself was an underground lake, with a flotilla of small wooden platforms stretched throughout the dark waters. Above, the cavern ceiling dripped with stalactites wrapped with green and red and blue Christmas lights, illuminating the area below. Torches in brackets lined the distant cavern walls, and the water itself lay at rest, still and glassy in the dark.

The main floating, wooden dock was the size of a small warehouse, expansive and covered with tables and stools. I spotted a few felt tables, crowded with poker players nervously guarding their cards and thumbing their chips. Another group leaned over one of the wooden rails, throwing darts at a floating board wreathed with fire in the water. One of the dart players landed a shot and a shower of sparks erupted from the board. The fellow in question loosed a hearty guffaw and jammed a dirty hand to another man, shouting "pay up!" The second fellow crossed his arms though and stuck out his chin. The chin in question received a straight right hook, and the two men hit the deck, rolling about in a flurry of drunken punches.

Behind a bar, a woman with pure-red eyes glanced towards the fracas but seemed to deign it unworthy of attention and gave a small shake of her spiky head to a muscle-bound bouncer leaning against the varnished wooden counter. The woman with the red eyes leaned over the counter, extending a hand towards a patron. A second later, there was a puff of smoke—which even from here smelled like lingering sulfur—and a silver goblet studded with black stones was extended to the man. The patron grabbed the drink, slammed a small brown bag on the table, shouted, "Open a tab!" then downed the glass.

The cavern air smelled fresher than one might expect, tinged with the moisture.

"Wow," murmured Dale, where he stood a few steps ahead of me, reclining against the wooden railing encircling the platform. He peered into the water, leaning closer.

Preacher yanked Dale back just before a large, gray shape with a sharp fin and gnashing teeth ripped through the space he'd been standing. The fish landed back in the water with a splash and the dorsal fin cut through the black, circling once, twice, then moving off into the darkness again, away from the illuminated platforms beneath the Christmas-light stalactites.

Dale gasped, pressing against Preacher. "What was that?" he asked, looking up at the tall shooter.

Annie peered out into the waves, her eyes narrowed. It was far too dark to see, but she said, in nearly a whisper, "There are other things out there. Larger things in the water."

"Sharks," I muttered, stepping onto the platform and hearing the creek of the wood beneath my feet. "Merfolk, too. Also, I've heard Baron O'Shea keeps a hydra beneath the Loophole, though I haven't seen it myself."

"I used to love mermaids" Annie said, a ghost of a smile threatening her lips, a far away look in her eyes.

I felt a lance of grief, though I couldn't quite say why. So instead, I said, "We're not here to sight-see; we're here for supplies. Also, careful who you mention the job too. This place is rife with contract-poachers. They won't take no for an answer."

I peered along the slatted floorboards crossing the dock-like connector between one of the smaller platforms and the main hub of the Loophole. I watched as the red-eyed barkeep handed another drink to a customer with twisting dreadlocks, glancing at their wrists. No jade bracelet.

My eyes then scanned the smaller connecting platforms like tiny islands dotting a main continent. These wooden platforms, in the darker portions of the cavern, also had shadows and shapes moving about on them. One of the platforms, directly opposite us was encircled by a low, smokey fog, hiding the denizens from sight.

"A veil," I said, nodding to Preacher.

Annie glanced over. "Uh-oh. Trouble?"

Preacher snorted, and I shook my head. "Most likely for privacy. Anything can be bought in the Loophole. *Anything.*"

Annie looked at me, confused. Dale perked up at my comment and when he caught me looking, his cheeks reddened. But my inference seemed entirely lost on my childhood friend. Again, I was struck at the contradictions found in my new employer. She seemed shrewd, wise, but also doe-eyed at times.

The way she moved, with a childish energy, dancing from foot to foot as if she couldn't bear staying still for long, accompanied by the wide-eyed looks of wonder she flashed about the place got me thinking. The veiled platform in the dark of the Loophole would likely cater to patrons in search of a particular sort of pleasure. I knew Baron O'Shea's outfit even offered clients the opportunity to go *below* the waters and spend time in the embrace of the merfolk. Anything was on offer.

But there was an innocence about Annie—perhaps the word *naivety* was closer. Though she looked twenty-eight, at times, it almost seemed like she were trapped in a child's mind. Or, perhaps, more accurately, the experiences of a child. Then again, Grendel—of all people—had seemed fearful of her. And she displayed no fear whatsoever, as if something in her mind had been broken or removed intentionally...

None of it made sense. Where had Annie been all these years? At times, she seemed as unknowing as Dale, moving about this world with wonder. Other times, she seemed a matron of secrets herself, holding cards so close to her chest that any hope of uncovering even a fraction of what she concealed might take a lifetime of prying.

I studied Annie, my eyes moving along the soft prickle of her buzzed hair to the smooth slope of her neck. My gaze landed on the silver flask at her hip, which, as I watched, she lifted and took a small sip from while she also looked around the place, scanning wrists for jade.

I'd promised to help her break into the Hollow. And I would have to keep my word. What choice did I have? Annie would do the job without me if I tried to sabotage the break-in. This time though...

My hand curled around the hem of my shirt, twisting at the fabric and rubbing my thumb along the seams. This couldn't be like the last time I'd entered the Hollow. I'd succeed where I'd failed before.

I puffed a breath, gritting my teeth. Napoleon was a kind boy, a considerate boy. Not too powerful, nor too connected. Not even the Imperium would know what to do with him... unless they found out...

"*Found out* what?" came a voice from the direction of one of the poker tables.

I felt a chill of recognition shiver down my spine as I glanced towards the approaching figure. He had a gun in hand and was followed by two women who were also armed. All three weapons were pointed at my chest.

Chapter 21

My jaw set and my teeth clenched as the gun-wielding trio drew nearer. The Christmas lights dangling from the stalactites above almost seemed to brighten, illuminating my aggressors. I recognized the two women as the Sven sisters. Savants like myself, though far wealthier thanks to their ties to the Union. They were clad in dark biker leathers and thin bulletproof vests made of some strange substance that hung loose and light, allowing for rapid movement at a moment's notice. They were both super-model beautiful, with crimson hair, upturned celestial noses, and cheeks (and personalities) as sharp as razor wire. Curving emerald tattoos twisted over their left forearms, forming the letter U. The sisters were distinguishable only in that Bianca Sven had single scar tracing along her forehead, rounding the curve over her long-lashed left eye. Her sister, Margarita had no visible blemish, but—I knew from experience—both were best admired at a distance.

I swallowed. "Bianca, Margarita," I said, nodding to both women in turn.

"Leonidas," said Bianca, shortening the vowels with a soft, Eastern European accent. "Pleasure to see you again."

I chuckled nervously. "As you say. It would be even more delightful if you'd lower the Glock."

Bianca glanced at the gun in her hand, gave it a little wiggling motion, then reached into a small, black purse with a silver strap slung over her shoulder, brought out a small mirror and held it up, examining her face. She turned her head side to side, replaced the mirror in the purse and withdrew a tube of lipstick, applying it gently to her bottom lip. All the while, she kept the gun steadily pointed at my skull.

Margarita looked bored and crossed one arm over her impossibly toned stomach, while still keeping her weapon trained on me as well. "Leonidas, tell your big friend that if he moves any more, I will, *how you say*, ventilate you?"

"That *is* how you say it," I muttered. "Preacher, hang on," I said through gritted teeth, forcing a smile. "Let's hear them out first. What's this about?"

The two savants both nodded towards the third member of their trio who, up to this point, had maintained his silence.

I glanced at the middlemost figure. A tall, handsome man with slicked blonde hair pulled into a bun. He took a final step towards me, his own weapon lowering just a bit until it aimed below my belt.

I glared, and he grinned.

"Hello, Lenny," he said.

"Percy."

He moved with a lupine grace and poise, and his voice came soft and husky like a lazy purr. An emerald tattoo, thicker than the Sven sisters', wrapped around his forearm, twisting and curling into a similar ornate U, marking him as a member of the Union. One of the only organizations with similar power to Baron O'Shea's mob, especially as the Union worked tightly with the Hillbilly Godfather.

Percy's fingers were rough and calloused—the hands of a fighter, of a laborer. Strangest of all, jutting through his tied back, blonde hair, one of his ears was a rolled up, leathery thing—stolen from an ogre, it was said. A botched healing during a particularly dangerous job, treated with a smuggled miracle—contraband purchased from Kay Kelly himself. Percy had survived, and they'd restored his ear, after a fashion.

Now, Percival Twelftree was known as the ogre-eared man. He also hated my very soul. Percy flashed a smile, his rolled up, leathery ear twitching in his hair. I could sense Dale behind me, shifting uncomfortably. I extended my consciousness back and placed a thought in Dale's mind.

Don't stare at the ear. He'll smile, nod, then blow out your brains.

Dale began to fidget even more uncomfortably behind me, likely glancing in every direction except for Percy's now.

"Were you the one who put Contrua up to it?" I said, muttering. "Made it mighty hard to enter."

Annie tried to extend a hand between us, but Percy gave a quick shake of his gun in her direction, and tsked his tongue. "Please keep back," he said. "I wouldn't want Leon's blood to stain that lovely coat of yours."

Annie examined the gun with curiosity. "Hi! I'm Annie. Who are you?" she asked.

"His name is Percy," I muttered. "His daddy is a big shot at the Union."

"Oh? What's that? I think *maybe* I've heard of them."

"The Union?" I said. "A group of savants who take the most lucrative contracts and split the pay, most of it ending up in daddy's pocket."

Percy's expression remained calm, placid, smiling still, but a flash of sheer rage bolted across his eyes. "Percival Twelftree," he murmured, turning back to Annie. He gave a small little bow.

"Hello, Percival! Nice to meet you. Why are you pointing guns at Leon?"

"Ah, yes, well. I understand the confusion. See, Leonidas here owes me a great deal of money, don't you, Lenny?" He reached up and patted my cheek with his free hand, the gun swishing beneath my nose. "And he's been dodging me for a while. The last time I asked him about the debt, he shot two of my men."

I cleared my throat. "In the interest of veracity, Preacher shot them."

Percy's eyes flicked past me and up, focusing on my tall, make-up wearing best friend. For a moment, Twelftree's polite, docile expression became rather fixed. I wasn't sure why, but Preacher always had Percy's number. Perhaps, while relying so much on words and charm, the idea of someone who participated in neither left Percy with a sense of diminished control. Or, perhaps, and more likely, Preacher scared the skinting breathe out of Percy based on sheer size and killer instinct alone.

The rest of the Loophole didn't pay much mind to us. Gun-pointing and idle banter were a matter of course in Baron's establishment. But I knew in Percy's case, there was nothing idle about his threats.

"Now, now," said Percy, glancing towards Dale. "If you jump in that water, the beasties will eat you. It wouldn't be a pretty sight, Dale Rodrick."

I heard a quiet gasp behind me and slowly turned, keeping one eye on the pistol and another searching for Annie's assistant. Dale was leaning near the railing, gaping at Percival.

"Is he—is he," Dale stammered.

"A Wit too," I muttered.

"Is everyone here a Wit?" Dale demanded.

"No, we're the only two in the Loophole," I said softly. "It's a rare talent. Isn't it Percy?"

"Oh, I don't know," said the athletic, blonde-haired man. "Some of us get more use out if it than others." He traced a thumb along the grip of the pistol, like a man caressing the cheek of a lover.

"Some of us have standards."

"Which, Leonidas, is why you'll always lose. Now, enough lip. Where's my cash? I'll take genie treasure in a pinch."

"I don't have it."

"Now, see, I was hoping you would say that." He tapped the gun against my chest now, pressing hard against the wounds through my shirt.

I winced, gritting my teeth, but also took the pause to push on my fear receptors, diminishing any terror while hardening my defenses against Percy's intrusion. I considered my own abilities like a scalpel—a useful tool intended to get what was needed and leave without leaving much of a mark. Percy, on the other hand, used the Wit like a shotgun. He didn't care what or who he hurt as long as he got what he wanted. He wasn't nearly as trained as I was, but he was ruthless in the training he did have. My old Head instructor Nicolas Arthurias Drego, in my father's palace, would have adored a student like Percival. It was one of life's happy blessings the two had never met. Especially since Instructor Nico was still out there, having been one of the few in the palace to survive the Grimmest Jest.

"I once heard a story," I said, through set teeth, "of a young girl, no older than five. She claimed that *things,* spirits of a type, were appearing in her room. Nice spirits. Could have been nyads, or maybe wind fae, perhaps—the way she described it—even the angelic."

Percy snorted, wiggling a finger in a spinning motion, as if to say *get on with it*.

"She was a painter," I continued. "Became renowned, even showcased her on unknowing television. Said, from a young age, the angels taught her how to paint."

"What's your point?" Percy snapped.

I jabbed a thumb towards Preacher's chest. "The girl was taught to paint by spirits at the age of five. My buddy here. He has a similar story. Says God himself taught him how to shoot. Attributes his dead-eye aim to his faith and heavenly tutelage at a young age, I kid you not."

Percy snorted with laughter, but then paused, staring at me. "Corker's breath, you're being serious? You don't actually believe that trove heap, do you?"

I shrugged. "You've never seen that little girl paint. Masterpieces by the age of six."

"I see. And your sidekick paints with bullets, is that the moral of this story? Vyle's teeth, Leon, and here I was under the impression you were a subtle man."

I went cold. "My friends call me Leon. You may call me Leonidas."

That's when I struck.

I surged forward, my hand yanking the knife from my hip-sheath and shoving my body towards Percy. My defenses were in place, but most my concentration still stifled my pain, and—a split-second before I struck—Percival sensed my reaction.

He darted back, before my knife could press to his neck. He kicked out, slamming a boot into my kneecap and buckling my leg. Then, he whipped down with the butt of his gun, snarling as he did, all signs of the polite, mannered charmer from before fading to a lupine fury as the ogre-eared man beat me to the floor.

My head throbbed and my hands grated against the rough wooden platform. Now, a few customers' eyes darted in our direction and a smattering of mutters came from the nearest table. Two extremely large and round men lifted their entire table and dragged it away from us, closer to one of the railings.

I no longer smelled the odor of moisture or cavern water; my nostrils filled with the scent of sweat and a faint odor of blood—my chest wounds likely seeped through the bandages now. I gasped at the ground, but then, shaking my head, leaned back, kneeling, and looked up.

Percy growled and pressed the cool metal barrel between my eyes. "Shouldn't have done that, sneakthief," he muttered. "If you don't have my money, I'm going to have to get what I'm owed some other way."

"Percy," I murmured.

"No," he spat. "No more charming stories. No more stalling. Give me what's mine or the sharks dine!"

"It's just like you," I muttered, gasping once and reaching up to gingerly probe at my head. "To only think one step ahead. You trollskull."

Percy's eyes narrowed and then he looked up, just over me. His face actually seemed to drain for a moment, turning pale. By shoving him back, even though it had cost me a blow to the head, I'd interrupted the Sven sisters' line of sight and *also* had ducked out of the way. One had to improvise in situations such as these.

Now, Preacher stood over me, like a guardian angel, *both* his six shooters out, both barrels pointing towards Percival's stupid face.

"Ah," said Percy, licking his lips slowly. "I see."

I stayed on my knees, still ducked, still giving Preacher line of sight. Annie was standing off a way by Dale, murmuring quietly to him and rubbing his arm in a calming way. Dale's one hand gripped the wooden rail encircling the main platform, his knuckles the same pale color as Percy's handsome features.

Percival's own weapon was trained on my forehead, and the Sven sisters had now stepped back, leaving a distance between themselves and the Union boy.

"Percy," Bianca said, rolling the *r*. "You asked for our help in a little bit of fun..."

"This is becoming not fun at all," Margarita said, straightening her ruby bangs and lowering her gun for a moment.

Bianca sighed. "I'm bored, Percy. When are we going to play in the aquarium? You promised."

Percival, who still had two of Preacher's guns pointed at his head, grit his teeth. He straightened a bit from where he'd been taunting me, but kept his weapon pressed between my eyes.

"I've seen him shoot bullets out of the air before," I muttered, looking up at my attacker. "You sure you're quick enough?"

Percival licked at his lower lip, frowning. For a moment, I could see his mind whirring. I didn't bother to try to read him—his thoughts were written all over his features in heavy strokes of violent intent.

Chapter 22

"Careful," I murmured. "I don't have your treasure, Percy. But I can get it."

"That's what you said before."

"I mean it. I'm on a job now, in fact."

"What job? I haven't heard of any new jobs even close to what you owe me."

"The Union doesn't know *everything*."

"We don't? Perhaps not. But if there's coin involved, we sniff it out soon enough." I felt an oily presence descending on my thoughts, but this time I was prepared for it and I kept my fear diminished, my defenses high, focusing all thoughts on just one pinprick of an image. The more focused a mind, the harder to break it.

And so I poured my attention into Percival's gun. I studied the indention along the muzzle and the jutting safety just above the trigger guard. I didn't know guns well—I rarely carried one—but I'd seen their effect most my life. If Percy decided to pull the trigger, at point blank range, no amount of suds or elbow grease would fully extricate my brains from the wooden floor.

"You shoot me, he'll drop you," I murmured.

Bianca and Margarita watched with twin expressions of mild amusement. Bianca leaned in behind Percival, swallowed a gulp of air and then yelled, "*Bang!*"

Percival nearly jumped, and he glanced sharply back, cursing and hissing through his teeth like a startled tomcat.

"Oh, calm down, Percy," Bianca said. "Leonidas said he's good for it."

But the Union boy shook his head. "Lenny only comes here for two reasons. For new jobs he can steal beneath our nose, pretending to represent the Union—"

"That only happened *one* time!" I protested.

"And," said Percival, waving his free hand towards one of the smaller, darker platforms bobbing on the underground lake in the distance. "To visit Kay. And if that's the case, then it means he *does* have funds."

"Excuse me, not to interrupt, but I'll pay what he owes," Annie called suddenly, stepping forward.

Percival glanced at her with a renewed interest. "Annie, you said?" he murmured. "Do you have a last name, Annie?"

She repeated, "Huh—what an interesting question. I'll let you know if I ever find out." She beamed at him.

"But like I said, I'll pay what Leon owes."

"He owes me a lot."

"The way you say it is really scary." She wiggled her fingers, and for a brief moment, it almost seemed like she was mocking him, though her tone remained sincere. "But that's fine—I'll pay it!"

I felt a slow flutter of relief in my chest, but it quickly faded as Percy's eyes narrowed. "Lenny owes me, Lenny pays. Simple. I'm not interested in *your* money. It's about the principle."

"That principle is going to end with a bullet in both our heads," I growled.

Preacher grunted, and, above me, his arm swayed and the metallic reflection off his six-shooter flashed beneath the Christmas lights.

"I'll pay," Annie insisted.

"Don't bother," I retorted, my glare fixed on my nemesis. "It's pointless. Percival doesn't care—do you, Perce?" I cleared my throat, then louder, so Annie could hear, but still fixated on the Union boy, I called out, "He's always hated me in fact. We once both went after the same contract; an old codger lodged in one of the underwater prisons in the Glass Lakes to the misty north. I beat Percy to the score, escaped the prison before he managed to track me. Later, when his goons found me sleeping in my RV at a campground, they tried to fleece me for the pay. Isn't that right Percy?"

I was goading him successfully, it seemed, judging by the narrowing of his eyes. But for now, if he allowed me to talk, it meant I was still alive... Maybe Preacher could find a shot. Despite Percy's poised look, I continued, my mouth dry.

"It doesn't end there, though, Annie. I bested Percy in a battle of Wits and caused him to *glimpse* fire ants crawling all over his body. In a bout of terror, he stripped naked and flung himself into the freezing Glass River."

The Sven sisters were giggling now, and Percival looked downright murderous.

I knew I was on thin ice. An injury, a man like Percy might forgive. But a slight to his pride? Nothing could make up for that, and so the ogre-eared man had hated me ever since.

The consequences were now playing out beneath the muzzles of tightly gripped weapons. I could see Percy's mind whirring as he steadily reached a decision. I braced myself, preparing to lunge back, hopefully avoiding the first bullet, giving Preacher a chance to drop him. The Sven sisters seemed to grow more and more bored, so maybe they'd stay out of it. One could never tell with Bianca and Margarita, though—they had their own brand of humor, which, when directed elsewhere, I found equally amusing. But now, as Bianca faked another yawn and Margarita checked her nails, some of the humor was lost on me.

"You know, Lenny," Percy said, his voice soft as he leaned in, so only I could hear. "You could settle this another way..."

"I'm not joining up, Percy, no chance." I could remember one of Instructor Nico's little lessons even now... *Swear not allegiance to disloyal actors.*

"That's how it's going to be?" I noted his finger now tightening on his trigger. I knew it would be easy enough to agree—to sign on the dotted line. But I'd spent most my life avoiding *sides* of any sort. I wasn't fond of being controlled. I'd grown up under the iron fist of a master manipulator. I'd once been promised a kingdom in exchange for my freedom. A boost in contract pay wasn't nearly so enticing. And in neither scenario was the exchange ever worth it.

"I heard about one of your recent contracts, Perce," I said, matching his quiet tone. "An old general for the Endeavor, am I right?"

"I wouldn't know, Leon. I take many contracts. Something you aren't accustomed to."

"I do fine."

"Hmm? I saw your RV when you came in. Doesn't look fine."

"The bullet holes are a new addition. I'm fine with my level of work. You know what I'm not as fine with?"

"Pray tell."

"That general you boosted from The Roost, do you know what happened to him?"

Percy's ogre-ear twitched in his bound blonde hair. "I don't ask questions."

"Which is why I'll *never* join your outfit." I spat on the wood between us. I still knelt, but glared up at Percy and his gun. "The contractor? An Imperium courier. That Endeavor general apparently hurt one of his family members."

"Pity."

"Not nearly as pitiable as what the courier did to the general. Nearly two months of torture from what I'm told. Dropped his corpse off—at least, what was left of it—from one of the Stormer gateway trees."

Percy's eyes narrowed. "I'm not responsible for what a client does with the cargo."

"Clients and cargo? Is that it to you? The Endeavor general's name was Silas Gestalt. He used to live near here, you know? Was a local boy—a teacher's son. Town of Leavenworth."

I glimpsed Annie's eyes flash with grief where she stood by the railing; she let out a little gasp of horror, one hand gripping Dale's shirt sleeve so tightly he winced.

Percy ignored her and snorted. "How could you possibly know all this?"

My eyes blazed, and I could feel my lips press firmly together. "Because, Percy, I *ask*. But you don't. The Union doesn't, and your father doesn't. Because at the end of the day, you don't care. A contract is a contract. If it ends in two months of horrific torture for the person you break out, then what is it to you?" I spat again. "So no, I won't be signing any golden contracts."

"On your head be it," said Percy, with a sigh. "A contract is a contract. And you're refusing to honor your end. Goodbye, Leonidas."

I noted him wiggle his fingers behind his back and the Sven sisters instantly became a lot less coy. Their fake yawns and bored expressions melted like ice from granite. Their eyes went cold and hard in their beautiful faces and their weapons aimed at Preacher.

Percy's own finger tightened on the trigger, and I realized my mistake. He hated me more than I'd first thought. Enough to risk his own fate. Enough to think the twins could drop Preacher before he dropped Percy.

Enough to think he could put a bullet in me and get away with it.

I reached out, desperately. In the minds of everyone around me, I glimpsed imminent violence. Bullets already flying in their thoughts, bodies dropping. In Percy's mind, I glimpsed a single image slip through his adrenaline-heightened defenses. A projected hope—a dream. The image saw Preacher's corpse draped over my own—my lifeless eyes staring up at the cavern ceiling, two bullet wounds in my skull.

Percy's intentions were clear.

I braced, preparing now to leap forward, *under* the gun. Not much of a chance. Not much at all. Three guns to Preacher's two. Normally, I'd peg my money on Preacher. But Percy was a Wit, and while Preacher's defenses were strong, they weren't perfect.

It was in that moment, bordering imminent violence that I heard whistling.

For a moment, all of us froze. The whistling was a quiet, gentle tune, a fluttering sound like a twittering bird, out of place in the underground cavern.

"I do not mean to intrude," said a new voice, from behind us on the platform, carrying a deep Alabaman accent. My neck prickled at the voice, but it took a moment for my thoughts to catch up with my memories, my eyes remained fixed on my current threat as the voice continued, "I must request, though, we lower them weapons and allow cooler skulls to prevail in this here imbibement induced atmosphere."

"Shut up," Percy snarled, without looking back. "Mind your own business."

The voice had a smiling quality to it, not at all put off by Percy's rage. As for me, I kept my eyes fixed on Percy's gun. The voice said, "This *is* my business."

"I said shut up!" Percy roared.

"Ain't much of a conversatin' sort, is you?" came the new voice. "Well then... fire in the hole!"

A second later, I heard a clunking noise, followed by a rolling sound. Then, a small, metal item spun to a stop between Percy and me on the floorboards of the wooden platform.

We both looked down. I heard the whistling return, beyond us, coming from near one of the circular wooden tables. The item that had rolled to a perfect stop between us was a ridged, metal oval.

A grenade.

And the pin was pulled.

Chapter 23

"Grenade!" I shouted.

I jerked back just as Percy fired a desperate shot. A hot bolt shot past my cheek, searing my skin. The Sven sisters wheeled, lunging behind an abandoned table near the edge of the platform.

Percy *kicked* the grenade, sending it skittering towards me and my companions.

Preacher, with a growl, grabbed me from behind, lifted me bodily and dragged my aching body toppling over the railing. As I fell, I heard a loud *bang!* A wave of hot air struck me and I spun like a rag doll. An angry orange flare blinded me for a moment, and a shower of splinters and wooden boards geysered and came fluttering down in a rain of wood. Then the underground lake claimed me, the cold suddenly dousing the heat on my flesh.

Dark water surrounded me, an inky black. The water curled into my nose and I sealed my lips. My eyes were open, but I couldn't see a thing.

I tried to scream, but air exploded from my lips and fled past my cheeks in a parade of bubbles. For a moment, I struggled to place which direction was up. I sensed *things*—large, inhuman things—approaching through the liquid, venturing towards where I kicked and struggled.

I reoriented by focusing on the minds above then attached to the thoughts of the Sven sisters, using the direction of the thoughts to aim myself and begin to kick.

My whole body screamed in pain—old wounds meeting new agony. I forced my concentration back, again, desperately suppressing the pain, gripping it like a rider holding the horns of a bull.

I could sense the other minds in the water, unguarded, unprotected and hungry—swimming faster now, jagged teeth ripping through black water.

My head broke the surface, my lips parted with chill droplets as I gasped, projecting my chin above the freezing liquid. I kicked, eyes wide. For a moment, I felt an inky presence settle on my thoughts. Percy. The skint. Never the sort to let an opportunity go to waste. He could sense my fear and was now taking full advantage.

I felt him sifting through my thoughts and forced myself to calm. The fear fled slowly, like blood leaving a corpse. Eventually, stonily, I kicked him from my presence. What had he seen, though? No time to tell.

Ahead, I glimpsed the wooden railing—a section of it blasted to splinters and charred with ash and fire. A large hole now settled in the wooden floor, also singed. Small fires pockmarked the floorboards, encircling a gap in the platform which stared down at the dark water. Through this gap, I watched Annie pulling Dale, tugging his sodden form onto the planks.

Preacher tread water, his back to me, looking frantically around. For a moment, he froze, and I also spotted the source of his sudden consternation.

A large fin was cutting through the black, streaking towards us and sending out twin ripples of white on either side. The fin was at least the size of a car door.

Preacher redoubled his frantic search in the frothing water. He made to dive, arching his back and dipping his head. But I gasped out a shout, "Preacher! I'm fine. I'm here behind you!"

He stopped mid-dive, bobbing on the water and spinning around, scooping water with one large, calloused hand. His make-up was now completely streaked, half-washed from his dark features. His auburn eyes settled on me, then he zipped forward, gripped me by the arm, and began to drag me towards the blast hole in the wooden platform.

"Careful," I gasped. "Behind."

Preacher didn't bother to look back. The enormous fin cut across the chasm water, beneath the Christmas light stalactites. I glimpsed the very edge of a large nose and glinting red eyes—the same red as the barkeep's—stared out from just beneath the glassy gray.

"Preacher!" I shouted, my voice rising.

The thing was almost on us. At first, I thought a giant wave was rising from the water, but then I realized it was a head.

A misshapen, lumpy, gray-granite head speckled with barnacles and strands of pearlescent silver. The thing looked like a cross between a shark and the bottom of a poorly tended ship. *Things* and vegetation and all manner of small plants *grew* from the monster's head. It opened its mouth—silent, no scream, no growl.

The teeth, though, were all too real. The mouth gaped as wide as I was tall. At least that way it could swallow me whole, though it might take a couple of chomps to completely down Preacher.

"Hey!" I screamed, if only to distract the thing.

Its eyes—which took a moment to find amidst the barnacles and encrustations—were milky white. Blind. And yet it could still sense us.

The teeth scooped towards us, swallowing water and creating a small vortex in its wake, threatening to drag us in. Preacher grunted in exertion, latching onto the wooden railing above. He tried to pull, dragging me along behind, but then his hand broke through the wood, pulling the charred and ashen remains down. The monster was on us. Too large to dodge left or right. I glimpsed other nasty protrusions speckling the back of its dark, pink throat. Mandibles, and *moving* tentacles, like tonsils, except thinner and streaked with puss dangled in the pink flesh.

Yuck.

"Tomb's trove, Preacher *down!*"

My friend trusted me enough to react instantly. We couldn't go left, couldn't go right, couldn't go up.

So we dove, both of us surging *back* beneath the blinding, dark water, dipping *under* the scooping jawline of the oncoming lake monster.

My back scraped against the barnacle belly. Bubbles swam past in swarms; my eyes stung from the murk and my arms and legs kicked out in desperation, trying to find my way around the thing, back to the platform.

For a moment, I thought I might drown, kicking and yet finding no way to break the surface; my head bumped against the monster. The thing was far longer than I'd anticipated. In my desperation and swirling anxiety, I found it impossible to breathe, my lungs aching. I kicked, refusing fear purchase as best I could, but my vision swam, darkening.

I shoved off with my good hand, trying to distance myself from the lake monster. The water churned and swirled as the thing rerouted, likely searching for the morsels that had slipped beneath it.

A second later, I glimpsed the dim outline of the Loophole's Christmas lights above. I screamed in desperation, kicking off the monster's corpse-like flesh.

My head broke the surface and I gasped. I could feel waves now, caused by the beast, thrashing around me and I swallowed a mouthful of dark water. Spluttering, I kicked a couple more times, leaving a trail of white froth.

"Leon!" Annie's voice called.

I spotted my friend dangling an arm over the edge of the platform and could faintly still hear whistling from the direction of one of the tables.

Cursing, I refused to look back towards the monster and instead kicked out. But something sharp closed on my heel. I yelled and lurched forward again.

My shoe nearly ripped from my heel, and I felt something tear along the laces. I yanked my leg, pulling free, barely.

I swam rapidly towards the wooden platform. Ahead, coming *under* the gap in the platform, also in the water, I spotted more eyes moving towards me—six sets—and they were moving faster than the hulking behemoth behind me. Sharks? Hydra? Corker's breath.

I heard a roar and a sudden splash as a fin slapped the water behind me and a geyser of spray erupted, showering my already drenched head.

Now, I spotted Preacher, pulling himself with herculean effort out of the liquid. He paused, clinging to the railing like a sodden hound. He scanned the chaotic scene, and his gaze settled on me. His eyes bugged, and he abandoned safety, diving back into the water in my direction.

The monster created more waves now as it torpedoed forward, but this also propelled me closer to Preacher.

The backwoods boxer grabbed me, pushing me closer to the platform.

"Don't," I gasped. "You get out. I'm good."

But Preacher shoved me ahead of him. Annie's hand dangled through the wooden bars, her fingers gesturing wildly above the water. I spotted her other hand gripping the strange silver flask and she took a quick sip just before I reached her.

I grabbed her—her fingers so very cold—and she heaved, pulling *hard*.

She was strong. Far stronger than I would have thought. I managed to latch onto the railing with my free, albeit injured, hand. I screamed in pain but refused to let go.

Next to me, Preacher surged from the liquid like a sea monster himself. Together, with Annie's help, our two sodden forms were dragged from the murk. I'd lost my shoe, my ankle was scraped, my bandages soaked, my hand on fire, but—for now, at least—I wasn't in the belly of some monster.

Said beast wasn't so delighted by this news. Just before tumbling over the rail, I spotted the enormous, crusted head breaking the waves, jaws flashing. The barnacles and strange growths glimmered dully beneath the Christmas lights above. The open jaws gave full display to the wiggling pink tentacles in the back its throat.

I yelped, rolling further to safety.

I avoided the blast hole in the platform just in time, managing to hang onto the railing, my arm jolting as I rolled onto a charred, but solid portion of damp wood.

Gasping, in pain, I felt a flutter of relief, but also a trickle of fear...

I didn't know who'd thrown the grenade. But the whistling, the location, the last words, *this is my business*, gave me enough of a clue. I wasn't sure who I'd rather face, the sea monster, or the grenade-thrower. What sort of psychopath used a grenade to get someone's attention anyway?

I breathed heavily towards the ceiling, the dewdrop lights blinking above. But I didn't have long to relax.

The monster below us seemed in a frenzy, furious its two mouthfuls had escaped. It lunged at me again, but this time, sending its large head into the railing, splintering wood.

I heard more whistling and the sea monster suddenly stopped its efforts to get at us.

"Whoa," said a voice in a soothing tone. The same voice with the deep Alabaman accent. "Whoa, calm down, girl. Calm down." He whistled again and the creature splashed beneath the waves. "Good girl," the voice said, and the head slipped beneath the surface completely now, along with the red eyes.

Soon, the waters had stilled completely, and I was left on the wooden platform of the Loophole, gasping and staring up, blinking against the pain in my body which had returned from my injuries.

We weren't free yet. Reluctantly, I pushed to my feet, tugging on Preacher to help him rise as well. A second later, the two of us, hunched, dripping—me without one of my favorite shoes—faced across the platform.

Annie and Dale had made it to safety by retreating back, avoiding the water entirely. Percy and the Sven sisters had also survived but were no longer totting guns. Now, they stood off by the railing, sheepish, hands at their sides, guns tucked away. They glanced at the ground like schoolchildren reprimanded by the headmaster.

My attention settled on the source of the whistling noise and, most likely, the grenade.

The man across from me wore a banker's suit, but had wild, jutting hair sticking out at all angles. His eyes were hooded but unblinking, as if staring into my soul. The sleeves of his banker's suit were stained with ash, but everything else was nearly immaculate.

He dusted off the edge of his sleeves and regarded me with eyes the color of gunpowder. He didn't smile, he didn't frown. He didn't try to project confidence, nor did he try to commiserate or comfort.

This wasn't a man who cared one lick about my opinion of him. He exuded a confidence of birthright. Not earned, but owed—a confidence as certain as DNA. In one hand, he gripped an ornate walking stick, pearl white, with a thin black string wrapped around it from the base to the top; the carvings in the walking stick were hard to determine. At his hip, he had a long, silver tube like a painting sheath.

I shivered as the hooded eyes regarded me with the cool calculations of a warcat observing a field mouse. I tried not to let my fear show as I met the gaze of the Hillbilly Godfather.

Chapter 24

"Baron," I said, swallowing. "Was that incendiary present yours?"

The mob boss looked me up and down, his gunpowder black eyes unblinking beneath his wild, untamed mess of silver-speckled hair. He leaned on his carved walking stick, lips pursed. "Everythin' down in this here place is mine. Pardon my failin' memory, but did I not caution you?"

"I'm not saying you didn't tell us to stop." I shot an evil look towards where Percy still leaned against the railing like a chastened child. "It wasn't my idea. I wanted to get in and get out—nose clean."

Baron gave a crocodile smile and an airy little wave of his hand. "A little swim does wonders for the sinuses, I reckon."

"Doesn't mean I'm looking to be blasted to pieces."

His smile turned into a good-natured grin now, quickly shifting from headmaster to schoolboy in an instant where he stood near the hole he'd blasted in the floor of his own establishment. "I figure, right out, you were quick on the move. Long fuse on that sucker. I recall hollerin' a warnin'."

I breathed slowly, still dripping water, trying to gather my wits. I was in more danger now than I'd been in the water. "I appreciated the warning," I murmured. "And the long fuse."

Baron's bodyguard, a Mr. Meadowfax—who I'd met briefly before—sat at one of the round tables, his feet up, reading through spectacles a small detective novel, seemingly indifferent to all of us, or, perhaps, deciding the seven of us, armed though we were, didn't pose enough of a threat to his boss to warrant his attention. Mr. Meadowfax had average features, was of average height, was lean and built solid, but not so solid he would tire in drawn out combat. Luckily, I'd never had to test this theory. The stories surrounding the Baron's bodyguard's prowess in combat were dwarfed only by the Hillbilly Godfather's own legacy. Notably, beneath Mr. Meadowfax, I spotted a long rectangular suitcase, like for an electric guitar, wedged against the table where he sat.

Rumors abounded around Baron and his outfit. Some I couldn't verify. I'd once heard Baron was a twi-talent, an exceptionally rare gift where someone held two eternal talents at once. Then again, I'd also been told by the same source that Mr. Meadowfax was a dragon in disguise. A stupid theory, in my estimation. I'd never seen a dragon.

Baron had been in charge of his outfit for more than two decades. He looked in his mid-forties, which meant he'd been a mob boss in his early twenties.

O'Shea's people had their hands in most the black-marketing outfits of the magical world. They provided protection for those like Kay—my supplies contact—for a cut, but also were a steady supplier for all the businesses they protected. Dead heart's ash was easy enough to get if one had a graveyard nearby, a lighter, some time and an indifference to all things *ick*. But other things were harder to snare. Gemdust from genies would take a barter or a burglary. Baron's folk were also rumored to have worked with some disgruntled angels, who sold bottled healing miracles—like the type used on Percy's ogre ear. Demons also worked with Baron's outfit, usually trading in illicit secrets, hidden fears, or long-forgotten curses. Some rumored O'Shea's outfit even bartered souls.

Baron gestured with his fingers, whistling softly to himself. Meadowfax looked over, folded his book into his jacket pocket and, rising, strolled over towards the Sven sisters and Percy first, one hand extended.

The three savants put up little protest as Meadowfax's hands moved deftly over them, retrieving firearms and knives hidden in places I wouldn't have even thought to check. He moved dispassionately, almost with a bored expression. He didn't smile once, but by the time he'd finished, a small pile of dangerous objects littered the ground at Meadowfax's feet.

He pointed at the pile, then pointed at Percy. "Don't touch those," he said. His voice was as boring as his face—no intonation, nothing remarkable at all. He turned away then, deciding his simple command would be followed without question.

And he wasn't wrong. Neither Percy nor the Sven sisters made any move towards their confiscated weaponry. As Meadowfax approached us, though, Preacher grunted.

Baron whistled softly, examining the weapons Preacher had procured and held butt first up and out of reach of Mr. Meadowfax. "Homemade, are they? You smith them yourself? Beauties," Baron said. "You can retrieve them on your way out. I ain't lookin' for O.K. Corral down here."

Growling, Preacher allowed Meadowfax to take his weapons. To the bodyguard's credit, instead of putting them on the pile, he tucked the revolvers into his jacket pocket and said, "I'll look after these for you." He nodded once. "You have my word."

And though Preacher's chest heaved in frustration as he watched Meadowfax retreat with his two babies, he didn't put up a fight. Meadowfax returned to Baron's side and once more pulled out the small detective novel from his jacket pocket and, peering through his spectacles, again seemed engrossed with the story.

Baron turned to my other companions now. He leaned on his ornate walking stick and smiled. "Ah, pleasure to see you again. My apologies, I didn't recognize you at first."

Annie looked pleased at his words. "Hi! Nice to see you again, too! You've been getting sun, recently—it suits your face. I'm going to keep my toys, if you don't mind."

"Of course not," he said. Then he looked at Preacher. "But the rest of you are on warnin'. Next time, there'll be a short fuse."

Percy glared. The Sven sisters tried to pinch him from behind, grinning when he slapped at their hands. I just nodded once. No sense prolonging it—we needed to see Kay and then get out. Already we'd wasted too much time and I couldn't keep my pain at bay forever.

"Glorious," Baron declared. "Now that we've relinquished the crayons, maybe we can sort a thing or two. Percival, for your daddy's sake, I won't feed you to the lake. Mind tellin' me what in the tarnation you were thinkin', though?"

Percy's face had gone pale, and he shook his head, his ogre ear shifting in his blonde hair. He stammered, "L-Leonidas owes me. Ten grand. Refuses to pay. This is Union business." Then, quickly, he added, "*Sir.*"

O'Shea turned to look at me now, raising one eyebrow beneath his wild hair. "This true, Three?"

"I told him I'd have the money. It's just taking time."

Baron crossed his arms over his banker suit, displaying the ash-stained cuffs. "Not fitting for me to get betwixt a man and his business," he drawled, speaking with the cadence of someone on a pleasant, meandering stroll on a sunny day. "Wouldn't be equitable."

"I don't have the pay now but will in a few days' time. I have a job." I didn't glance at Annie, refusing to even *think* in her direction with Percy so nearby. "It pays well—double what I'm used to. I'll be able to give what I owe."

"Percy?" said Baron, turning to my nemesis. "What about it—I feel near certain you're able to wait a week."

Percival cleared his throat. "He's here to visit Kay. Which means he has money. He's just holding out to spite me!"

"Untrue," I snapped back. "Besides, I'm not paying for supplies. Annie's taking care of it."

"Is that how it always is? You hide behind someone else's purse strings?"

"I prefer it to hiding behind a gun," I snapped back.

"You're a nothing, Leonidas. A nobody. Even your alias," he sneered. "Stealing the name of the lost prince—pathetic. You'll never be a tenth of the man the heir is!" As he said it, he gestured wildly. My eyes bugged as I stared at his wrist.

There, visible just past his sleeve, were jade beads.

My heart sunk into my toes. Percy Twelftree was the confidant, the location-keeper of the Union for the Unlocated prisons. I stared at the beads, my skin prickling. Of all the thrice-hexed skinting bad luck... Without the confidant's participation, we wouldn't find the Hollow. If we didn't find the Hollow within the next couple of days, there was no entering it for another year.

Which meant I couldn't end this once and for all, and I'd also fail to uphold my word to Annie.

But Percival would rather eat lice than give me the location of the Hollow. Not even for a bribe...

I let out a shaking, trembling breath, but tried to hide my horror.

"Careful," I said, my voice only slightly shaking while addressing his last comment. "You're letting your allegiances show. This is neutral territory here, remember?"

"Eat skunk, Lenny."

"Insulting you is beneath me," I retorted, forcibly looking away from the bracelet on his wrist.

Annie had noticed it too, judging by the way she kept nudging at me from behind.

As Percy and I bickered, Baron started whistling, softly, one hand moving into his suit, near his ribs.

Immediately, we both went quiet and glanced nervously over. Baron, still whistling, withdrew his hand. Instead of another device that went *boom,* though, he held a checkbook.

"I'll cover it," he said. "How much does Three owe?"

"Sir, I don't need *you* to pay. I'm—"

"How much?" Baron's voice still remained patient, curious. He still leaned a bit on his ornate, carved staff. His black eyes weren't indigo, suggesting twi-talent rumors were overstated at best, or—he'd held back his gift long enough the telltale color had faded.

Still, in our world, looks are always deceiving.

"Sir," Percy growled. "I don't want—"

"Money. I know. You want leverage. But as you were about to open fire in *my* establishment, do you want to hear what I want? Anyone?" He glanced around.

Mr. Meadowfax folded the corner of his page and glanced up, peering through spectacles with his unremarkable features. Other customers looked over from their seats, but then quickly glanced away lest Baron notice their attention.

"I," Baron said, "would like to not feed a Union Chair's offspring to them sharks. Then again, I honestly may have to. Do you want to ponder why, Percival?"

Percy swallowed. The Sven sisters were carefully distancing themselves now, stepping back a bit from the Union boy. Percy cleared his throat. Hoarsely, he said, "Fine. You can pay his—"

"I asked if you wanted to know *why.*"

"Why?"

"Because no one kills on these premises without my permission. Do you need a reminder of that?" Baron's tone remained calm, curious. He adjusted the sleeves of his banker suit and ran a hand through his wild, jutting silver hair. He clicked his tongue. "No? You're sure? Good. How much?"

"Ten thousand," Percy said, still hoarse.

"Let's make it twenty, and we'll bury ill will too."

Baron extended a hand, and a pen appeared from within Meadowfax's jacket pocket which he handed to his boss. Baron wrote the check, signed with a flourish then handed the paper to his bodyguard. Meadowfax took it and dutifully marched over to Percy, handing it off.

Baron said, "Redeemable at any of the genie vaults, or the neutral drakin banks. Are we good?"

Percy held Meadowfax's gaze for a moment and must have seen something he didn't like in the shorter man's dark, dull gaze, because at last he said, "We're good."

"Right, well... I can only think of one other thing that might take off the competitive edge between you two. Savants like yourselves ought to be workin' together. People in my line rely on your help." He winked and gestured towards a darker part of the cavern behind the bar. "Competitive edges can be worn through without bullets flying, you know?"

At this Bianca Sven looked delighted all of a sudden, her beautiful features transitioning from a mask of uncertainty. "The aquariums," she said. "You said we would, Percy. Well, Leon?" she asked. "Are you game? The big one can be your buffer."

I peered over the bar in the direction of a series of stone steps which led up alongside the wall, disappearing into the back of the cavern, through twin tunnels on either side. At the foot of the stone steps there was, what seemed to be, a boxing ring and two piles of coiled rope.

"Percy only has one thing I want," I said.

He sneered at me. "I'm not giving you squat."

My eyes flicked towards his bracelet. But then I shrugged. Instead of addressing him, I said to Baron. "I'm not feeling myself. Injuries from a job. I'd happily compete, just not today." I'd have to find another way to get the Hollow's location.

While O'Shea was a dangerous man with an iron will, he was also just, after a fashion, and regarded as even-tempered for the most part. He shook his head and said, "Well, that is a disappointment, no doubt. But some things can't be helped. And Leon," he said.

"Yes?"

"You don't have to play in my aquarium today if you don't want. But it might allow Percy to take some of that aggression out without any of your companions catching lead, if you see my meanin'."

"See it clear as day."

"And that check," he said, nodding towards Percy's hand. "Ain't free."

I gritted my teeth. I'd suspected as much. "I'm not partial to price tags after purchase."

Over his shoulder, Baron said, "Well, if it makes you feel better, imagine you have no choice. You owe me one, Leon." Then, he moved back to the table, across the wooden platform and away from the blasted hole in the floorboards. Meadowfax followed, moving towards one of the tables where three other large, armed figures waited, sitting and watching. All three sets of eyes blinked with indigo.

Owing Baron O'Shea anything was a recipe for disaster. But right now, at least, it cleared my debt with Percival.

I shot a hateful look towards Percy, which he returned in double portion. Then, beneath my breath, I muttered to the others, "Let's go see Kay and then get out of here. I've had enough of the Loophole for one day."

The Sven sisters were ignoring us now as they tugged on Percy's arm. Bianca kept saying, "You promised, Percival. You promised. Let's bleed—it'll take your mind off things."

Percival just leaned against the wooden railing, trying to burn a hole in the side of my head with the intensity of his glare.

Preacher strode next to me, shooting shifty glances towards where Meadowfax now sat by the bar, next to the table with the three indigo-eyed mobsters and their wild-haired boss. Once again, the rumored dragon bodyguard was reading.

"You'll get them back," I murmured beneath my breath.

Preacher looked at me.

"I'll make sure of it. Why would they want to keep your guns? They just don't want any more trouble."

Preacher didn't look half convinced. Thankfully, instead of bum-rushing Meadowfax to retrieve his beloved tools, he allowed me to lead him, Annie and Dale across the main wooden platform, through the tables, beneath the blinking Christmas lights, away from Percy's venomous looks and towards a row of small, black wooden canoes.

"Kay's platform is just over there," I murmured towards Annie. "Two to a canoe. The things in the water should ignore us if we're slow and steady."

"Did you see?" she whispered. "On his wrist?"

I let out a faint sigh and nodded. "Yeah. Percy's the skinting confidant."

"So—so where does that leave us?"

I scowled and kept my voice quiet. "I was planning on bribing him for the location, but as it's Percy..." I shrugged. "I'd rather mug him instead. We'll figure something out, but not here. Not now. Later, under the cover of night."

"We don't have much time left."

"We're fine," I said. "Finding the location-keeper was half the problem. The rest is going to come down to a bit of creativity in our sales pitch. We've got time."

"Alright then, if you're sure. So what about his Kay fellow?" Annie said, already untying one of the watercraft. "He'll have what we need for," she looked doubtfully at my bruised and battered form, and whispered, "the job?"

I winced and pressed a gunshot hand to my bloody, sodden chest. "He'll have anything he shouldn't."

Preacher untied a second canoe and together, the four of us eased into the wooden vessels.

We were doing this in reverse order. Buying the supplies before we even knew the Hollow's location. But solving the Percy problem would take some doing. One way or another, I had to get that location from him.

But I pushed this from my mind, forcing myself to focus on the problem at hand while we began to paddle across the underground lake, leaving the scent of ash in the air behind us as we headed to meet my black-market dealer.

Chapter 25

The black-marketer's business hid behind a row of stalagmites protruding from the dark water. Torches in deep brackets lined the stone teeth, displaying flames that changed color to match the Christmas lights above.

Dale cursed. "Are those bones?" He indicated the unnerving torches.

The multi-hued flames sputtered from within the recesses of upside-down skulls. The topsy-turvy leer of the skeletal faces glared out from eye-sockets and gaping mouths.

"Don't worry," I murmured. "Kay's harmless... well, mostly. Well... To me. On second thought, worry a bit. And Dale, whatever you do, don't accept *anything* for free. Understand? Not even a postage stamp."

Annie's assistant went pale at my comments and Preacher pulled on the paddles a final time, bumping our canoe against a mooring post. I reached a helping hand to Annie as Preacher roped us off. "You offered to pay for supplies. What sort of budget are we talking?"

Annie took my hand and stepped onto the dock. Then she reached into her peacoat, and for a moment, I thought she might procure her strange silver flask. Instead, however, she withdrew two small brown bags the size of golf balls, tied with white ribbon.

"Mostly silver," she said.

"Treasure packs? What weight?"

"Three ounces each."

"Junkstuff, halfthing or purenice?"

"Mostly halfthing. A diamond in one. Uncut, though."

I closed my eyes, doing a bit of quick calculation, then nodded. "That puts us at about two grand. Not ideal, but workable."

Then, marching against Kay's platform with satisfying *thumps*, I moved between two stalagmites and stepped into the black marketer's secondhand shop.

More flaming skulls meandered lazily across the chamber, illuminating portions of the cramped store. Piles of weapons ranging from crossbows to sniper rifles rested in stacks by wooden stands behind a row of glass display cases. Inside the cases rested old treasures and artifacts. Some boasted labels written in cramped, cursive writing, while others simply read: *See attendant for details.* I spotted a tea kettle wrapped with barbed wire and secured by two hefty padlocks. The label read: *A miniature pandora's box rests within.* This item had been here for nearly five years without purchase. Even the daring sorts in the Loophole knew better than to mess with a sleeping fury, no matter how small it might be. Another display case boasted a golden crown ornamented with black gemstones reflecting the light from the flames above in odd and interesting ways. The label to this one read, on closer inspection: *Crown of Sorrow. 18- only. Adults beware.*

Next to the Crown of Sorrow, there was a single wooden stick. The label read: *The Bough*. I shivered in fright and gave the twiggy thing a wide berth.

Dale's breath fogged the glass of what looked to be a medicine cabinet. Within, it carried all manner of potions, bottled wishes and the Kelly family's novelty energy drink *BeeBuzz*. Of all the things in the store, in my estimation, the most dangerous was the Kelly family's entrepreneurial spirit. In liquid and carbonated form this meant double the caffeine, half the taste and a few floating chunks for texture.

I wrinkled my nose in grim recollection. Behind one of the counters, in front of a row of polished armor, ranging from medieval to Kevlar, I spotted the shop owner himself.

Kay Kelly winced, staring at an item beneath a magnifying glass, rotating the thing with tweezers and muttering to himself. I'd long suspected Kelly needed glasses, a suspicion increased by the way he squinted and leaned too close to the magnifying lens. But Kelly thought glasses made him look less "tough," so he avoided them.

The black marketer didn't glance up, but continued examining the glittering item and called out in a hybrid accent seemingly combining parts of Boston, Texas, Alaska and a mild speech impediment. "Peruse, ponder and price—I'll be with youse in half a pinch."

The scrawny black marketer's spiky brown hair adorned a head taller than average, which only emphasized his mild frame. Even squinting, he had smiling eyes and the sort of mouth on the verge of a defensive smile, hoping to beat the world at large to a punchline at his expense, as if certain everyone were laughing behind his back.

He wore a biker t-shirt two sizes too large for his scrawny frame with skulls and a silver chain around his neck and two black spike earrings through both ears and a hooped nose ring. As we drew nearer, a tattoo in the middle of his forehead became apparent, displaying a single word in black ink: Oops. Kay was a Napoleon complex packaged in a six-foot-three frame of mostly bones and skin.

"Kay," I said. "We're in a bit of a rush."

The tall man glanced across the counter now, blinking as his gaze readjusted in the poor light of the shop. When he spotted me, though, a grin split his face, displaying perfectly white teeth—perhaps a bit *too* white.

"Leonidas number three!" he said. "You're back—so soon, too!"

He placed the item he'd been fiddling with back behind the glass case and leaned across the counter, extending a hand in greeting.

Kay had the hands of an inventor, ornamented by strange scars, burn marks and one oddly colored patch of skin on his thumb. As a part time crook, part time chemist of the arcane, it was testament to his genius that he still possessed all his fingers after being in business so long.

"Greetings Kay," I said fondly, gripping the hand. He squeezed back, a bit harder than necessary, but I braced myself, prepared for the familiar grasp.

He winked at me, releasing my hand to spread his wide and indicate the shop. "Selling or buying today, Three?"

"Buying, actually."

"Oh? Stocking up for a job then?"

"Mhmm. I'm looking for more of the usual." I winced as I spoke, and added, "Especially anything for a quick physical fix."

Kay mirrored my wince and rubbed at his pointy chin. "Gawd, you look like dung. Ah, well, about that— we're fresh out of miracles, and my new shipment of imagems won't be in until..." He hesitated, glancing at one of the skulls, which flashed a strobing pattern of lights and Kay nodded. "Won't be in for a few days. You got time to wait?"

I tried to stave off a welling gloom. "'I'm afraid it's urgent, Kay. Don't you have any in reserve?"

"Wish I could, Three, but Twelftree reserved the last of it and picked it up this morning. Clean out." He waved a hand towards an empty portion of one of the glass display cases.

"Percy's a skint," I muttered darkly. "That makes two things he has that I want."

"What's the other?"

"Percy's a skint," I repeated, ignoring the question.

"I ain't agreeing, nor disagreeing. Say, Three," he said, leaning in and squinting. "You don't look airtight. Been through a storm or two?"

"Something like that. Do you have *anything* for the pain?"

"I mean... there's always devil's bramble, but you're not a user if I remember."

"No, no. Fine. I'll figure something else out."

Kay was glancing past me now. Preacher had come to a halt at my side, eyeing some of the firearms on the wall with a critical eye, occasionally nodding as if impressed or snorting in derision. Kay seemed to take note of Preacher's attention, but then his gaze was drawn to where Annie and Dale lingered in the back of the shop, still near the glass case of potions and energy drinks.

"Who are the two rooks?"

"Friends," I said vaguely.

"Contract?"

I nodded. "Don't let Percy hear, though. The Union has enough of a monopoly."

Kelly grinned. "They pay well too. Well, no healing gear—no pain-relievers. So, what can I do you for?" his eyebrows lifted, along with the *Oops* on his forehead.

I glanced around, rubbing at my chin. "Protection, mostly. I'm looking for some of those tiger's eyes, too, if you have any left. And especially something against," I cleared my throat softly, "dreaders, if you've got it."

Kay had been nodding as I spoke, stooping to reach beneath the counter, but at this last part he stiffened. Still half bent, he looked at me over the counter, eyes searching. "Dreaders?"

I shrugged.

"Three, you're not planning on taking the Hollow, are you?"

"I can't tell you the target."

Kay straightened again, lifting an entire drawer and placing the wooden container on the glass. Blue and pink flames reflected off his skull necklace and chains to glitter like veins of ore.

"Can't help much if I don't know the target," Kay said. "Sides, if it is the Hollow—you might want to hear a thing or two I've learned."

I bit my lip. "Someone put you up to asking?"

Kay crossed a finger over his heart. "I'm no rat—if I be, cut my tongue. Nah, just trying to help, Three. Well?"

I sighed, massaging the bridge of my nose and glanced up to Preacher. My hulking companion shrugged in reply.

"See," Kay said. "Even ol' deadshot knows mums the word."

I paused again, staring at the black marketer, but then my eyes narrowed. "Kay..." I said slowly. "Why are you pressing?"

"No reason. Like I said—"

"Don't lie to me, Kelly. You have a bet, don't you?"

At this, the scrawny, six-foot-three shopkeeper glanced off to the side, rubbing at his sharp chin.

"Kay..." I said, my voice hardening.

He huffed. "Cursed mind-readers. It ain't a thing, Three. Just a little wager. Said you'd be back to the Hollow in the year is all."

I stared at him, hard, resisting the urge to reach out and read his mind. Partially, because most my efforts were now focused fully on holding back the pain. But also, because Kay was a friend—after a fashion. A dangerous friend—but which of my friends weren't?

Besides, I believed his excuse.

Kay Kelly had a thing about betting tattoos with others over the jobs the savants performed. The *Oops* tattoo was from a bet with one of the Sven sisters: Kay was certain they couldn't break a famish out of the Crooken Hen in under three days. The sisters did it in thirty-six hours. Granted, Kelly had wanted to tattoo his own name on their chests—in his estimation the risk was worth the reward. And now he had a stupid tattoo and the Sven sisters' skin was as flawless as ever.

As I stared at him, he began to cough, cursed, reached into his pocket and pulled out a black inhaler with a silver skull on the front. He puffed on the inhaler for a moment, breathing deep and coughing before releasing it.

He shook his head, embarrassed and quickly jammed the inhaler back into his pocket, out of sight as if hoping no one had seen it. He didn't meet my eye right away, but instead looked across the store, spotted Dale poking at one of the glass cases and shouted, "Hey! If you knock that over, I'll cut your tombish foot off!"

Dale's hands shot up and he stood stiff as a board. Kelly, though, seemingly satisfied he'd taken his own embarrassment out on someone less threatening in the room, turned back to me, shaking his head. "Tell me, and I can help. Plus, if you're doing the Hollow, my daddy has to get a gumdrop on his keister." Kelly giggled now, but cut the sound short as he started wheezing again and his hand inched down his pant leg towards the pocket with his inhaler.

"Never let me get between you and a gumdrop tattoo." I frowned. "Your father still works here?"

Kay waved a hand. "Yeah, we hashed it out after...well, you know..."

"He tried to steal from you and blame it on your older brother? And then when you confronted him, he stabbed you and ran?"

Kelly grinned sheepishly. "Family," he said.

"Family," I muttered. "I wouldn't know. Look—fine, Kay. I'll tell you where; you can get that tattoo depending, and in exchange you can help me resupply. But you have to let me put a timer on the memory."

"Ah, Three, come on. You know I hate it when you thinkers start rooting around my skull."

"That's the deal. I'll be gentle. But I get to timer the memory. Can't have it getting into the wrong hands. Final offer."

Kay nibbled on his lip, weighing his options. He traced one acid scarred finger across the countertop, but then sighed and seemed to determine that a butt-cheek tattoo was worth allowing a savant to root around his head. Plus, he trusted me, after a fashion.

"Fine. Deal. Where is it?"

"The Hollow," I muttered.

"Ha!" Kay declared. "Ha!" he shouted at one of the skeletons that came too low. He pointed at the orange flames over the floating head. "Go tell daddy I need to see him. Urgent!"

The skeleton bobbed as if nodding and then zipped away, flying past the stalagmites, over the canoes and out across the underground lake towards a series of tunnels in the far cavern wall.

I took the moment to reach out, grabbing the memory and stretching it thin, placing it in the realm of dream recollection. Kay didn't feel a thing.

"So?" I said. "What did you hear?"

Kelly's smile faded a bit, and he leaned in now, whispering conspiratorially. "A saboteur was killed recently," he murmured. "Murdered outside the Hollow's region, only a few days before it opened for locating. Like having a street address, but not being able to find the door—that poor thing. Everyone's talking about it. Well, *whispering* about it." He glanced around, visibly shivering for a moment, his necklaces rattling. "Never know when one of those wereblade wielding skints is nearby, you know?"

I nodded once. "Kay, I knew that. That's not new news, it's history. I see dream imps too."

"Yeah? Well did you hear that another saboteur is holed up in the Hollow? February herself. The lieutenant of the whole troving order."

I nodded again. "I knew."

He looked a bit flustered now. "Yeah... well... did you also know that since a saboteur was murdered in the district, they shut down the Hollow? As in, complete."

I felt a flicker of anxiety. "Hang on, shut down how? They already have it Unlocated."

"Yeah, but I'm sure you know the window is opening in thirty-eight hours. They took even more precautions."

"More? Like..." I felt my eyes widen.

"You know..."

"Not a Threshold Seal?"

Kelly shrugged. "That's what I'm hearing."

"Vyle's teeth. How long? Pardon my swearing."

"Psh—you swear all the time, Three."

I scowled. "I would hardly say I do it *all* the time..."

Before Kay could reply, though, I felt gentle fingers on my shoulder. "Is everything alright?" Annie asked, her green eyes fixed on me, but then moved to Kay. She pushed her hands against his glass counter suddenly, and then, to Kay's astonishment, she vaulted onto the glass, sitting butterfly legged on his counter.

"I—hang on, no—" Kay spluttered in protest.

I flinched, knowing how particular Kelly could get with his things. Annie, though, completely oblivious to Kay's discomfort, stared past him towards his workbench. "Oh, *wow!* That looks awesome. What is that?"

"Excuse me—could you not sit—"

"Oh, of course!" Annie exclaimed, and then she hopped off the counter, on Kay's side. She glided over to the workbench, leaning in so close her nose nearly touched the stained and gouged wood. "That's a *lot* of cut marks."

"Annie," I said, cautiously, watching Kay's face turn different shades of pink. "Could you please leave Kay's things alone?"

"Customers are not allowed behind the counter!" Kay managed to eke out, taking a quick puff from his inhaler.

Annie looked at him, bright-eyed. "Oh, okay, then. Hmm... It's a *really* nice place you have here, by the way. Oh," she giggled, "don't turn red. I'll leave." She skipped past him again, patting him on the arm and vaulting the counter in one easy leap, landing back on my side of the table.

I massaged the bridge of my nose, wondering if I ought to apologize for my friend's behavior or just gloss over it. Annie was my employer after all.

I settled on answering her earlier question, hoping to refocus everyone. At least for now, Kay wasn't throwing things. "Everything is *not* alright, Annie," I said, carefully. I folded my hands in front of me, hoping that by modeling good posture, she might follow suit. Instead, Annie slouched against a weapon's rack, causing it to tip precariously. I winced, proceeding, "It isn't alright. The job's a bust. It's not possible."

Annie quirked an eyebrow, straightening a bit and mercifully allowing the weapons rack to resettle. "Oh no... Hmm, so what changed?"

I waved a hand towards Kay. "Is February really that scared?" I demanded. "What can possibly scare a saboteur? Why would she hole up like that? You're sure—a Threshold Seal?"

"That's what I've heard," he said, his cheeks still tinged red while he watched Annie with equal parts alarm and curiosity. Still watching her, he directed his words at me, "Umm, not to mention they got another remnant of the Banes to move in. Whole place is lined with glass now, and that's only *if* you get an invite in. Which, given the Seal, we both know is imposs—"

Eyes wide now, Annie breached communication etiquette by interrupting, "That sounds horrible!"

I was too busy shaking my head and muttering to myself to reply. Kay, though, ever the ladies' man, seemed to have overcome his distress at my friend's behavior and instead winked at Annie. "Don't trouble yourself, doll. Look, see this," he pulled out a stone tray and placed it on the table. The tray had intricate carvings of vines and pine needles up the edges. Kay called to Dale, "Oi, squeaker, grab me a BeeBuzz."

Dale looked frantically around for a moment, but, when he realized he was being addressed, he began to stammer.

"The yellow can, in the fridge," I called.

With trembling fingers, careful not to touch anything else, Dale opened the potion case, grabbed one of the energy drinks and hurried over, handing it to me. I passed the cold beverage to Kay. He popped the tab, took a long sip, sighed, then poured the rest of the contents into the stone basin. At first, the bubbling, fizzing liquid had a vibrant, pink hue to it, with odd chunks floating around.

But as the energy drink sloshed across the carved stone bowl, it began to turn clear. And finally, the liquid settled into a glassy, smooth, translucent form.

"What is this?" Annie asked, leaning in.

"Information," Kay said, tapping his nose.

She watched him, curiously. "You know, you're good-looking, in a way... A bit like a dapper ferret." She bobbed her head once, beaming at the comparison. "Yes, yes, that's exactly it!"

Kay blinked, staring at her.

For my part, I resisted the urge to groan. One moment interrupting him, the next insulting him—Annie wouldn't have lasted a minute at one of my father's masquerade balls. Thankfully, Kay was a bit more easy-going than Imperium court life.

The black-marketer met Annie's gaze. "You think I'm good-looking?"

"Mhmm," she said, wagging her head. She reached out, patting the man, who was a stranger to her, on the chest. "Very. Good for you!"

Kay raised his brow in my direction, his *Oops* tattoo shifting.

"Don't let your imagination get away with you," I snapped. "She's friendly with everyone. Can we just get on with it?" I waved a hand towards the stone basin.

Kay shot Annie another hopeful look, but now my odd companion was distracted by a couple of bracelets inside the glass counter, like a jackdaw at the sight of something shiny. Kay sighed, but then, in order to regain the attention of the room, he declared in a loud, authoritative voice, "The Hollow!"

A second later, the clear liquid in the stone basin shivered and shimmered. A picture began to form, coalescing in a sudden tremor of ripples.

As I stared at the image, an icy gust suddenly erupted down my spine as two, bright blue eyes stared up and out at me. The eyes vanished a second later, and I glanced around, wondering if anyone else had seen. Before I could gauge their reaction, though, Kay let out a low whistle and pointed one, bony finger towards the basin.

"That," he muttered, "is the Hollow."

The image in the basin was clearer than an HD television. Within, spiky trees adorned jagged mountains circling what looked like a volcano crater. Around the crater, walls soared into the sky—nearly fifty feet of stone and tangled roots and thorns. The stone slab walls encompassed an area larger than an unknowing football field, and the walls towered as high as some mountains.

The chasm itself was deep but, with the added depth of the walls, it seemed an endless pit into the heart of the earth itself. Sheer blackness stared out at us, like a giant, gaping demon eye.

"You wouldn't happen to know where it is, would you?" I whispered.

"Psh—not how it works. You know that, Three. Thing is Sealed and Unlocated. I mean, you went in once before, didn't you?"

I flinched at the dark memories prompted by this question. Memories of a gun, my brother, and when I'd gone to kill him the first time.

***

Two years before...

...the wild sprint through the labyrinth, the three-eyed guardian behind us, thrashing in the dark. The blood dripping down my fingertips... the distant chatter and giggling and howls coming from cracked mirrors lining the underground shafts. And then, stumbling, I reached my little brother's cell.

"Leonidas?" I could still hear Napoleon's voice, inquiring in the dark. I couldn't see him—a mercy that. "Is that you?" he'd called, his eyes better adjusted to the pitch black than mine. He'd been there since he was four years old. A decade entombed in the prison, held by a banished clan of genies.

Preacher had fallen behind, lagging. He'd never been as quick underground. I stood outside my brother's cell made of twisting iron; I gasped, not speaking, hearing his voice usher out into the black. "Leonidas? Are you there?" he'd asked, a soft sob creeping into his voice.

My twelve-year-old kid brother, at the time, had been buried for eight years. My doing. My fault. But I couldn't allow him to escape. I couldn't let him loose... Not after what I'd done on the night of the Grimmest Jest. He was too dangerous, because of me. Too dangerous because of my actions. And he suffered for it.

I stood in the dark, waiting, trembling. I wanted to cry but had never learned how. I wanted to scream. My whole body shook as if chilled to the bone. My hand had slipped into my waistband, towards the gun. I'd felt the smooth metal, pulled the weapon, gripping it tight. Just one shot. All it would take to put him out of his misery...

No one could unleash him then. Devastation would die in darkness, forgotten...

My fault...

I gasped, hyperventilating now.

"Leonidas..."

I raised the gun, trying to adjust. I'd purchased a potion from Kay when I'd first visited the Hollow. A potion to allow sight in the darkest places.

But I didn't want to see those familiar eyes staring out at me. Napoleon had been the one brother who was normal. Not a particularly strong eternal, but none of the Rex siblings had been weak either. He'd been kind, though. A kind child—a superpower in its own right, given how we'd been raised. Compassionate as an instinct. Only four by the time of the Grimmest Jest and the assassinations. Only four, so they hadn't killed him—even the Endeavor occasionally postured to maintain their reputation. So instead of murdering a four-year-old, they'd dragged him off to the darkest corners of hell, hiding him in the mountains, burying him deep. The Endeavor would likely execute him when he came of age, at sixteen.

But I couldn't wait for that. Who knew if *they* might discover him. Discover what I had done.

My finger trembled, gripping the trigger, the gun raised, pointed towards the pitch black, towards the cell he was trapped in.

"Tomb's trove..." I'd gasped to myself. "Do it. Do it!"

My finger tightened... I tried to suppress my compassion. Suppress all the emotions Nimue had been resurrecting in my husk. Tried to repress any emotion against the inevitable necessity of letting the bullet fly.

I stood in the dark, shaking like a leaf in a gale, gun still raised.

And I couldn't pull the trigger.

I couldn't do it.

Once upon a time, at the height of my father's training, I would have been able. I was near certain of it. But no longer...

Standing in the dark, gun throttled in my grip, I threw my head back and screamed a bloody, inhuman howl at the darkness.

"Leonidas?" the voice had asked. "Please... please, is that you?"

His pleadings had echoed in my ears as I'd turned, cursing myself in my mind, and then I sprinted away. Failed... the rumors had circulated. Leonidas Rex, the third with that title in the Loophole. The third pretender, adopting a name not his own. He'd failed. He'd failed a job in the Hollow.

The whispers had spread like ripples on a still pond, reaching the deeper corners of my world, the realm of the savants and the saboteurs.

But I hadn't failed the job. I hadn't been there to rescue anyone. I simply had lost my nerve at the most crucial moment.

And now...

Now, I had to go back and finish the job.

Annie didn't know. Only Preacher knew. And he only knew the what, not the why. No one could know the why. Not even Preacher... Vyle's teeth, I'd never even told my adopted mother. No... some secrets were best left buried two graves deep in the lapsed memory of an indifferent night.

Chapter 26

The memories flitted away, and I snapped back to the moment, my ears tickled by the slow whisper emanating in quiet spurts from Kay. He entranced his captive audience in Annie by murmuring and waving his fingers over the basin.

"...A murdered saboteur, only three nights ago," he said, chuckling softly. "And so a Threshold Seal has been raised. No living thing. *No living thing* may enter the Hollow without a direct invitation from February herself, the lieutenant of the saboteurs. Do you understand now, doll?"

"Our key is useless, basically," I muttered. "At least, useless for getting in. The moment we enter—we get zapped. Instant death."

Kay shot me a look. "I mean... not that any of it matters if you haven't *located* the hexed prison... You have located it right? Three?"

I wrinkled my nose. "We're working on it," I muttered. "Percy's the confidant."

Kay winced. "You've got less than two days to—"

"I know! Don't worry about it, I'm figuring it out." And in a way I was telling the truth. I could think of *one* thing Percy wanted that I could give him in exchange for the prison's location. But it would hurt like hells.

Annie's normally chipper expression flickered now, and the faintest of frowns creased her brow. As it did, I noticed her shadow shimmer and shift at her feet. Annie looked from me to Kelly. "There has to be a way. You have all manner of magical artifacts lying around here. Something can make us seem dead."

"I don't know if such a thing even exists—but *seeming* dead isn't the same. Without a direct, verbal, *intentional* invitation from February herself, there is no entry. And if you're within eyesight of February, you might as well be dead anyway."

Now, Annie's expression darkened even further. For a moment, her voice almost seemed to change, going deeper, harsher. Her shadow swelled across the ground like spilled ink. She scoffed, "You speak of this lady as if she's some sort of god..."

I watched my old friend, my eyes fixed on her shadow. Slowly, it receded again, and Annie's expression lightened.

Kay and I shared a look. Neither of us smiled, neither of us spoke for a moment. Then, in a hushed voice, Kay whispered. "No, not a god... A killer of gods. And angels. And demons. And the Hidden Kingdoms. An assassin trained and raised to balance the mortal powers against those that might crush them. A saboteur is an army in a body. They're unnatural, married to darkness, wielding a wereblade."

"What's that?" Dale asked.

At this, Kay did smile, his skin around the inky *Oops* shining beneath the flaming skulls above.

Watching his reaction, my eyes narrowed shrewdly, and for a moment I forgot my childhood friend's strange mannerisms. "You're *joking*," I said. "There's no way. No *way!* You didn't get it. You couldn't have..." I stared at Kay, trying to read his face without reading his mind.

He ducked behind the counter and I heard the sudden spinning of a metallic lock. A *click*, another lock, another *click*. And then, with a practiced flourish, as if he'd anticipated just such a moment, he reemerged, gripping a thin, wooden box.

He placed the box delicately onto the glass counter, holding the corners of the simple container as if afraid he might smudge it. Kay reached down, unhooked a metal latch and, still carefully, opened the box.

My eyes bugged. Preacher actually emitted a soft breath of surprise behind me. I could feel the heat from Dale's body as he leaned in next to me, swallowing, seeking a closer look.

Black velvet cradled a single gleaming dagger.

The blade in question seemed made of pure glass. And as Kay shifted the container, the weapon caught and reflected the light from the skulls above in twinkling patterns. A flash of many colors, through the refracted glass, spread across the counter and touched Kay's knuckles.

He grinned, staring at the thing, then looked at me. Dale marveled at the weapon, but I could tell from his posture, he didn't truly know what he was looking at.

"What... what is it?" he said.

"A living blade," I murmured, my eyes transfixed. I took a step back, feeling a sudden shiver along my spine. Briefly, I even forgot about the impossible prison-break. The shadows around me loomed larger; the prickle along my neck intensified.

"Forged by the ancient djinn," whispered Kay, grinning now. "Made from pure gemstone—but not like the diamonds and sapphires and emeralds we're accustomed to..."

"That's diamond?" Dale asked.

"No," Kay said. "It's far, far more. The genie grow it in their vineyards, in the baths of molten rock, near the base of the cratered nurseries. Some of the gems grow to be eaten, juiced. Others, though, continue growing—tended by the matrons—they develop something of a... *personality*."

Kay reached in now, plucked the knife up. As he did, sparks danced over his fingers and he winced. For a second, it seemed like he might drop the blade, as if it had grown suddenly very heavy.

He grunted, hefting the weight, and he murmured, "This is why they call it a wereblade."

We all watched as the dagger, gripped in his whitening knuckles, began to shift like fluid. The many crystalline facets moved like the scales of some snake, twisting suddenly. The light cast in different patterns now, and what had once seemed solid, now seemed fluid, pouring into an invisible mold, while still gripped by Kay. I yanked Dale back as a sudden flashing blade jutted through the space he'd been standing.

The dagger reformed, and now, in Kay's hand, he held a broadsword. Just as quickly, though, Kay focused—sweat beading on his forehead, panting now—and the weapon shifted again. The crystalline facets made a tinkling sound, like wind chimes, and the blade itself seemed to glow as it reformed once more, liquid crystal seeping back in on itself with immaculate craftsmanship driven by some unseen force. A second later, Kay now held a pure diamond pistol. He pointed it in the air and, with a crazed grin on his sweaty face, the *Oops* tattoo standing out in the flaming skulls above, he fired twice.

The weapon barked and a sudden downpour of dust and stone trickled and pattered against the table. Dale sneezed and I waved a hand before my face.

Kay was gasping now, though, as if he'd run a race. With a grunt, seemingly taking all his energy, he placed the blade back in the velvet case and lifted his hand. As he did, he massaged his fingers, wincing. "Takes the wind right out of you," he said, gasping.

I stared at the box, the prickle along my spine still intense. "Maybe you should put that away," I muttered.

Kay looked from me to Dale, who still stood wide-eyed, then shrugged, closed the lid and slid the box out of sight.

"How much is it?" Dale said, stunned.

Kay looked at him. "Fifteen, maybe twenty..."

"Twenty thousand?" Dale gaped.

"Million."

Dale let out a strangled little sob of a sound, as if unsure whether he should breathe or wheeze. I closed my eyes for a moment, shaking my head. I'd encountered the saboteurs before—seen their weapons. But it had been years. The memories weren't pleasant ones.

"Alright," I murmured. "It may be a bit out of our price range..." Then, pausing, I looked at the black marketer. "You know what you're doing, yes? Keeping something like that—"

Kay waved my comment away. "The saboteur is dead. She doesn't need it anymore. Besides, who's going to get it down here? Thank you, Three, but I'm quite content to take care of myself. Anyhow... As for you, forget about the werbeblade, let's do business."

"Business indeed. Right, well—with a Threshold Seal raised, I'm not even sure what the point is..." I frowned, glancing to Annie, who just watched me, waiting. I'd given my word, but with a magical veil protecting the prison, we couldn't enter *even if we did locate it.* There was no way in. At least, none I could think of. Still, I supposed while we were still here, we could supply anyway. "Hollow it is, I guess," I murmured, "So..."

"Gold dust cylinders?"

"Probably."

"Tiger's eye, you said?"

"Definitely." As he said it, I felt a flicker of curiosity. Tiger's eye, or teleporting stones as they were also known, could transport a soul over short distances. Could a teleporting stone break through the Threshold Seal? Perhaps... We'd have to test it first without putting our lives on the line. But where could we test a teleporting stone against a powerful veil? I wrinkled my nose, falling deeper into thought.

As I considered our options, Kay moved deftly, his skull chains shifting about and his earrings glinting as he ducked and grabbed items from beneath the counter. In one case, he reached up, slid a glass pane into a hidden compartment behind the wall, and pulled out two small brown bags before placing them on the counter in front of me.

Dale's expensive shoes shuffled closer, paused, then moved a step back, seeming caught between his brimming curiosity and overall unease around Kelly.

Like a shark smelling blood, Kay's eyes zeroed in on Dale's fidgeting form. The black marketer reached into one of the brown bags, procuring a single item which resembled a gold and auburn gelatin pack. As he held up the item, the small lines of gold seemed to sway in the mesmerizing fire. Kay squeezed the thing and it squished like a dish detergent bulb.

"What's that?" Dale squeaked, clearly unnerved by the sudden attention.

Kay extended the detergent pod-looking thing to Annie's intern. "Here, take it."

Having learned his lesson with Grendel, though, and remembering my admonishment against accepting anything for free from Kay, he quickly shook his head. "Er, no thanks."

"It won't hurt you. Go on," Kay insisted.

Dale glanced at me, and I shrugged. "He's right. It won't hurt you. It's tiger's eye."

"Like... an actual eye of—"

"No. Tiger's eye, like the semi-precious stone from South Africa. Its molecular structure is altered, though—alchemically."

Dale rubbed at one of his sideburns. "Altered to do what?"

Kay pushed the tiger's eye into Dale's hand and then gestured at a far corner of the strange shop, waving a hand. "Throw it," he said. "Hard."

Again, Dale glanced at me. Preacher and Annie simply watched curiously. For my part, I muttered, "I'm not paying for that one."

Kay, though, seemed too interested in making Dale squirm to hear me. At last, reluctantly, Dale took the item, hefted it and flung it into the far corner of the shop. The thing rebounded off a glass display case with a full suit of armor and then landed on the ground where it rolled to a halt against the stone. One of the flaming skulls dipped low, as if to investigate.

"Umm... Nice," Dale said, glancing around and probing at his face as if worried he might have sprouted a third ear.

"Didn't work," Kay said, frowning.

"It didn't break," I replied. "Faulty product, perhaps?"

Kay bristled and took a puff from his skeleton inhaler, his mood souring at the accusation. "Not my troving fault he throws like a girl!"

Annie patted Dale consolingly on the shoulder. Then, she skipped over to where the tiger's eye had fallen, picked it up, held it to the light from the skulls, one eye narrowed, examining the thing. "You mean like this?" she said. Then Annie launched it *hard* across the room. It shot like a bullet from one of Preacher's six shooters and slammed into a jutting stalagmite, smashing against the stone column. The tiger's eye burst like a dew drop. A sucking sound, as if from a straw dragging the final bits of a slushie, followed a cry of surprise from Dale.

A second later, Annie vanished from where she'd been standing and reappeared next to the stalagmite. Normally so graceful on her feet, Annie yelled in surprise and stumbled against the stalagmite, tripping and nearly falling.

Dale rushed over, calling, "Are you okay!"

Preacher just frowned, crossing his arms, allowing his distrust of Annie to cloud his countenance. But then, with a sigh, he walked over, reaching out to help her back upright.

I glanced from the floor where she'd been standing, back over to the stalagmite.

"She teleported!" Dale exclaimed.

"Defective wares my skinny arse," Kay muttered darkly.

"Sorry," I said. "You were right."

"And don't you forget it."

"I'm still not paying for that one."

"Whatever—there are nine more in the one bag and a few in the other."

I reached out, accepting the two small brown containers which resembled coin purses. Gently, I pocketed them in my left pocket which didn't have the knife slit.

"Are the bags reinforced?" I said.

Kay waved a hand. "Won't crush, even if a rhino sat on 'em. Delicate though, once the tiger's eye is removed. Same as the ones I gave you last year."

"*Gave*," I snorted. "For the price of a small car."

Kay chuckled, wiping at the inked *Oops*. "Right," he said. "Here's your gold dust. This one we won't be testing, if you don't mind."

I took three small vials of powdered gold, like glitter tubes, and put these in one of my jacket's interior pockets.

"Also... here, we'll call this a bonus," Kay said, wagging his head. "Half price for new inventions."

He pulled out a small jar with a black lid. Inside, a grayish dust sifted about like grains in an hourglass.

I frowned, leaning in. "What is it?"

"Alchemical thermite. And if that's a note of pride you detect in my voice, it's because it's earned. Do you know how hard it was to make this stuff? Just... careful it doesn't touch metal."

"What happens if it touches metal?"

"Completely harmless to skin. Can even drink the stuff and it won't hurt you. But the moment it touches metal. Boom."

I pursed my lips. "Boom? Understood. No metal. So it might work on locks, on gates, bars..."

"Exactly. Quite useful in a pinch. Can keep it tucked beneath your tongue, for instance, while dragged away in cuffs, then use it to break out. Just remember—harmless on skin, but if it touches metal..."

"Boom."

"Exactly. Anything else?"

"So no healing?"

"Like I said, none. Sorry."

"Well," I winced, massaging at my bad hand and glancing around. "Do you have anything defensive? Protective?"

"Against dreaders, yeah?"

"I mean... it is the Hollow."

Kay held up a single, bony finger. He hobbled along the edge of the counter, taking a moment, with his body shielding his face, to duck and puff from his inhaler once more. He kicked out at a skull that had hovered too close, exerting dominance. Then he reached the tall glass display case with the suit of armor. He wrapped his knuckles against his pocket.

A second later, a small, skeletal hand—pure white, with tiny bones, little more than that of a baby—poked out of the pocket, extending a ring of iron keys up towards Kay.

Dale squeaked, staring at the infantile, skeletal hand.

Kay looked over, grinning wickedly. "Anti-pickpocketing device. You like it?" Then, he used the ring of keys to open the display case. He ignored most the armor, but removed the shield and, with a grunt, hefted it. He waved a hand in front of his face, clearing some dust, then marched back in my direction.

"A bit large for my taste," I said.

Kay frowned, tipping the shield towards me. "Didn't take you for a priss, Three. This here is Lancelot's own shield."

"Lancelot's? How'd you get the Knight-Commander's shield?"

"Oh, you know those Round Table sorts," Kay scoffed. "All of them upgraded. Ever since that deal with Hephaestus. Human made armor just isn't good enough for them anymore." Kay snorted and shook his head. He glanced off, muttering... "Never can trust a blacksmith god, though, can you? Remember Brokkr? That little dwarf weirdo? Cursed all the items he sent out. No, but of course, and if they ever work with an enchanter—do they pay them well—I think not. What a bunch of stodgy, uptight, elitist—"

"Kay?"

He coughed. "Erm. Sorry. Yes. The shield. Lancelot's *old* shield, I should say. Before the glory days. But still quite serviceable. You, squeaker, come, try to hit me."

Dale shook his head.

"Aw, come on, you priss. Do it!"

"No, thank you," Dale said.

Kay turned to Preacher. "What about you, big guy? Think you have what it takes too—"

Preacher reached in one swift motion behind Kay's counter, his fingers latching onto something hidden beneath the glass. His hand reemerged with a firearm—likely Kay's own protective device. I tried not to roll my eyes—my mute friend was like a bloodhound where weapons were concerned.

He aimed the firearm swiftly at Kay's shield and fired twice without hesitation.

Chapter 27

Twin blasts. The moment the bullets struck, though, they didn't seem to quite *make it* through to the shield. Instead, they hit a blue, vibrating barrier, about an inch from the surface of the metal.

The bullets, completely unharmed, fell to the floor, tapping against the stone and rolling to a stop under Kay's foot, where he trapped them.

Kay grinned over the shield. "See—repels magic, too. Not much use against a Wit," he said, shrugging in my direction. "But, you know. Serviceable for most physical types of attack."

"It's large, isn't it?" I asked.

Kay waved away my protest. "Aw, come on."

"Do you think you could make it smaller?"

"What, you mean like cut it in half or something?"

"No... Just..." I waved airily towards Kay's workbench behind the counter. "Smaller. You're always bragging how you're an inventive Picasso. Do work on it."

Kay shrugged. "You saying you don't want it?"

I glanced at the bullets lodged beneath his feet, then at Preacher. "How much?"

"For you? A grand."

I narrowed my eyes. "Really?"

"Friendship discount."

"Alright, now I know something's wrong. What is it?"

Kay looked scandalized. His mouth unhinged and he clapped a bony hand to his black shirt, shaking his head. "I—I *what?* Wrong? How... how *dare*—"

"Kelly."

"Ah, tomb's knockers. Right, it comes cursed," he mumbled in a quiet voice, lowering his hand from his chest. But he hefted the shield again. "Still, stops bullets."

"What type of curse?"

Kay brightened. "Barely even noticeable."

"What type of curse?"

"Really, quite a manageable one. Honestly, hardly even a curse if you think about it."

"What type of curse?" I repeated for the third time.

"It's Lancelot's shield," Kay said hesitantly. "You know how history has a way of embedding itself in enchantments. Let's just say..." He hefted the shield again, displaying the emblem in the center of it. "It effects certain carnal urges."

I hadn't noticed the silver etchings at first, but now, as I leaned closer, I noticed two intertwining fig leaves etched in silver and, seemingly, fluttering to the ground.

I looked up. "The shield makes me horny?"

"That's one way to put it." Kay shrugged. "Seems to have a penchant for infidelity. But honestly, given that it saves you from bullets, is it really too much to ask—"

"Kay, I don't want a shield that makes me horny."

"*And* protects from bullets."

"It does protect from bullets..." I said hesitantly. What was the worst a shield that tempted infidelity could really do? I needed defenses for the job, didn't I?

"Only a grand," Kay added, seemingly sensing me wavering.

"What about eight hundred?"

"Done," Kay said without batting an eyelid.

Preacher coughed.

I glanced at my gun-totting friend. "He has a point," I said. "It does protect from bullets."

Preacher glared.

I knew my friend was a stickler for this sort of thing. As far as I was aware, Preacher was a virgin. As for me, I like hanging around virgins; it gives me insight into how the other half lives.

"Come on," I said, with a bit more whine in my voice than I liked. "I could use the protection!"

Annie giggled at this, and Preacher's eyes narrowed further.

"You know what I mean," I muttered.

Preacher closed his eyes, murmuring a silent prayer and waving his hand in my direction as if to ward off evil.

I turned away in a huff. "Don't you try and pre-exorcise me!" I grumbled some more but shook my head sadly. "Sorry, Kay. If you can figure out a way to make it smaller and remove the curse, then I'd take it. But, as it is, no dice. Dad won't let me."

I glanced back at Preacher, glaring. He'd stopped warding off evil and gave a small nod of contentment. Annie, meanwhile, was still smiling and desperately trying to hide it by covering her mouth. Genuine smiles in my line of work were so rare nowadays, I just watched it for a moment, enjoying the sight.

Kay sighed, leaning the shield against the counter before turning and moving back around the display case. "Fine," he muttered. "Remember that guitar I gave you?"

"The twelve string? I still have it in my room back on the RV. What about it?"

"Did it ever turn out to be cursed?"

"You said it wasn't."

"I said *most likely*. Was it cursed?"

"I don't think so... Why?"

Kay nodded, seemingly pleased about something. "In that case, if you pay upfront, I can remove the curse on this shield, figure out a way to make it more... luggage-sized. I'll have it hand delivered, by rizzle-post."

"Deal. Get it to me in a couple of days, though."

Kay made a crossing motion over his heart, hefting a breath as if he'd just completed a race. "Will that be all?"

I began to nod, but as I did, hesitated. I swallowed, glancing at Kay. "These... tiger's eyes," I said, patting my pocket. "Do you think they'd at all get through a Threshold Seal?"

Kay frowned over the glass display case. "You mean teleport you straight through?"

"Possible?"

"Anything's possible, Three."

"Likely?"

"Bout as likely as your friend over there giving me a kiss." His hand waved towards my six-foot-nine companion.

Preacher frowned again. Kay, indifferent to the effect of his words, played with one of his pendants and shrugged. "Dunno, might get lucky—like *really* lucky. If I were you, though, I'd test it on a lesser threshold first. Just to be safe. 'Sides, the way you're looking, you'll be chewed to pieces before you even get to any Seal.

Anyway—is that all? I've got a couple of pixies to feed or they're gonna start knocking things over again." He shook his head and extended a hand towards a shaker like a fish-food dispenser, except filled with strange glowing, green orbs. As he did, the floating skulls throughout the room began to congregate, moving towards the shopkeeper.

Taking this as our cue, Annie handed over the required payment, while Kay distractedly contended with the floating skulls.

"So what now?" Annie murmured in my ear as we walked away, lighter of purse and heavier of heart.

"Well..." I winced. "The Threshold Seal is a problem. We need to find a way to get through it."

"These tiger's eye might do it?"

"Seems very unlikely. But we need to test it."

"Oh. Okay. How?"

"Well..." I stepped into one of the canoes, watching as Annie moved into hers as well, her shadow strangely rigid as she did. "I need to take care of some of these bleeders," I said, waving my bandaged hand. My back was still numb from my pain-suppression, but was also sticky and slick. The bandages were doing what they could, but heading forward like this was ill-advised.

"So we need to test the tiger's eye against a barricade, and we need to get you healed," said Annie. "Any idea where to do that?"

"Actually, yes," I grunted. "Two birds with one stone. Plus... we have to stay local until nightfall." My mind moved back to the Percy problem, and I frowned. I knew what I had to do. There was only one barter the ogre-eared man would accept. If I told the others what it would cost, they'd never let me do it.

I cleared my thoughts and shot a look at Annie. "Afraid you'll have to wait in the RV, though."

Annie frowned. "Why?"

"The place I have in mind is private property."

Preacher stiffened next to me as he also got into the canoe, causing the boat to rock. His auburn gaze burrowed into the side of my face.

"Sorry friend," I muttered. "But do you have a better idea? My hand is killing me."

Preacher scowled, tapping his head angrily.

I pretended like I didn't understand. "What?"

He tapped his head even harder.

"What?"

He gripped me by the collar and lifted me into the air with one hand until my feet dangled towards the bottom of our now swaying boat.

I swallowed. "Oh, *that*." I extended my consciousness reluctantly, probing towards Preacher's mind.

I refuse, Leonidas, he said, the moment he sensed my presence.

"Be reasonable," I muttered. "We need to test the tiger's eye against a veil. And I need to be patched up. Where else can we do that?"

No. Not him.

"I don't get it. What's your feud with—"

No!

But even as he said it, Preacher's shoulders slumped and he released me. I dropped, nearly falling out of the canoe, but my large friend caught my shoulder and shook his head before sitting back down with a sigh.

I sat gingerly, feeling a stirring of guilt in my stomach at my friend's reaction. If only to make myself feel better, I murmured, "We'll get your weapons back from Meadowfax. That'll be nice, won't it?"

Preacher didn't answer, and I didn't blame him. I knew how much he hated visiting his father.

But my brother was still in the Hollow—Annie still had a mission I needed to prevent at all costs. And there was only one way to guarantee no one ever went after Napoleon again... I couldn't do that unless I was healed, and nothing would matter anyway if we didn't find a way into the Hollow. It was now sealed by a powerful veil and guarded by a saboteur and all manner of monstrous watchers.

Less than thirty-eight hours before the Hollow could be located. We were running out of time, so sacrifices had to be made... Even if it came at the cost of estranged relationships and old war wounds.

Chapter 28

Preacher shifted uncomfortably as we approached his father's farm. I, on the other hand, found it easier to breathe as I moved over the hill, down the trail and past a row of blackberries lining the dirt road. The dark pines bristled; the fresh air swaddled the sweet fragrance of berries, and a trickling stream moved through the hilly terrain, over which I could hear splashing and the laughter of children.

As we moved beneath old, flaking boughs, along the dusty path, a thin wreath of fog arose from the ground. The mist hovered, wafting on the air, stretched thin like cotton on a spinning wheel.

Innocuous enough to the eye, such things often held powerful protection magic, or veils. We'd have to test the tiger's eye against it soon enough. And then, when night fell, I'd have to handle the Percy problem.

But first things first—I needed the faith healer. Besides the veils themselves, the single greatest protection against harm for the denizens of Mr. Gallows' farm was the man himself.

As if sensing my thoughts, I heard another burst of laughter. Two children suddenly darted across the path in front of us, chased by another duo. All of them brandished water pistols, shouting and spraying each other as they hotfooted from tree to tree, bare feet slapping the detritus-padded ground.

They didn't even seem to notice us. Yet, even in their joyful play, the children made sure to stay *within* the boundary of the foggy circlet.

"Is your father still taking on new charges?" I murmured as we approached the wreath of low-hanging white.

Preacher shrugged.

"Is he still taking *all* charges?" I asked, feeling a slight shiver across my spine.

Preacher lowered his head, murmured a soundless prayer, his lips barely moving, crossed himself and then moved through the mist.

We moved up the trail and paused at the top of a hill. As I beheld the view, thoughts of the Hollow, of Percy, of our dwindling time frame faded. I sighed in a wistful, contended sort of way, wincing, but ignoring the pain for a moment. Below, centering a grassy landscape, an arching bridge split two ponds. The air held the fragrance of fresh cut grass, and I spotted and old tractor-mower by a red barn. Sun poked over a two-story white farmhouse, and a second home, about the same size, was under construction near twin oaks twirling to the sky.

Ducks flapped over the pond. The group of four who'd been squirting water pistols had now made it to the wooden platforms and were watching another group of children take turns backflipping into the water. Their grace and ease seemed unnatural... *inhuman* even.

Then again, most of the Gallows orphans weren't human at all. Many could only be seen in their true forms, once the sun dipped—another one of the protective measures of this oasis.

Another two children were scaling the side of the white farmhouse and scrambling onto the roof. One of the kids had pure green skin, visible even from this distance, suggesting the veil didn't *completely* manage to hide the nature of the children.

Preacher slowed a bit, and despite his lengthy strides, he began to fall behind as I moved over a bridge, across a stream, and towards the porch of the white farmhouse. "Are you going to be alright?" I said, glancing back at my friend.

He just frowned. A single form sat in a rocking chair on the porch and Preacher's hands balled into fists as he stared at the figure.

The old man on the porch had choir-boy hair, parted at the top. An easy smile split his cheeks as he listened to the children playing in the pond and on the roof. After a moment, he seemed to hear me drawing near as I limped along, breathing heavily. He perked up, turning in my direction. With a fluttering wave of a wrinkled hand, he beckoned me onto the porch of the old farmhouse. His eyebrows were like white clouds, fluffy and angled, reminding me of a glimpse I'd once had of Zeus. Also, the old man was blind. His eyes were closed behind dark spectacles, barely visible through the thin shade of the reflective glass.

Two of the children I'd spotted earlier, including the one with pure green skin, continued to swing from the railing lining the wooden porch. Every time I tried to look at the children, though, to get a better glimpse of their features, it almost seemed like staring into a heat mirage. Their faces would shimmer, their forms would go foggy and I would blink, feeling a headache coming on.

A powerful veil, then. I could feel it settled over the entire farm. I knew it would lift when the sun slept. Usually, though, the children under Mr. Gallows' protection would already be in bed by then. We'd have to test the tiger's eye before sunset.

Nestled against the white and blue siding of the porch wall, I spotted an old-fashioned popcorn machine, the type we used in Amazin' Bandini's Travelling Circus. One of the children, a girl with pigtails, perhaps only fourteen, wearing a quizzical expression and mud-stained overalls, reached a hand covered in dirt into the machine, grabbed a handful of popcorn and began munching.

Children often made me nervous. Not just because of the form my poltergeist took. Rather, children shared my penchant for unapologetic honesty. Though kids could be frightful liars at times, they also had a way of speaking without the everyday skill of deception developed over a lifetime. Faced with children, I was often confronted by the discomfort my own speech often prompted.

The old man creased his wrinkled fingers over each other. His dark skin seemed soft and smooth where palm met finger, and I detected a faint aura extending from his mind. Not everyone has an aura. Usually, I have to engage my eternal gift in order to pick up on someone's thoughts. But some few are more thermostats than thermometers. They carry a mindset, a thought pattern so deep that it can't help but leak out from them.

In Paul Gallows' case, he emanated peace. I took a step towards him without even realizing it. Preacher's old, blind father smiled at the sound of creaking wooden plank. I placed a hand on the rail, wincing as I did, glancing towards my red-stained bandage wrapped around my fingers.

"It's good to hear you, Mr. Rex," said Paul, beaming again, and rocking back and forth on his chair. He held a glass of homemade strawberry wine.

Preacher shuffled uncomfortably next to me. He prodded me with a thick finger, ushering me up the final step towards his father. Again, my mind was assailed by a pulse of pure peace from an untroubled mind. Not a mind *without* trouble, but one calcified against its effects. Someone might not know it, looking at Paul, but his mind was as strong as granite.

He took another sip from his wine, swishing it around and inhaling deeply.

"Hello, Mr. Gallows," I said, clearing my throat. I winced as I spoke, feeling the wound in my back beginning to throb again. The painkillers I'd taken before visiting Kay were starting to wear off and my concentration was slipping.

Paul's sightless gaze shifted, directed towards the rafters. I reached out and sensed a couple of small minds, spiders, I guessed. And also the hungry, vapid, airy thoughts of a sparrow.

"Is Preacher there with you?"

I glanced towards my tall friend and waited. I'd seen the father and son interact a few times, and Preacher had yet to break his silence. My tall friend shook his head, remaining a few steps away from the bottom of the porch.

I coughed, wincing as I did. "He's, umm, he's here, but doesn't want me to say."

Preacher glared daggers at me, and I shrugged back. He'd known me ten years—he should've known I wouldn't lie.

"Oh," said Paul, sighing softly. "Alright. Hello, son!" he waved a bit off to the left of where Preacher stood in silence.

I wanted to reply on his behalf, but decided it wasn't my place to try and reconcile the old revival tent preacher and his dead-eye son.

Preacher took a quiet step away from the porch, his arms crossed and his eyes fixed on the distant tree line across the bucolic scene. I'd seen my large companion take down monsters and demons without breaking a sweat. But every time he came near his father, he fidgeted and worried his lip like a little boy.

For a moment, a look of sheer pain gouged into Paul's wrinkled countenance, and his lips went taut with grief. Some of the peace I'd sensed earlier slipped and, in a frail voice, he said. "Do you think he'll come by for supper?"

I looked to Preacher as did the young girl with her hand in the popcorn machine. She began to speak, but Preacher put a finger to his lips and gave a quick shake of his head. The young girl in overalls glared and stamped a foot. But Preacher shook his head adamantly and looked away again.

The look of pain on the old man's face caused my stomach to ache and I turned, glancing back at Preacher and giving my tall, musclebound companion a long look. I reached out with my mind and placed the words in his head. *Come on. It's your father. He misses you.*

But Preacher shook his head once. *Stay out of it, Leon. We're here to get you healed and test the threshold. No supper, nothing else. Get on with it.*

I glanced back at the old man sitting in the rocking chair. I wasn't sure what a blind faith-healer could have done to rouse such feelings of hurt and anger which I sensed emanating from his son. Mr. Gallows seemed so harmless, sitting there, his expression half hopeful at the prospect of enticing his eldest child to supper.

But Preacher was no longer looking, again, standing a way off from the house, his feet at shoulder width in the dirt path. He glanced back and his eyes flicked towards the young girl in overalls, and I glimpsed a sudden flash of guilt across his face, but just as quickly he looked away, still staring off. The girl sighed but didn't speak. She wiped one hand on her dirty overalls, the other still gripping a handful of popcorn as she skipped down the patio stairs with thumping footsteps and gave Preacher a side-hug, which he returned, leaning down and kissing her on top of the head.

I sighed. "Sorry, Paul but we won't be joining you for supper either. We're busy, but also Preacher doesn't want to."

Paul directed his face towards the rafters. "Well," he said at last, "if he changes his mind, we're having blueberry crisp. His favorite."

For some reason, this only seemed to frustrate my large friend further; Preacher huffed and stomped off, moving up the dirt path in the direction of the chicken-shaped mailbox, past a row of geese floating on the quiet pond.

I watched him retreat, wincing against the pain in my hand as I did, but then returned my attention to Mr. Gallows.

The look of grief on Paul's face was so strong it nearly made me gasp. At last, though, Gallows took another sip of strawberry wine. Then, quietly, he said, "We cleared the thorns in the east blackberry grove," he murmured. "Did he at least notice? He used to talk about those thorns all the time..."

Preacher was far off now, still quiet, tossing blades of grass into the pond and watching the geese chase each other in an effort to reach the ripples in the water, suspecting food. Then, wiping at his face again, Preacher glanced back, frowning to me. I noticed his mascara had smudged a bit.

"Mr. Rex," said Paul.

"Mhmm?"

"My boy, has he still not found his voice, child?"

"He's still quiet, yes. I..." I paused, biting my lip. I could still feel the pain in my body, but also a question come to mind that I'd never had a private chance to ask the old faith healer before. I'd only visited a few times before. "Did he ever tell you why he took a vow of silence?"

Paul gave a small, sad smile. "Preacher doesn't tell me much anymore."

"Fair. Just thought I'd ask."

Paul's hand lowered from the glass of wine and shook a little as if suddenly cold. But then his smile returned and he said, "Will you be staying the night in the area?"

"I'm afraid not. Actually... we're here for a bit of help."

Paul still seemed to be listening, but he reached down, winced and begin to rub his hand against his lower back. The same spot I had my wound. My chest was still on fire from the glass injuries, and I found my hand gripping the rail even harder now, holding tight.

"Are you hurt?" said Paul.

"Pretty badly," I said, gritting my teeth.

"You should have come straight here." Paul rose suddenly from his rocking chair and placed the strawberry wine on the table next to him. Unfortunately, the glass just missed the edge and fell, shattering against the wood and spilling reddish liquid across the floorboards.

"Oh dear," said Paul. "I hate to be a bother, but Sussanah would you mind grabbing a broom?"

The girl in the dirty overalls was still on the dusty ground at the base of the stairs, watching Preacher with a sad expression. At her father's words, though, it seemed a spell was lifted and her previously lively disposition returned.

"On it!" the young teenager declared, rushing back up the stairs with bare feet and racing into the house. The door slammed shut with a loud *thud*.

Paul shook his head, chuckling as he said. "That youngster is a perfect combination of the practical and... and what's the word... *ethereal*?" he paused, frowning. "Did I say that right?"

172

I tried to hide a smile. "Yes sir, ethereal is a good word."

"Thank you, Lord!" His face split. Then, he beckoned to me. "Let me put my hand on you, child."

Gratefully, I limped away from the steadying support of the white painted rail and leaned towards Mr. Gallows. He winced again, massaging at his lower back where my own gunshot wound had occurred. I'd long since grown accustomed to Paul's premonitions about other peoples' pain.

A penchant, I called it. All sorts of oddities often cropped up among the eternals. While there were only six recognized eternal talents, I'd often heard of adjacent abilities, though rare, appearing among the knowing. *Impure* abilities, according to some of my father's friends.

Paul Gallows was a revival preacher who spoke out of a giant white tent on the outskirts of Picker's Lake. He had a bit of a reputation for himself. The Blind Healer, they called him.

"Do you have faith, Mr. Rex?" Paul murmured as he reached out with his rough, work-calloused fingers. Despite his disability, Paul was a man who valued working with his hands.

I winced and swallowed. I'd seen Mr. Gallows operate before. In my estimation, everyone had faith in something. And while Gallows and I didn't always see eye to eye on the big picture, I knew enough in this moment to put my faith in him. "Of course," I said. "It's mostly my chest and back. If you could get to my hand too, I'd be much obliged." I leaned with my good hand braced against the white patio barrier and sighed, releasing some of the concentration for the pain I'd been holding over the last twelve hours. As I did, like silted water flooding a ditch, the pain came back in a swishing scrape.

I grit my teeth and gasped sharply.

For his part, Mr. Gallows actually yelped, and tears began to trickle from behind his darkened glasses, meandering down his wrinkled cheeks towards the edge of his chin.

"Oh, child," he said. He placed a hand on my shoulder more firmly now.

I felt heat on his palm emanating through me. I'd often wondered the source of Mr. Gallows' power. The same source as mine, albeit. I knew enough about the world not to discount the miraculous. Hell, I'd once bartered a smuggled miracle on the doorstep of Hades in my youth. Of course, now I knew better than to go messing firsthand with angelic contraband. Bad business that. More firepower than was worth attracting. But I wasn't so inexperienced to think there weren't *other* sources of power in the world. Some of them darker, some of them mysterious, many of them powerful.

Paul wasn't the sort of man to blame another for their *lack* of faith. Most likely because he had more than enough faith to spare for the both of us. Which was why, most Sunday nights, his revival tent was surrounded by parked cars and overflow crowds of the sick and wounded, hoping for a glimpse of the Blind Healer.

"Lord," said Paul, simply, "heal my friend, Mr. Rex. In the name of your beloved son, Jesus, I ask for his full restoration."

I shifted uncomfortably as he spoke. More out of habit than anything. There were some names under heaven and earth that attracted far too many eyes of the unseen variety. Sometimes friends, but more often than not, simply sources attracted to power. And faith in a name increased power in the thing itself. Such has always been the case.

Paul Gallows' faith was the strongest I'd ever known.

I noted Preacher by the lake, bowing his head in respect and crossing his heart. Again, I shifted uncomfortably, wishing for a moment Kay had something a little less potent for my wounds than faith in a resurrected God. It felt a bit like a full surgery for a paper cut.

As I was thinking this, and then, desperately, trying not to think *too* loudly, lest I get myself cursed instead— tomb's trove, I don't know how this stuff works—I felt a prickle of heat begin to spread along my shoulder where Paul touched. Everything seemed to narrow, darkening. Across from me, blue eyes reflected in the glass window that peered into the kitchen.

My poltergeist stared back, merely a reflection for now, his eyes hungry. A small, pink tongue darted out, licking his chapped lips as he watched me. Like I said, all sorts are drawn to raw power.

The heat continued to spread through me and as it did, I gasped, feeling a tingle along my lower back, where the bullet wound was. My chest also heated, almost uncomfortably. I winced, gritting my teeth, expecting a sudden surge of pain, but then, a moment later, a swell of relief flooded through me and I breathed a slow, steady exhalation. An easy breath, the likes of which I hadn't drawn in days.

At last, gasping, my whole body buzzing with fire and heat and a chill wind swirling around me, I heard Mr. Gallows murmur a soft, "Thank you, dear Papa." He lowered his hand. "Well? How does it feel?"

I glanced down at my chest and reached up tentatively with my hand gripping the patio rail. I probed at my body hesitantly, wincing, expecting a sudden flash of pain. But it never came. I pulled the collar of my shirt down, revealing the bandages beneath, which were stained with flecks of red. I tore one of the bandages, staring towards a portion of my chest that had been wreathed in criss-crossed cuts from the glass.

Only smooth flesh stared back. I tore another bandage, eyes widening further.

Also smooth, no more wounds.

"Holy shi—ps in the night." I coughed. "It worked."

Paul nodded, smiling. "You have a strong faith, child."

"Not sure I can take credit for this one, Mr. Gallows."

I reached behind my back, fully dropping all concentration on numbing pain now. I half expected a surge of agony, but this also didn't come. I poked and prodded beneath the bandages on my lower back. Smooth flesh, no wounds.

"Wow." I grinned now. "Thanks!"

I reached out to clap Mr. Gallows on the shoulder with my bandaged hand. As I did, though, I suddenly winced. With a soft, little yelp, I peeled back the bandage around my hand.

I could still see the faint outline of the bullet wound, a wreath of angry red and dried black against my palm. I flexed my fingers and they moved but felt tender.

Paul massaged his own hand and sighed, shaking his head. "Oh dear. Nearly got it all. I can try again in the morning, if you'd like."

I glanced towards where Preacher still stared across the water and said, "No, sir. Really. It's fine. My hand feels better—don't worry about it." I shook my palm a bit and wiggled my fingers, gritting my teeth. "See, nearly as good as new. A couple days and it'll clear up on its own."

Mr. Gallows tilted his head back, sighing towards the ceiling.

"Hey," I reached out and placed my good hand on his shoulder. "Sir, it's fine. You've nearly made me a new man." I checked inside my shirt again. "A couple of scars from a few years ago vanished too!"

The blue crown tattoo remained, however, and I quickly pressed my collar back against my newly healed skin.

But Paul looked even more troubled now. He brushed at his neat, choir boy hair and lowered back into his rocking chair.

I hesitated, uncertain what to say. "I... I mean it's more than I could have healed," I ventured, hesitantly. "You got ninety percent. That's something."

He shook his head. "It's not my ego I'm worried about, child."

I leaned against the porch now, flexing my still tender fingers on my nearly healed palm.

Before Paul could comment further, though, the door to the patio banged open again, and Sussanah stepped back onto the porch, carrying a broom. Next to her, a much younger girl came flouncing out as well.

It took me a moment to realize this new girl wasn't one of Preacher's sisters. In fact, she wasn't even human.

Chapter 29

Sussanah couldn't have been much older than fourteen. Her mud-covered overalls and bare feet darkened by familiarity with the sun suggested a lively personality interested in splashing through creeks, chasing frogs, or throwing clumps of mud.

The girl with Sussanah, though, had to be at least half her age. The child in question had pure blue eyes, larger than a human's, with no pupil to speak of. Her pale skin, like moonlight, twisted with pearlescent designs and patterns, which, on closer inspection, one would realize weren't tattoos, but—strangely—the nature of her skin itself.

Despite her age, she had three piercings, golden bands, in one ear, and a nose ring stud in her tiny left nostril. Most genies could be spotted by the piercings and skin patterns, even young ones like this. The child had the features of a chipmunk—her large eyes both playful and nervous, and her pudgy cheeks seemingly accustomed to smiling. She had a glistening purple barrette in her pale blue hair and a small braid tied in the shape of a knotted rope swing, upon which a small stick beetle was resting and moving about near her cheek.

Every so often, the girl's hand would rise and pet at the stick beetle in her hair as if to sooth it.

"Papa!" Sussanah said, leaning the broom against the wall near the shattered glass and placing her hands on her hips. "Grace doesn't want to drink the blessed water."

The wishmaker child shifted and glanced shyly off to the side. If I knew anything about genies, this child was older than me in human years. Genies age at a seventh of a mortal's rate. The girl in front of me was no older than six-years-old among her kind, but among mortals, she would have been at least forty-two.

"Grace?" said Preacher's father. "Why not? The water keeps us all safe here. Hiding us."

Grace sighed, her small lips bunching up on one side of her face. She opened her mouth as if to speak, but then glanced over at me, her cheeks reddening a bit around the swirling, vine-shaped patterns in her skin, and she quickly looked away.

Sussanah frowned. "Oh," she said. "I forgot. Mr. Leon, can you cover your ears please? Grace doesn't like speaking in front of strangers."

I hesitated, but then, at the hopeful look on the miniature genie's face, I turned and covered my ears. Despite myself, and probably much to my shame, I still extended my consciousness, lightly grazing the minds around me.

The peace from Mr. Gallows intensified, and I could feel a fatherly, protective kindness extended towards the two children on the porch. Sussanah's mind echoed with a hidden laughter, but also a pain every time she glanced from her brother by the lake to her seated father. At the same time, her mind raced a mile a minute, as if it couldn't quite be bothered to remain stuck on any one notion.

The genie child, one of the Smith clan if I wasn't mistaken, seemed curious and shy. Most her attention, though, kept diverting towards a portion of the rafters. I couldn't quite spot what she was looking at, but whatever it was seemed to cause her a modicum of sadness.

"Well, Grace?" Mr. Gallows pressed.

My ears were still covered, but the combination of the faintly muffled speech, coupled with the light extension of my mind picked up the genie's response.

"I... It makes me *fuzzy*," she said crossly. "The spitting lizard king didn't know who I am!"

"Excuse me, child?" said Gallows.

"He spat on me!" Grace said, her voice rising. "We were friends. But I got fuzzy. So he spat on me!"

Mr. Gallows' mind swam with confusion. I could feel him clearing his throat and waiting. Jumping on the opportunity, Sussanah filled in the details. "She really likes the lizards in the swamp."

"They're my friends," Grace's small voice piped up.

"Right. Friends."

"The humpback toads too."

"Yes, the toads too," Sussanah said patiently. "But Papa, the blessed water makes people fuzzy if they're not human."

"It veils them, yes," said Gallows. "For all our protection. It isn't perfect, I know, but given the things that come near, it's the best we can do."

"But the lizards don't know me," Grace said, crestfallen. Again, I could tell she was glancing up into the rafters, saddened further by whatever she saw.

I snuck a peek. There, curled on one of the rafters, I spotted a daddy-long legs spider, dangling against a web, clearly dead.

Grace sighed in tandem with my attention.

"Gracey," said Gallows, "you don't have to drink the water, of course. But... your siblings, they do, don't they?"

Grace wrinkled her nose. "Yeah... But they don't *like* the lizards."

"Well... That's a shame, isn't it? Lizards are noble creatures."

Grace wagged her head up and down.

"Still... Could you think about it a bit? I'll drink the water too. It's perfectly safe. It is only a danger to those who might try and harm the innocent. It's powerful you know—a blessing."

"I know," Grace said, moping. She sighed again.

While I couldn't quite track, or understand the politics of this water, the lizards, and the small genie child, I did feel a bout of sympathy. I turned around now, clearing my throat.

Grace looked up, her cheeks reddening and reminding me of Annie, once upon a time. The only friend I'd had at that age. What I wouldn't have given to grow up on a farm like this, surrounded by friends, by love, by safety...

I felt a lance of regret and pain, but pushed it aside. I had been deprived, but that didn't mean others had to be.

"I couldn't help but notice you glancing at the spider," I said.

The child stared at her feet, also mud-stained like Sussanah's, but then glanced at me again. "Yeah..." she said hesitantly, seemingly deciding—stranger or not—we shared an interest worthy of a response.

"Do you like spiders?" I thought back to my RV and the tarantulas on the ceiling.

"Yeah..." she said, hesitant. Then, she looked me in the eyes, as if trying to decide whether she would ignore me. Her mouth bunched in the corner again. She glanced at Sussanah, not quite looking to me, and, addressing her older friend, but directing the words to me, she said, bouncing up and down in delight, "I really, really like the fuzzy *big* ones. They're like small puppies. You can pet them and everything! And if you're nice, they don't even bite you!"

Sussanah tried to maintain an older child's imitation of mature, gracious approval, but she couldn't hold back a small snort of laughter and a wink towards Grace.

The genie looked back at me, frowning. "Do you like spiders? Your beard is fuzzy like a spider's legs you know. And you have lots of bites on your face."

I blinked and reached up, tracing my fingers through the scars on my chin. I shook my head. "I mean... I guess so. But my, er, bites, aren't from spiders. Look, though. See that fellow?"

I pointed to the rafters. She followed my gaze, staring at the dead spider in the web.

I reached out with my consciousness, extending my thoughts towards the thing... Spiders are soulless beings. It's one of the reasons, including how small they are, that I'm able to keep a connection with them at such a long range.

Up close, though, even dead, I can enter their tiny minds. "Watch closely," I murmured. Then, I pressed into the remnants of the spider's decaying motor capabilities. I took hold of the tiny thing's legs and eyes. It was still dead. Yet, with things this small, moving them required no more effort than a puppeteer's exertion.

Grace stared, wide-eyed as the spider began to twitch and move. She beamed, staring up as the daddy long legs suddenly disentangled from the web. I focused, moving the spider down one of the wooden beams and across a web.

Even with something this small, I could feel the *puppetting* begin to drain me. The initial effort came easily, but maintaining it was costly—especially with someone out of practice with such tricks.

Grace, though, watched wide-eyed as the small spider disappeared around one of the wooden columns. I quickly moved the spider, tucking it into the shadows beneath another beam, out of sight from the young genie.

"You brought it back to life!" she crowed, no longer bashful. Apparently, I'd made her 'nice' list.

She paused, darted forward, giving me a quick hug around the legs, then she scampered off.

"Grace, please think about the water!" Mr. Gallows called, hearing the thump of her small feet on the wooden steps.

"Okay, Papa Paul!" she called back.

"Really, I mean it—it keeps us all safe!"

His words were lost, though, as Grace raced towards the small bridge over the two lakes, joining some other children who were tossing pieces of bread to the ducks and giggling each time they managed to bounce their breadcrumbs off the ducks' feathered heads.

I stared at the idyllic scene, glancing towards where Paul Gallows sat. The sunlight dipped over the distant ring of trees, sheltering his hundred-acre farm. The mists of the veil rose above the leaves as if to meet the final rays of warming sunlight. Night was coming, and soon, the warmth would fade.

I shook my head, glancing towards where Preacher stood, his arms crossed, watching me. He regarded the rising mists and I sighed, nodding once.

We needed to test the tiger's eye against the veil before it got too dark. Our only hope of crossing the Threshold Seal of the Hollow was if we could move *into* the dungeon uninvited. But the Seal was strong—nothing living could enter without express permission from the queen of assassins herself—the Saboteur February.

Not to mention, I still had to *find* the blasted prison. But I'd thought up a solution for Percy. One that had been a long time coming.

"I have to go, Paul. Thanks again," I murmured. As I glanced down, I noted my hand, which had healed slower than the rest of me, seemed whole again. I winced, flexing my fingers, feeling a residue of ache.

Sometimes the healings took time, it seemed.

I waved goodbye, though he couldn't see me.

"May the Lord watch over you, Leonidas!" Paul called after me.

"Hopefully not too closely," I muttered.

And then, I hurried off towards Preacher, joining him by the lake and fishing into my coat pocket to pull out the small bag of tiger's eye I'd purchased from Kay Kelly.

Preacher grunted as I pulled up, glancing more significantly towards the fading mists now. The children on the bridge were now, as the sun-dipped, standing out clearer. I spotted scaled skin on some, slender necks tapered to pointed ears on others, even one child that had the lumpy, thick gray body—like molded rocks—of a tiny troll.

I shivered, glancing back towards the Blind Healer where he reclined in his rocking chair on the porch. The warmth of the orange light emanating from the two-story white farmhouse shone out into the dark, meeting where the first bits of shadow rose from the dusty ground.

I shivered, staring at it all, feeling as if, somehow, with each step I took away from the farmhouse, the colder the wind felt.

"Let's go test this thing," I muttered.

Preacher didn't speak at all, but moved with gusto, kicking up dust with his boots as we both hastened away, back up the path in the direction of the first ring of veiling mist. Preacher glanced at me, raising an eyebrow as we strode side-by-side, my legs moving double-time to keep up with his gait. He signed with a hand in front of his mouth. He inched his eyebrows.

"Yes," I said. "Nearly good as new. He didn't quite get the hand, but it's healing itself. I barely feel a thing."

Preacher nodded.

"You know, most people would kill to have a father like yours."

Preacher stared straight ahead. He went rigid as he walked now, doubling his pace.

"I mean it," I said, growling and refusing to speed up out of spite alone.

Preacher ignored me, his large shoulders hunched as if against a sudden chill wind as he strode towards the nearest ring of mist, and I reluctantly followed.

My frustration with Preacher was short-lived, though. The tiger's eye would *have* to work against the farm's veil. If it didn't, it certainly wouldn't work on the Threshold Seal. We'd be left with no way into the Hollow. And once night fell complete, I'd have to deal with Percy.

That particular part of the job, though, I'd have to do on my own. Preacher would lock me in the RV if he knew what I was planning in order to get the location of the Hollow.

Chapter 30

Preacher stationed himself on one side of the dusty farm road. I stood on the other, one shoulder pressed to the sap-slicked bark of a bleeding maple. The tendrils of mist seemed to have dissipated for the most part beneath the final rays of sun as darkness came complete. The glimmers and glances from moonlight extended over the farm road, bathing the ground in blues and grays.

Preacher paused, frowning into the shadowed woods.

The veil would be weakest in the dark—the best way to at least test our only shot at entry. The tiger's eye would teleport its thrower a short distance. But could it pass through a magical blockade? If it didn't work on this veil, it certainly wouldn't work on the Threshold Seal of the Hollow.

"Nothing for it, I suppose," I murmured. "If we wait any longer, the veil will be completely gone."

The distant sound of children playing had faded somewhat as the Gallows orphans retreated under the cover of night. The farmhouse itself carried its own, deeper protections which could even stand against the encroaching darkness, but now, out among the farmstead itself, we stood exposed.

I pulled a single gelatinous pack from inside my jacket pocket. The small tiger's eye felt squishy and soft beneath my fingers. It was little larger than a dishwasher pack where the gold and brown shimmer trapped within swirled and strained against the thin walls of its confines.

I dabbed my tongue against chapped lips, feeling the dry ridges. "Here it goes," I murmured.

Preacher simply watched.

Then, I hefted the tiger's eye and tossed it *through* the mist, aiming just to the left of where my friend stood. It slammed into a nearby tree, exploding on impact. Instantly, I sensed a familiar sucking in my belly, as if a hook had been wrapped around my navel.

I felt myself lessen, lightening like vapor. My vision swam, and my eyes dotted with black spots. Everything seemed to spin and swirl, and I felt myself sucked forward, jettisoned as if by a sudden beam of light.

A second later, as my vision cleared, though, I realized I hadn't moved an inch.

The final flitter of the passing mist veil seemed to twirl and wave, like the cheeky gesture of a teasing hand.

My brow darkened. "Well... that's not a good start," I murmured. I pulled a second, squishy pouch from my pocket, hefting this tiger's eye and aiming towards the mist a second time. Had Kay given me a bad batch?

I threw this tiger's eye as well, aiming towards the faintest portion of the lifting mist veil.

Again, I felt the swirling sensation, again, my eyes darkened, and again, nearly instantly, I re-emerged standing exactly where I'd been moments before.

"Bad batch," I said out loud, growling now. "It must be."

I turned, facing up the road, pulling a third pouch from my pocket and tossing it in the opposite direction of the mist. This time, however, my vision swam, my stomach twisted, and I blinked out of existence in one location and was teleported twenty feet ahead towards where the burst detergent pod had left a wet streak against the dirt beneath the moon.

I spun around, staring at Preacher. "Vyle's teeth," I snapped, my stomach twisting in sheer disappointment. "What's the use of these cursed things. Can't even breach a weakened veil. Pathetic. No way they'll pass a Seal."

Preacher watched, an eyebrow raised.

I could feel my stomach twisting, feeling the full weight of our predicament settle on my shoulders like the leprous grip of death. "Corker's breath," I cursed. "There's no way in other than dead. No living thing can enter the Hollow without the saboteur's permission... It's impossible."

Preacher shrugged, waving his hand like a conductor's wand in a single flourish indicating East and West.

I scowled. "I know we still have to locate the thing. I have a plan."

He quirked an eyebrow.

I sighed, glancing up. "Thought about ambushing the blighter, but he'd see it coming. No... I've got another idea." A far more *painful* idea, but I didn't mention this part. "But even if we locate the thing, what's the point? We can't cross the Threshold Seal. These things sure as hells don't work." I tapped the remaining tiger's eye.

Preacher pointed at his head and I extended my own mind.

Preacher thought, *Permission?*

"How, though? We just waltz up and ask February herself if she wouldn't mind a cup of tea and a tour?" I snorted. "She'll kill us before we get within ten miles. Don't forget, someone murdered a saboteur. She's not going to take strangers in. Especially us. There's no controlling that scenario. For all we know, she'd torture us and find out..." I shivered. "Well, find out *what* she actually has inside that prison of hers."

I felt a blossom of cold in my chest. "No..." I said, "We can't risk letting anyone else know the goal."

What then?

"I... I truly don't know."

We have to think of something. You gave your oath as a Wit.

"Don't know what?" said a sudden voice from near the portion of woods Preacher had been glancing to earlier.

My companion and I both turned sharply, staring into the dark shadows.

Stepping from the forest, gliding through the trees, Annie emerged, her gray backpack slung over one shoulder, her green eyes fixed on me in the night, and her peacoat settled around her. One hand gripped the silver flask she always carried, tipping it and taking a slow sip.

She swallowed once then lowered the flask. "Don't know what?" she repeated, staring at me.

I blinked, feeling a slow shiver up my spine. Preacher, though, wasn't watching Annie. Instead, his eyes were fixed on her shadow. A shadow which was *moving* far too much. For one, the shadow seemed *larger* than the moon should have allowed, than the cover of trees above her should have permitted. For another, the shadow seemed to twist and curl, like a fluttering curtain in an open window.

I stared at the shadow, my eyes darting back up to Annie. A few things could affect shadows in such ways... none of them nice.

"I didn't see you there," I said quietly. "I thought you were waiting back in the RV."

"I came to see what was taking so long," she replied simply, her usual smile lessening somewhat, the ever-present dimples on her cheeks fading. And yet now, I could just glimpse *things* beneath the surface of her calm facade; something in her gaze.

"I... What do you want with my brother?" I said, switching track now and going on the offensive. I wasn't sure how much she'd heard. Only the last part? I couldn't lie either way.

Her shadow distracted me again. It fluttered around her, as if bathing her feet in darkness.

Preacher had gone rigid, staring at the back of Annie's head. His eyes narrowed in the same suspicious glare they'd held back in the upper floor of the Jester's mansion. Now, though, his hand was moving towards one of his shooters.

"Wait a moment," I said quickly.

Annie glanced back, twisting her head, one eye now on Preacher, her silhouette cutting an imposing profile against the night.

"I wouldn't," she cautioned sharply.

Preacher went for his gun.

"Don't!" I shouted.

Two six-shooters now rose, pointing directly at Annie's shaved head. She went still; Preacher stood like unassailable granite. I felt my own heart hammering desperately in my chest.

"You don't understand," Annie replied, breathing heavily. "Neither of you. Don't do anything rash."

Her shadow was moving again. This time spreading *out* like oil on a slick floor, moving, covering everything it touched, and heading towards Preacher.

He growled, eyes narrowed, taking a step back from the extending blackness. Was it just me, or did the shadow almost resemble an opening maw? Like the mouth of some great whale, teeth displayed against the detritus of the forest in wispy black streaks of absent light.

The three of us stood on the dusty farm road, beneath the rising moon and the fading mist.

And then Annie spoke again... Except this time, it didn't seem as if she were addressing either of us. "No, no I've got this," she murmured beneath her breath, tucking her chin against her chest and speaking quietly. Her cheeks reddened a bit as if she were embarrassed by our attention. She twisted slightly, staring off into the trees, one foot tapping energetically, one hand twisting around a small ring of woven pine-needles she had made.

"No," Annie said, a bit more insistently. "No, please. You don't have to. I'm okay. They're friends."

I stared, unblinking, my heart thundering. Preacher also watched; his weapons still raised.

And then...

A new voice entered the clearing.

A voice from Annie's lips, but deeper, colder. Not the cheerful, playful voice of my gregarious friend. Not the curious, inquisitive tone, friendly and accommodating. Annie suddenly went still. Her foot stopped tapping, her fingers stopped twisting. She stood taller, prouder, her chin angled. Even the red flush in her cheeks at the embarrassment of having us watch this strange spectacle faded.

The colder voice said, "Hush, child, I will attend this."

A prickle sped up my spine.

Just then, Annie ducked her head once more, and her physical transformation reverted. She twitched and fidgeted again, all the more; her voice was gentle, soft and pleading again. "No, no it's fine," she said. "He doesn't mean it. He's Leon's friend. He's just scared for him."

The other voice returned, Annie's own lips moving. "No, dear. These are dangerous folk, like I told you. Allow me to speak with them."

I stared, eyes bulging as one of Annie's hands went still, reaching up and caressing her own hair. The same, stiff hand lowered, patting Annie above the chest as if she were consoling herself.

Her body seemed at war with itself. An energetic, excited, twitching and playful nature suddenly conceding to rigidity, to an iron bearing, to a proud posture.

"Please," Annie's voice whispered one last time.

"When have I ever led you wrong, little one?" came the ominous reply of the dark, deep voice. The same voice I'd briefly heard her use on Grendel. The same voice in the mansion when she'd demanded my oath.

And then, Annie looked up, suddenly.

She was no longer sniffling, no longer pleading. She didn't blink, didn't fidget. It was as if someone had installed a rod of ice in her spine. She stared coolly from me to Preacher, then back.

"Leonidas," she murmured, nodding her head once at me. "Curb your ape, before I do."

I swallowed, my throat parched all of a sudden. I could feel the prickle still spreading across my skin. Could feel my gaze fixated on Annie, trying to search out my old, childhood friend. Her eyes were still green, but different now. Darker, brooding, suspicious.

"Who—who are you?" I murmured, one hand straying towards the knife at my hip.

"I am Annie," the proud voice replied.

"I—I don't understand."

She let out a weary, impatient little sigh, her shadow still swirling about her feet. "I am the part of your childhood friend, Leon, that kept her safe for the last twenty-three years." Her fingers still lingered near her collarbone where she'd been gently patting Annie's chest. Now, though, those same fingers curled into a fist and the hand fell to her thigh. She murmured, "No one else would keep her safe. So I had to."

"You're... you're what? A demon?"

The woman in front of me scoffed. "A demon? Do you really believe I would allow a *demon* any level of favor in my life? Pshaw! For a mind-reader, your imagination is quite limited."

"What then?" I said, forgetting, in my own shock, my mounting fear.

"I am Annie," she said simply. "That's as clear as I know to make it."

"You're a split personality?" I asked.

"Call me what you want. I am a protector, first and foremost. And you," she said, her eyes suddenly rounding on Preacher, "need to stop aiming your weapons at me."

Annie had turned fully to face Preacher now. One of her hands moved into her gray, military backpack. The other darted into her peacoat, replacing the flask, but staying hidden from sight as if reaching for a weapon of her own. I didn't remember seeing her armed before.

"Annie," I said sharply. "Preacher!"

But my two friends ignored me. How much had Annie heard? Who—who was this? Like my poltergeist, perhaps? Except her personality had fractured rather than her spirit? We were always made of similar stuff, her and I. I could still feel the chill across my skin as I stared at my strange friend and her even stranger shadow. What did she want with my brother, anyway? She'd been cryptic back in the Jester's mansion.

Preacher's distrust seemed to have reached a crescendo. Despite the spreading shadow, despite Annie facing him, completely absent of any strain of fear, he kept his own weapons raised, pointed at her head.

"Don't..." she murmured, her voice almost echoing as if carried by whispers from the trees and grass.

Preacher cleared his throat, his fingers taut on the triggers.

Preacher! Don't! I yelled in his head.

His auburn gaze flicked over Annie's shoulder, fixed on me for the faintest moment. *She's not what she seems, Leon. This is all wrong.*

"Annie! Please—stop! Let's talk!"

Her back was to me now, her face directed at my large friend. "I am not the one pointing weapons," her voice resounded clear and crisp.

She's a liar, Leon, Preacher pressed, hard. *A devil's agent in disguise.* He paused for a moment, tilting his head as if studying her. *What if...* his thoughts echoed in my mind's connection. *What if I shine a light beneath the rock? Hmm?* A sudden look of iron certainty crossed his expression. He nodded once, and then he shot her.

Both barrels flashed, light streaking the dark. My friend didn't miss—he was the single best shot I knew. And yet, suddenly, as he fired, the shadow pooling at Annie's feet rose up like a wave. The bullets slammed into a suddenly solid wall of shade. Sparks flew, shadows swirled, and Annie moved.

Except... she stepped *into* the wall of shadow as if it were a doorway of sorts.

She moved through the shade and at the same time, half of her body was still in the shadow while the other half emerged from the darkness beneath an oak tree behind Preacher's back. It was like watching someone step through a portal.

Preacher, though, whirled around, firing again.

Annie moved once more, this time *dropping* through a pool of shadow beneath the tree as if falling through a manhole, then slipping out of the darkness in the lowest boughs of a tree on the opposite side of the road.

Her own shadow reformed, creating steps, which she took, slowly, moving down the black stairs towards where Preacher stood, his guns whirling about again.

He didn't fire now, but he flashed a wicked grin. *Told you,* he said in my mind. He crossed himself, murmuring a silent prayer to ward off evil.

Annie had pulled something from within her peacoat, and it now glinted and gleamed in the moonlight, sending a cascade of rainbow colors sparkling across the ground.

A dagger at first—seemingly made of pure green crystal. But, as I watched, the emerald, glassy blade reformed. Portions and pieces of quartz bled on top of each other, flooding forward like a sudden glaze of ice overtaking a rail top. The emerald crystal extended now and a single, wicked spear spread from Annie's hand, pointing out across the path in Preacher's direction.

Her voice seemed hoarse, ragged now, echoing with the many whispers spreading from the shadows in every corner she touched. "You shouldn't have done that," she hissed, something serpentine about the whispering, echoing quality of her vibrating voice.

My mouth lay unhinged and I stared at the emerald wereblade in her hand. I glanced towards her gray backpack, which lay discarded in the lowest branch of the tree she'd stepped from.

There, just visible over the lip of her backpack, I spotted two prongs of a horned, metal helmet. Difficult to determine in the dark, but even from here, I could see the furious molten orange scrawl twisting and swirling in serpentine patterns over the cast iron headpiece.

A helmet I recognized—the stories abounded.

I breathed slowly, sucking air through my teeth until they hurt. Suddenly, I felt exposed, vulnerable. I remained rooted to the spot, my eyes the size of coins as I stared at my childhood friend.

"Satyr's hooves," I said, my own voice echoing. My face felt numb, my hands twitching near my waist. Every muscle in me seemed poised for action, but simultaneously drowned in an emotion I loathed: pure fear. I gaped. My eyes traced from the horrifying helmet, barely visible on the branch, and its evil, swirling scrawl, darting over to the emerald wereblade held loosely in a practiced hand, and at last, settling on the shadows which were now waving and twisting and undulating like snakes at her feet.

Through numb lips, I managed to eke out the words, "Dear gods, Annie, you're a skinting saboteur."

Chapter 31

"Leonidas," Annie said, her voice echoing once more with a thousand whispers. The foliage above shivered with the sound, and the ivy along the bark trembled. "Let me explain!"

I stalled, stuck between horror and grief. My friend—my childhood friend—A saboteur? A demon with a devilish blade, the bane of the eternals. I stumbled back, scattering dirt and trying to suppress the rising tide of sheer terror reverberating in my chest. This odd combination of sweet and gentle one moment, cold and deadly the other didn't echo in any of the stories of the saboteurs. I supposed this split-personality was something unique to Annie herself, just like her gift of *seeing*. But even more than her trauma-induced coping mechanisms, even more than some secret gift, the fact she was a saboteur demanded most of my horror and shock.

"Leonidas," she pressed.

I stood on the precipice of terror and stared unseeing at Annie. I'd been blind; allowing my own allegiance to cloud my judgment. Annie hadn't been resurrected. She'd been reforged.

A weapon now stood in front of me, amidst a slew of shadows and shade, an emerald blade in one hand. Her mask remained on the branch, jutting from the backpack. A small part of my conscience tugged at me, trying to point out the mask. If she really was a threat, wouldn't she have armored herself? If she meant us harm, surely she would have attacked before.

But horror rose just as quick to snuff out the gentle flames of reason.

Annie was a weapon forged in the Twilight Citadel, the hidden home of the saboteurs. A pocket realm, it was said—accessible only by the order itself. The saboteurs were assassins, trained by the Shademaker and chosen by their fabled wereblades. They weren't eternal kin—their talents, their powers went deeper, darker. Magic from the gates of heaven and the bowels of Hades.

A vile order. The saboteurs saw themselves as the defenders of the unknowing, but their defense took the form of a culling. They hunted creatures and beings in the Hidden Kingdoms as much as they hunted eternals. Their code of justice and duty was impossible to fathom.

Now, I knew why Grendel had called her mistress. Now I knew why the Hillbilly Godfather had treated her with respect, refusing to confiscate her weapon. The wereblade of a saboteur was dearer to them than their own fingers or eyes. They'd sooner part from their heart than their blades.

"Leonidas," Annie called, her voice pulsing from behind the trees, carried on the whisking mist. It came from nowhere and everywhere all at once, like streams of wind forming a gale. "Please, hear me!"

My hand went instinctively to my thigh strap as I continued to backpedal, fingers groping towards the cold metal of the dagger.

She's a demon! Preacher's thoughts came reverberating in my head. *You can't trust one married to nightfall!*

I glanced over at my friend, blinking and trying to adjust, trying to catch my raging thoughts, my slicing terror. I wanted to run towards him, to cry out. Preacher had been suspicious from the start—I should have trusted him.

Now his weapons still pointed at Annie. He seemed waiting for her attack, or for my call for violence. As the congealing darkness slithered about her feet, moving and cocooning her footsteps, I felt the urge to shout. But at the same time, her voice met me, and my eyes attended her gaze—glinting blue flecked with indigo meeting flashing emerald above a dusty farm road.

"How could you..." I murmured, my voice strained.

The shadows moved like waves and swallowed Annie whole. They pooled on the ground like spilled ink and spread rapidly towards me. Then, reemerging from the very pool of darkness, Annie reformed, covering the distance from the trees to my feet in the blink of an eye.

A million voices now whispered in my ear. "Leonidas... *listen.*"

The pool of darkness suddenly rose around us like walls, cutting off sight from the forest, of Preacher, of the road itself. I stood as if in a jail cell, surrounded by absent-light. And Annie stepped from the folds of the shade, standing in front of me.

Her wereblade was no longer a spear, now reforming, the glinting green crystal melted back like ice beneath hot water, forming a simple knife, which she then stowed in her coat.

"Tell your ally," this cold version of my friend murmured, "to stay his triggers. I don't want this, Leonidas. I'm not here to hurt anyone."

At the same time, I could feel Preacher's wild thoughts. I could hear the sound of his feet scraping in dirt, could hear him grunting and cursing as if fighting through a deep thicket. Even as I had the thought, around me, portions of the room of black twisted, and sharp thorns and roots of sheer smoke protruded through the walls, like a sea beast swimming through an otherwise still lake.

I heard more shouting. A gunshot.

"What are you doing to him!" I yelled, extending my mind.

"Nothing, holding him back is all," she whispered. "Please, Leonidas, listen to me. Calm your friend. *Listen.*"

I stared at her, not blinking, my mind grazing Preacher's. She'd been honest; he wasn't hurt. I could just feel the surface thoughts, the wild action. He was frightened for me, contending with a never-ending hydra of thorny roots extending from a wall of shadow on the other side of my black cell.

"Preacher... care... I'm fine," I murmured, pressing the words to his mind.

I could feel my companion go still, his mind still racing. *Leon, get out of there! She'll kill you—she'll harvest your soul!*

I looked into Annie's eyes. I knew the stories of the saboteurs. Though I'd only ever met one close-up once before—nearly a decade ago. Little more than a dark memory. I'd forgotten what I'd seen, mostly. Forgotten the things I'd encountered. As if, like shadows themselves, the memories of the saboteurs would flit away quicker than usual.

"Are you here to murder me?" I whispered.

Annie blinked suddenly. Her cold, rattling voice was replaced by a sudden sobbing sigh. She shook her head as if shaking from a dream. For a moment, she stared at me, her foot tapping again, her fingers twisting around and around the band of woven pine-needles still wrapped around her fingers. Her shadow went slowly still, like gossamer cloth dropped by a dying wind, though the small room of darkness remained.

Then Annie began to cry. Tears slipped from her eyes, tracing the inside of her nose and dripped down to her chin. "No," she said at last, still crying. "Oh gosh, I'm so, so sorry. I—I didn't mean to scare you. No, hang on. Let me talk to him. No—I want to." She shook her head, addressing these last comments to some unseen voice. She winced as if against a headache, but then looked at me once more, her eyes still soft. "Please, Leon. Please, believe me. I need your help. I didn't lie about that."

"Who are you talking to? Who was that just now?" I said, my chest rising and falling rapidly.

Annie stared at the ground again, her cheeks red. "I—it's so embarrassing. She's, I mean—well, I don't know how to say it, so I'm just, yeah, I'm just going to say it. I guess she's me. Or, I'm her. Or... It's strange. I know." She winced, staring at me as if bracing for a blow. In her eyes I glimpsed foreboding of a kind.

It wasn't a physical sense of fear, nor was it some type of anxiety on the cusp of danger.

She seemed braced for what my response would be. Worried I might dislike her now that I'd seen beneath the mask.

I swallowed again. "Annie... It is strange, but I am fine with strange. A fractured part of my spirit haunts me. Preacher hasn't spoken a word in ten years. Trauma does strange things to people. I'm not angry with you."

She beamed. "Oh yay! You're not!" She rushed in, hugging me tight. She seemed to sense me stiffen, though, and quickly withdrew, a hurt look in her eyes.

"Whatever she is... or... or you are... I don't know—"

"She protected me," Annie said quickly, not even pausing to take a breath in her rush to speak. "She came to protect me when I was little. When I couldn't take care of myself. She said I wasn't tough enough. And—and I guess I wasn't. I don't think I would've survived without her..."

"I understand that," I murmured. "But you're also a *saboteur*." Here, my words went hard.

"I... I—yes..." She stared at her feet, one hand clasping at her arm, looking so small all of a sudden, even in this cocoon of shadow she'd created.

I refused to look towards the roiling walls of darkness. Instead, I murmured, "Which one?"

"I—excuse me?"

"There are twelve in your order, yes?" I said, my voice shaking. "The Regent January, the Lieutenant February, down through murdered July and to the youngest December. All of you killers. Who are you?"

"I... November. I'm young too, Leon. They only let me out two years ago. You have to understand."

"Let you out?"

She stood outlined against the backdrop of swirling shadow, her tears still slipping down her cheeks, but I refused to be entranced so easily this time. I could feel my heart hardening. At the same time, I pulled my consciousness, extending my mind to hers.

No fear. Again, as if somehow the capacity for fear had been cut from her. I'd heard similar claims of the saboteurs. They weren't natural—weren't normal.

But still, even without fear, I glimpsed *things* rising to the surface.

"Your helmet," I whispered. "It makes you invisible to the eternals, doesn't it?"

She nodded once, still staring at me. "I don't need it, do I? I'm not trying to hurt anyone. I just need your help, please," she sobbed.

The helmets of a saboteur carried the swirling molten letters from an ancient, forgotten language—the helmets were protection against my kind. The Wit couldn't break through the helmets. A saboteur in their *full* armor, couldn't be affected by *any* of the eternal talents. Not the Kindred, nor the Potents, nor the Alchemists, nor the Wits, nor the Blessed nor the Elementalists. The armor made them immune to magic, to power.

This coupled with their own dark devices—now witnessed as a tornado of shadow around me—and their wereblades, plus years of dedicated training to the art of murder, made them near insurmountable foes. Perhaps even enough to contend with the archangels. Some supposed Regent January—with a bit of luck— could even kill one of the lesser gods.

As my mind grazed Annie's, though, I glimpsed images, thoughts...

Again, in the swirling darkness of her mind, I spotted a child, chained to a cold floor. I heard the slithering sound of some serpent, then the scream of the child in agony. A tattered, dirty shirt clad the child's trembling form. The image swam, and I found myself peering at two green eyes in a tiny cell.

Annie. She couldn't have been older than six in the memory. Her body covered in bruises, the cobblestone floors dappled wet from tears. I suddenly heard a clanging in the memory, and a door flung open, causing light to stream in, rising up around the body of a man in a hat and a cloak. The man in the hat stepped into the room—he had a heavy walking stick in one hand.

The small child in the cell whimpered, pulling back.

A voice echoed in the dark, just audible to me before the memory faded. *"You'll thank me for the pain, one day... Be grateful. Agony breeds greatness... Now hold out your hand."*

The last thing I heard was a terrible scream and then the memory vanished.

Chapter 32

I stared at Annie, wide-eyed, wondering if she'd realized what I'd seen.

Her eyes brimmed with tears, and she was trembling now. As if sensing her pain, some of the shadows lifted from the wall and moved towards her, sliding up her legs, and over her arms as if trying to soothe or protect her.

I felt a chill of revulsion at the undulating darkness.

"Why are you really going to the Hollow?" I growled. "Tell me! No more lies..."

Annie swallowed, staring now, her green eyes turning gray for a moment. She blinked and they flashed back to emerald. Her features went stony once more, her shadows moving once again. Her voice hardened and now it was November speaking to me, "I need your help. Let that suffice. I mean you no harm!"

I scowled back. "I don't know you anymore. Tell me the truth. Why are you interested in the Hollow!"

"You gave me your word!" she reminded me.

"I gave my word to a liar."

"I am no liar. I really do need to find your brother..." The saboteur trailed off, as if glancing over her shoulder and watching something *in* the shadows. She tilted her head, listening. Her voice once more thrummed in the darkness, like a million whispers coalesced, and yet the tone still held pain.

"July was murdered," I said. "A saboteur, dead. Now another saboteur wants to break into the very prison the murdered assassin was rumored to be headed to. Why do you want my brother? Why not just go to February yourself. You're one of her orders, aren't you? Enter the prison of your own volition."

"I can't," November whispered... "Not now. Not even when it's locatable."

"Why not!" I growled.

"Because!" she screamed, "I have to find who killed July! I have to find them before I go to February or I'll be killed. Tasked with protecting July, I was told to escort July safely to the Hollow. Something is going on, Leonidas. Something stirring in the dark. Not just among the eternals, but also in the Stormer region, the Hidden Kingdoms, the Celestial heavens—armies are rising, whispers of war have reached even my ears. Things best left sleeping are waking."

"What does any of that have to do with me?"

"I need your help to reach your brother!"

"Why!" I screamed.

"Because I think he killed July!" November retorted. She exhaled now, her thin chest rising and falling, her hands at her side, fingers loose. She stared, pleading. "If I can't prove it—if they don't believe me, my life is forfeit. I failed to protect July. A superior was murdered."

"You saw my brother kill her?" My face felt numb as these words left my lips.

She glanced off and shook her head. "I wasn't with July. I was supposed to be but I thought she would be fine with six cordials guarding her. The soldiers of the Twilight Citadel and the servants of the saboteurs are usually more than enough to protect their masters. It was July. She's stronger than me. I'm only November."

"I don't understand."

"You don't have to. The politics of the Twilight Citadel are irrelevant. Suffice it to say, cracks have been forming in my order."

"Your order? The saboteurs—you claim them so lightly."

The shadows now roiled around November, rising and bubbling and spreading even further towards the sky like a jutting finger meeting the clouds. "Ought I not?" November said, her voice booming now. "Am I not of their breed and breaking? Do you not see me, Leonidas, as I truly am?"

As she spoke, her voice echoing, I heard a slithering sound. Behind her, there was movement in the black wall. Like the hand of a satyr through wood, an arm of shade moved through the darkness, carrying something hooked on its tentacle.

Annie's backpack. She reached out with imperious fingers, lifting the scrawled helmet from within the open bag, holding it on the edge of two fingers, and staring at the molten letters twisting and writhing across the naked metal.

The helmet itself seemed like the head of some decapitated horned eagle. The three horns encircled the skull, jutting up and pointing like the prongs of a crown at the sky. The helmet itself had no visible eyeholes nor mouth opening. Red letters, gouged into the metal as if by magma, continued to shift and spill around the helmet, circling over one side, down the other. The words were indeterminable to me. I'd heard rumors the letters themselves were ancient curses circling like halos. I'd also been told the lettering scrawled names of the dead, an endless spiral testifying to the pillage of the Twilight Citadel and the Shademaker.

The truth, though, was likely something worse.

November donned the three horned helmet. No visor, no eyes, no mouth. The helmet swallowed my friend's face in metal and magma and horns.

"Stay out of my mind, Leonidas!" she said now, her voice deeper still, resounding from the darkness. "You *must* help! You must find and enter the Hollow, break into that cursed prison. I cannot be seen by the lieutenant of my order, or it would spell my *death*. The death of two saboteurs, Leonidas—do you know what that would mean?"

Her voice increased in volume, the swirling molten scrawl continuing to spin and spin in dizzying patterns. I even found myself glancing away, my head aching, my eyes strained as I stared, in near relief, at the shadowy ground. Even the shadows, though, seemed to have gone still, as if out of respect for November's cry.

"The saboteurs stand between the third heaven and the second!" She called, her voice echoing. "They stand against the celestial hosts—against the sons of the gods themselves. They stand against the children of Hades, defending the plight of mankind!"

"You murder eternals!"

She scoffed, her voice hard all of a sudden. "We protect the sheep from vengeful shepherds. A person is a person, Leonidas. We simply champion their cause."

"You've killed creatures too—Sphinx and minotaur."

"They are allied to humanity," November said, her voice still deep and dark. The molten scrawl of the helmet seemed to have slowed a bit, leaving me staring at old, glowing runes etched into cast iron. I missed my friend's eyes. Now, as I reached out, my mind collided only with darkness—I winced against the absence. There was no mind before me, no mind I could see. The helmet had erased her from my grasp.

I snarled and tried to reach out again; I could still sense Preacher just outside the wall of black, poised and waiting, wondering if he should try to break through. He couldn't see us.

But when I returned my power to Annie, again, I was held back by an entire absence, not just of fear this time, but of all memory and thought. The helmet of a saboteur, then, did exactly as I'd been warned.

If November wanted, I'd die in this dust.

And yet, she hadn't killed me. Certainly not the kind-hearted, gregarious, prattling friend with ill manners. But also not this cold, cruel queen of shadow. Could she be telling the truth now? The saboteurs saw themselves as soldiers against the demons, the ancient gods, the angels, and any of the magical creatures or beings which might set themselves against mankind. I supposed it made sense, then, they might go after the eternals too. Those of the Imperium weren't particularly kind to the unknowing. In fact, I knew firsthand that one of my father's cousins had been taking humans captive from the towns around Seattle and dragging them to the mountains as slaves.

A saboteur—March, if I remembered correctly—had killed him and all his minions in the mineshaft. But now that I thought of it, I did remember the saboteur hadn't harmed the unknowings. When I'd been told the story, the captive mortals had warranted little more than a passing comment. I stared at my friend's iron-encased head, my eyes darting from the magma scrawl to the jagged metal horns.

"You believe my brother killed your saboteur, then?" I said. I waited, watching, wondering if she *knew*. Truly *knew* what my brother's release would mean. "How?" I said quietly. "He's trapped."

"He still remains imprisoned," Annie answered, her voice dropping again to a calmer tone. Her shadows stopped moving so wildly. Her words softened suddenly, and she winced, massaging at the back of her neck. "Sorry, Leon. I'm—I'm sorry. I don't know how he left the prison—I really, really wish I did. But I don't. I don't know how he," she dropped her voice to a whisper, shuddering as she spoke this next word, "*killed* July, then returned. She was guarded by cordials, guarded by shadows, and armed with her own blade and helmet..."

Annie shrugged helplessly. Something about the gesture coming from one clad in that helmet, carrying that hidden blade didn't seem right.

"I... You're sure it was him?"

Annie hesitated. "I have to check, Leon. Please, please, I have to. I just know I do. It's the only way! You're so good at helping people. I know that about you. But I have to *know.*"

I stood on the edge... Was she telling another lie? I couldn't reach out and see. Her helmet had erased her from my grasp. But either way, her eyes were set on my brother. If he had found a way to escape, even temporarily, to murder a saboteur, then I needed to know. How would he have, though? The Unlocator spell couldn't be avoided... It didn't make sense.

"Leon," Annie said, "we still don't even know where the Hollow is."

"I'm working on it," I said. "I—I have a play. Just me, but I needed nightfall."

She shrugged. "It's night."

My stomach twisted at these words. The Percy problem couldn't wait much longer. She was right. I had to find the location of the prison, or all of our work would be wasted. Then again, didn't this change everything? Annie wasn't who I thought... But if anything that only made it more urgent I sabotage the mission. The only way to stop Napoleon's release, this year or the next, was to put a bullet in his skull. Annie's lies didn't change anything. I still had to finish this.

"Drop the shadows," I whispered. "Please. I need to talk with my friend."

November stood still. A cold voice, "Tell Preacher not to shoot and I'll lower the walls."

My fingers probed into the smokey substance and came away without sensation, as if I'd simply waved my hand through a beam of light. "Curious..." I murmured. Then, louder, I called, "Preacher, don't shoot! We're going to talk!" Quieter, I said, "As long as you don't hurt me, he won't."

Then, Annie's hands dropped to her sides. At the same time, the walls of shadow, the undulating thorns and roots all fell, like water pouring to the ground. The shadows shifted and rolled, then, all at once, fled back into Annie's own shadow, leaving the three of us once more standing exposed on the lonely road. I could only hope

Preacher wouldn't shoot first—he could be quite obstinate where my safety was concerned. But the last thing I needed now was for Annie and Preacher to come to blows.

I didn't need another corpse on my conscience.

Chapter 33

Off to the side, Preacher watched me, hard, his eyes widened.

"I'm fine," I said, feeling parched.

Preacher kept his six shooters still half-raised, though, for the moment, angled off.

"She says she's investigating the murder of the saboteur outside the Hollow territory," I murmured. "Says she's sorry she misled."

Preacher gave me a hard look and an adamant shake of his head. November snorted, and Preacher turned his glare on her, his right hand twitching, the weapon glinting in the rising moon.

"If you attack," she said darkly, "I'll remove my protection from you. The only reason you're not in the belly of that Kindred right now is because I vouched for you!"

Preacher didn't look impressed. His suspicion and distrust were scrawled across his glare.

"Maybe she's..." I began, but Preacher cut me off with a look and another sharp shake of his head.

Come on, I said in his mind. *She lied, but now we know. She hasn't killed us. Besides, she's right about Grendel. He'll come for us again without her.*

Preacher scowled. *Think with your head, Leon. She's a saboteur. She'll kill us. She's not right in the head— look at her!*

"Preacher," I murmured. "Which of us is? You don't have to trust her. But what choice do we have?"

For a moment, he glanced over his shoulder again, in the direction of the forest. Was that a shadow moving in the trees? A glint of golden eyes amidst the woods?

I shivered, but shook my head. I extended my mind, but found nothing. Grendel wasn't nearby. He couldn't be. Just my imagination playing tricks.

Still, Preacher returned his attention to Annie, then me. Again, he shook his head.

"We can't abandon this," I said, pressing on the words now. In his mind, I added *my brother can't fall into the wrong hands. You know this!*

Preacher huffed a breath, his auburn eyes turning, his large frame strained as he rolled his head, shifting back and forth from one shoulder to the other. He danced from foot to foot for a moment, like a boxer warming up for a bout.

For a moment, I thought he might even lower his six shooter.

And then...

My poltergeist appeared.

Directly between Annie and Preacher. As luck would have it—or, perhaps—as my evil, six-year-old self had calculated, neither of them was looking at the other. Preacher was still staring up at the moon, lost in thought. Annie had glanced off towards the forest in the same direction Preacher had watched before.

My blue-eyed poltergeist stood in the dusty road. The child, wearing the uniform of an imperial academy, grinned at me. His ghostly face winked. My poltergeist snapped my guitar strings to rob me of joy. I should have known he wouldn't allow me the wealth of friends. He reached out, one tiny finger moving towards Preacher's trigger fingers.

"Don't!" I said sharply.

The Poltergeist pushed *hard* then vanished in the middle of the road.

Preacher's gun went off. At the same time, Annie spun as well, her wereblade emerging like lightning from her coat. This time, the reforming emerald crystal created a medieval shield which caught the bullet in a shower of sparks.

November howled, "Coward!"

Preacher growled, his fingers flexing. *That* girl *touched my gun, Leon!*

"No—no!" I said hurriedly. "It wasn't him!"

My own mind panicked. My poltergeist would often tear or break things that were important to me. My guitar strings, yes, but also smashing my mirror. Now, though, he was intervening with my companions... He was escalating.

No sooner had the thought occurred to me, accompanied by a horrified shiver, I had to put the consideration on pause to prevent bloodshed.

"It wasn't Preacher! She didn't touch your gun!" I yelled. "Stop!"

November glared at me, her eyes fixed. "This won't work, Leonidas," she said firmly. "Not with him!" she jammed a finger towards Preacher. For a moment, though, I felt like I detected something *else* beneath the words. Not just fury, not just frustration... But jealousy?

My face pressed in a frown at the thought. Those bankrupt for friends, I knew from experience, guarded the few they had fiercely.

I swallowed, glancing where Preacher was still standing, his fist curled protectively around his shooter. November glared back.

"Choose, Leonidas!" she demanded. "Remember who we were! Remember how we were born! This lumpy-eared *thug* is nothing! He's only dead weight!"

I swallowed, hesitating, shaking my head. "Annie, it's not like that. Please... just calm down. Look, that was just a poltergeist. I—I know it sounds strange. Let me explain."

But my childhood friend seemed to have made up her mind, and I wasn't sure anything I said would even matter. What bothered her seemed to go deeper than anything my poltergeist had caused. She pointed a finger over her shield at Preacher. "Because of Leonidas—you live." Then, she turned to me. "You wish to stay with your *friend*. I'll do it on my own. You're released from your word and bond. Go live your life, Leonidas Rex. Enjoy it, while the rest of us work to prevent a coming calamity. Bound to none, bound *for* none." She snorted and shook her head angrily. Then, shield still raised towards Preacher, her eyes hard, the shadows swirled around her feet, lifting and sliding up her legs, her thighs, over her coat, along her abdomen, up to her shoulders, then neck. Then the shadows fell like a collapsing cloak.

"Wait!" I shouted.

But the darkness fell in the mud, swirling as if pouring into a drain, and then vanished completely. Annie was gone. Her protection now gone too, which meant Grendel would come for us again.

Was it my imagination, or could I now hear movement in the trees?

I spat off into the dust, growling and shaking my head.

It wasn't me, Preacher said, speaking through the remnant of our connection. *I didn't fire... I thought it was her.*

I shook my head. "Skinting poltergeist," I muttered. "Vyle's teeth, Preacher. She's gone. She's gone to meddle with the Hollow, and there's no way to beat her to it. What if she confronts Percy on her own? Even if we get the location too, we can't cross the Threshold Seal any easier without her."

Preacher glanced off now, shaking his head. He turned, slowly, and began to move up the road, his long strides carrying him away from his father's farm. He paused at the top of the dusty hill, glancing towards me and quirking an eyebrow.

I just shook my head, closing my eyes for a moment, allowing grief, frustration, exhaustion to all wash through me. I wasn't sure where my poltergeist had disappeared to, but I muttered a string of oaths just in case he was in earshot.

"You head on back," I said. "Get some rest. If Dale is still at the RV, tell him we're no longer employed and send him on his way. If he needs money for a hotel, give him some."

Preacher nodded in approval and resignation. It wasn't long ago that Preacher had been forced to model generosity for me. We'd been teenagers when we'd first met, and it was a lie to suggest my adopted Sphinx mother was the only one who'd had a hand in my rehabilitation.

Even so, I could feel the *need* returning.

A need that caused me to cast my eyes off into the dark, my cheeks turning red. If Preacher could feel my thoughts, I wouldn't be able to bear his look of disappointment.

My hand clasped and unclasped at my side as the need rose in me... I looked towards the trees, but Annie was gone. I glanced across the road, but the golden eyes I thought I'd seen were also gone.

All I was left with was exhaustion on a dark forest path, beneath a rising moon. The need clawed up to my throat and I could feel my tongue dry. It started as an itch in my stomach, but I knew it would only grow. Besides, it was time for me to meet with Percival Twelftree. Time to locate the Hollow was running out. No more stalling. I knew what I had to do.

"I..." I couldn't lie. But I certainly wouldn't tell him the full truth. "I need to think a bit," I said. "I don't know if we can beat Annie to the Hollow. And if we do, we need a much better plan. A way through the Threshold and a way to survive a saboteur. In the meantime, guard the RV and keep a watchful eye for Grendel and his children. We're no longer under *the mistress'* protection."

Preacher sighed, still watching me. *What about Percy?*

"I... it's handled. It will be, anyway. Just—do you think your dad will let me use his phone?"

Why the phone?

"I have to make a call." I flashed a smile, which I didn't feel whatsoever, so I let it die on my lips instead of risking the deception. "I'll be back as soon as possible. Don't wait up, I'll use my own key."

Preacher gave me another long look, his silhouette outlined across the road. His own shadow remained still then moved when he did, giving me an odd sense of relief.

A strange thing where a man can find comfort.

But natural shadows wouldn't suffice for the night. I turned, waving a hand over my head. Annie had lied then left. My poltergeist had meddled, and if Preacher knew where I was heading now, he'd tackle me and tie me up, dragging me screaming back to the RV.

No. Best he didn't know.

Chapter 34

The old farmer didn't even know I'd crept into his house. Now, in the dark, I had his old, corded red phone pressed to my cheek, the plastic cold against my skin.

But my cheeks prickled for another reason entirely.

Fear.

I swallowed, finger hovering over the small buttons. Was this really the only way? Very risky. *Very* risky. Percy couldn't be trusted to do anything besides hurt me. But that was the plan, wasn't it? The ploy.

Was I just being arrogant?

I could feel my need still rising in me. A desperate, cloying desire...

I let out a shaking, rattling breath, my nerves frayed, my skin prickling. I could outwit Percy, couldn't I? Part of me wanted to complete the call just to prove it. How else was I going to find the Hollow's location?

I knew I wasn't thinking straight. Knew the night's events, Annie's revelation, the ticking clock for the Hollow to Unlocate again... It was messing with me. I was frazzled, tired and... deeply sad for some reason. The pain I'd seen in Annie caused my heart to break.

I sniffed, then reached a rash decision, rapidly dialing the number I'd snuck from Kay a few years before. I waited as the phone rang.

And then... after another ring.

"Yes?" A cold voice. "Who is this? How did you get this number?"

"Percival?" I said, a shiver moving down my spine.

A long pause. Then the ogre-eared man's voice took on the hiss of an adder. "So, Lenny, calling to apologize are we?"

"Not exactly. I want something from you, Percy. And you want something from me."

It was a stupid plan. A brash plan. Not really even a plan. But still, I needed the Hollow's location. I needed to deal with my brother. I needed to beat Annie to it. Was she already en route to speak with Percy?

"You have nothing I want, Leonidas."

"That's not true."

"What could you possibly offer me?"

My throat felt very dry. "Myself," I said simply. "Without Preacher. Unarmed." Even as I said it, standing in the old, creaking wooden farmhouse, I felt prickles up my spine.

After a length of silence, I thought he'd hung up.

But then... "I'm listening... In exchange for what?"

"The location of the Hollow," I said simply.

He snorted. "That's it? You'd give me a crack at you for a job? My, my, you really are desperate."

"Do we have a deal?"

"You want me to tell you the location of some stupid prison in exchange for me kicking the snot out of you?"

"Yes." I winced.

Percy let out a giggle like the bray of a hyena. "Ha! I'll tell you where to meet."

"Promise me first," I said. "Promise me you'll tell me the location before anything else happens."

Percy was a Wit. He wasn't an honest man, but his abilities prevent him from becoming a liar.

He scoffed. "Promised. I'll whisper it into your ear before I drive my fist into your gut. Leon, I hope you understand, I'm going to hurt you, very, very badly."

"I know," I whispered. "One criteria. We have to meet at an Endeavor bar."

"Endeavor?" he snorted. "You really have gone soft."

"It has to be Endeavor," I whispered faintly. "Your choice. Send who you want. But that's my one stipulation."

"Fine," Percy sneered. "Deal."

***

I moved along the dusty street with low, rolling steps, stray fragments of asphalt crunching beneath my feet. A bar's windows reflected the orange street lights back across the cobblestones, embracing the stems of old-fashioned lantern-tops and marrying them with shadow. I reached into my pocket, my hand slipping through the slit in the fabric to the thigh strap with my knife. I pulled the blade, balancing it on my fingertips, watching the cold steel level like a teeter-totter. I hated guns. Even as a child, I'd never been trained to use one. Rather, I'd been taught how to command those who could.

A knife was a weapon of culpability. Everyone knew whose hand was stained red in such proximate scenarios.

I tossed the blade clattering into the shadows beneath one of the lantern posts.

Exhaling slowly, I steeled myself for what came next.

I strolled across the street and looked through the windows of the watering hole. Pausing, I removed my handkerchief from my pocket, and used the silk to push against the glass as I entered the bar.

The cool of night was met by the warmth of the business. A clean enough establishment, and yet my eyes were inevitably drawn to a small portion of the floor, wedged against the counter, where mop and broom hadn't reached a thin layer of dust and grime. I wrinkled my nose, but forcefully looked away.

Eyes glanced up, regarding me. Perhaps ten customers in the small, scattered room. Neon lights wreathed a corkboard covered in photos. Old photos. Family photos. All of them with dates pinned beneath the portraits.

I'd seen the like before in other establishments. I leaned in, studying the cork board. One man was depicted staring with bright eyes from a clean-shaven face. His arm held a pretty brunette to his side. They both beamed at the camera. The names beneath read, *Justin & Deborah Monroe. 1992.*

A young married couple. Killed nearly two decades before the Grimmest Jest. My eyes slipped along to other portraits. They lingered for a moment on the face of a child. Perhaps only eight. *Bennie Porter, 2009.* Only one year before the overthrow of the Imperium. He'd nearly made it.

More than twenty faces covered the corkboard. Thin, block letters beneath, in peeling paint read "Never Forget."

And they never would. Neither would I.

Next to the words, against the wood of the wall itself, someone had painted an indigo-colored eye. The symbol of the Endeavor. A beacon to all—untalented and talented alike. The thing the Imperium valued most, they wore first mockingly, but then as a claim of nobility and equivalence.

I opened my eyes, facing the corkboard. This bar was for Endeavor sympathizers, frequented by those who'd lost loved ones to my father's regime. *My* regime. I could smell the smoke, the drink. But my vices were of a different variety.

I faced the bar now.

The need was so strong now, I could feel it twisting in my gut, like cold iron. I'd chosen to meet Percy for the Hollow. But I'd chosen an Endeavor bar for me.

I scanned the gawkers seated around the bar. The three closest to me, around tri-legged stools and a circular wooden table glared over thick mugs.

"Piss off," one of them snapped.

Instead of answering, I gripped the hem of my shirt and pulled, peeling it up and over my form. No sense in ruining my top; it was seamster-made after all. I draped it carefully over the back of one of the least dusty stools next to me.

I knew what I looked like beneath my garments. Not just the muscles, tightened from a lifetime on the run. A woman behind the bar let out a small little gasp, reminding me of the severity...

Scars upon scars laced my body. The ashen black pendant of a leering skeleton rested against my chest, the chain cold on my neck, next to the leather strap with the blunt key. Two of the men sitting next to the pitbull just frowned, no longer drinking. An older man, leaning against the counter turned and said, "Young man, this isn't the place for trouble. Sheriff Atticus Sawyer lives only a half mile down the road."

"Atticus works for Percy," I called back. I looked around the room. Twelftree wasn't here. He was too cautious for that. "Which of you did he send?" I called out, glancing at the denizens. No takers.

I rolled my shoulders, flexing. It took me a moment to locate the tattoo of my blue crown. Sometimes, it moved of its own volition, whether or not I tried to remove it. Now, it was over a particularly nasty, three-pronged gash healed crooked across my left pectoral.

"You lookin' for trouble?" said the pitbull. He rose, swaying a bit, but supported by his friends.

The older man raised his voice. "Care, Alex—don't be a fool!"

"Alex," I said quietly, staring the man in the eyes. "Is that your name?"

The pitbull had close-cut hair and thick muscles, but not those of a bodybuilder, rather the steely, corded sort that came from a lifetime of fieldwork. Farmer strong, they called it. A world entirely alien to my own, both past and present.

"Greetings, Alex. Pardon the intrusion, but do you know who I am?"

He blinked beneath the dull lights and neon glow from the corkboard. A small fire pit settled in the middle of the bar, beneath an iron grate. Sparks and smoke lifted on the air, meandering to the skylight above, whisking out into darkness.

"Pshaw! Shouldn't wander in here with a mark like that," Pitbull growled, his voice rasping.

At this, Pitbull's two friends seemed to notice the tattoo as well. The flames behind them almost seemed to grow, reaching hungrily towards the ceiling, framing them against a backdrop of orange and angry red. They nudged each other, and Alex's pitbull eyes narrowed to mean slits. He ran a hand across his buzzed head, down his inflated chest and the fingers curled in front of a labor-stained t-shirt, forming a fist as he looked at me.

Percy was watching. I knew that much. At least, someone in Percy's hire. Maybe even Alex. One could never quite tell with the Union boys. But I'd come here for one reason. Percy had given his word. One way or another, this night ended with me in Percy's grasp, and the location of the Hollow whispered in my ear.

The path to that destination? Only through pain.

"You don't know where you are, boy," said the older man by the bar. He gave me a quick, cautioning look. "You'd better leave." He had kind eyes and laugh-lines around his forehead and cheeks. He was also missing his left hand, apparent by the plastic appendage resting on the cool glass of the auburn counter.

The need was on me. I'd tried to fight it, once upon a time. But now I knew any effort to push off the desperate, cloying desire only forestalled the inevitable. Each day of discipline ended in a far more horrible collapse beneath the pressure to give-in. And give in I did. Always.

Now, I'd learned to manage the need. The cost was worth it, in my estimation. Though, if Preacher found where I was... he'd be furious with me. How many times had he found me after? How many times had he found me saying I'd try to never do it again? And how many times had he forgiven the known failure?

Even if Percy hadn't agreed to meet me, even if Percy hadn't been involved at all... I couldn't honestly say I wouldn't still be in a place like this. Looking for my type of trouble. My type of release.

In part, this dark little secret pleasure of mine was my advantage over Percy. Fists and pain didn't scare me nearly so much.

"Did you lose it in the war, old man?" I said, nodding towards the kind-eyed gentleman by the counter. He was staring at me now, pleading. He gave the faintest shakes of his head and gestured with an urgent nod towards the door.

"Not a good night to be here, friend," he called back.

I stared at the missing limb for the moment, my mind jolting, memories—cursed memories I'd tried to carve from my brain—drifting to the surface.

My father, smiling. The screaming of a talentless, captured soldier. Always on their birthdays. Always. He would make a note, when they were taken, pretending they might have a chance at release as a show of mercy on their birthdays... a lie, of course. Just another psychological torment.

The more powerful captives he might send to prisons or try and recruit.

But the untalented? Those without magic of any kind?

He would take their birthdays down. Some of his generals would join to watch on the days—for a bit of sport. I once remembered seeing a schedule in a small notebook on my father's favorite desk. A schedule with the birthdays of the prisoners he kept personally in the palace dungeons. Hundreds of them beneath my home.

Then, every birthday, he would give them a choice.

Which limb?

He would watch as it was done. Still smiling, always...

It was one of the tamer things my father did to those who didn't have a magical gift. By the fifth year, my father's guards had to get creative. But they always found a way. And my father, when stressed, or tired, or simply in the mood for some entertainment would head to the dungeons, his little booklet with the schedule tucked in his pocket. He'd find a birthday, find a prisoner, and enjoy the view and the screams...

My mind snapped back, gasping, feeling nausea swirling in my stomach.

Pitbull was still staring at the blue crown tattoo on my chest, as if he couldn't quite believe his eyes. A loathsome symbol. Not just to him, but to me as well. But also part of my legacy. Part of the legacy of the names and faces pinned to that corkboard. Family, friends, loved ones who'd perished in this small town. The corpses of Picker's Lake gifted by my family in wooden boxes wrapped in bows of crimson and planted six feet deep.

Sparks and smoke spat up, fleeing towards the grate in the ceiling, disappearing out into the night sky.

The older man still kept trying to shoo me towards the door, but eventually seemed to realize I wasn't getting it, or wasn't interested in his advice. He slumped in his seat a bit and took another long sip from the glass in front of him before saying, "All of you, calm down, alright? Just wait a moment."

Pitbull snapped towards him, "Leave it alone, gray one. A fox has wandered into the chicken coop."

I smiled softly, thinking of the Endeavor who'd chased me and Preacher over the last few days. Thinking of the bounty hunters they'd hired, of Euryale, Grendel and his offspring.

"Chickens?" I said. "Is that how you see yourself? Percy?" I called louder. "Come out—where are you hiding?

A couple of other patrons had begun to edge around the room at the increasing tension, and they now slid through the door, disappearing out into the night.

Pitbull slammed a finger into my chest. "Shouldn't have come here!"

I wrinkled my nose at the touch of his dirty fingers.

"Look, if you're going to cause trouble, take it outside!" snapped the older man by the counter.

One of Pitbull's friends scoffed. "And give the fox a chance to flee? I think not, geezer. You stay out of this."

"This is my bar," he returned, frowning. The fire swished and swayed, and a flutter of sparks burst up now. The old man was no longer looking, contenting himself to lower his head, stare at the counter and nurse his drink. Head down, say nothing, see nothing. Just how most of my father's subjects were taught to behave. Keeping your nose clean, keeping out of trouble: this was considered the lesser of two evils. The alternative? Your friends, family, everyone you'd known thrown into jeopardy.

"Let's step outside," I said softly, studying Pitbull's mean eyes. "No sense ruining the man's livelihood."

I knew this part well. The calm before the storm. They were like hounds, sniffing me out, looking for tricks. Had Percy hired them? Perhaps... Not that I really cared in that moment. My flesh screamed.

Pitbull pulled a small, jagged knife from his belt suddenly, jutting it beneath my chin. "You're Imperium?" he demanded, his aggression rising with the brandished weapon.

I grinned. Now we were getting somewhere. I allowed the leer to linger, flashing through my beard. That's when Pitbull seemed to have enough. Trust the drunkards to find hidden courage first.

"In a war, it's them or us." He tapped his blade against my tattoo again, then hissed, sharply, his breath smelling of liquor. "So let it be."

His knife gouged at the tattoo, ripping through my skin. A flood of pain burst through my chest. Not a deep cut, just one meant to hurt.

He danced back, seemingly expecting me to lash out in response. But I didn't, my hands hanging limp at my side. Some say everyone has a fight, flight, or freeze response in dangerous situations.

But for my needs, my urges, there was a fourth option.

Enjoy. Some men had frailty in women, others with needles, others in drink. And though my vice could be found in a bar, it wasn't the sort discovered in the bottom of a glass or in companionship on the cheap. It was just happy accident that Percy would give me both my desire and the location of the Hollow. Where was that skinting Wit, anyway?

I forced a smile as Alex noted my lowered hands, my defenseless posture. A blow struck me from the back, one of his friends who'd snuck behind. Pain exploded across my skull and sent me reeling. A series of kicks lashed into my ribs where I fell beneath a table. Pitbull and his friends shouted in fury.

Fear swirled through me, pain exploded all around me. And in that moment, I felt the release, the need being lifted, carried away. My offering of flesh and blood a suitable sacrifice. Blows rained down on me. I felt another sharp cut as the knife now gouged into my chest again, trying to completely tear the tattoo away. Of course, it would reappear again. But I wasn't here for anything less than the pain itself administered at the hands of my family's victims, whether Percy had hired them or not. It didn't matter.

I tried to push up, momentarily. Mostly, because resistance motivated further punishment. Resistance elicited fury. People often talk about how crowds affect them. Groupthink, or mob mentality they call it. They never stop to consider perhaps that's what people *really* are. They aren't affected by the crowd, but liberated. Perhaps we only let our true selves show when there is safety in numbers. I've found companions are the perfect camouflage.

A fist collided behind my ear, sending my head buzzing. Another fist caught me in the back of the neck and my head snapped in a gout of sudden white-hot pain. Kicks aimed at my ribs, between my legs and at my spine.

Pain wouldn't do it. Only a *type* of pain. A pain at the hands of those my family owed.

Woe, woe, heavy is the head that wears the crown. My arms buckled and I fell under the full weight of the legacy of the house of Rex.

Not once did I even catch sight of Percival Twelftree. The confidant hadn't shown himself.

Yet. But he'd come.

One way or another, our paths would cross tonight.

After all, Wits don't lie.

Chapter 35

I groaned in my dream, my body aching with the reward from a night of pain and stupidity. My eyes fluttered, and I began to wake, but as I did, some apparition—still in my dream—placed a furry foot in the center of my chest and shoved.

I didn't quite fall as physics in dreams aren't actually physics. Instead, I began spinning like a dizzy top. At the same time, I spread my arms, trying to catch my windmilling, subconscious self.

A second later, I found myself hovering above a gray cloud. A single rizzle now stood in front of me on the cloud, with a brown paper parcel under a single arm. The creature cocked its fuzzy head, its enormous eyes reflecting my own form back.

I could see, even in my dream state, my body carried the bruises and cuts from my night time beating. The need that had felt so urgent, so important had now faded, replaced only by the predictable dull ache of shame. Especially after everything Mr. Gallows had done to heal me that same afternoon.

"What?" I snapped, staring at the rizzle.

"Delivery for the third pretender of the Loophole," squeaked out the creature's voice. This rizzle was chubbier than the others had been and wore his Dracula cape like a bib. He also wore a onesie stitched with cartoon scenes of me getting my teeth kicked in from all angles at the Endeavor bar. There was even one scene of someone smashing a chair across my back. I didn't remember this—it must have happened after I'd fallen unconscious.

"Package?" I said suspiciously.

"Are you the third pretender?" asked the rizzle in its obnoxiously squeaky voice. The imp danced from foot to foot, passing the brown package around his back, to the front, and back again, like a section of some lumpy hoola hoop.

"Just give it," I groaned. Only Kay referred to me this way. Not that I could blame him. He had so many clients in the fringe of the magical world who claimed the name 'Leonidas Rex,' he'd numbered us in his mind, just to keep the John Doe's separate. And as much as I liked Kay, I wasn't going to correct him on the assumption of my actual identity. It was a favor, really, that so many in the knowing world had adopted my name as their camouflage.

"Relinquish it here," I snapped, some of my old speech pattern coming out as I wiggled my fingers impatiently.

The rizzle hesitated. I noted he had a banana cream pie hidden behind his back now and was inching towards me one step at a time.

"If you try that," I growled, "I'll give you vestiphobia."

The rizzle froze in place, one foot still raised, eyes darting side to side. I clicked my fingers and extended my hand. "I consent to the delivery and claim all consequences as my own."

Normally, rizzles were a news source. They couldn't meddle with the physical world without express permission from every party involved. Kay would have given permission on his end. Now, at my words, the rizzle sighed reluctantly and tossed the package at my chest.

I caught it deftly, waved goodbye and—as a banana cream pie came arching through the air, narrowly missing me—I blinked awake, lying on a cold floor.

I groaned, wincing as my head scraped against concrete. Slowly, I tried to push up and found metal bars against my back. I blinked against lancing light which only further exacerbated my pounding head.

I was in a jail cell, sitting on the opposite side of a thin cot and a metal toilet. Huffing as I tried to sit upright and recline against my cell, I peered out through the bars across a small office space with two desks, one of them tidy and neat, the other scattered with papers and old folders.

Next to me, a second cell was occupied by a rail-thin woman with raven black hair and bony features. Her eyes were closed, her form still, and, for a terrible moment, I thought she might be dead. But then she rolled over, slapping a bare, tattooed arm against the second cell's cot, and she burped, loud.

I winced against an odor like eggs and flat beer.

I'd been thrown in the drunk tank. Still no sign of Percy. At least for now—I could imagine him hiding somewhere, watching me sweat and fret. I refused to give him the satisfaction of seeing me scared.

As for pain? Nothing I could do on that front.

Though, my new collection of bruises from my nighttime beating seemed lesser now than usual. Another one of the lingering gifts of Mr. Gallows' abilities. I pulled at my shirt, examining the crown tattoo. A thin cut, still bleeding, displayed where Alex's knife had gouged. The crown tattoo itself, however, had migrated near my shoulder. I glared at the cursed thing and pulled my collar back down.

Through an opaque door, at the opposite end of the room, I spotted shadows moving, and detected muffled voices. A camera centered the ceiling. I glared at this. "Come out Percy!" I shouted, shaking a fist. "A deal is a deal!" I'd taken my beating, now he owed me the location. He'd given his word, and as much as he hated me, there was no way he'd willingly give up the Wit just to screw me over.

But the door remained shut. The camera didn't move: it wasn't angled to watch the furthest corner of my cell, though, so, on hands and rump, I scooted out of its line of sight and then turned my attention to the strange package.

A lumpy, weighty thing, wrapped in twine and brown paper, no larger than a baseball. Hesitantly, I ripped the parchment to reveal a clunky metal wristwatch.

Curiously, I twisted the metal band, and—there on the side—spotted the same etching I recalled from back in Kay's shop. Two fig leaves, entwined together, twirling as if falling from a tree. My eyebrows ratcheted up, and I rested the back of my head against the cold bars, shifting a bit to avoid a bruised shoulder. At least my hand seemed to have healed fully by now, thanks to Mr. Gallows' expedited restorations.

"Kay, you genius... did you really..." I murmured, distracted from my current predicament. I fitted the watch to my wrist. Where the clunky silver touched my arm, a biting cold prickled my skin. "Alright, you tease... where's the..." I pushed the button on the side of the watch.

And nearly lost my head.

Lancelot's shield shot out like an umbrella. A flap of metal streaked towards my neck and I ducked just in time. The shield's edge clanged into the bars behind me with a resounding *gong.*

I cursed. The voices through the opaque door paused for a moment. The woman next to me on the cot, blinked a couple of times, but then seemed to relax once more.

Groggily, I regained my feet, wincing but gripping the shield. Grateful for this distraction from a nighttime of shame, I moved about, rotating the defensive device. It was heavy, but not unmanageable. I chuckled, nodding and muttering, "Cool." A word my father had loathed—just another one of my little rebellions against daddy dearest.

Another black button had been placed on the inside of the handle. Written just above the button was the word *Oops.*

A smile replaced some of my churning emotions, and I pushed the button with my thumb. Instantly, the metal closed, again like an umbrella, and the shield folded itself back into a watch.

I nodded and hefted my wrist—clunky, but bearable. Kay had promised to reduce the thing's weight and size, which he'd done. I'd also asked him to remove the curse...

Before I could recollect the exact nature of the curse, though, or allow myself to descend into the embrace of regret over last night's choices, the opaque door suddenly swung in.

The first man to enter the room wore a ten-gallon hat and a glinting silver star on his blue flannel shirt. The man had a snowy, walrus mustache, and a lean form, save a small belly just above his leather belt. He was likely in his sixties, and walked with a long stride across the small office space towards the neater of the two desks. As he moved along the cages, he glanced over.

"Oh, hello there. You're up."

I watched the man. A sheriff? A deputy? I knew the Sheriff of Picker's Lake was a man by the name of Atticus, but I'd never met him myself. Though his deputies had chased me and Preacher off from the Jester's mansion more than once in our youth, thinking us loiterers. I also knew the sheriff was in Percy's daddy's pocket. He might keep Percy's behavior within the lines, but he wouldn't stop Twelftree from causing me damage.

So that had been Twelftree's plan. The coward was too scared to show himself, so he'd sent a couple of thugs to get me thrown in the drunk tank. I let out a little hiss of air. Confronting Percy in a bar was one thing, but *behind* bars... Hardly the ideal location.

The man pulled at his neck skin, twisting it. The skin seemed loose, reminding me of a man I'd once known who'd lost a great deal of weight. "I suppose you know why you're here."

"Percival," I said simply.

He nodded, still tugging at his loose skin. "Mr. Twelftree wants a word. What's your name—just for the file."

"Leon," I said quietly, watching him through hooded eyes.

Atticus cleared his throat. "Do you have a second name, Leon?"

"Rex," I said without batting an eyelid.

He snorted, rolled his eyes and glanced towards the neat desk with the stacked papers. "Fine, then," he said. "Don't tell me. You won't be here long."

I paused. "I won't?"

The sheriff continued sifting through the papers on his desk, muttering to himself, "Where is... ah, here we are." Then, he pulled a folder and turned, his polished brown boots clicking against the floor as he moved towards the opaque door.

The state of the man's desk and dress gave me a vague appreciation for the fellow himself. A certain bond existed for the order-inclined. The second desk, messy and scattered as it was, reminded me of my own arrangements with Preacher back in our RV. For a man as physically disciplined as Preacher, his tidying habits had often left me befuddled.

Thoughts of my friend sent a jolt of shame through me. I winced, feeling the premonitions of a stomachache, and massaged my wrist with the watch.

As I did, I glanced through the bars to the drunk woman now snoring on the cot. She looked quite lovely, lying there, drool dangling past one lip.

The watch on my wrist—Lancelot's shield turned mobile—now seemed even colder than before. I found myself staring at the sleeping woman, trying to make out her features beneath her sticky, dark hair.

But did her features even matter? I could feel my heart pounding. She was the single most beautiful woman I'd ever seen.

I could feel a longing growing in me, rising in my chest. I wanted to reach out, to hold her hand. I wanted to kiss her, to tell her everything would be okay. I wanted to sing songs to her, composed on my own guitar, declaring my affections with reckless abandon.

The watch on my wrist felt downright frigid. I winced, rubbing at it.

The woman snored a bit more—what a lovely, delicate sound, like the vibrant notes of some songbird flitting on blue breeze.

She snorted and scratched at her stained pants. Every motion seemed a melody, only further emphasizing sheer grace. She twisted about and then, with a grunt, rolled off the edge of her metal cot and *thumped* onto the dirty cell floor. What dexterity! She continued snoring, one hand draped awkwardly over the cot, her lower lip and chin jutting against the concrete if only to better present her lovely silhouette.

"I adore you..." I murmured softly, the words springing unbidden.

I shook my head, trying to concentrate. I didn't even know the woman, but still, I knew beyond everything I'd ever known, she was the one for me. Soul mates existed, and I had found mine. I reached through the bars now, if only to touch a strand of her hair—the sticky sweat and oily grain only added character.

As my fingers touched the cool cot, near her fingers, though, I didn't venture further. She was my bride-to-be, I was certain of it, and I was a gentleman—to touch even the edge of her pinkie while she slept would be a poor introduction. I would simply have to wait while my Sleeping Beauty slumbered. Once she woke, then I'd have ample chance to declare my love. But what would I say? I'd have to think of something—spend some time reciting...

The watch on my wrist felt heavier than before. And for a moment, I glanced down, staring at it. The prickles along my skin were spreading up and over my fingertips, practically causing them to buzz.

The curse...

I blinked, and then, as if doused in ice water, I remembered what Kay had said. Lancelot's shield carried a curse of infidelity, likely bled into the metal by some fae or immortal nyad. They often liked tempting mortals with power and protection if only to then ensnare their minds for the fairfolk's own amusement.

"You chain-wearing little skint," I muttered to myself in a moment of clarity.

Kay had left Lancelot's curse on the shield. And now, I was madly in love with a drunk woman I'd never met—was that a puke stain on her shirt?

And yet, even though I became aware of it, I couldn't shake my absolute adoration for my unnamed songbird.

One hand moved slowly to the watch, angling to remove it. The other, though—wearing the watch—moved away. I was torn between love and sanity, adoration and clarity.

I gritted my teeth, cursing Kay in my mind and wondering if the skinny black marketer was giggling even now at the thought of the affects his device would have.

My existential crisis, though, didn't last long.

The opaque door opened a second time, this time with Sheriff Sawyer entering the office ahead of two other men.

The silver-mustached sheriff, in his shiny brown boots, came to a halt by the neat desk, leaning on it and watching the other two entrants. Sheriff Atticus was saying, "That's the form... You'll have to look it over. Haven't had dealings with the Union in a while."

I went suddenly cold. Part of me still felt torn, my attention absorbed by my Sleeping Beauty. But another part perked at these words, trying to focus.

The second man had terrible posture, his back hunched, but his arms heavy. His biceps were the size of bowling balls, but his legs were as thin as rails. He had a silver star, slightly smaller than the Sheriff's, over a yellow pocket on his beige shirt. One hand of the hunched deputy rested on his sidearm in its black leather holster.

He moved over to the messy desk, and snared a set of metal keys, which he hefted and dangled. "Here they are," he muttered. His voice came high-pitched, not matching his strange topsy-turvy physique.

The third person, though, is where my attention landed.

I cursed, my heart jolting. Not just for myself, but also for the fate of my beloved... I needed to protect her. Protect her, especially, from this new threat.

Last night's decisions all came rushing back.

Only a day remained to locate the Hollow. I'd made a deal...

With a devil.

The ogre-eared man stepped into the sheriff's office. Percival Twelftree, Union-boy and the only other Wit around, was standing framed in the door, his arms crossed. The Sven sisters weren't with him this time, and his firearm was out of sight. But his eyes landed on me, and he smirked widely. He gave a little wiggling wave in my direction and then turned to Sheriff Atticus.

"Yes, that's the fugitive. Do we have an accord?"

I stared, watching through the bars like a caged rabbit at the sight of a wolf. Twelftree pushed his blond hair behind his ogre-ear, and scratched at his perfect jawline, waiting as Sheriff Atticus pointed towards the single piece of paper gripped in Percy's hand. "Fill that out, then, when your credentials are called in, we can complete the transfer."

"Tomb's trove," I muttered to myself. I glanced over to my would-be lover lying on the ground. "Get up," I murmured as gently as I could afford. "Please, dear. We have to go!"

I'd only thought the plan this far through. Percy had given his word to tell me the location of the Hollow. But afterwards... I'd already gotten a beating. I should've known Percy would want to give me another. The skint.

"Oh, I don't think we need the paperwork," said Percy, his eyes twinkling indigo.

Sheriff Atticus paused for a moment, frowning and scratching at the side of his head. Then, slowly, loose-lipped he said, "I don't think we need the paperwork."

"We had a deal, Percy—you gave me your word!"

The ogre-eared man gave a taunting little wave beneath his chin with fluttering fingers. He pulled his coat tight around himself, buttoning the loose top button and said, "Hello, Lenny. You seem to have found yourself in a tight space."

I didn't reply, my mind whirring. The last place I wanted to be at Percy's meager mercy was trapped behind bars. I looked sharply at the small window above and behind me, but this was barred too. I patted my pockets, but realized my tiger's eye was gone—my knife I'd discarded. My coat, with all its pockets, was dangled over the back of the deputy's chair, far out of reach.

The deputy was still dangling the keys in front of Percy's nose.

At the same time, I felt another swirling sense of longing in my gut. My fingers were stroking something sleek and grainy...

I looked over, horrified to find I was stroking the sleeping drunk's hair. Part of me wanted to whisper soothingly, to tell her everything was going to be fine. I yanked my fingers back through the bar, reaching up to rip the watch from my wrist...

But the chill sensation along my arm spread even further now. The curse wouldn't bend so easily...

My fingers went still, pressed against the watch. True love was hard to find after all. I didn't even know her name, and yet I knew we were as star-crossed as two could be.

I needed to get out of here, though. Percy was a threat to me and my true love.

I snarled and lowered my fingers from the watch, leaving it against my wrist for the moment. At the same time, I extended my consciousness, angling towards the deputy's mind. I couldn't let him give those keys to

Percy. But the deputy's back was to me.

Eye-contact wasn't strictly necessary for what I needed, but it made things easier. And Percy had eye-contact, while I was still dazed, waking from a beaten stupor.

Percy snatched the keys from the deputy and, at the same time, erected a mental barrier against any intrusion. I tried to reach out, but winced, feeling the mental equivalent of gouging my fingers into what I'd thought was sand, but turned out to be cold concrete.

Grinding my teeth, I withdrew my thoughts.

Percy smirked, crossing his arms over his sculpted chest. "He won't be on your hands much longer, don't worry." Percy patted the deputy on the head, like a child ruffling the ears of a puppy—knowing Percy, he thought of most unknowings as little more than animals.

He skipped past the deputy with a delighted bounce to his step, and the keys in his palm jangled with the motion. Humming softly, he approached my cell.

I snarled now, meeting his gaze. "Back off, Twelftree! Give me the location!"

But Percy winked. "I'm going to, Lenny. I already said I would. But we are going to have some fun—that was the deal."

"You already gave me a beating!"

He eyed me. "You do look a bit battered, but no, Lenny. I didn't do hex-all to you. My turn is coming up. Besides, your big brute isn't here to protect you now."

"You don't know where he is," I retorted, gritting my teeth.

"Is he nearby?" Percy asked, making the question direct. His eyes flashed above the glinting keys.

I froze, swallowed, tried to think of an answer. One of the downsides of being a Wit—no lying, not even with lives on the line. If I deceived, my own abilities would weaken substantially, if not vanish. Sometimes only for a few hours, sometimes for a day or more—depending on the level of the lie. And sometimes, I'd heard, on breaking an oath, Wits could lose their powers permanently.

But Percy chuckled and tapped a key against the bars. "You know, I was worried about him. So I sent some friends of my father's to investigate your... *mobile home,*" he said, making no effort to conceal the sneer in his voice.

I froze, my lips numb now, feeling a sudden desire to swallow, but refusing to give Percy the satisfaction of even the simplest reaction.

"The thing is..." he murmured, his eyes now split by a single metal bar, both of his pupils dilated in the well-illuminated sheriff's office, "when they arrived at your RV... The whole place was destroyed. Blood streaking the metal walls. Claw marks and bullet holes everywhere. They found the corpse of your bodyguard, draped over the threshold of the RV." His lips twisted in a horrible leer. "Dead, Leonidas. Your friend was found dead. Slashed to ribbons."

Chapter 36

Percy clicked his tongue, shaking his head. "A real pity that. If I was feeling generous, I might bring you by, so you could bid farewell. But I'm afraid I have other plans for you, Lenny. Lovely, lovely plans." He lodged the key into the lock with a satisfying *click*. The Sheriff and his deputy watched, wearing vague looks of confusion.

"Did you say someone was murdered?" Sheriff Atticus called.

It took me a moment, though, to register Percy's noncommittal grunt of a response. My own mind was reeling, my eyes staring sightless at where my nemesis had begun to open the cell door.

It couldn't be.

Can't it? Percy's voice whispered in my mind. *Truly? You want to know where the Hollow is? You're the second seeker in as many hours, Lenny. Not even special in that way. Fine*—here.

I felt a weight descend on my mind...

And suddenly *I knew*. I could see the Hollow in my mind's eye, picture where the mountains cradled it. Hours north of our current location.

"And that," Percy murmured, "is my end of the bargain fulfilled."

I could still feel his presence in my mind.

He'd broken through my fear. With a snarl, I suppressed my horror, my mind still spinning. Then, vaguely, I remembered Percy snatching something from my memory back while I'd been thrashing in the dark waters of the Loophole. I hadn't known what he'd seen then...

But now it made sense. He must have realized where I was headed. Must have realized Preacher's father owned the farm. Or, at the very least, where we'd parked my RV. So he'd sent minions to find me... but instead...

I shuddered.

It couldn't be.

Percy leered now, his indigo-flecked gaze still split by a single metal bar and his head surrounded in a halo of fluorescent light.

"I can show you..." he murmured. "Look... Lenny." He clicked his tongue and shook his head in mock sympathy. "But I have to warn you. It's not a pretty picture."

I knew the Hollow's location.

But it didn't even matter now as I felt something pushed against my mental defenses. Percy was strong, but he'd never trained as deeply as I. He'd grown his powers like a beast, a lone wolf, scratching and clawing and fighting with naked ferocity and sheer cruelty. I'd been a weapon, honed—unwilling to use most the tools at my disposal for fear of shattering my tender and newly budding conscience. Percy, on the other hand, used every underhanded blow at his disposal—he was the Wit equivalent of a boxer who flung dust or sand in his opponent's eyes before kicking them in the jewels.

And yet still...

I slowly lowered my defense, just enough to reach out and probe at his invading thought.

He didn't rush in. Instead, he dangled the thought, just out of my reach. I moved towards it, and, with a sheer sense of joyful vindictiveness, he pulled it away again.

I snarled, and Percy winked, his hand still gripping the keys in the cell lock. Then, he flung the memory at me.

I gasped as it came on me like ice-water. For a moment I was seeing through someone else's eyes—a memory Percy had ripped from the mind of one of his Union enforcers.

I glimpsed a small clearing, trees swaying in a night-time breeze. I glimpsed the moon full and fresh, peering down on a valley. In the distance, I discerned the large, white revival tent Preacher's father used. I spotted an old stack of rubber tires which marked the entrance to the dirt road leading to the farmhouse and the Gallows orphans.

The eyes in my stolen memory turned towards the RV. The aluminum sides and glass windows reflected back the moonlight.

But...

I froze.

The RV was no longer upright. The wheels were still spinning, slowly, as if kept in perpetual motion by a particularly insistent breeze. One of the tires was missing completely, ripped from its fixture. Another had been slashed to pieces.

I stared, horrified, the memory playing out. Worst of all—Percy was a Wit like me.

It meant he wouldn't lie.

And so, I watched with a mounting sense of terror as the memory played on. I'd only just left Preacher—how long ago? A few hours? More? What time was it?

I frantically tried to pry my gaze away in search of a clock on the wall, but just as quickly, my attention snapped back to the torn memory.

Blood... Blood everywhere. The eyes of the Union enforcer had circled the toppled RV now and was staring at the roof. Something had ripped a hole through the ceiling, claws tearing through the metal.

Blood scattered across the RV, blood across the blades of grass which drooped under the crimson weight. Blood speckling the windows I went to such effort to keep clean. Blood and gouge-marks. Not just the bullet holes from earlier, but new destruction.

And then... I spotted the body.

My eyes remained dry as always, but a sheer sound of strangled, feral pain ripped from my mouth.

Preacher had been ripped to pieces. He dangled, impaled against a jutting branch which had been driven through the RV like some sort of flagpole.

His body had been ripped, torn. Judging by the blood, I felt near certain he'd been alive for most of it. My dear friend had clearly put up a fight, but it's difficult to pull a trigger when you're missing all your fingers.

Preacher had been mutilated beyond recognition, his corpse dangling over the edge of the RV.

I heard slow murmurs in the memory—the Union enforcers stammering to each other, and then beginning to turn. At the same time, I heard howling in the distance. Then laughter from the line of trees.

Large shapes moved about in the darkness. Then, the enforcer's memory switched focus. His eyes darted up, staring at a low branch upon which sat a human form wearing a top hat and Sunday suit.

Golden eyes peered out from the dark branch. Teeth flashed in the night.

I heard the strained scream of *Run!* from the memories. Then the memory's gaze twisted away, and I heard thumping footsteps, howling laughter and horrible screams.

The memory ended.

I blinked, feeling icy shivers along my back, down my spine, over my arms.

A lump lodged in my throat, and, for a moment, I didn't think I could breathe. Preacher was gone. Grendel and his children had destroyed my home, killed my friend. They'd hunted me but taken my companion instead.

"It can't be..." I growled, shaking my head. "It can't..."

"But it is," said Percy, shaking his head in mock sympathy. The leer twisting his cheeks like taffy, though, communicated his true emotion. He delighted in my hurt and horror. Knowing Percy, he was probably aroused by it all.

I flung forward, slamming my hands against the bars and barring my teeth as my nose nearly jammed against Percy's cheek. He jerked his head back, one hand still gripping the keys in the lock.

"You did this!" I snarled. "I'll rake you to pieces. I'll make you wish..." I could feel the cold rising, but still suppressed some of the words hoping to rip themselves from my throat. I snarled, though, a guttural, canine sound. I knew the location of the Hollow, but it didn't matter now.

Grendel was on the hunt. He'd killed my friend. For all I knew he'd hit the Gallows orphans next. I pictured Paul, his wife, his daughter Sussanah, and the young genie, Grace, who'd I'd just met. I pictured them treated to a similar fate as my friend.

I had to get away. I couldn't wait here. Grendel and his brood were on the move.

How could I have been so stupid to let Annie leave? I hadn't trusted her. She'd lied. But she'd also been protecting us. Of course Grendel would have respected a saboteur. I should have known she'd been more than she'd seemed. Nothing short of a demigod assassin would have curtailed Grendel's bloodlust.

Now, though, I was open, exposed. And I'd walked right into Percy's grasp. His thugs had already pummeled me, and now Percy was going to take his turn. I'd agreed to this, hadn't I?

But now Preacher was gone. My chest pounded with grief.

The Gallows orphans would be in danger.

At the same time, Annie and that split personality of hers were on the move, heading towards the Hollow, hoping to release my little brother from his prison. Had she managed to gain the location herself? Had she bribed Percy? Annie suspected my brother of murdering a saboteur. But she didn't know what she was walking into. A trap, undoubtedly.

A strangled snarl burst from my lips again, the sounds of a wounded animal.

I'd ruined it all. The night of the Grimmest Jest, I'd ruined everything... Preacher... Preacher was gone... The sheer thought threatened to collapse my legs. But I couldn't dwell on it—not now, not yet. What would I tell Mr. Gallows? *Not yet!*

Grendel was hunting me—everyone I knew was in danger. But if I didn't stop Annie, then far more would be threatened.

But what options did I even have? Percy stood across from me, a nuisance, but a deadly one. An enemy and a blockade. Until I got away from him, I wouldn't be able to help anyone else.

And so, I reached up and in, muffling my grief, suppressing my guilt. The emotions wouldn't be useful now. I flared my anger.

"You really think you can take me?" I said, still barring my teeth, the moonlight casting my shadow across Percy's body. I rolled my shoulders in a very Preacher-esque way. "Think you've got what it takes, knacky?"

The light of mirth died in Percy's eyes at my words. "What did you call me?" he hissed through clenched teeth.

"You heard me. You're nothing more than a little knacky, playing at eternal. You wish you belonged among the Imperium, but you're a mere waste—nothing more than an unknowing with a vague abnormality. You little *knacky!*" My words pressed on Percy, cutting deep. Even as I spoke to them, I felt a flash of guilt. They were words from another life, words calculated to cut Percy where it hurt most, to push him off his game. This epithet was most used by those strolling the highest courts of the Imperium. We were taught not to swear nor to use vulgar speech, but to speak against humble heritage in the foulest terms? This was considered fair play.

I knew a man like Percy hated his heritage, his background. No eternal talents in the rest of his family, which made him—in the minds of most Imperium—little better than an unknowing with a knack.

Percy had gone to great lengths to prove his strength, his power. He'd claimed wealth, honed his craft, declared his loyalty to Imperium in every action save speaking too loudly in a neutral zone like the Loophole. But I knew he loved the Imperium, and so I knew my words would sting.

"And what are you, *Three,"* he spat, the spittle arching through the bars and landing at my feet. He stared wild-eyed. "A pretender. You stole the name of a man ten times what you are. A hundred times!"

"You like Leonidas Rex, hmm?" I returned, holding back a flash of vindictive pleasure at his words. Part of me wanted to know how he'd react if he knew who I was. If he knew I wasn't a pretender at all. But that, I was certain, even in my horror, my fear, my grief would be a terrible error.

"The heir to the throne is a true eternal," he spat. "Like me. You wouldn't even be worthy of kissing his boots!" Percy chuckled now, licking his lips. He pressed his thoughts against me, shoving hard and giving me the faintest glimpse of Preacher's ripped corpse, before turning and gesturing towards the opaque door. "I didn't come alone, though. Thank you for reminding me. I'm not here because I think I can *take you,* Lenny," he said. "Though I'm certain I could."

"Prove it," I said sharply, feeling a rising sense of fear. "Prove it, or it's just words."

"Well..." Percy said, waving towards the opaque door now. "Words have power. You should know this. For example..." He cleared his throat, raised his voice. "Come on in!" he called.

Then the door pushed open. Six Union enforcers crowded through the office space.

And I realized we'd now reached worst-case-scenario.

Percy hated me... *truly loathed me.*

A beating wasn't enough. Not once. Not twice... He wasn't going to pummel me. No—I could see it now. See it in those six men in the door. Percival had *other* plans where I was concerned.

I'd known this was an option. Known he might just take me and torture me.

The one advantage I had, what I was counting on, was he wouldn't just put a bullet in me. Not now. Not while I was under his control. No—Percival would take his time. I knew my enemy—I knew that much. I'd been counting on time. Counting on space to make good my getaway.

But physical punishment would be a part of it. That much was clear.

Sheriff Atticus frowned, but didn't speak, suggesting he'd known they'd been waiting outside. Percy was always a sly one, a master of garnishing truth with inferred deception. Unable to lie, but more than willing to allow willing minds to fill in dishonest blanks.

The Union enforcers all had emerald, arching tattoos displayed on their forearms. None of them were indigo-eyed, but they all carried weapons: an assortment of pistols and one submachine gun on a leather strap. Not nearly as outfitted as the Endeavor. For one, none of them had body armor—but all of them with narrowed, harsh gazes, and rough bearings. These were tough folk that made up for their lack of equipment with cruelty and will. A couple of them sported wounds—fresh, by the look of them. One man had a slash mark across the back of his neck, which he kept reaching up and tenderly probing.

"You need friends to take me?" I said, trying not to let my fear show now.

I needed to get out of here, but my chances seemed to be wavering. Even as I thought this, the image of Preacher's body was suddenly pushed roughly aside by thoughts of my new bride-to-be. She was slowly waking, as if the arrival of all these new folk had finally stirred her. She sat groggily up, glancing around.

She looked at me, and, with a faint French accent said. "What is going on?" She stared at me. "Who are you?" she said slowly, rising on wobbly legs.

A strange mixture of emotions this. True love brought on by a cursed shield, true horror brought on by a scene of carnage and my dead best friend, true fear brought on by Annie's intentions and my inability to prevent it. Percy had said someone else had come to him for the Hollow's location. It had to be Annie.

I felt dead in the water.

I stared across Percy, towards the six armed enforcers. I knew if I went with them, I wouldn't like where they took me. I'd be lucky to make it out alive.

"Do you trust me?" I said, leaning through the bars and extending a hand towards the lady.

"I... er, what?" She reeled back now, staring at me with a horrified look.

"Do you trust me," I insisted.

"No. Who are you?"

I grit my teeth.

"Enough, Lenny," snarled Percy. The keys twisted completely, the door to the cell suddenly opened. "Come quietly, or painfully. I don't care. Well, actually, I'd prefer the second. Hurry along now."

I stepped further back into my cell, away from the ogre-eared man outlined in the doorway.

I had to think... think....

But what? How could I escape? What could I...

I grit my teeth, shaking my head. Nothing for it—the only option I could think of. It took all my will and focus, but I reached down and—spurred on by my would-be lover's rejection—I ripped the watch from my wrist. Hell hath no fury like a savant scorned.

I didn't stop there, though and instead, I tossed the watch towards Percy.

"Catch!" I called.

Percy reacted quick—lightning-fast movements. He was a savant after all. His fingers snared the watch. For a faint moment, I thought I glimpsed a shimmer of blue sparks extending down his fingertips.

"Gifts won't help you here, Leonidas," Percy snarled. "You're coming with me. *Now!*" He wiggled his fingers, gesturing over his shoulder. Three of the largest Union enforcers began moving towards me, fingers flexing, bodies poised for action.

I needed to buy some time... Just a bit—some time for the curse of Lancelot to take effect...

The enforcers shouldered past Percy, glaring at me now. They stepped into the cell, carefully, hesitantly. The one who had the wound across the back of his neck reached up and pulled away bloodied fingertips. He wiped them off on his royal blue shirt.

"Were you the one who saw the carnage at my RV?" I asked, slowly, pointing a finger towards the man. "Did Grendel give you that? How did you get away?"

"None of your business," the man snapped, raising the submachine gun around his neck and pointing it at my chest. "Come... *now."*

Chapter 37

I was beginning to think more clearly. The tingling cold on my wrist had faded. I no longer beheld the urine-soaked drunk in the next cell as an object of affection. Some of my normal sense of decorum and hygiene had returned, and I was hastily scrubbing my hand—which had stroked her greasy hair—off on the wall behind me.

I was literally backed into a corner. Nowhere to go. No more weapons. No more tricks. My own powers here would be limited as Percy would block most of what I could do. The images of my RV had been intended not just to inform, but also to disarm. The horror of what I'd seen was wreaking havoc on my concentration.

Memories of my own, memories of Preacher, of my friend, kept trying to rise in me and I—with snarls—was forced to shove them down, trapping them beneath the dark waters of my subconscious.

"Come on then," I snarled, curling my fingers on my newly healed hand into a fist. "Come on."

The middlemost enforcer stepped in, his muscular forearm braced, displaying the swooping emerald tattoo of the U. The man with the gun narrowed his eyes. "Get on the ground!" he snapped.

But I'd never been much in the habit of kneeling. Not to my father, not to his regime, not the Endeavor and certainly not to Percy's goons. I stood still, one hand bunched, all of me poised, preparing for action.

I could feel Percy's own mental barrier rising, like a linebacker on a football team, trying to anticipate where I might strike next. His gun-totting enforcer, though, seemed to have ideas of his own. He lowered the weapon's barrel, pointing towards my knee. I could see the violent intent in his shrewd gaze.

"Get on the ground," he said, through pursed lips. *"Now."*

I knew he would fire. He didn't care that a corrupt sheriff was watching, didn't care about a deputy. That's Union for you—they're so used to being in control; they assume they're entitled to their way wherever they go. Power-addicts, through and through.

And yet, my knees weren't made for kneeling or shooting.

So I moved *fast.*

I wouldn't make it out—that much was clear. But I wasn't about to go down without swinging, and, at least for the moment, I saved my leg.

Instead of allowing Mr. Submachine to blast my kneecap to shards, I surged forward, lunging at the man to my right. I shoved into him, hard, grabbing him by the lapel, but instead of sending him reeling, I held on tight, using his stumbling momentum to spin, putting him between me and the Mr. Submachine.

The other enforcers cursed. The three who'd remained in the door broke into a sprint, racing to the small cell.

Now, I flung the man backwards, sending him stumbling into the other two. For a brief moment, I had a clear shot at the cell door and at Percy.

I took it.

If I was going down, then I at least wanted to give the ogre-eared man something to remember me by. I lunged at the other savant, hands outstretched like tiger claws. I snarled, grabbing at his ear and trying to yank *hard*.

Just as quickly, though, Sheriff Atticus yelled. "Stop!"

There came a booming sound, and, now, over Percy's shoulder, I spotted the walrus-moustached law enforcer of Picker's Lake hefting a double barrel at the ceiling. Plaster and dust trickled from where he'd unloaded one of the chambers.

For a moment, everyone went still. I could feel my stomach tighten, my heart pounding. I wanted to run, but knew if I moved too quickly, I'd entice a second blast—this time, likely between my shoulder blades. Besides, where could I go?

The three other enforcers still blocked my line to the door. Percy, though, was gripping the watch I'd thrown. He stared at me, wide-eyed, his nostrils flaring. He seemed caught in some emotional tug-of-war, the turmoil of his thoughts written across his features...

"Leon?" he said softly.

He was still holding back my wrist while I attempted to get at him, but his other hand moved out and traced a finger along my cheek.

I shivered in revulsion—the thought of Percival Twelftree suddenly finding me alluring made me want to spit. I couldn't think of a man I loathed more. His eyes softened, and I could see slow silver sparks still spreading over his fingers where he gripped Lancelot's reformed shield.

"Leonidas?" he repeated, quietly. Then, in a strangled voice, he screamed, "Don't hurt him! Please—don't hurt him!"

The Union enforcers pulled up short. One of them had grabbed my shoulder and was trying to drag me off Percy. The three in the door had their weapons raised, taking aim. Sheriff Atticus seemed stunned by the whole thing, his double-barrel still pointed at the ceiling, and his deputy had scrambled behind the messy desk, staring with wide-eyes and making his hunched form even smaller.

"Don't hurt him!" Percy shouted, seemingly unable to believe his own words. I could see his eyes widen even further as he tried to make sense of his now warring emotions. I could detect, faintly, just on the surface level of his mind, the thoughts rising up, caused by Lancelot's infidelity curse.

I slowly released Percy's lapel and stepped back, hands up. "Let me go," I murmured, then, through gritted teeth, I added, "We can talk later, sweetie." These words directed towards my arch-nemesis would have struck me as comical in any other situation, but now they fell like desperate, hollow appeals.

And yet, the cursed watch still seemed to have an effect on the Union-boy. He held up a halting hand towards the men behind me and they slowly backed away, uncertain. One of the enforcers said, "Boss, you sure?"

But Twelftree just snarled and kept a hand upheld. "Leonidas," he said, his voice whimpering. "Please... please don't leave me..."

I took a couple of cautious steps backwards. My eyes darting from a slack-jawed Mr. Submachine and moving over towards where Sheriff Atticus seemed entirely bemused. I stepped back, then back.

One of the enforcers grabbed my wrist. Instead of resisting, though, I shouted, petulantly, "Owie! Percy—he's hurting me!"

"Stop that—stop it now, how dare you!" Percy screamed.

The hand released me as if I were electrified. I took another step towards the open door. Percy grit his teeth, wide-eyed. He seemed like a hound with a treat balanced on his nose, caught between one command and a deeper instinct to pounce.

I spun around, bolting through the open Sheriff's door and leaving my two would-be lovers behind. Nothing like a love triangle to really stir things up.

"Mr. Twelftree, the watch," a voice suddenly said behind me. It sounded like Mr. Submachine. "It's sparking. Look! Oi, Hardy grab that from him. He's bewitched!"

I cursed, glancing back in time to see one of the more courageous enforcers reach out and slap the watch out of Percy's hand. The band thudded to the ground, and I spotted Percy standing there, shaking his head for a moment. I was already outside the office, my feet padding against the dusty ground of the Picker's Lake outskirts.

Percy's eyes widened and he shook his head, the effect of the curse suddenly clearing. He stared over the gathered henchmen, eyes fixed on me and they widened in horror.

I winked, blew him a little kiss then broke into a sprint.

Twelftree howled, "After him! Get that skinting savant!"

A commotion burst from within the small town sheriff's office as armed thugs tried to be the first to tear out the door, like hounds finally released from their leashes. But I was picking up the pace, sprinting across the cobblestone streets, racing away from a couple of the other small town structures lining the road and angling towards an alley. I rounded the street, turning along the sidewalk at an intersection—

"Stop right there!" snarled a voice.

I came to a dead halt.

Normally, I would ignore a command like that.

Except this time I found myself facing something entirely unexpected. I could hear the pounding footsteps behind me, closing off the gap. But ahead, I was blinded by headlights.

A jeep on one side with five armed men inside, all of them aiming heavy weapons towards me.

Five motorcycles also lined the road, also blocking my escape. The headlights cast shadows, but also outlined the silhouettes of more gunmen sitting astride their lowriders. The streets throbbed with the grumbles of the bikes themselves.

Worst of all, though, flanked by the five bikes on one side and the jeep on the other, was the *massive* gray-green, armored vehicle sitting smack-dab in the center of the road. A few cobblestones had been dislodged, and portions of the street crushed and permanently rearranged from where the thing had traveled. Behind it, lining one of the sidewalks, I spotted two light poles completely bent and angled off over a white fence. A sidewalk had been smashed.

I remembered this vehicle from back in front of the Loophole. At the time, I hadn't known it belonged to the Union, but I supposed I should have figured. Percy's father and his outfit had a certain flair about them.

Plus, the giant painted green U on the front of the vehicle should have been hint enough.

An M4 Sherman tank sat in the middle of the road.

The giant, armored, World War II tank grumbled and growled along with the motorcycles and jeeps, the cannon, as thick as a telephone pole, jutted across the cobblestones, aimed directly at my skull.

Clearly, I'd underestimated Percy.

My feet wouldn't move. I just stared at the heavy artillery all pointed in my direction. I turned, glancing desperately back, but now Percy and the six other enforcers had arrived, all of them pointing their weapons at my head.

"Skinting little knacky!" cursed Percy. "Move a muscle, and I'll eviscerate you! Get on the skinting ground!"

The ogre-eared man had lost his temper, and I knew he meant it this time. Hesitantly, cursing quietly to myself, I slowly raised my hands, locking them behind my head. I glanced back, and spotted one of the guards, Mr. Submachine, had my jacket draped over his arm. I narrowed my eyes.

"That's mine," I said.

But my words received a vicious blow to the chin as Percy sent me reeling. I tried to get up, but he slammed his booted foot into my back. "Stay down, pretender," he spat. "Think you're clever, hmm? Think you're funny?" He ground his boot against my back.

I felt blood on my tongue and spat into the cobblestones, hearing voices and the sound of thumping feet as even more Union enforcers emerged from their vehicles or left their motorcycles to hurry over and help contain me.

Vyle's teeth. Percy had brought a small army. Couldn't fault the guy—he always did come prepared.

Rough hands dragged me up. At least two gun barrels jabbed into my spine as I was shoved *hard* in the direction of the jeep.

Stumbling forward, I could feel my heart hammering a million miles a minute. I couldn't shake the images I'd seen back at the RV, couldn't shake the fear I felt now for Gallows' orphans. And Preacher... I swallowed a lump in my throat. The grief alone was taking most my concentration to hold back. I also couldn't ignore my old childhood friend. A saboteur now, perhaps—but Annie was still heading into things unknown.

I could only hope she was wrong. Could only hope something *else,* something powerful, had killed the saboteur. Could only hope my little brother was still locked away in the belly of the Hollow, guarded by an insane clan of genies and February, the lieutenant of the assassins.

I was shoved into the jeep, pushed between thickset guards carrying full on machine guns. I glimpsed the armor of the Sherman tank through the window on my right. Heard a shouting voice as Percy gave instructions to his mini army.

And then I felt the vehicle jolt, heard the grumble of motorcycle engines and the squeak of a tank's caterpillar track against the cobblestones as we began to move.

"Where are you taking me?" I demanded. Clearly, I'd overplayed my hand. While I'd succeeded in ascertaining the Hollow's location—I could still feel I nestled in my thoughts—that phone call from the farm was seeming more and more suicidal.

Percy had climbed into the front seat. He turned back, jamming his chin past the headrest, his mean eyes fixed on me. His ogre-ear in his blonde hair twitched. "You'll see," he murmured. He flashed another trademark leer intending, and fully succeeding, in raising my blood pressure. "I always thought you were unprofitable to me, Lenny. But I think I may have found a use for you after all. I do have to warn you, though—it's going to be magnificently excruciating. You can handle a bit of pain, though, can't you?"

He chuckled and turned back, peering out the windshield as the jeep led the way, followed by the motorcycles and the skinting Sherman tank up the cobblestone roads, away from the small village of Picker's Lake, leaving the old mining town behind us as we angled up and deeper into the mountains.

Chapter 38

The jeep rocked and jolted on the old roads carving the larger mountains in the forgotten terrain of Northwest Washington. The surrounding trees were larger, now, deeper, the shadows wider, more belligerent in the ground they claimed. On one side, a sheer drop off—no guard rail to speak of.

I glanced in the rearview mirror, watching the Sherman tank chug gamely along, maintaining pace with the jeep and crushing dislodged pieces of rock beneath its tracks.

The motorcycles pressed together just behind the tank, but I could only make them out from their headlights now. As we rose, the mist descended to meet us until we circled into a bank of fog.

The wisps of white fluttered through the open windows, and soon, as we continued to circle the mountain, I could barely see ten feet through the windshield.

"Careful," Percy was muttering to the driver, "Don't take us off the cliff."

I scowled at the thought, trying not to picture a sudden plummet and a fiery crash. I'd be no use to the Gallows orphans or a prison break with a snapped neck. But what could I do? An armed man sat on either side of me. Three more sat behind us. Two pistols still pointed at the back of my skull, and if I so much as twitched a muscle... *bang*.

Percy kept glancing into the back seat, keeping an eye on me. I could feel his thoughts grazing past me like submarines beneath a merchant ship. Already, my concentration was slipping, allowing grief to rise at my old friend's bloody death. I knew if I tried anything, Percy would give the order to have me shot. Then the window ahead of us wouldn't simply be streaked in fog.

"Where are we going, Percy?" I said, breathing slowly, trying to think. I now had the location of the Hollow secure in my mind. Even with Preacher gone, I still had to stop Annie from freeing my brother. And if she was right, if Napoleon was killing saboteurs, then it was potentially already too late.

"Shut up—" he snapped but then suddenly he reached out with a shout, bracing his hand against the leather dash. The jeep jolted. My own stomach leapt into my throat.

The front of the jeep suddenly dipped. My head banged into the seat in front of me, my body jolting as the vehicle seemed to drop and go suddenly still.

The jeep squeaked, the tires whirring uselessly beneath us.

"Tomb's trove," Twelftree screamed. He slapped the back of the driver's crewcut head. "Idiot—you nearly took us off the mountain!"

Indeed, as we slowly rocked back and forth, my heart in rhythm with the motion of the vehicle, the floodlights from the jeep itself illuminated the tops of trees *far, far* below as if we were angels peering from a cloud.

Panting, I winced, trying not to picture a Sherman tank slamming into us, crushing whatever hopes of survival remained. The jeep continued to rock back and forth, tires spinning, scraping where it dangled just over the edge of the jutting chasm.

"Get out, out!" Percy howled at two of the goons. "We need a push!"

Both men nodded quickly and reached for their respective doors. As they did, I felt a flicker of hope. With everyone distracted, now might be my chance. Percy wasn't watching me either, his gaze fixed on the imminent tumble.

I still didn't know where he was taking me and didn't much feel like finding out.

At the same time, I needed my jacket. It held the gold powder—my only defense against the Hollow's guardians—and also the tiger's eye. On top of that, I'd seen Mr. Submachine place the silver Lancelot watch into my jacket before passing it, and my newsboy cap, into the back seat.

Now, a particularly wide-hipped guard was *sitting* on my stuff.

I shot a glance back but went stiff.

The men charged with keeping me in their iron sights maintained their diligence. Two gun barrels leaned in now, pressing above both my eyes.

"Eyes front, savant," snapped one of the Union henchmen. His muscled forearm, boasting the swooping emerald tattoo, flexed, suggesting he was prepared to fire at a moment's provocation.

"Do you mind?" I said through gritted teeth, trying not to let my anxiety show. "You're squashing my hat."

In answer, the wide-hipped goon wiggled his rear. I puffed a horrified breath, vowing inwardly to make sure I had it dry-cleaned *twice*.

"Shut up and eyes front," the guy snapped.

By now, the two henchmen on either side of me had managed to push open their doors. The one on my right moved a bit quicker and began to hop out of the car. As he did, though, the jeep groaned and *tilted*, moving even further over the edge of the unguarded drop.

"No, stop, stop!" Percy screamed. "Get back in—back in! You'll make us fall you imbecile!"

The guard was hesitant at first. I could see his mind churning, trying to decide if he was more scared of Percy or gravity.

"I said," Percy screamed, "Get back in!" I felt his thoughts suddenly move, swelling up like a wave and crashing horribly against the hesitant henchman. Instantly, the goon went slack-jawed. He twitched, shaking a bit, but then I could feel Percy hook into his mind, ripping at his self-will, controlling his thoughts. It was a ham-fisted, brutal assault.

The man bled from the nose as, still slack-jawed and vacant-eyed, he slid dutifully back into the jeep and buckled himself in.

"Stay there," Percy snapped. Now he screamed at the driver and jabbed a finger towards a walkie-talkie wedged into the dash above a curling wire. "Hurry up... hurry it up!" Percy was snarling.

I felt a flush of frustration. The henchmen flanking me had shut their doors again. And while Percy was still distracted, the two guns behind me still pressed to my skull.

Should I move? If I did, would I cause us all to plummet?

I waited, desperately searching for my opportunity.

"Yeah, behind us!" Percy was shouting into the walkie-talkie, one finger pressed against a red button. "Hurry it up. And... I swear, if you knock us off, I'll bleed your brains. Get us on the path. *Now!*"

I glanced into the rearview again, staring at the headlights behind us. The bright yellow lights cut through the mist, and I heard the creak and groan of the hefty vehicle.

A few seconds passed, and then I felt something nudge against us. The whole jeep jarred forward.

"No, you imbecile!" Percy screamed. "You'll knock us off! Use the gun, dummy!"

I blinked in surprise, also mildly impressed at Percy's forward thinking. Vicious, cruel, horribly tempered though he may be, he was also clever. I heard a whirring, mechanical sound. Then, what seemed like a tree branch suddenly struck us from the side. Not hard enough to crush metal, but the windows rattled.

"Don't move," Percy commanded suddenly. Then, into the walkie-talkie, he added, "Not you. You need to get us on the path. Hurry up!"

The gun barrel of the old tank began to push us with a creaking groan, sliding our jeep back onto the road. The men around me muttered darkly. I heard one of them, in the back seat, loft up a prayer—but the words seemed hollow on his lips compared to Paul Gallows' entreaties.

Our salvation, though, came in the form of 1940s craftsmanship from the U.S. Army Ordnance Department.

The tank's gun barrel finally pushed our jeep fully back onto the path. I heard the whir of tires, felt our vehicle suddenly grip the ground again, and with a jolt, we began to move forward once more, probing into the mist.

Percy let out a long breath.

"Nervous?" I asked innocently from the back seat.

"Shut up and stay quiet," he snapped. "I'll deal with you soon enough. Someone's willing to pay a pretty purse for you."

I frowned, staring at the back of Percy's head, my eyes flicking from his curled, leathery ogre-ear, down to the nape of his neck, resisting the urge to reach out and throttle. "What do you mean by that?"

"Ah, worried are you? Good. You should be."

I felt a prickle along my chest. "I don't enjoy speaking with you, but yes, I am worried. Someone's willing to *pay?* Percy, what are you talking about?"

He sighed as if in pleasure, resting his chin on the shoulder of his seat now, and turning his body like a serpent, if only to get a good look at me. "Ah, Lenny... You never were a profitable fellow. That's your biggest failure, you know."

"And yours is vagueness. Who's paying for me, Perse?"

"Don't call me that."

"Fine. Mr. Twelftree," I said. I could feel my apprehension rising. There were a few people, I knew, who would pay for me. And only one of them, in recent memory, had gotten close enough to try.

I was no longer under Annie's protection after all.

"Percy," I said sharply. "Grendel? The Endeavor bounty hunter? Are you insane?"

"Endeavor?" Percy snorted. "Please. We've worked with that bloodthirsty Kindred before. He's a mercenary. And, like all men of forethought, he values the weight of coin."

"Percy!" I exclaimed, suddenly trying to reach for him, to grab at his shoulder, to shake sense into him. But both henchman on either side of me slammed forearms into my chest, sending me snapping back into my seat like a helpless waif caught on a roller coaster.

"Now, now, Leonidas," said Percy. "I'm sure he'll eat you slowly. Plenty of chances to use that big brain of yours to escape." He winked. "Besides, you weren't willing to pay me what you owed. Grendel is."

"Baron paid for me!" I snapped. "Are you insane? What happens when Baron finds out, hmm?"

Percy snorted. "You pay far too much credit to the *Hillbilly Godfather.*" He sneered these last words. "Baron will get what's coming to him soon enough. And you, well... you're going to help line my pocket." He chuckled. "I've been looking into one of the elvish homes. Rare for them to go on sale. But I prefer paying full price, anyway. I'd like to thank you for your help."

I could feel my heart threatening to escape my throat now. Percy was taking me to Grendel. He'd made a deal with the Endeavor bounty hunter. On one hand, this was good news—it meant Grendel wasn't off tormenting the Gallows farm. On the other, it meant I was being carried at gunpoint and tank barrel into the waiting arms of a psychopathic shapeshifter and his children.

"Percy—I shall recompense you. Come now, see reason here!"

"*Shall?* What do you think you are? Though, Lenny, this is how I prefer you. Will you beg? I'll pull over to the side of the road if you'd like to kiss my feet. Hmm?" He was smiling widely now, clearly enjoying this. "Should we? Driver, one second, I think Leonidas would like to lick my toes."

I glared.

The road had straightened out now, and instead of curling *up* the mountain pass, we were now cutting between two peaks, barely visible against the white mist spreading across the sky.

"Percy," I murmured. "You're making a mistake. You can't reason with Grendel. He's Endeavor. You might not see it, but he is."

Percy snorted. "I don't believe you. You're just trying to trick me."

"I'm a Wit, you cretin! We don't lie!"

Percy shrugged. "You're desperate and stupid. No knowing what you're willing to sacrifice."

I actually jolted forward now and even managed to grip Percy's shoulder, trying to twist him to look me in the eyes again. His gaze was once more drifting off through the windshield, tracking the mist-covered path.

But no sooner had my fingers touched his shoulder, then a hard elbow caught me in the stomach and I doubled over, gasping. Another hand gripped my throat, dragging me back, squeezing and choking me until my hands went limp and motionless.

The henchman on my right released me, and I coughed, gasping into my lap.

"He's Endeavor," I said through a choked breath. "He's working with them. He's only using you, Percy. And if he has even *a whiff* you're Imperium allegiant, he'll hunt you down too."

Percy shook his head, snorting. "You don't know what you're talking about, imposter. Now shut up. We're drawing near."

I glanced frantically though both windows. Behind us, I could still hear the steady rolling grate of the tank's tracks. The grumble of the low-rider motorcycles also carried on the air. Nearly fifteen henchmen in all, by my estimate. All of them heavily armed, protected by a moving artillery and a brutal Wit.

He thought he had the upper hand. He thought he was untouchable. At first, I'd thought he'd brought all the reinforcements for *me*. But now it made sense.

I remembered the scrape marks on Mr. Submachine's neck. With a jolt of pain, I remembered the bloodied corpse draped over my destroyed RV. I remembered the howling, the sound of pursuing footsteps. There was no way the Union enforcers had escaped without cutting a deal. And now, I knew what they'd bargained.

Their skin for mine.

But Grendel was a hunter. Caliban, his dear friend, was hungry. And Grendel's children were vicious, but when coupled with their father, they were downright terrifying. Percy thought he'd brought enough firepower to protect himself.

But I couldn't shake the feeling he'd sorely underestimated the threat posed by an entire pack of Kindred.

The surrounding vehicles were picking up speed, now, moving rapidly through the mist in a straight path and beginning to descend, cutting down the mountain slopes into a deep, green valley, visible amidst the mist on either side of the road. Portions of the path were still unguarded; every few moments, it seemed, we blurred by another mountain of boulders, pile of stones, or open drop-off, leading to a horrible plummet.

Nothing for it, guns to my head or not, I'd have to make a bid for freedom. If—and it was a big if—I managed to get out of one of those doors, flinging myself over a henchman, then maybe I'd be able to roll under the Sherman tank and snag one of the motorcycles. In the confusion and the mist, they'd be hard pressed to take aim.

I glanced surreptitiously from side to side. The man who Percy had *puppeted* was still bleeding from the nose, his eyes still vacant. He'd be the one I'd lurch past. He was still dazed, confused. Who knew what Percy had broken.

But by the way Percy leaned forward, his eyes widening with anticipation, it seemed we were getting closer to whatever rendezvous he'd set up with the Kindred bounty hunter. Grendel would be near, along with his brood.

I couldn't wait.

I needed to act—now.

I exhaled slowly, summoning my courage. And then I lunged towards the door handle, placing a *glimpsing* of mist in the guard's mind. I made it seem like the mist had flooded the jeep. The more natural the *glimpsing*, the more chance to deceive. The guard reacted causally, waving a hand in front of his face. For the moment, I knew, he couldn't see.

"Hey, watch it!" Percy said, suddenly, sensing my mind trick.

But I didn't wait, instead lunging towards the door, my fingers scrambling against the handle.

Then I heard gunshots.

I froze, one hand still gripping the handle, the rest of me stiff, waiting for the inevitability of splitting pain.

But it never came.

The gunshots weren't coming from behind me. Well, they were, just *further* behind. And not from pistols either. I heard the chatter of automatics, then the spray of a submachine. I heard a sudden, horrible and desperate scream.

Percy slammed a finger into the radio receiver. "What is it?" he screamed. "What's happening?"

No response at first. A few voices, probably from the tank, said, "Don't know, boss. Something big—something chasing the motorcycles."

I heard more gunfire, another horrific scream of pain.

And then, echoing above it all, there came a blood-chilling, bone-rattling howl.

Percy's face went suddenly pale. More gunfire, and another scream. This time, I watched as a motorcycle flipped over the top of our jeep and slammed onto the road in front of us.

The bike tumbled and twisted, carrying the mist in swirling patterns but, finally, like dice settling on a number, it came to a sudden and impressively upright halt. Both tires were on the ground. The rider was still in his saddle.

The jeep screeched, and our bumper just barely grazed the motorcycle.

The rider on top of it remained upright, but the helmeted head fell completely off, severed at the neck. Blood stained the corpse as it also, at last, fell, taking the bike with it. The motorcycle and its headless rider slid a bit down the angled mountain road and came to a slow stop in the middle of the dusty ground.

The howling grew louder. More screaming and more gunshots. Two motorcycles ripped past us on either side, avoiding the jeep narrowly on the mountain and tearing down the path.

I stared bug-eyed through the windshield as something *large*, and covered in fur, something the size of a small elephant burst from tree cover on one side of the road. Like a killer whale jumping from the ocean, the shadowy shape snared one of the motorcycle riders directly off his bike and carried him out of sight into the trees and shadows on the exact opposite side of the road.

There was a sudden crunch; then the screaming died.

Chapter 39

The final motorcycle rider aimed his weapon into the lower branches and fired; a jet of hot metal met the boughs and leaves.

Amidst the mist and smoke from gunfire, a blurring shadow darted from branch to branch, jumping with hellish agility along the boughs, dodging the bullets.

At last, the motorcycle driver cursed, squeezing the trigger, but finding it unresponsive.

Out of bullets.

I felt a sensation of blood-thirst, glimpsed a mind bent solely on carnage and feasting. Then this biker was carried off into the trees as well, his scream dying before it even started.

Two bikes remained crumpled heaps of metal on the path. One rider, headless, draped over his vehicle.

The jeep had halted, and the M4 Sherman behind us had also stopped. I heard one of the goons behind me hyperventilating. Another man gasped beneath his breath. "Mr. Twelftree, we have to go. Now!"

Percy, though, held out a silencing hand, his own eyes fixed on the trees. He had senses these guards didn't. Undoubtedly, like me, he could detect the thoughts around us.

Three...

Five...

Seven...

Shadows began to move and emerge from the tree line. Large shadows, but they shifted like snowmen melting in the sun. They stepped in the mist as giant *things* but, as they drew nearer, the Kindred had taken—once again—their human forms.

Eight now...

Ten...

Ten sets of indigo eyes flecked with gold emerged on the dusty path, walking slowly, like a wolf-pack approaching a downed doe. All of them were spattered in blood.

Almost as alarming to me: all of them wore dusty, ragged clothing. Jackets fluttered around them against the wind. Wild, ragged hair dangled over ravenous eyes. Teeth covered in blood, lips streaked with crimson stood out in mud-streaked features.

Most of them were smiling. Others, though, seemed far too hungry for delight.

Then, emerging amidst Grendel's children, came the top-hat wearing bounty hunter himself. He moved with a slight dance and a skip to his step, whistling as he came. He dusted off one sleeve, and wiggled a hand, like he was shaking it free of wet. A few red droplets scattered from his fingertips.

Grendel still wore his Sunday best, streaked and ripped as it was. He tilted his top hat in greeting then pulled himself up to his full height, puffing out his chest and exhaling softly. The mist around his mouth swirled and twisted from the pressure.

Grendel paused for a moment, holding up a hand in a fingerless glove. Reluctantly, his children—many of whom I'd never met before—came to a slow halt, peering hungrily through the windshield.

Grendel cleared his throat, then, in that musical, sing-song way of his, he called out, "Companions at heart—I bid thee forgive us our momentary indiscretion. Only that my children had grown peckish in the waiting." He flashed a blood-streaked grin of his own. "We are now here, your humble servants." He tipped his head in a mock bow. "We acquiescence to aforementioned barter. Where, might I inquire, is dearest Leonidas Rex?"

He straightened up, his eyes fixed on the windshield to my jeep, his gaze peering straight through the glass, over the seats, past Percy's shoulder and landing directly on where I sat trying to make myself as small as possible in the back seat. Our eyes met, and his smile widened.

"Percy," I murmured, staring through the glass, fixated on the Kindred sire standing in the mist. "Don't trust him. Whatever you do. Don't. We have to get out of here."

A couple of Percy's henchmen were also seemingly cowed by the Kindred whose human forms were little more than stage dress. Gone were the blurring shadows, gone were the scything claws beneath indigo and gold.

Now, ruffians, vagabonds, the like which often turned the nose of Imperium sympathizers. And yet, instead of disgust, it was fear which trembled the interior of our jeep. Percy glanced to the mirror, his eyes darting to the reflection of the Sherman tank, its gun pointing out above the jeep.

He sneered, then, and, with a great show of bravado, opened the jeep door and slid out of his seat, coming to stand in the mist. "Grendel," he called, his voice echoing in the mountain pass. "You killed my men."

"Ah—only a fleeting misunderstanding. We thought they gave chase to your person," Grendel returned.

Percy stiffened, clearly aware it was a lie. But caught between a precipice of pride and pay, I knew in the end what would win out. Those henchmen's lives meant nothing to Percy. And now, he was obviously doing his own arithmetic. They were outnumbered, even with their tank. And at the same time, he'd come here to ransom me...

At last, Percy glanced away from the beheaded motorcyclist on the road's edge. He sniffed. "Not normally how I conduct business, beast man. But regardless, we have the package. Do you have payment?"

"Allow our eyes to witness the claim," Grendel returned, one grubby hand fidgeting with the brim of his top hat.

Percy turned, glancing back through the glass, and gesturing towards me. The henchmen grabbed my shoulders. One of them pushed open his door. I could still feel the guns behind me fixated on my head. I was dragged out of the jeep, onto the dusty mountain pass amidst a curtain of pale mist.

The two Union-boys pushed me forward, one of them now carrying my jacket draped over his arm, with my newsboy cap jammed unceremoniously in the pocket. Grendel's eyes never left me.

"I bid thee an early morrow, Leonidas," he said, his eyes dazzling like gold.

"Greetings," I replied, my voice rasping.

"Pray approach."

"I'd rather not."

"The time for requests is fleeting."

I tried to keep up with the flow of conversation. Grendel had more funds in the word-bank, however, and I ended up simply holding my tongue. Oftentimes, silence best adorned an otherwise naked noble bearing.

The two henchmen behind me gripped my shoulders.

"As for payment," Percy called. "You first, beast man."

Grendel's eyes flashed for a moment, darkening at Percy's words. A couple of his children behind him grinned. I spotted Euryale standing next to Mago, who still wore his loose-fitting gray cloak. Beneath the hood, he had wild Charles Manson eyes, and an equally untamed beard jutting in every direction and now, it seemed, streaked with intestines.

I shivered and looked away.

"We do value your service," said Grendel. "Allow my youngest daughter, Scylla, to bequeath the agreed upon sum."

He waved his hand, his dirty digits flowing over the fingerless gloves. One of the silhouettes in the mist stepped forward. The girl looked no older than a teenager, maybe even Sussanah's age. She glanced about shiftily, sniffing at the air as she did. Her hair was matted and tight to her face. She wore shreds of gray and white silk—suggesting perhaps they'd once been a wedding dress. In one hand, she carried a single brown backpack, which she hefted and then, at an encouraging nod from her father, she scampered forward—far too fast.

"Careful!" Percy snapped.

Scylla pulled up shortly, sniffing at the air. Her golden eyes spun from Percy to me, to the henchmen, barring teeth filed to sharp points. The gunmen next to me muttered an oath and took a step back.

"Steady," Percy snapped. "Don't let the little skint scare you. Come on, beast. Drop the satchel here. Hurry along, your stench is nauseating."

Scylla tilted her head, hair shifting about like the mane of some lion as she regarded Percy. Her father stood still, his eyes hooded, watching.

At last, Scylla darted forward with the quick, cautious movements of a hyena, then jerked back out of reach, tossing the satchel *hard* at Percy's feet. He grunted where it hit his shin, then, cursing, leaned down to unzip the package. His fingers were steady, but his tongue darted out to lick his lips.

For a moment, I wasn't sure who was more hungry—Percy or Scylla. Their appetites, after all, weren't that different.

He unzipped the bag then whistled.

For a moment, I half expected there to be something nasty inside. Maybe guts, or severed heads. But now, as I peered over Percy's shoulder, I spotted stacks of cold, hard cash. American green.

Percy nodded slowly, looking up. "Let us count it," he said.

Grendel, though, narrowed his gaze. "It is all there."

"I don't know you, beast man. I'll count it first."

Grendel paused, tilting his head for a moment, frowning as he did. Desperately, part of me wanted him to refuse. Right now, I stood trapped between a rock and a hard place, hidden in the mountains, without help to speak of and surrounded by enemies. I'd only get one shot at escape, so I needed to make sure it counted. But the guns behind me and the clawed Kindred ahead were only part of the problem.

I was still all too aware of the tank at my back.

No help was coming this time. The only person who'd be able to track me this deep into the mountains— who'd *want* to spend their time doing such a thing—had died back at my RV, ripped to shreds by Grendel and his brood.

I could feel anger rising as Percy probed at the bills.

At last, though, to my surprise, Percy's pride gave way to caution. I suppose there's a first time for everything. "Alright," he called out, his voice booming over the road. "But every cent better be in here, beast man, or you and I will have words."

Grendel nodded once, his top hat tipping. "I'm fond of words. Bring the savant to me, if you don't mind."

Rough hands shoved at me, sending me stumbling down the road. The mist almost seemed to curl out as if to snare me, to drag me closer. Grendel grinned, nodding to two more of his children. One of them, Euryale, the other I didn't recognize. He had a flat, hammer-blunt face and a missing nose. Only a gouged indentation of flesh remained where nostrils would have been.

I winced at the facial wound but winced even further as Euryale sauntered forward, her hips swaying, her lip even hairier than I last remembered. In that horrible southern accent, she said, "My, my little Leonidas. I have missed you. Daddy says I get first bite."

I swallowed. "Well, just so long as you're gentle," I replied, trying to keep my voice from squeaking with fear.

She seemed to sense my terror, though, and winked as she approached. I didn't even bother to suppress my emotion—sometimes, it was best to allow the sensation itself to motivate. I was walking like a man to the gallows.

In that final moment of desperate horror, I felt due for a good turn.

A flutter of wind swept through the mountain pass, sweeping aside the mist for a fleeting moment. There was only one person I knew who could track anything through the mountains, and who'd spend their time in search of me. And for the briefest moment, I could have sworn I spotted that very same person crouching on a mountain ledge, far above where Grendel and his children stood.

I frowned, stunned. Preacher?

I blinked, but then the mist came back, descending on the gathering once more and nearly blinding me.

At the same time, I heard a gunshot.

It came from the same ledge.

Euryale suddenly screamed in pain, spinning like a top in the mist. Her father snarled. "Treachery!"

"Who did that?" Percy yelled, his voice shrill.

"You *dare*!" Grendel howled. *"You daaa—ROOOOAR!"* The second half of the attempted word was drowned in a guttural growl as Grendel reformed into his truer form just as the mist came rushing back, hiding him. The mist continued to sweep, and I spotted the other shadows begin to twist and form.

"Who did that?" Percy was screaming.

But confusion abounded. I heard another barking gunshot. Had that really been Preacher? How was that possible? I'd seen the RV. Seen the bloody body.

There was a screech from in front of me. I could no longer make out much as the mist seemed to have returned with a vengeance. But whoever was shooting had eagle eyes even in the murk.

Percy was now screaming, "Back to the Jeep! Back!"

Grendel's roar shook the mountains. Thumping paws and claws beneath growls and snarls tore up the path.

I couldn't stay here. But if I turned, I was doomed too.

A dark shadow suddenly hurtled through the air, snarling and screaming like a wounded jaguar. Claws and dark fur flashed towards my neck. Teeth the size of razors cut at my skin. But just then, a deep, deafening boom echoed behind me. This one definitely not from a revolver.

The beast was stopped mid-air by a cannon shot and then sent reeling backwards with a horrible howl. The creature crashed into the trees, lost in the mist, but releasing a sound of snapping boughs and cracking branches.

Another boom and then the dust in front of me exploded in a geyser. I cursed and wheeled around. The tank was firing blind into the mist.

"Go! Go! Go!" Percy screamed.

The headlights of the jeep flashed, and the tires churned, the engine roaring. I jumped out of the way just in time as the jeep ripped through the spot I'd been standing moments before. Dust and mist met together, twirling about, blinding me. At that moment, I thought—briefly—I spotted Percy slipping off around the mountain, in the opposite direction of the Jeep. I frowned, but then the mist swallowed the image.

One of the henchmen had thrown my jacket to the ground in his haste to flee and I quickened over, snatching and hastily donning it. Then, I closed my eyes, abandoning my physical senses. I sensed the fleeing minds of those in the Jeep whoosh past. I could feel the thoughts of the henchmen in the tank, loading and preparing to fire again. The idiots were going to hit the jeep if they weren't careful.

More importantly, though, I could sense the minds of the feral beasts in the mist, moving, on the hunt. The howls cut through the wind, the thumping paws and ragged gasps sent chills along my spine.

Two of the beasts were now hurtling towards me. I opened my eyes again, able to see them in the mist like sharks scything through dark water. I cursed and spun, racing back towards the tank. At the same time, I heard another gunshot from the cliffs. Another howl from behind me.

I didn't have time to reach out to this mind. Was it Preacher? Someone else?

The Sherman was moving too. The giant caterpillar track crushed a motorbike discarded on the ground, leaving it crumpled in a screech of metal and fuel. A fire burst out across the tracks of one of the Sherman wheels. Some of the flames illuminated the surging tank and, noting the two blurs of shadow moving towards me, I sprinted with all my might towards the war machine.

I flung myself at it, scrambling up the side, my feet slipping on cold metal, gripping rigid handholds. I clung tight as the tank picked up pace. The grainy cold metal beneath my fingers gave me adequate purchase, my body bouncing along the curved dome of the rotating artillery piece.

Then, gritting my teeth, I reached down with my mind, extending my thoughts towards the driver's inside.

I hated *puppetting* of any variety—it went against my convictions. But while I refused to take complete control...

...I did the next best thing. I snared the thoughts of the gunner, my eyes swimming as I probed through the naked fear clouding his mind. Shadows rose around me, flashing across my own gaze as if I'd suddenly entered a dark tunnel.

Delicately as possible, but with increasing urgency, I snared the gunner's fingertips. For a moment, I heard him yell in surprise, fearful at the invasion of his mind. *I'm helping!* I thought, loudly. This only further frightened the gunner inside the metal hull.

I growled in frustration, battling for control... I didn't want anything more than his hand. Just a single...

I closed my eyes, wind whipping around me as I focused even harder, sending the full weight of my thoughts against the frightened mind beneath me.

And then...

The fingers flexed, and I waited until I spotted movement in the mist...

Then pressed on the mind below.

The tank boomed again. A blast of fire in front of me, a sudden squeal in the trees. Smoke gusted over, catching me in the mouth.

The shadow I'd seen darted out of the way as the shell slammed through a row of trees, toppling three of them in a cascade of splinters. I'd never mind-controlled a tank in misty mountains before, and I wasn't sure I liked where this was heading.

I gripped my metal handhold and refocused. Still controlling the gunner's hand, I aimed once more, my eyes stinging against the whipping air.

"Come on!" I screamed. "Show yourselves!"

Two more shadows darted across the road. Again, I made the gunner fire, aiming for the largest shape.

This time, a loud *yowl* met my efforts. "Yes!" I screamed despite myself.

I aimed again, rotating the speeding tank to track the second figure I'd spotted.

But just then, in the distance, I heard a quiet keening whistle. A whistle I'd heard before.

Grendel...

Summoning Caliban.

Chapter 40

Percy's soldiers didn't know what was coming, but now, full of terror, I realized we were all doomed. Caliban was near... But where? Up ahead, Grendel and his children were running alongside the Jeep, moving along the road, looking for their angle to take down the vehicle.

The Sherman continued to pick up pace, running over a corpse in the road. Kindred or human, I couldn't tell.

The angle of the mountain slope gave us even more speed now. The tank raced recklessly down the path. Now, even if we'd wanted to stop, we couldn't have. The gun boomed a fourth time—this time outside my control. My ears rang with the sound, mist streaming over me. And then, a shadow suddenly surged from the mist.

A horrible, clawed creature slammed into the side of the tank. It scrambled up and over the metal surface, howling and snarling, flashing teeth. It looked like a cross between a hyena and a white wolf. The fur was matted and odorous. The creature was smaller than some I'd seen. Grendel's youngest?

The thing had *two* heads. Both hyena heads' golden eyes blazed with horrible fury, fixated on me. The thing howled in protest and began scrambling, twisting its tawny body across the top of the tank. The artillery piece rotated, in a slow, mechanical movement, trying to find a new target. I'd lost control—now, the gunners were making their own decisions.

For myself, I gripped the handle on the side of the tank, desperately trying not to fall. I'd be crushed and then eaten.

But I couldn't stay either. The double-headed hyena was nearly on me, snarling and snapping towards me as the cannon moved about, trying—it seemed—to shake the beast loose.

I spotted other shadows moving through the mist. And then, suddenly, the mist seemed to clear. We'd traveled far enough down the mountain that I could see along the road again.

Ahead, Percy's jeep was still moving. The chatter of machine guns erupted the moment we had vision. Two more Kindred in beast form ducked back into the treeline, avoiding the salvo of bullets.

The two-headed hyena screamed some more. My one hand still gripped the metal hold, while the other darted desperately into my pocket. I felt my newsboy hat, rolled up and flat. I winced at the treatment of my favorite headwear.

Pushing past this momentary frustration, I jabbed my hand deeper, feeling cold metal against my fingertips.

The hyena, though, chose this moment to lunge.

Two bloodied mouths slashed towards me. Razor claws scythed at my face. I screamed and lifted the watch all at once, desperately slamming my fingers into the button.

Lancelot's shield opened like an umbrella. The hyena screamed in surprise. For a brief moment, I felt its horrible weight slam into my shield, and then, the beast ricocheted, tumbling over the top of the protective device. I heard the scrambling sound of claws desperately trying to find purchase. The sheer weight of the enormous beast crushed down, and I groaned, nearly losing my grip on the tank.

But the momentum of the creature spared me. It flew off the other side of the shield with a scream, landing amidst the trees behind us. I exhaled in slow relief, lowering the shield and hastily placing it back in my pocket before I accidentally fell in love with a cursed beast from hell.

The Jeep continued to race, continued to fire bullets in a steady stream. The Sherman tank did its best to keep the other Kindred at bay as they hurried alongside us. I was reminded of a documentary I'd once watched with Preacher—he'd loved the nature channel. Wolves would often track their victims slowly at first, allowing the prey to tire itself. Then... at the last moment, they'd pounce.

I could still hear the strange whistling from Grendel, somewhere unseen in the forest. I glanced around, desperate. Where was Caliban?

Suddenly, I spotted a shape on top of a low cliff ahead of us. Percy's Jeep was moving into the shadow of the cliff. I stared up, eyes narrowed. Was that a small house?

No...

It was moving.

I stared, stunned.

"Deadman's teeth," I cursed...

Percy's Jeep never even saw it coming. The giant shadow on top of the cliff *jumped.* It arched through the air, nearly fifty feet and then *slammed* like a meteorite into the roof of the Jeep, crumpling it instantly, like a tin can.

Everyone inside the Jeep would have been killed instantly.

For a moment, the Sherman tank squealed as the brakes were applied. It continued to move, though, sliding at a side angle, now, down the hill. Ahead of us, standing on top of the Jeep and growling softly, my eyes found the horrible form of Caliban.

The thing was twice the size of a garbage truck. Like Grendel's accent and country of origin, Caliban looked like something that ought to have gone extinct long ago. I'd seen similar skeletal structures in museums, or even renditions in movies.

In person, though, the beast wasn't nearly so charming.

It had pink, fleshy, human-like skin—perhaps the oddest and most chilling part of its appearance. The rest of it, though, resembled an obese T-Rex with saber-tooth tiger incisors jutting from its pronounced lower jaw. Hot slobber fell in sticky stands to the crushed metal of the jeep. The teeth alone were larger than an entire human body. Portions of calcified protrusions, as sharp as jagged stone, jutted from its neck, and around its joints, sharp enough to filet mammals to the bone. Legs thicker than redwoods stomped against the ground, leaving indentations in the dirt. Two golden eyes flashed, unblinking like the gaze of some shark. A rattling, rasping, *wet* sound gurgled in the beast's throat.

The obese, human-skinned dinosaur with the teeth of a saber-tooth tiger stood over the crumpled jeep, tilting its head and roaring at the sky. Even the clouds, it seemed, parted a bit as if to flee the monster below.

A tail the size of a telephone pole swished in the air behind where it sat on the crumpled Jeep. Three ancient trees smashed in half as if they were kindling from the tail. A single talon pressed down, crushing a metal frame as thick as my legs, bending it like a plastic straw.

The giant beast emitted a clicking, rasping sound. I watched in awe and horror as a small, wiggling form, gasping, tried to crawl from the wreckage—one of Percy's men, somehow miraculously surviving the crash. He groaned, dust swirling as he dragged his bloody form towards the trees.

Caliban tilted his head briefly, staring down at the helpless fellow. It was like watching a killer-whale eye a passing minnow. Caliban continued watching, though, seeming almost to enjoy the wretched squeals of pain, the sheer agony of the fellow beneath him. Slobber dripped in clumps now, some of the strands even larger than the crawling man's fists.

Caliban shuffled a bit, just watching, watching as the survivor reached the edge of the road with a gasp. The man was crawling faster now, emboldened by the distance from the jeep. I could sense his survival instinct, awed by the sheer courage and willpower, despite his horrible injuries, to drag his crushed body to the trees—though he still remained in Caliban's shadow. Over the roots now, still gasping with pain.

Then Caliban made a sound, almost like a purr, and darted forward *far* too fast. Something that size shouldn't have been able to move that quickly. But a blur of bony protrusions, jutting teeth and pinkish flesh darted in.

Caliban's head jerked down. I heard a wild scream, and the man was lifted off the ground like a doggy treat. I spotted two feet slurped past enormous, fleshy lips. For a moment, the man's sneakers jutted out, twitching and kicking. Then a *crunch*, and the scream stopped.

I looked away, feeling sick.

At the same time, three black blurs burst from the trees, racing wildly towards the crushed vehicle in ecstatic hunger. All three of the Kindred—large as they were, one even the size of a horse—would have only weighed half of what the muscle and tooth and claw of Caliban did.

The saber-toothed monster tilted its enormous, over-sized head, roaring at the sky. Boulders trembled from the cliff and fell. Trees shivered and leaves fluttered to the ground.

I could feel the minds inside my tank going into panic mode. They'd just seen their boss' Jeep body-slammed by a Frankenstein creation. Of course, unlike me, they hadn't seen Percy slip off behind the mountain earlier.

Caliban was snarling at some of the Kindred who were getting too close to his crushed prize. The feast to be found amidst the crumpled metal was his and his alone. The Kindred were hungry, but not stupid, and they retreated with snarls and shuffled paws, leaving Caliban to his prey.

For my part, I realized my initial assumption had been correct. The tank wouldn't be able to stop, not even if it had wanted. We'd been careening too quickly down the side of the mountain.

And now, though the drivers tried to halt the Sherman, we were spinning out. My whole body rattled along with the tank itself as it twisted sideways, now skidding down the hill horizontally. Then, the tank began to topple.

I heard muffled shouts from within the contraption. With a cry of my own, I flung myself free as the tank twisted on its side completely.

I slammed into grass, air whooshing from my lungs, and I rolled a good thirty feet, mostly hitting moss and small stones. At the same time, I heard the roar and rip of metal slamming into the woods. Tree trunks cracked and groaned beneath the unwanted burden. The tank barreled through the forest, spinning, crushing vegetation and bark in its wake, sending a shower of splinters up wherever it struck.

I rolled to a halt along a grassy portion of the ground. The tank had slowed enough that I hadn't killed myself by leaping free, but my body which had already been through a bruising felt like it had suffered another night-time beating.

I lay with my chin pressed into dirt. Low leaves tickled one of my ears, and I could detect the faint odor of turned earth and clover. Groaning and shaking my head, I pushed up.

I knelt in the forest now, trying to regain my senses. Through a trail of crushed trees, where white spokes of wood protruded against a backdrop of green and brown, I spotted the smoking, dented shape of the tumbled Sherman.

Two figures were crawling out of the hatch. Both henchmen were shaking and bleeding. One of the men fell off the side of the toppled tank, landing with an *oomph* in the grass. The second sat upright, groggily shaking his head.

At least, as long as he kept his head. Which was only for a second longer.

A creature like a cross between a mountain gorilla and a horned bull suddenly leapt from a tree, whacking the man off his perch and sending him like a rag doll, head over heels, careening into the trees beyond.

A second later, there was a snarl, and two more furred, shadowy shapes erupted from the undergrowth, ripping into the fallen fellow. His screams died instantly.

The second tank driver cursed, rising to his feet and breaking into a sprint.

...In my direction.

Crap. I surged to my feet, pushing off my wobbly knees and turned, stumbling away back up the hill. A blur of shadows was now chasing the tank driver. Five of them, seven...

It wouldn't take long for them to spot me next. Even at an all-out sprint, they were all far faster.

Then, I heard a grumbling sound...

Not a growl or a roar, though.

An engine.

I whirled around, looking up in stunned surprise as a motorbike, parts of it dented beyond repair, smoke spewing from the front, came to a sliding and dusty halt in front of me. Coughing, choking on the dust and smoke, I waved a hand, preparing to jump away in case a machine gun was aimed at my head.

A second later, though, I spotted a familiar outline. A giant, muscle-bound form, one six-shooter clutched in a fist, aiming over my head. Handsome, stern features outlined against a backdrop of ash and dust.

Preacher growled, fired once.

There came a squeal from the trees. He looked at me and jerked his head. *Hop on,* he mouthed.

For a moment, my feet remained rooted to the ground, my eyes as wide as saucers.

"You're alive?" I said, a giddy flash of joy flooding me with a flare of strange hope. "But... but..." Then I realized my stupidity. Preacher hadn't been the only person back in my RV.

Dale had been there too.

I felt a sudden flash of grief, followed by a confusing bout of relief. The competing emotions didn't sit well with me, but now wasn't the time to plum the depths of morbid favoritism. I lunged towards the motorcycle, sliding onto the back.

I heard more snarling and growling from the trees. A few of the Kindred had broken off from their chase of the tank driver, distracted by Preacher's gun shot.

He tapped my leg hard as if to say *hold on.* I did, gripping him around the shoulders, my arms like a child's in comparison to his enormous, muscled form. It felt comforting to feel my friend, to see him, to hear him breathe and watch him move. Very much alive. I swallowed a lump in my throat as Preacher spun his motorcycle around and released another two shots over his shoulder before stowing his weapon; he twisted the throttle and we tore away, ripping back up the mountain, fleeing the pursuing Kindred.

"You're alive," I kept muttering. "Thank gods, your alive... Er... I mean, sorry, thank God."

Preacher glanced over his shoulder, one eye fixed on me, but then he twisted a bit more and frowned. I turned, also following his gaze. The Kindred were now racing after me, having ripped their other prizes to shreds.

The howls and ferocious screams ripped the air. Our motorbike continued to fizz and sputter, dented and beaten as it was. Preacher removed his second six-shooter coolly, switching hands on the bars. He twisted, firing off another two shots.

More screams of pain. He never seemed to miss. But at the same time, he was nearly out of bullets, and we were running out of time.

I could feel the hot breath of something almost on me, could hear the sound of paws and grinding teeth. I could hear the ragged, ferocious panting in my ear, sensing the speckle of warm spit land on my cheek as something tried to snarl and snap at my head.

I jerked low, pressing against Preacher as we continued to angle up the mountain. But now, the slopes were sharper. We slowed even further as the worn bike tried to compensate for the angle and the burden of two passengers.

We had nearly stalled completely; Preacher's rescue attempt had only thrown himself in danger right along with me.

Chapter 41

Preacher growled in frustration and spun the bike around, angling *back* down the mountain. He'd sensed it too—ascending the steep road would get us killed. The bike was already on its last wheels. Smoke sputtered from the engine, grazing my cheeks in acrid puffs, and flames had spread, spewing up in scarlet and orange streaks from the front tire.

A shadowed form just missed us, scything over in a flash of teeth and slobber. The thing whimpered where it slammed to the dusty road, rolling past like a whirling dervish.

At the same time, five more golden-eyed beasts charged up the mountain. Two of them snarled, lunging through the air—the double-headed hyena and the gorilla-bull. Preacher fired.

Two bullets for the hyena, one for each head. Two bullets for the gorilla.

Both beasts screeched. Such small caliber weapons wouldn't incapacitate the Kindred for long. But it didn't look like it mattered either way.

Preacher made a good go of it, steering the bike towards a gap in the final two beasts. I spotted Caliban in the distance, distracted by his tasty prize wedged in the metal of the jeep. At least the giant beast hadn't joined the chase. For now.

Where was Grendel, though?

As we cut through the opening between the Kindred, they moved in to close the gap.

A fat, thick-bodied snake—as wide around as a car tire—with the head of a lion, jolted forward, cutting off our path with its scaled, corpulent flesh.

My heart jolted and my fingers dug into Preacher's shoulders, trying to direct him by force of will.

But too late.

Our front wheel slammed into the snake. With a yell, I found myself flying over Preacher, over the handlebars.

The moment we hit the ground, we'd be dead.

But we never did hit the ground.

For a moment, I thought a pillow had caught me... But that obviously made no sense. I winced, and waited for impact, my head still below my heels. But I was now swaddled by something black. Darkness held me as if a hand from the earth had plucked me from the sky.

Death?

Preacher dangled next to me, having followed a similar trajectory, also held aloft by a fold of black fabric.

No, not fabric. Shadows.

Shadows probed up from the ground, sprouting from beneath the glare of the mountains like inky mushrooms blossoming in dirt, and now held us aloft, suspended. Blood rushed to my head. Preacher kicked, vying to dislodge himself.

The shadows fell, slowly, carrying us gently to the ground.

The Kindred around us snarled and spat, but paused, circling for a moment, sniffing at the shadows. The motorbike Preacher had used lay in a crumpled mess, burning and sparking where the thick snake-lion had crushed it.

The two-headed hyena and the gorilla with a bull's skull were both huffing and grunting, standing amidst other furred atrocities.

Grendel stepped from behind the gorilla, back in his human form. I hadn't glimpsed his creature self in the chaos. His children waited, poised, staring at the shadows with severest suspicion. Grendel cleared his throat then raised an eyebrow as he tugged on the brim of his hat, twisting it about. Instead of his normal diarrhea of words, though, he simply said. "What?"

The shadows slipped back into the ground, fleeing into the shade of the mountain. I sat in the dust, but quickly regained my feet. Preacher had already beaten me and was standing, both of his six-shooters looped through his fingers in club-like grips. He was out of ammo.

I was mostly unarmed. One hand probed slowly towards my pocket for my Lancelot shield. If I accidentally kissed Preacher in the process, or—worse—Euryale, I'd have to apologize later.

But for the moment, the strange, unexplained tide of shade had brought the battlefield to a tentative silence.

We were surrounded on all sides by Kindred, surrounded by tooth and claw. I reached out with my mind, wondering if I could break through the defenses in time. Grendel stamped a foot in frustration, raising his voice and repeating, *"What?"*

A cold, steely voice called from the path behind us. "I'm what."

Golden eyes, indigo eyes, blue eyes and auburn eyes alike all turned to face the saboteur standing in the middle of the road, her emerald wereblade clutched in one hand, pointing towards Grendel's face.

Instead of a dagger or a sword, though, the wereblade had taken the form of a small handgun—a six-shooter, in fact, not that much different than Preacher's. Had the two of them paired up to find me? Preacher certainly didn't seem surprised by her appearance. I supposed I was the only thing the two of them had in common. My breath choked in my throat. Annie had come back for me.

"Ah," Grendel said, dusting off the front of his shirt and forcing a smile. Some of his would-be charm, though, was lost in the growl behind each word. "It has reached my attention these two no longer abide under the shadow of your wing. As such, I'm here to collect."

Annie wore her mask now, the molten scrawl twisting and turning about over the cast iron. The three curving horns groped to the sky. She had her gray backpack slung over one shoulder, and her voice echoed with a thousand whispers, vibrating from every crook and cranny of darkness available in these slopes.

"I'm afraid you're mistaken," November said.

Grendel grit his teeth. "I think not, mistress. Your words reached attentive ears. Two squirrels and a cricket attest your released bond."

"I changed my mind."

The Kindred were all shifting uncomfortably. Eight of them in total, including Grendel. I wasn't sure where the others had gone. Dead? Perhaps by the blasting tank. Or, more likely, off somewhere licking their wounds and the wounds of the dead.

Over Annie's head, I spotted Caliban still poking and pawing at the distant jeep. I shivered as something the size and shape of a leg was lifted, tossed into the air by thick jaws and then swallowed whole with a slurp. The enormous, pink-fleshed monster's hunger trumped any desire to intervene with further prey... for now.

Grendel's own eyes slipped to his companion, and he sighed. But he didn't whistle, nor did he beckon. "My friend is feasting," he murmured, "but he'll have room for more in a few moments. Perhaps it's best for all if you were to reconsider your claim to the lost prince."

November's coat fluttered about her. The shadows at her feet moved and swayed like sea grass in the Mariana Trench. Her wereblade aimed off to the side for the moment, and she didn't move a muscle. Her tone came somber but fearless as ever. "Leonidas is a friend of mine," she murmured, her voice echoing from within the recesses of her iron helmet, as well as from the shadows around us. "I can't let you harm him, Grendel."

"I see. A friend? Well, mistress, that alters the terrain. One way or another, the heir must be mine."

"No, Grendel."

"A simple no? That offering won't suffice. I no longer face you alone, mistress... Euryale, Scylla, Mago..." Grendel flicked his fingers, his head swaying now, back and forth, as if to some unheard music.

His children gathered around him began to growl, their feral, beastly forms flashing teeth and claws. Black lips arose over gouging fangs and ripping incisors. Slobber speckled the dusty ground.

Annie twitched for a moment, then a far softer voice called out, desperately, "Please, you guys. I really, *reallly* don't want to hurt anyone. Please stay back." She sobbed briefly, shaking her helmeted head, seeming awkward and ungainly all of a sudden.

Grendel's children didn't respond, though. Perhaps they were well accustomed to beings with two disparate natures.

The two-headed hyena, the gorilla-bull and a wolfish-lioness all began to stalk forward with careful probing paws. Each of these creatures was easily three times the size of any human. The Kindreds' golden eyes flashed, acknowledging Annie with scorn and hunger.

Annie didn't speak anymore, straightening again. I heard a murmured voice mutter, "It's okay, child. I'll take it from here." One of Annie's hands patted herself on the forearm in a comforting gesture. Then, Annie went still once more, calm, poised, waiting.

The hyena struck first, flashing forward, claws stretched. The mangy wolf-lioness, Euryale, followed as a close second. Simultaneously, the gorilla-bull lunged towards Preacher, trying to use the distraction to crush my friend.

November moved quicker, though.

A wall of shadow rose behind her, catching Scylla. The hyena beast crashed into the shade wall as if it were made of granite. At the same time, November fired her wereblade—a streaking hot shard of crystal caught Euryale in the cheek, blasting into her mouth. The monstrous lioness screeched.

In a following motion, November reached out, planting a hand on Preacher. Shadows bled from her fingertips, swelling down my companion and covering him like tar. A second later, he seemed to melt, vanishing beneath her hand, and, a moment later, I spotted him materialize in the low branches of a distant tree, emerging from the shadows there and blinking in confusion.

"Kill the saboteur!" Grendel howled.

More of the monsters darted forward. November danced around me, her wereblade flashing in unyielding emerald. The gun reformed, crystal swirling and shifting until November raised a two-handed axe, swinging the pure gemstone weapon at the writhing form of Mago.

She cut deep across his flank, but at the same time, flipped backwards, over the top of a lunging snake-creature.

She landed on the other side, her wereblade reforming once again into a crossbow, which she aimed at Grendel, firing. The beastmaster howled, snaring Scylla by the tail and lifting his own daughter as a shield.

The bolt of emerald struck the wiggling hyena beast, and Grendel flung her aside. He still maintained his human form, screaming, "Kill her! Rip her! Kill them all!"

Six of the Kindred coalesced as one, charging November from all angles, trying to land on her like a football team sacking a quarterback. But November was no longer there. As quick as thought, she melted into a pool of shadows at her feet, and reemerged ten feet to the left.

She lashed out with an emerald sword.

The beasts whirled about, charging again. And again, November melted into a pool of shade, emerged, now—at the edge of the path, dust flying about her as she reset her feet, aimed a crystalline rifle and fired.

The gorilla beast howled and tumbled to the ground, motionless. An entire pack of ancient and trained eternals against a single saboteur... And she was winning. My neck prickled at the thought.

The monsters seemed to realize how slippery their prey was. At Grendel's screams, though, they rerouted. "The savant! Grab the savant!"

I took this as my cue. I didn't know quite what to make of Annie, but for the moment, she was the only ally we had. I sprinted straight at her.

Her eyes weren't visible beneath the sheer iron surface of her visorless helmet. I could hear heavy breathing, monstrous panting. November barked a command, "Leonidas, *jump!*"

I hesitated, briefly, but felt a claw slashing at my ankle, and so I flung myself *up*. One foot extended before me.

In a flash, November waved a hand and a shadow rose from beneath my own leg. The shadow shifted sideways, forming a thick apparition, resembling plank wood. My foot struck the thing, and it felt solid.

"Keep going!" she ordered, her voice steady as if she'd only been for a light jog.

A moment later, another shadow ripped from its proper location beneath a tree branch. This shadow rose above and ahead of me. Again, I leaped forward, and my foot landed onto a second materialized step made purely of darkness.

Like this, I stepped one plank of shadow at a time towards the tree where Preacher still dangled, watching in stunned silence. I shoved off the final shadow step, lunging towards the lower branches.

At the same time, I heard a ferocious scream like from a jaguar, and felt something thick snap beneath my foot. I yelped, my fingers latching onto the lowest branch just in time. I kicked, huffing, then glanced down.

Two beasts, twins, it seemed—identical in make and mark. They resembled blubbery hippopotamuses with the forelegs of enormous spiders; molars the size of my fists and bits and pieces of bone—human if I wasn't mistaken—lodged between their giant, crushing teeth. The giant hippo heads snapped and chomped beneath me, and they lunged off their thick, fuzzy spider legs, trying to snag my feet.

I yelped, scrambling, nearly falling.

A firm hand gripped my wrist. Preacher groaned, dragging me onto the lower branch with a heave. I nearly slipped off the other side, but with a yelp, blood smearing the bark beneath, I held tight, gasping and staring down at the twin monsters. The hippo-tarantulas began to skitter, their golden eyes peering up, moving towards the base of the tree.

"Surely not..." I muttered.

The enormous monsters began to climb sideways, their spider legs propelling the enormous bodies up the bark. Slow-going it seemed, but they continued rising.

"Corker's breath," I muttered. "Are you seeing this?"

Preacher, though, seemed to decide the hippos weren't an imminent threat just yet. It would take a moment, even with their spider legs, for their blubbery bodies to ascend the large tree. Now, he gripped my arm, *hard,* and pointed.

I followed his gaze, then stiffened.

November was using the same shadow steps she'd provided me. But now she was using them to hop skip and jump around slashing claws, scything fangs and whipping tails. She dove in a somersault over Euryale's snapping jaws and, before hitting the ground, rebounded off a lily pad of shadow and jumped up to another materialized disc of shade in the air. At the same time, a monstrous Mago lunged through the space she'd been standing, jaws as wide as any shark's.

But November fell *through* the dark disc now, disappearing into the shadow and reappearing in the shade beneath an old pine. She stepped from the base of the tree, her wereblade shifting into a long, Spartan spear.

The molten scrawl circling her helmet flashed and shivered as if somehow the words themselves were experiencing delight.

Grendel screamed even louder, "Kill her!"

Five monsters spun in confusion, trying to spot where their prey had scampered this time. Once they rounded, noting November on the side of the road, they howled and with scrambling, scraping steps, burst forward in renewed gusto, leading fangs first.

The molten scrawl went suddenly still. November's spear traced the ground in front of her, and then, pine needle-shaped shadows hovered about the saboteur, like a hundred small porcupine quills.

She flung a hand forward and the needles swept through the air.

The lunging, charging monsters screamed, suddenly, faltering and stumbling back, struck and pierced by the flying barbs.

"Kill her!" Grendel kept screaming. "Kill her! Caliban!"

A reluctant lull fell over the battlefield.

"Caliban, *now!* Leave the cursed jeep!"

It took a moment, but then, with an air of reluctance, I heard thumping, shuddering footsteps. The titanic fleshy, T-Rex finally followed his companion's screams.

My own attention redirected, though, as I heard a snap and a rip and glanced up to see Preacher had torn a thick branch with his bare hands. He flung it at the two climbing hippo monsters beneath us. Some of their molars were the size of my skull, and their grayish faces were scarred and ripped and torn. Still with a demonic ferocity, they continued to ascend the tree, scrabbling up the bark and sending pine needles scattering to the ground.

Following Preacher's lead, I cracked a branch as well—smaller than his—and tried to fling it towards the eyes of our assailants. The hippo I'd aimed for just opened his mouth, swallowed the stick and chomped it whole with a popping, snapping sound. Mean, golden eyes glared out from the enormous head.

Yikes.

"Leonidas!" November screamed.

I looked down. She now stood beneath our tree amidst a large pool of shadows now swirling, circling like drain water. She gestured once then fell, tumbling through the shade as a claw slashed through the air, just missing.

More of the Kindred raced towards our tree.

"Preacher," I muttered, feeling my anticipation rising. "I think we have to jump." I pointed towards the swirling vortex of shadows.

My large friend looked at me and shook his head adamantly, before returning to poking at the nearest Kindred with his big stick. The monstrous jowls were now chomping at our branch, gnawing through the wood with crunching ferocity.

"That's not going to work!" I screamed.

He simply poked all the harder.

"Preacher!"

He shook his head more adamantly. More poking.

I huffed, then grabbed his arm and shoved him *hard.* He blinked as he tottered, stunned—then he fell, his arms waving as he toppled backwards towards the hole.

I jumped just as the branch cracked beneath me.

One of the spider-legged hippopotamuses screeched, trying to snag me from the air, but its corpulent body provided little in the way of agility, and it failed to reach us.

Other waiting jaws and flashing claws probed at the dark vortex of shadow itself. Preacher fell through first, past fuzzy shoulders and bowed heads, swallowed by the shade. The Kindred looked sharply up. Four sets of golden eyes fixed on me as I tumbled.

Jaws opened. One of the monsters leapt. I yelped, my fingers already ripping a tiger's eye from my pocket and *flung it* hard.

The small squishy pod exploded against a tree behind the Kindred. My stomach twisted, and I was ripped from my fall, teleporting fifteen short feet to where the tiger's eye had smashed.

The Kindred whirled, howling and snarling, confused. I pulled a second tiger's eye, gasping, but waiting.

The monsters began to encroach, pine-needles crushed beneath their horrible forms. The snake-thing, as wide as a tire and as long as a whale, began to weave through the trees, crushing small plants and hissing with a forked tongue through its lion head.

"No thank you," I muttered, shivering in revulsion. I aimed my next tiger's eye, then flung it *up*.

I didn't expect the monsters behind me to know what Kay Kelly's inventions did. I turned, hotfooting in the opposite direction of the swirling vortex of shadows. I sprinted, dodging through the trees, trying to count in my head, estimating how long I had until the pod tumbled back to earth.

The slithering grew louder behind me. Roaring and snarling and stomping came after it.

Ahead, I found myself racing towards a horrible scene. A pink-fleshed T-Rex, the size of a small house stood at the edge of the forest, watching me with hungry eyes. Its head was as large as a car.

Standing between the talons of the enormous *thing* that had somehow avoided its rightful extinction, a man in a suit and top hat stared through narrowed, golden eyes flecked with indigo. He looked like a toy beneath his massive friend's shadow. Grendel seemed puzzled for a brief moment, watching as I raced towards him. No hesitation now. Twenty feet until Grendel. Ten feet.

Caliban above lowered on his haunches, preparing to pounce, his two little arms swishing about like withered limbs tipped with callous and claw. He'd be able to rip a tree from its roots if he wanted. Grendel's form began to shimmer and swim. Fur sprouted from his arms; dark claws extended from his fingers.

I was too close. I pulled up short, wondering what on earth had happened to the tiger's eye. Had it failed to smash? I swallowed in horror, staring down the bounty hunter.

"The Hollow," Grendel said, his voice half growl, half scream. "That's what you said back outside the Sleeping Dwarf Inn, isn't it? And what do you want with the Hollow, Leonidas?"

Grendel lunged at me. Caliban jumped, leaving deep gouges in the ground. Behind me, the pack of Kindred, by the sound and clamor, had reached me too.

No way out. I'd mistimed—

My stomach twisted, I felt a sucking sensation.

The last glimpse I had of the Kindred bounty hunter was a half man, half beast—mid-shapeshift leaping in the shadow of his nightmarish friend.

Then I was snapped back, as if by a rubber band, to where the tiger's eye had smashed against pine needles.

It took a moment for me to reorient, teleporting the short distance as I had. I blinked, looking around. About fifty feet ahead of me, I spotted the wounded and furious Kindred skidding on pine needles and leaves, looking around in horror, trying to locate me.

Before my feet there opened the gaping black vortex of shadow and darkness. Behind me, I heard groaning and thumping.

I spotted a Kindred in its human form. One of the hippo's most likely. A large man, with a big belly. He was bloodied and groaning, but his golden eyes fixated on me in fury. One pudgy hand reached out, trying to snare my leg.

I squeaked in fright then lunged into November's shadow portal, vanishing from the mountain forest.

Chapter 42

A hand clapped over my mouth, and strong arms pulled me close. My back scraped dusty stone as my elbow grazed a cushion of moss and mold where we sheltered in the shadow of a jagged ledge, Annie on one side, Preacher on my other, his calloused hand clasped over my lips and a finger pressed to his own.

Annie's shadows crept up from the ground, concealing us in darkness.

Through the trees, down the hill, over a scene of carnage and burning vehicles, I spotted limping Kindred sniffing through the forest. The corpulent twin Kindred scrambled in the grass where the vortex of shadows looked to have vanished.

"Wherefsh—" I tried to speak, but Preacher tightened his grip, muffling the sound.

Annie's elbow brushed mine and, with the faintest motions, she sipped from her strange silver flask. Her horrible, eagle-head helmet was halfway removed, still covering her eyes. With slow movements, she removed her helmet, revealing her sweat-streaked olive complexion, and wiping an arm across her brow; she leaned back until her bristling head pressed to the mossy stone, more shadows rising over her sharp cheekbones and gently crooked nose.

Something howled in the distance; clawed feet pattered the forest floor. Creatures sniffed at the air then whirled about, moving in the direction of a keening noise, leaving us lodged in our precipice, hidden in the folds of the mountain itself.

Hesitantly, Preacher removed his hand, still holding a finger to his lips. He gestured, then moved with quiet footsteps around the edge of the mountain, down a slanted ridge of undergrowth and tangled weeds.

The three of us made way in relative silence, Annie's shadows still enshrouding us. My breath coming in worn gasps as I soldiered through the undergrowth, ripping aside brambles and thorns, wincing against prodding branches venturing from the canopy. The three of us retreated from the precipice, away from the sounds of our hunters, away from the battlefield.

Preacher led us to a small clearing, still carried only by our silence and the murmur of leaves against gentle wind. Eventually, my feet crunched a gravel road, and I looked up, my eyes tracing the familiar contents of the small gully, beneath the dangerous precipice trail.

My RV.

The gouge marks and bullet holes still ripped through the metal sides. One of the windows had been smashed, covered now with flattened cardboard and red duct tape. A wheel was missing and another slashed flat. Blood streaked the off-white paint job and I felt a tremor of grief as I pictured the corpse from Percy's pilfered memory.

"Dale?" I murmured, softly.

"Dead," Annie replied at my elbow. I glanced at her, surprised to discover tears in her eyes. She shook her head, her shoulders hunched, both arms wrapped tight around her thin form. "It's so—so horrible," she said, tears leaking from her eyes now. As if she couldn't help herself, she flung forward, snaring me in a hug and crying into my shoulder, her shoulders shaking.

Her skin was cool to the touch. I stiffened as she embraced me but let out a little puff of breath. I was getting emotional whiplash from the two natures my childhood friend seemed to hold in tandem. Now, though, the killer from the mountain pass seemed to have receded, leaving behind the Annie I remembered. She'd always had a far bigger heart than anyone I'd known. She'd cared for strangers and friends alike. It had seemed a super power to me then.

Now, as she shook, her arms wrapped around me, her face buried in my shoulder, I forced myself to relax.

I remembered, when we were five, how she'd stared over my shoulder. Her eyes grey and wide, *seeing* something behind me when the cold had overtaken me. Remembered how scared she'd look at first.

But in the end, I also remembered what she'd done.

Instead of allowing her fear to hold her back, she'd come right up to me, embracing me.

Now, Annie had her own dark passenger.

If anyone deserved compassion, it was my childhood friend.

With an act of will, I growled to myself, severing any of my own fear, my own reservations. I didn't do this with my power, but rather I did it by sheer choice.

My body became looser, and I hugged Annie back, holding her as she cried. "I'm very sorry," I murmured. "I didn't know the man. But I'm sorry."

I sighed wearily, unsure what to say in response. I'd known the bespectacled man was in over his head. Known he'd been treading in a valley of bones. I'd tried to warn him...

Too late. The Eternal Wars and its subjects had claimed another soul.

"I'm sorry," I repeated a final time.

Annie's head lifted from my shoulder, the prickle of her close-cropped hair brushing my cheek. She blinked back her tears, wiping her sleeve beneath her eyes. The simple motion gave me pause. Through my mind, images of her—the saboteur November—flashed. I glimpsed the wereblade spinning about, her shadow spreading as she moved with expert precision across the battlefield like a choreographed dancer. And yet, despite what I'd seen, as I stood next to my friend in the quiet clearing, facing my devastated RV, thinking of her lost employee, I couldn't see anyone but my old childhood companion.

"I'm sorry," I repeated, a bit louder, clearing my throat. I carefully extricated my door-handle handkerchief from my pocket. "It's clean," I murmured.

Annie looked at the handkerchief, a ghost of a smile crossing her lips. But the smile faded as she took the silk cloth and dabbed at her eyes. "He went badly," she said, still crying softly. Her eyes went suddenly gray, and she frowned, waving a hand in front of her face at some unseen entity. "Get away from me!" she snapped.

"Umm..."

"No, not you," she said quickly. "Just... a spook—a nasty one. They like grief. Feed on it."

I blinked, shaking my head, and Annie seemed to calm a bit, stepping closer to my RV, her eyes turning emerald once more. "Sorry," she murmured. She glanced to Preacher. "Thank you," she said. "For your help."

Preacher crossed his arms, standing in the shadow of a large fir.

I turned to Preacher now, finally allowing the dam of adrenaline to release pent up relief. I grinned and took two quick steps towards my friend, snaring his massive frame. "You're alive!" I said as I embraced him, hard.

Unlike Annie, I'd never fully mastered the art of a hug. A foreign thing for all my childhood and most my teenage years. I'd never known what to do with my chest. Even still, I angled awkwardly, my arms sort of limp and loose like strands of pasta. I wasn't sure how long one ought to hug. I wanted to hold him close, feel his warmth—my best friend was still alive! But at the same time, I didn't want to bother him. What was hugging etiquette? I'd have to remember to ask Nimue.

Preacher, though, a practiced embracer, pulled me tight. My face buried into his chest, the rough cotton of his duster rubbing my cheek. For a moment, it felt like a million little burdens tumbled from my shoulders. He patted my head affectionately.

A few seconds passed... Perhaps that was too much. Bother... I quickly released Preacher, stepping back and clearing my throat uncomfortably. I could feel Annie's eyes on me, amused despite her grief.

"You escaped before they reached the RV?" I said

Preacher glanced at me, but it was Annie who answered. "He went looking for you," she said. "I found him watching the RV after Grendel had come through. I'd returned for Dale... but..." Sorrow ripped her voice again. "Too late, I'm afraid."

I shook my head sadly. "I really am sorry, Annie."

"Me too." She handed my handkerchief back, and it was tribute to our lifelong bond that I accepted it, stained with another human's fluids as it was. Still, I folded it daintily, trying to avoid the tear-stained parts before tucking it back in my pocket.

I said, "Dale knew the risks. I warned him. A few times."

Annie sighed, a long, sad sound, bunching her mouth up to the side. "Gosh, that was very nice of you. You're a very nice person, Leon. I warned him as well... Like a lot. But, you know, he just seemed so eager to help."

"Curiosity is dangerous in the wrong hands," I murmured. "Grendel killed Dale, not you."

She shook her head again, closing her eyes and tilting back, as if to stare through a sightless gaze at the sky betwixt the boughs. "If not for Preacher, you might have also..." She cut herself off, wincing. "I can't even say it! Oh man, you guys, that was so dangerous up there! But you both were so very, very brave. Preacher," she said, looking at him now and staring with genuine awe. "You're so *amazing*! You traced Leon to the Sheriff's office."

I glanced at my companion. "Nice going. I guess you saw the tank leaving town, too, huh?"

Preacher grunted, examining the backs of his fingernails.

Annie closed her eyes against another wave of regret, but then looked back down. "We didn't have time to think up much of an escape plan. But thanks to you guys it all worked out really nicely!" She sniffled. "We didn't have a chance to clean the RV but... I do appreciate you, Preacher, taking the time to bury my friend."

I winced. "Dale's buried?"

She stared off again. "Yes," she murmured. "I'm going to miss Dale. He was such good company. I loved having him around..." She sighed again. "It wasn't a very deep grave. He deserved better than that. But, you know, we were running out of time to find—find you," she said, glancing at me sharply, and looking away again. "Didn't even have time to fix your home—I'm so sorry about that. The RV nearly went off the road twice on the way here."

"Not really meant to drive on three wheels," I said. "Especially with one of them flat."

Annie shrugged. "I don't really know much about cars. Never driven one."

I stared at my strange friend, struck again at her mass of contractions.

"I..." she began, hesitantly. "I'm still thinking what I was thinking before... I—maybe I shouldn't say it, but I think I have to say it, so I'll say it: I need your help, Leon. Both of you," she added, glancing to Preacher.

I quirked an eyebrow at my tall muscular friend, prodding at his thoughts. *Well?*

Preacher tapped his trigger fingers against his thigh, but his mind held firm. *I still don't trust her, Leon. Something doesn't add up. She's still lying to us.*

She just saved our lives...

Preacher frowned.

Lying about what?

He shrugged his thick shoulders. *I don't know. Personality quirks are one thing. I can look past those. The good Lord forgives all of us. But it's her story that doesn't make sense. Ask her. Ask her specifically. You'll see.*

I frowned at my friend's thoughts but returned my attention to Annie. "You're still intent on breaking into the Hollow?"

"I am," she said. "No more dawdling, though. Only a day left—and even that's quickly disappearing. I'm running out of time, Leon. I have to reach your brother. I have to find who murdered July. If I don't, February will kill me."

"That's what you said. You were meant to protect July. But you didn't."

"I didn't think she needed it," Annie said, her expression vague. Her tears had stopped now. "I need to break into the Hollow. Your brother has the answers. I'm like almost crazy certain of it, you guys."

"And requesting February's help—it isn't an option?"

"It's so horrible, but she'll kill me, Leon! She's no friend. She's a tyrant. She'll kill me as soon as Grendel would."

I blew cool air through pressed lips, trying to find the angle. My body ached, exhausted; I wanted to lean back and fall asleep. But we didn't have the luxury of rest. *We.* I supposed my mind was already made up. Annie had saved us—she needed our help. Besides, entering the Hollow would be easier with her. I couldn't let her reach my little brother.

I yawned again and shook my head. I'd have to sleep on the drive.

"I have the location," I said simply.

Annie stared at me. "I—I thought you might. With the confidant there..."

"Percy, yes... a bit of a risk, I'll admit." I winced at Preacher's disapproving scowl. "But I now know where the Hollow is."

"To the Hollow, then," Annie said excitedly.

I held up a hand. "There's still a Threshold Seal. Only living things allowed entry *must* be invited by February herself."

"There has to be a way around it, Leon!" Annie said, chipper all of a sudden and beaming at me now. She patted me on the shoulder, giving my arm an affectionate squeeze. "You're a renowned savant! You will figure something out—I believe in you! Those tiger's eye of yours, do they—"

"Don't work. We tried on a weaker veil. Not an option."

"Well..." Annie began fidgeting from foot to foot in front of my RV, shaking her head. "What about... what about some sort of feigning? We could fake dead? There are potions, roots, herbs that can slow a human heart." She wrinkled her nose. "Sounds nasty, I know."

"Faking dead is not the same thing as dead," I replied. "Not even the eternals have the power to resurrect. And necromancy deals only with the dead, not with resurrection. Unless you want to become a mindless, thoughtless, enslaved sort of zombie, then such things are out of the question."

"But there has to be *some* way!"

I hesitated, looking at Preacher. His eyes were still hard, cold, glaring towards where Annie paced back and forth. He stood resolute, tall, like a stony pillar in contrast to her hyper movement.

"Then what?" Annie exhorted. "Jeez Louise, this is why I need you, Leon. What do you think we should do?"

"I... I don't know exactly. But, it isn't going to be easy. Grendel said something as I vanished. He knows we're headed to the Hollow."

Annie and Preacher finally looked at me for once, both of them staring. "He did?" Annie said.

I nodded. "We mentioned it—or," I coughed, "Well, I did, when you first saved us from him back behind the Sleeping Dwarf Inn. He remembered. He knows where we're going. Surrounded by his children, he's not as scared of you as he was before."

Annie grit her teeth, dragging both her hands across her face in an expression of frustration.

"Whatever we decide, Grendel will head to the Hollow too. I wouldn't put it past him to have gotten the location from Percy as a backup plan. He might even warn February we're coming..."

Annie raised her voice before I could continue. "Grendel or not, we have to do this. We *have* to."

"Or you die?"

She winced, glancing off.

Preacher nudged my shoulder insistently. "That's all, Annie?" I said softly. "You'll die if we don't? For failing to protect July... You're holding nothing back? You wouldn't lie to me again, would you?"

Annie held my gaze for a moment. In her eyes, I spotted something and I reached out with my mind, grazing her thoughts. I felt a flash of... of something... a strong emotion she tried to bury just as quickly.

It took me a moment to realize what it was.

Guilt.

"No," she said simply, no longer meeting my eyes. "I'm not lying. Why would I?" She shrugged nonchalantly and then moved back to the RV. "Take us to the Hollow, Leon. I can help you get out of these mountains. And you can help me break into the Hollow."

"There's no way to enter," I called after her.

She paused in the threshold of the doorway. "You'll find a way. You always do. How long of a drive to the Hollow?"

I glanced to Preacher. He knew these mountains better than me.

Preacher looked reluctant, but at my insistent glance, he slowly extended five fingers.

"Five hours," I murmured.

"Well," Annie replied. "That gives us five hours to rest. I need some shuteye..." She murmured quieter, "Guess I'll just hope the nightmares leave me alone."

"Nightmares?"

She blinked as if startled I'd heard this last part. "Oh, no, don't worry. It's nothing. You're kind to care, but really, it's fine. Just... well, every night since I can remember I've had scary dreams. But don't worry about me: look, Leon, five hours isn't long. But it's what we have. What *you* have to come up with a plan. Please! I need you to figure out a way to break into the Hollow or my life is over." She looked me in the eyes, and for a moment, all signs of guilt, of doubt of anything faded to a stony, certain resolve. "Leon, please. If you do this," she said gravely. "I'll give you what you want."

"And what do you think that is?"

"I—not to presume, but... Freedom? Anonymity. I know an old druid, lives near the Indiana crossroads. She's good—the best I've ever seen. Really, really pretty hair, too. Beautiful hair. But anyway, she can change your appearance—not how savants do it, with dyes and colors and plastic, but permanently. She can change your fingertips, even your DNA. She can change your name, your vocal cords, your height, your identity— everything, Leon. You'll be free at last. No one will know you, no one will find you. You can disappear into the wind, like a ghost!"

I stared at her. "A druid? I've never heard of her."

"You wouldn't. Not to sound all high and mighty, but saboteurs have contacts of our own. But she'll do it for me—she owes me a favor."

"If I help you," I said, my voice husky, "You'll give me my freedom?" For a moment, my mind flashed back to the Gallows farm. I'd never considered I might be able to build something similar one day—not with my name, and my face. Settling down, slowing down wasn't an option. But this...

"The lone ranger, bound by none, bound to none," Annie said, an ironic tinge to her voice. "Isn't that what you want?"

I licked the corner of my lips, feeling the dry ridges and exhaling slowly. "You're telling the truth?"

"I give you my word, Leon. The druid is real. Help me, and I'll bring you to her."

"What cost?"

"I'll pay the cost..."

"My friends," I said softly, thinking of Kay, thinking of Preacher, of Nimue...

Annie paused. "You'll have to leave *everything*. Your enemies will use your friends to find you. The best thing you can do for all of them is to leave, isn't it? Bound by none..."

"Bound to none," I said. "I heard you the first time."

I considered her words for a moment. What she was saying seemed impossible, and yet, I knew there were druids of the type. Old magic, Celtic magic. The sort of thing that could reform a man, rebirth him in his own flesh—but different. I'd lose my old identity. No one would know who I was. I could move to Argentina. I could move across the world. Hell, I could live wherever I wanted, unseen, unknown, unwanted. A nobody. Maybe even buy a farm of my own...

I smiled softly.

A nobody... just like I'd always wanted. I could bury my crown... Bury my father's legacy. Imperium and Endeavor both be cursed. I needed nothing from them, and I had nothing to offer in return. Annie was offering me my freedom, a new life, a new start.

It was everything I could dream of.

"Do this for me," Annie said, fully aware—it seemed—she had me hooked. "And I promise you, I'll take you to this druid. You'll never suffer the name of Rex again. You have my promise." Her eyes flashed and then she turned, entering the broken, slashed, RV.

I stood in the forest, beneath the ancient trees, staring at the mobile home set against a backdrop of dark brown bark and rusty pine needles. A hand descended on my shoulder, tugging insistently.

I glanced back and Preacher tapped a flat hand beneath his chin.

The sign was one of the first I'd learned.

Lying.

I held my friend's gaze and dipped my head in a slow nod. I couldn't help but agree. Annie wasn't telling us something. She'd hidden a truth within a truth, but even so she'd held something back. I knew the tactic well. I'd used it myself before. People think I'm honest when I reveal stuff two layers deep, gouging out hidden truths and buried secrets... They think a man who'd reveal such things must be an honest one.

They see me reveal my junk and think me authentic, because their worst secrets match my second layer. But what they don't realize is that revealing the things two layers deep is only a defense mechanism. A trick.

Men like me have tens of layers, revealing the second is sheer camouflage, a bluff.

Annie had told a portion of the truth... A dark portion.

Which meant whatever she was hiding, I knew in my gut, was far darker still.

One way or the other, though, I wasn't willing to risk Preacher, or my own life, to brave these mountains on our own. Grendel was still coming after us. Besides, Annie was determined. I couldn't let her lose my brother.

Did she know about Napoleon? Was that what she'd hidden?

I frowned, considering this for a moment. But then shook my head, scraping one shoe along the pine needles and tracing the toe of my other boot.

I supposed there was only one way to discover Annie's own secret.

I'd always known I'd have to return to the Hollow, the most wretched of mutinied prisons... I had simply hoped it wouldn't call my name so soon.

With a sigh and gesture, I stomped back to the RV. "We need to get a tire at that station outside Picker's," I muttered. "Then fix up what we can and patch up the rest."

Preacher grunted and moved swiftly after me, trying to catch my attention. I turned to him, looking him in the eyes, pausing with one hand braced against the frame of the RV. "We have to," I said firmly. "There's no choice. We have to."

I waited for an objection, my jaw set. But then Preacher just sighed, shaking his head then pushed past me into the RV.

Give me the location and I'll drive. You sleep, his thoughts pressed as he passed. *I'll take care of the tires. If we're going, then she's right. You have five hours to figure out a way to break past the Threshold Seal, to avoid Grendel—who's coming after us—and to trick February herself.*

"Don't forget the insane clan of genies," I replied with a quiet grunt.

Preacher tapped his nose and then entered the RV, moving towards the driver seat, his scowl deepening, it seemed, with each step.

Chapter 43

Five hours north, through twisting roads, across abandoned logger lanes and paths hidden by bramble and thorn and shadow, a lonely stretch of forest and ancient wood claimed the desolate mountains.

The Wilderness, we called it. An old, deeper portion of the million-acre forests. Untouched, virgin land, much of it—unseen by mortal eyes. I knew places where the Prometheus flowers grew, sputtering cold flame against mountain snow, surrounded by trees twisted in avalanches, the vegetation unknown to human botanists. Species of bird and squirrel and larger animals, never before seen could be found. Not just critter and creature, but also denizens of the Kingdoms of Pilfery roamed the Wilderness, traveling through the Stormer gateways hidden beneath the ancient oak.

Our destination, sequestered in the furthest reaches of this forgotten land, came visible after nearly six hours of travel.

In the distance, it came like a blemish against greens and browns. Cresting walls, twisted with thick vines and corded ivy; thorns and prickles and brambles of every nature twined up the colossal structure, circling the walls which seemed as large as those of a football stadium.

"Pull over here," I muttered, placing a hand on Preacher's arm and gesturing off to the side of the road. I leaned back in the passenger seat, my feet resting on the dash. Annie was taking her turn sleeping in my bedroom, recovering from the sortie with Grendel's offspring.

The RV jolted along the trail—the two tires Preacher had attached not quite suiting but serving their purpose for now. I winced as we bounced over a particularly cracked portion of the dirt road, and Preacher carried us off to the side of the trail amidst the trees.

"On foot from here," I murmured, peering through the windshield at the distant prison walls visible over the treetops and thick forests.

Preacher grunted and waved a hand to the West.

"Well, yes, but we'll give the gateway portal a wide berth, won't we?" I said, glaring. "The vermin keep to their tunnels and torture devices anyway. They won't see us."

Preacher indicated the barely visible wall of the distant prison. I sighed. "Yeah, we'll have to be careful. They'll be watching the roads."

Preacher put the vehicle in park on the side of the road, cutting the engine with a twist of the keys. Together, he and I shared a long look, and then he adjusted his wide-brimmed hat with soft motions, a strangely gentle gesture for such rough fingers. He raised his eyebrows, regarding me a final time.

"I'm sure," I murmured, responding to his thoughts. "We have to." I felt a cold jab of unease in my belly. I swallowed, though, pushing it down. "What other choice is there? Come, let's get Annie. It only gets worse from here."

***

Annie jolted awake beneath my hand. She didn't startle, so much as attack, rolling off the bed in one swift motion, a hand darting into her jacket—which she'd worn while sleeping—pulling her wereblade in dagger form and pressing the emerald tip to my chin all in one smooth motion.

She blinked, her gray eyes turning green once more, and shook her head, swallowing. "Sorry," she murmured. She looked around, glancing back at the disheveled bed and one of the blankets which had been kicked off onto the floor.

"You're a restless sleeper," I murmured.

She gave a sad little shake of her head. "Nightmares—I have them whenever I sleep."

I winced in sympathy. "You mentioned. I'm sorry."

"Oh, that's quite alright! Thank you. Are we here? Is it locatable now?" She glanced back to the window, this one boarded up with cardboard and duct tape. A gouging claw mark had ripped through half the wall and gave glimpses of green foliage and summer sunlight just beyond.

"Yes. It's open for the next twenty or so hours," I murmured. "Walk from here. The prison guards mostly keep to the Hollow itself, but other things watch the roads."

Annie massaged the bridge of her poorly set nose, but then nodded, moving over towards her gray backpack and hefting it over one shoulder. She took a sip from her silver flask and then gave me a long look, her fingers twitching against the strap of her bag. "Do we have a way in?"

I glanced at Preacher, but quickly looked away. "We've been discussing it," I replied. "If we go and speak to February—"

Annie's eyes flashed. "I told you," she moaned. "This is not an option, Leon. She'll really, really kill me. I didn't protect July—that's my fault. Unless I figure out who *really* murdered," she shuddered, "her... then I can't go back."

"Right, well... you seemed adamant about that. Which means I can think of only one other way into the prison."

"Oh?" She perked up, eyes bright.

My voice darkened, and for a moment I didn't dare to speak. It felt wrong, standing in my RV across from my shattered mirror. The twelve-string guitar which I hadn't yet restrung leaned in its black, rubber stand, as if reminding me of who I was.

At last, I forced the words to come. "We have to destroy the Threshold Seal *from outside,*" I murmured, shaking my head in resignation. "Most likely an impossible feat..."

"Wow—that sounds really smart but how can we do that?"

"We'll have to lure one of the guards near enough to us without being seen."

"Can't a guard just invite us in?"

"No. According to Kay, only February is bound to the Threshold Seal—only she can invite anyone in. Anyone or anything trying to cross the boundary will die instantly without a direct invitation."

"I see. Well, so, like how does this guard help us?"

"Well," I murmured, "it's a long shot. A very long one. But..." I glanced at Preacher. "If I can get a guard close enough, I may be able to puppet them."

"Take over their mind?" Her eyes widened to saucers and she nibbled her lip. "I thought you didn't like doing that. It sounds kind of mean."

"I... yes, how do you know I don't puppet?"

"Oh," she said with a would-be casual wave. "I've done my homework, Leon. I wouldn't have hired you if I hadn't. You're known for having a conscience! Which is so cool."

"Yes... well. Desperate times."

"You'll puppet a guard, what then?"

I swallowed, feeling a slight shiver down my spine. "You'll need to give me your wereblade," I murmured. "The only way to kill a saboteur, I'm told, is with greater power, or one of their own weapons."

Annie stared at me now, gaping. "You... you want to *kill* February?"

I looked her in the eyes. "It's either her or you," I said. "I'll use the puppeted guard to carry your wereblade. If February dies, then the Seal breaks. Preacher will cause a distraction, gathering attention to a breached portion of the prison wall. February herself will have to come investigate, I'll make sure of it with my puppet."

Annie swallowed, and for a moment I thought she might scream. Something about her gaze seemed frozen, locked on some distant image neither Preacher nor I could see, nor fathom.

"You'll kill February?" she murmured.

Of course, I'd known this would be a sticking point. Why on earth would a saboteur agree to a murder of their own order while simultaneously investigating another killing? July was dead. February hiding. Annie investigating. No way she should agree...

Unless, like Preacher said, she was lying.

I pressed on, my voice still even, quiet, "It's the only way to break the seal. The only way to give us what we want. We won't be able to kill February without your wereblade, though. You'll need to grant permission for Preacher and me to wield it."

Annie stared between the two of us now, and I could see her thoughts spinning. She didn't shake her head, nor did she protest. She didn't get up or shout in my face. Instead, she simply said, more somberly now, "You need my wereblade for this? It sometimes has a will of its own."

Preacher glanced at me again, but I kept my eyes fixed firmly on Annie. I knew Preacher was thinking exactly what I was. Why would she agree to kill February? She'd said the lieutenant of the saboteurs would execute her if she was found trying to investigate July's murder. She'd said she'd been responsible for protecting July and had failed. Was February now out for blood... None of it made sense anymore.

Annie was still lying...

Another note of concern: this plan would never work. Too many contingencies. I couldn't kill a saboteur either, not even with a wereblade. What would Nimue think, even if I tried?

No... I couldn't kill February.

I just needed to break the Threshold Seal. And for that to happen, Annie needed to believe the lie.

But lies were costly... Even now, I could feel my powers slipping, fading away. Would I lose my powers for a few days? For months? Forever?

To lie is to muddy the mind. At least I hadn't taken an oath...

Annie continued staring at me, as if trying to glimpse beneath the mask. But I kept my face impassive, my eyes fixed. I knew what had to be done. One way or another, we were going to enter the Hollow.

I thought briefly of Annie's promise. A druid at the crossroads. A new face, new identity. No longer hunted by Endeavor trying to crush the Imperium. No longer hunted by the Imperium trying to restore the lost heir. An ability to start over, to disappear, to drop my weary head and allow the crown to slip.

First things first...

We needed to enter the prison.

***

Two hours we trekked through the darkened woods. Two hours we hacked our way through undergrowth and untainted forest. We moved as silently as possible. I only had six tiger's eyes left—some of them lost, having tumbled from the protective pouch and squished by an oversized hip of a Union-enforcer, the others used.

I still had three vials of gold dust, shaped like glow sticks. I also had Lancelot's shield, which I wasn't wearing for the moment. My knife was still missing, discarded back beneath the old lantern outside the Endeavor bar, while Preacher's six-shooters were beneath his trench coat, jammed into the stitch-seamed leather holsters, once again refilled with ammunition. But twelve bullets would do little for us now.

Annie hefted her backpack over one shoulder, occasionally using shadows to carry us forward, through portions of the dusky trees.

Once, she lifted all of us to a low branch of knotted wood, then, like stones skipping across a pond, she whisked us from shadow to shadow, avoiding the undergrowth entirely. Another time, we'd been forced to use three tiger's eyes to cross over a particularly sun-streaked creek with no bridge. Beneath the light of the sun reflecting off the sparkling water, Annie's own shadows had seemed weaker...

It was beginning to make sense to me. The more light, the less Annie's powers worked. The more shadow, the more material she had to play with, sometimes stepping into it as if through a portal, other times solidifying it into a substance. Baffling really... Unlike any of the six recognized eternal talents.

Preacher had his own backpack. A hefty thing, weighed down with materials for our breaching attempt. As we hopped over a smaller stream, angling along the natural path cut by forest creatures who'd made their way to the source of freshwater, Annie glanced past me, breathing softly, her olive features standing out against the sunlight. "What's in the bag?" she asked.

"Bomb," I said simply.

Preacher nodded.

Annie blinked. "Wow, really? A bomb? What for?" She stiffened suddenly, and her shoulders straightened. Her shadow began to shift and shimmer, and a whispered voice murmured, "Allow me a moment, child. This is where I may be of use."

But then Annie shook her head adamantly. "No—no," she said, whispering back to herself. "It's fine. I've got this."

I just stared at the odd exchange, my skin prickling. I chose not to comment and instead replied to her earlier question. As I spoke, Annie's green eyes rounded on me, wide and earnest.

"We need to get February's attention some way," I whispered back, delicately stepping over a pinecone to make sure it didn't *crunch*.

Annie winced, biting her lip, but then nodded. She took the lead again, pulling her wereblade; it reformed into a machete which glinted in the sunlight as she hacked and cut through any twisting shrubs or low hanging branches impending our tiresome trek towards the old prison, the cursed Hollow.

Breathing heavily now, dripping with sweat, feeling my lower back sodden against my dark shirt, I suddenly froze, listening. Preacher heard it too, going very still.

"Wait," I cautioned.

Annie paused, her wereblade overhead, beneath the canopy. The emerald machete glinted in the sun, but then, slowly, melted back into a dagger. She placed it back in her coat, and turned slowly, head cocked curiously as she peered up the small incline towards a row of green bushes covered in small, bright-yellow berries. Without a care in the world, she began to stride towards the bush.

"Hang on," I whispered, reaching out and snagging her shoulder.

She stopped, glancing at me, looking at my hand, and then patting it. "Are you alright?" she said, her expression quizzical, and excited, even. She glanced back towards the bush, where the sound had originated from, an eager look in her eyes, as if somehow the threat of imminent danger was nothing more than a passing entertainment.

"Just wait," I replied. "We need to be careful."

Crouched low, I moved towards the small thicket. My hands pressed to soft mud, knees to old, rotten vegetation, the sweet scent of the yellow berries lingering on the air; I crawled beneath the tiny branches and star-shaped leaves.

Annie crawled next to me, her shoulder brushing mine, twigs snapping beneath her fingers in the mud as she giggled beneath her breath. Preacher moved more cautiously and quietly on my other side. The three of us looked out from beneath the bush, staring across a wide, two-lane road leading towards...

The Hollow.

Chapter 44

A stone's throw away, thick, thorny walls soared to meet the sun. Large, purple gates, etched with old runes and dappled with fragments of strange glass, reflected sunlight in resplendent patterns back along the dusty ground.

"Avoid the reflections," I whispered as quietly as I could. "It'll set the alarm."

The sound I'd initially detected was growing louder. Suddenly, I cursed and pulled my friends back, holding them behind berries.

"What is—" Annie fell silent as she also spotted the source of the noise.

A horse-drawn chariot was coming up the road from the opposite direction, heading towards the prison. Figures sat in the chariot, dark, hunched beings, indeterminable from this distance.

I knew, of course, what they were. My eyes narrowed.

Annie leaned in, then gasped. "Sons of Ares," she said. "Look at them! They're adorable!"

I began to nod, but then frowned. This wasn't the word I would've chosen. I held a finger to my lips, allowing the chariot to approach. The chariot was made of ornate, whitened wood and golden trim. Glistening emblems boasted from gilded wheels. The Sons of Ares in the rider's seat guided the horses.

The carriage behind wasn't nearly so ornamented. No gold, no gilding, no etchings or carvings whatsoever. Rather, it seemed a hunk of metal with angry, crude bars the size of telephone poles.

"What is it?" Annie murmured.

"Prison transport. I've seen its kind before."

In fact, I'd seen this *exact* carriage before. The scene played as if from memory. As the chariot and carriage drew nearer to the Hollow, the gates began to creak, then open slowly, grinding against the dust. The purplish metal and the glinting fractions of glass protruding from the wall itself reflected the sun across the trees.

Annie ducked even lower, but we were still too far away to be spotted by the guards of the Hollow.

"It's opening," she whispered. "Now's our chance!"

But I gripped her shoulder, holding her back. "The Threshold Seal doesn't require a physical boundary," I hissed. "It'll kill you as soon as you set foot on the premises. No—not yet. Wait—watch!"

The chariot and carriage suddenly went past and Annie looked suddenly excited, suggesting even more familiarity with the riders and coachmen. The Sons of Ares were made of ebony bone.

No flesh, nor muscle on them. The dark, pristine skeletons had a strange beauty about them. Stormfolk, some called them. Skybanes, others said. The ebony skeletons were laughing and jeering, pushing at each other in their chariots. Three in the first chariot, two riding in the coach seat of the prison wagon.

"What are they dropping off?" Annie whispered a bit too loudly for my liking.

"Not dropping off," I replied in an even quieter tone as the chariot and its occupants trundled past. "Picking up."

She looked at me, quirking an eyebrow above her slightly bent nose, then glanced towards the thick, ugly metal carriage. It was empty behind the upright bars.

Next to me, a yellow berry had squished like bird droppings on Preacher's shoulder. My friend's scowl, though, remained fixed on the passing chariot. Preacher had never much approved of the worst kept secret in the Dwindling Imperium.

"Prisoners make good sport," I whispered back. "Especially if the Sons of Ares are involved."

"I—what?" Annie pressed, absentmindedly squishing more of the berries around her as if she were now bored.

The chariot and carriage were now drawing near to the opening doors. In the darkness of the giant stadium-shaped prison walls, I spotted movement.

Things poked and pushed a large creature forward from inside the Hollow. I glimpsed flashes of silver and glinting metal. Loud, unnerving laughter suddenly burst from within the darkness and some of the figures began twisting and moving in strange ways. I shuddered, staring through the giant gates, past the waiting skeletons.

"What do you mean, prisoners make good sport?" Annie whispered. "That sounds so horrible!"

I just pointed. "Looks like a thunder troll. This won't be pretty."

More maniacal laughter burst in peels from the open doorway to the Hollow. The massive purple and glass gates were now fully open. Thick black chains stretched from the ceiling and latched to metal rungs at the base of the gate—the rungs alone were the size of small canoes.

The Sons of Ares pulled their chariot and carriage off to the side. Only five of the ebony, skeletal creatures had come. Too few—or, at least, so I'd thought once upon a time.

Suddenly, pale figures shoved something *hard,* sending the large creature stumbling out of the Hollow gates into the sunlight. The enormous being held up a three-fingered hand, blinking against the sudden glare. The cackling, laughing guardians of the Hollow slipped back into the darkness, leaving the beast outside with the Sons of Ares and their chariot. More grinding, more groaning; the chains went taut. Then, the twin doors to the

Hollow began to close.

"Leon," Annie said quickly.

"Tell him we must go," she said, in a colder, deeper voice. "Tell him now."

Annie replied to her own comment, "I will, just hang on. That's what I'm *saying*. Jeez Louise, you can be so impatient sometimes."

"We must go," the cold voice snapped back.

Annie's face twisted from scowl to wide-eyed interest and back again. Never once, between the two personalities did a glimpse of fear even emerge.

I swallowed, but replied just as firmly as the iron tone, "Not yet. Just wait."

Already, I could feel my head aching, could feel my powers slipping. I blinked, and for a moment, everything around us seemed dark. I shook my head and grit my teeth. I felt a calloused hand grip mine.

Preacher squeezed, hard, and pain jolted up my arm. I blinked, but nodded ever so lightly, grateful. I needed to focus. Just... a bit... longer...

The thunder troll was still blinking in the sunlight, stumbling a bit and trying to catch his bearings. Sometimes, I could tell how many years a prisoner had been trapped based solely on how long it took for them to adjust to daytime once again.

The thunder troll was as tall as three men and wide as the carriage. Muscles sprouted all across it. A thin web of flesh stretched from its upper layer of arms, to its lower layer. It had four arms, two legs, and a skull shaped like a boulder.

One of the thunder troll's eyes was missing, another gift, I imagined, from the Hollow. It snarled now, looking around, spittle flying. It began to growl, spreading its arms. The fleshy mesh between its appendages expanded like the fabric of an umbrella.

Annie stared, going rigid as the Sons of Ares began to move towards it. The ebony skeletons called harshly at the monster, weapons of crude metal, darkened in fire and ash, jabbed forward. "Oh no," Annie murmured, her voice whining. "Leon, are they going to hurt it? We can't let them hurt it! Look, it seems so scared!" Her voice bled with genuine concern. And she actually made to move, forgetting, for the moment it seemed, why we were even here. Her eyes fixated on the troll in trouble, and she began to rise.

I caught her arm, though, yanking her back down. "No!" I said. "We can't help." This was true. For more reasons than she knew.

The thunder troll roared and then suddenly clapped its hands together. Where the fleshy sheet between its arms flapped, a sudden burst of sound and wind erupted like, quite literally, a thunderclap.

Two of the Sons of Ares were blasted to their bony bits, ebony fragments and teeth and femurs sent flying.

The three remaining ones charged forward, soundless, their skeletal feet pounding the ground.

Annie was now moaning, holding her head, and rocking back and forth in the mud, amidst trails of yellow berries she'd squished for fun. "No, no, no," she murmured, crying. "No, stop—they need to stop! They're hurting each other!"

I placed a hesitant hand on her shoulder, murmuring, "It's going to be okay."

She looked at me, tears down her face and gave me a quick side hug, holding me close, her shoulders still shaking with grief. In my mind, I glimpsed images of her thoughts: memories flitted in her mind. *A young girl trapped in darkness, shaking and sobbing. The same girl staring beneath the slit under the door, desperately hoping to see light. Her food tray empty, discarded in one corner. I could feel the hunger pangs, could feel the terror.*

The sobbing child tried to cry out, but no one responded. I watched the memories play in Annie's mind. *Weeks. Months. No one met her cries. When the door did open, it only brought pain.*

I watched in Annie's mind as she continued to shake and shiver, *still crying, months later, thinner now, face gaunt and streaked with dirt and mud and blood.*

I watched the memory as Annie's bent form huddled against a cold wall, concrete against her small spine. I watched as the door to her cell opened. A man in a hat entered the room, a thick stick in one hand.

"Come here," the voice said in darkness. "Little one, come closer."

Six-year-old Annie pulled in on herself, her arms tight around her knees, her frail body shivering in terror and fear, sweat on her small arms.

"Come here!" the voice insisted, louder.

Annie shook her head, desperately, still crying.

The man snarled and stepped into the room.

Suddenly, Annie straightened like a string pulled taut. The final tears trailed down her cheeks and cold, green eyes fixed on the figure in the door.

"No, I won't," a rigid voice emanated from the child's lips. A voice from someone far older, far colder.

Annie straightened then, standing upright in the dark, shivering, with only a thin shirt on her frail form for warmth. Annie stared directly at the man in the door. "You won't hurt me," Annie had snapped.

The man in the hat froze in the door, staring. Then, he snarled, lunging in, stick swinging...

The memory faded, Annie still leaned against me, still sobbing. "Stop hurting them," she whispered beneath her breath. "Stop!"

The Hollow loomed resolute and indifferent, the thorns and twisting vines lining the wall itself rising high into the air over the odd spectacle on the dirt road. The thunder troll swept two of its right arms through the approaching Sons of Ares. Another burst of bones and two skulls went flying over the first carriage.

The horses whinnied... Of course, they weren't normal horses either. Black, dark bones, not a stitch of flesh or meat on them. The skeletal sons of the god of war lay scattered across the ground and ditch. The troll stood huffing, twin jets of smoke puffing from each nostril as it glanced around, breathing heavily, its gray, fleshy chest heaving.

But then the bones began to rattle. Then grow. Skulls grew necks, necks grew arms. Arms grew ribbed abdomens, abdomens grew legs. Necks grew *more* skulls, *more* bones. They didn't just reattach, they *bred*.

Now, rising from the dust and dirt, where there had once been *five* Sons of Ares, now there stood fifteen of the stormfolk.

They were chanting now, their voices echoing in the sky. "You can't kill bloody death," they cried. "It comes for you all!"

The troll bellowed.

"You can't kill bloody death!" cried one chorus. The answering voices screamed, "It comes for you all!"

The troll thumped its arms together, slamming hands once more. Another thunderclap and another blast of wind.

More bones exploded, flying every which way. More skeletons rose from the earth, piecing together, but growing rapidly at the same time. Now fifty skeletons surrounded the troll, crude weapons growing from their own bones, or, in the case of others, leg bones were wielded like cudgels as some of the skeletons preferred to hop forward, using their appendages as weaponry.

"You can't kill bloody death!" they screamed. "It comes for you all!"

The troll lashed out. Another blast of bony pieces. It clapped its hands, another burst of skulls. But now, the wave of the Sons of Ares was growing insurmountable. Over a hundred of the things, all chanting and screaming. A small army of the stormfolk descended on the troll. It put up a valiant fight, wheeling about, windmilling its massive arms...

But perhaps it should have simply listened to the inevitability of its assailants' chant.

The troll was soon taken down, even as it scattered more bones, even as smashed ebony littered the road, and the Hollow's purple and glass doors stared indifferently at its once occupant.

Then, beaten into submission, but not dead, the thunder troll was dragged by the Sons of Ares into the back of their prison carriage. So many of the brittle, frail beings had grown from the fragments they were able to carry the troll over their heads on their spindly fingers.

"You can't kill bloody death! It comes for you all! You can't kill bloody death! It comes for you all!"

And then, the troll was shoved into the back of the prison carriage. The Sons of Ares locked the door. They continued chanting as they wheeled their skeletal beasts about, their ornate chariot and iron prison cart rotating in the dusty street before twisting and heading back down the path.

Annie was still crying out of sheer empathy. I supposed trauma made some of us cold, but others only more compassionate. I couldn't even begin to piece together my childhood friend's state of mind. Preacher and I stayed very still as the monstrous creatures passed, chanting, clapping, and screaming in delight.

We pressed to the mud and mold, quiet, watching with furtive and quick eyes as the last of the small army of skeletons passed us, led by the carriage and chariot. The chant continued up the road, continued as they rounded the switchback, moving through the trees. Continued even, for the next minute, for the next few.

At last, still listening to the now distant chant, Annie shivered and looked me in the eyes. "That was so, so awful. I hated that!"

"I'm sorry," I murmured, and I meant it.

She trailed off, inhaling shakily, "I never thought..." she stared after them. "Guardians help me," she murmured, one hand probing towards her gray backpack where she carried her helmet. "What a sight. What are they going to do with that troll?" Her voice tinged with heartache, and I felt my own stomach twist, my brow darkening with a frown.

"Nothing nice. The prisons have illegal gladiatorial arenas amongst each other. Sport for the gods and the more powerful Kingdoms. Ever since the collapse of the Imperium and the Endeavor's incompetent usurpation, the gladiatorial arenas have been stocked full of prisoners bartered and bought from the prisons. All in attendance, human and otherwise, bet ridiculous sums on the outcomes of the fights."

"The troll is going to be a gladiator?" Annie gasped, wide-eyed.

I shrugged. "Most likely. Maybe in one of the smaller, underground fighting cages, or—maybe—for Ares' birthday."

"Ares? As in the god of war?" Annie's nose wrinkled, and for the first time, I detected a note of scorn in her tone. I watched as her expression went rigid. I was beginning to note the physical differences when Annie's split occurred. It seemed Annie and November played an odd sort of dance—November never seemed to force control, rather waiting for Annie to give some sort of permission, spoken or otherwise. Now, a colder tone—the voice of November the saboteur, snapped, "Good riddance. These skinting creatures are a blight on humankind. They are a threat to all that matters."

Annie blinked, shaking her head. In a quiet whisper she replied to herself, "I don't believe that. That was just sad..."

I watched Annie, though, gauging her response. I murmured, "A natural enemy of the saboteurs, aren't they? The gods don't like you either, don't worry. But yes—Ares' birthday is coming up. It's going to be a tournament to rival any mankind or otherwise has ever known."

Annie shook her head, staring off in the direction the thunder troll had been taken. "What a waste," she said. "And people watch these things? The death and carnage—they enjoy it? That's awful!"

I held up my hands in mock surrender beneath the shrubbery. "I don't have an invite to Ares' birthday. Don't blame me."

Annie looked back to the prison, eyes narrowed. "And those *things,* the ones who were laughing, who pushed the troll out. What were they?"

I felt a flicker of fear at those words and swallowed. "Guardians of the Hollow," I said. "Banes, they're called. A cursed clan of genies. Banished from their own kind—every one of them insane."

"Insane?"

"Yes... I don't know exactly how.. Something to do with gold and dreaders—tampering with horrors instead of wishes. Regardless, the Banes now live in the Hollow."

"And these insane genies guard the Hollow? Might they help us for the right price?"

"We'll find no allies among the Banes. They're insane, which means *puppetting* one will come difficult. But if we want to enter the Hollow, to find my brother, we have to do what we can."

Annie gnawed on her lower lip. "Oh boy, I don't know... You're willing to kill February," she murmured.

I stared at her. "You're willing to let me?"

Annie glanced off towards the purple gates. "If we don't find who killed July, if I don't bring that information to Regent January, then my life is done."

"Simple, then. You or her, right?"

Annie closed her eyes, swallowing. Her shadow began to shift again, her shoulders set once more. She nodded once, and in so doing, confirmed my suspicions. "Yes," November said simply. "If it's the only way to enter the Hollow, to speak with your brother, I suppose we'll have to kill her, won't we?"

I looked at her fully now, frowning. "We'll need your wereblade. Do we have permission to use it?"

November winced, glancing off. Her fingers probed in the pocket of her peacoat. "Must I really?"

"Trying to kill a saboteur is impossible with human weapons. We need your permission. Even I've heard how fickle wereblades can be."

"My permission... yes... Well, if that's what it takes. Then yes, you have my permission."

I went very still all of a sudden, my eyes unblinking from beneath a searching frown.

November returned my look. "What?" she demanded. "If it's against your conscience, say so. You're the one who proposed the plan."

"Yes, I did," I said, my voice as cold as November's. My eyes fixed on her. My gaze flashed with dark spots again. I could feel my powers threatening to abandon me completely now...

The sound of the chant still came audibly over the trees and rushed to meet the air swirling above the dark canopy.

The saboteur dusted off her sleeves. "If you have a better plan... then just..." She froze, staring at me now. "Leonidas, what is it?"

I looked to Preacher, still glaring. "Do it!" I snapped. "Get me out."

Preacher nodded once, fished his gun from his side and didn't hesitate. He pointed it at my head and pulled the trigger.

My mind jolted with pain. Annie stifled a shout, her hand jumping to her mouth, her eyes bulging in shock. I blinked, shaking my head, still standing, a gaping hole having blasted through my ear, tearing off my jaw and ripping out the other side.

"I... Leonidas, Preacher, what..."

November cursed and reached for her wereblade, but when she raised it, nothing happened. She stared, stunned. The shadows around her feet froze in place. "Leonidas!" She snarled and rolled back from Preacher, one hand jamming towards the backpack, unzipping it, fingers groping for her devilish helmet.

Except, her fingers found only fluff. She yelled in horror, ripping the fluff out and sending it flying every which way.

"Leonidas!" she yelled. "What did you do? What's happening!"

I blinked one last time, reaching up and feeling the bullet hole that had ripped my head in two. My fingers probed towards a missing section of teeth. I was still standing, still alive...

The impossibility of it all jarred me, like ice water down one's neck. I exhaled slowly, closing my eyes, then opening them again.

Chapter 45

We were back in the RV, standing over Annie's sleeping form. Preacher's hand rested against my head where he'd smacked me a good one, rousing me from my trance. My eyelashes flickered, refocusing on where my right palm grazed Annie's forehead. Her own eyes were now fluttering; each time she blinked they flashed emerald or gray.

"Preacher," I said firmly. "Have it?"

Preacher nodded, pointing the wereblade at Annie's head. His fingers tensed, and sweat already beaded on his forehead. But he didn't struggle to hold it nearly as much as Kay Kelly had back in his shop. Kay's wereblade had been imparted by the death of a saboteur, ours by permission. The only two ways to access the legendary weapons.

Finally, Annie's eyes snapped open, and she stiffened, staring at the crystal gun in Preacher's calloused grip. She swallowed, eyes darting around the room, still flickering colors. "What—what—how?"

"A dream," I said simply. "No—don't move." I shook my head. "Wish it hadn't come to this, old friend. But you lied again. I should have suspected what you wanted a while ago."

Annie tried to rise, but then went still, her eyes tracing along her arm, up to her wrist.

Rope bound her arms to the bed frame and ensnared her legs. On top of it, two floodlights we'd once used to scare satyrs in a prison break at the Chasm now dangled from the ceiling where Preacher had rigged them; the hot, white light glared down at Annie and illuminated the room.

"No shadows either," I murmured. "At least not enough. Move at all, and Preacher has orders to fire." My giant companion leaned in, pressing the crystal barrel right up under Annie's neck. He crossed himself slowly, his eyes somber. For a moment, my insides wormed with guilt and fury.

"Leonidas... what do you think—"

"No. Quiet. Let me speak first."

She went still; as ever, her eyes held no fear. But waking fear wasn't the only weakness...

"Nightmares," I murmured, softly.

"Wh—what?" her voice gentle again.

"You said you have nightmares, every night." I shrugged, glancing off and wincing as the white light from the spotlights beamed down around me, emaciating shadows and sapping darkness from every corner. "Fear is a Wit's favorite entry," I murmured. "Nightmares, though, while sleeping—ten times easier."

"You... you mean all of that..."

"Made up. Make believe. Yes. I shared your dream—directed it. A memory, really. From the last time I visited the Hollow."

"I—I don't understand. What are you doing, Leonidas!" Her chest rose and fell now with rapid breaths. She sputtered, "You're meant to help me in. You—you *lied* to me!" Her voice swayed between frustrated and hurt and cold and furious.

I winced again, nodding slowly. "Yes... Already my powers are leaving. A lie in a nightmare isn't so devastating, but it will cost me. I don't know how much." I shrugged.

"Please! Pleeease! What are you saying?" She shook her wrists, trying to rip them from the ropes, but the lights only seemed brighter and Annie collapsed against the covers, breathing heavily.

Preacher grunted, still keeping the gun to her chin. He pointed to a corner of the room and waved a finger threateningly from side to side.

I looked over, watching where, in a particularly hidden corner of the bed frame, shadows were now rising up, slowly, like serpents.

"Don't," I snapped. "Stop it—I mean it. I might not want to pull the trigger, but Preacher's the one with the gun."

The shadows fell still again. Annie stared at me now, tears forming in her eyes as she shook her head side to side. "I thought... I thought you were my friend." Such an odd comment. She didn't protest my character, or my loyalty, but rather my friendship... The words of a wounded child, coming from the lips of a thrice-cursed assassin.

Again, my insides wormed with guilt, and I felt a lump in my throat. My own eyes, however, were dry. Perhaps a mercy I never cried... If I ever started, I wasn't sure I'd be able to stop. I tried to reach out, to test her emotions, but my brain swam, feeling foggy. My knees buckled and I turned sharply, retching towards the ground. Preacher tapped my shoulder and I spat; a trail of saliva extended from my lips towards the carpeted floor. "I'm fine," I gasped. "Fine... just... nauseous is all." I shook my head, blinking. Already, I'd lost my ability to enter human minds... Not good, the speed at which my powers were fleeing due to my dishonesty didn't bode well for their likelihood of return.

But I'd made peace with my decision.

Napoleon couldn't be allowed to leave. Annie had been lying the whole time.

"I know why you're here," I said softly, wiping a hand across my lips and breathing heavily before pushing off my knees and rising again.

"I—what?"

"You confirmed it in that little dream of ours. I had to make sure."

"Make sure of what, Leon. Preacher, put my wereblade down. You'll hurt yourself!"

"Ah, but no. Remember, you gave us permission, Annie. The only way to gain a saboteur's blade is if they die or surrender it willingly—even I know that. You thought we were going to use it to kill February, so you agreed."

"In a dream!"

"Yes, but permission of the mind is permission enough. The wereblade won't harm us—not now."

Annie strained, her bound legs lodged against the foot board, her head motionless against the pillow. "So what?" she said, breathlessly. "You'll use it to kill me?"

"To contain you," I murmured. "I don't normally like operating like this, Annie, but you gave me no choice."

"You're making a mistake!"

"And you," I said, "are here to kill February."

We all went quiet now. Annie didn't blink, her eyes fixated on me, ignoring the crystal gun beneath her chin. She swallowed, and a single bead of sweat rolled down the side of her face, likely from the heat of the lights above.

"Well?" I said, my voice whisper quiet. "Are you going to deny it?"

"I... Leon, you don't unders—"

"Don't I? You lied to me, Annie. You don't care about Napoleon at all, do you?"

"I—I do. I think he's the one who—"

"Stop it!" I shouted, slamming my fist against the bed-frame. My shadow extended now, cast by the light. Preacher reached out, ripping me back, allowing the light to illuminate the bed once more. He cautioned me with a hand to my chest, keeping me at bay.

Annie, though, seemed too stunned by my reaction to use the moment of opportunity. She was simply shaking her head wildly, her lips trembling. "You don't know what you're doing, Leon. Please. I know—I know I lied. But you have to believe—"

"Believe you?" I snapped. "Truly? After all this? Do you think I'm a fool, Annie? Hmm? You don't care about Napoleon at all. He was a ruse. You confirmed it when you gave permission for me to kill February. I wasn't sure what you wanted, but now it's clear to me."

"I don't—Leon—I just—"

"You killed July!" I screamed, jamming a finger towards her, once again casting a shadow, but this time Preacher didn't bother to lower my arm. "You murdered her! You weren't trying to protect her. February has locked herself inside the Hollow because she's afraid of *you!*"

My mind raced as I spoke, piecing together the fragments I'd seen, what I knew to be true. Only a god, or one of the angels would venture to kill a saboteur...

Or another saboteur...

I remembered Annie's scoffed words back at Kelly's. *"You speak of this lady as if she's some sort of god..."* From someone who didn't know of the saboteurs, the inflection of disbelief made sense. But from a saboteur? She knew... Yet she'd scorned. Not out of ignorance, but out of something else... Hatred? Fury?

"But I didn't know why you wanted to break into the Hollow," I continued, breathing heavily and lowering my arm once more. I jammed my hands into my pockets if only to have somewhere to place them where my trembling fingertips weren't visible. "You killed July. Which means my brother didn't. Which also means," I said, snarling, "You knew he had nothing to do with the murder."

"Leon, please..." she said, tears now spilling down her sharp cheeks. "Please... just listen."

"No!" I howled. "No more lying, Annie. I don't take well to it. It burns my stomach and twists my insides. I abide with Preacher because he's an honest man by choice. But you... you came to me and from the very moment we reunited your words were sewage. Weren't they! Vyle's teeth, Annie! How could you!"

I could feel the cold rising in my stomach, swirling up to meet my fury. I could feel my instincts bobbing to the surface, the breaking, my training. Annie's eyes widened where she lay helpless on the bed, her gaze illuminated by the blazing floodlights. Her emerald eyes shifted to gray.

"Leon, careful," she said, whimpering. "Please... stop... It's behind you. Please!"

She seemed so genuine. It seemed so real, for a moment I actually blinked, looking back over my shoulder. But nothing was there. The cold still swirled in me, swelling in my belly. Furiously, I rounded back on her, shaking my head. I didn't care. A curse on the ghosts she saw, a curse on it all. Saboteur and shade alike.

"You're here to murder February," I murmured. "You're here to kill the lieutenant of your order. Napoleon was an excuse, to get me involved. You knew my brother was here. You mistakenly thought I wanted him free. You thought I'd failed to free him two years ago."

At this, though, she seemed genuinely surprised; her eyes flicked back to green. "I—what? You don't want Napoleon? I don't understand..."

"Perhaps he could have made it a few more years. But by kicking over this particular hornet's nest, you've bound my hands. It's my fault. I know it. I wish I could change it, but I can't, and that's *your* skinting fault!" I shouted and turned to face the wall now. I couldn't stand to look at her.

Her refusal to approach February for help hadn't made sense to me. Her willingness to let us assassinate February had heightened my suspicions, and now, in the stark, stunned stare she'd only confirmed it. She wasn't here for Napoleon. She was here to murder the lieutenant of her order. She had murdered Saboteur July. She was killing saboteurs.

"I just don't understand *why?*" I murmured, staring at the wall and closing my eyes against the glare from the floodlights dangling from the ceiling. I didn't want to keep talking. I didn't think I could take any more lies. I could still feel my powers leaving me, sifting from my mind, retreating. Would they come back? I didn't know. But I was in too far now. No going back.

Regardless of Annie's mission of murder, I had one of my own. I had to see it through.

"Leon," Annie murmured. "Let me explain..."

"Don't," I said, stiff, quiet. "I don't want to hear it."

Her next words, though, caught my attention. "You're right."

I glanced back. She was no longer crying, her eyes fixed on the ceiling, resolute, her arms and legs tensed against the ropes as if readying to rip through the bed. Preacher maintained the emerald gun against my friend's throat.

"I did kill July," November snapped. "Not only her, but I killed April, too. Last week..." November shook her head. "My order went into hiding. They've been trying to find me. February knew I'd come for her next, so the lieutenant," she sneered, "hid herself in that cursed prison."

I turned fully now, staring. She'd killed another saboteur too? April and July? My mind reeled. "How... Why?" I said, breathing slow.

But the shadows went still again, and Annie continued, her voice increasing in volume and speed as she went, wresting control back from November. "I'm sorry. I'm a million times sorry, Leon, please believe me. I know you don't believe me. And I suppose if your powers are fleeing, you can't sense it. But if I could, I'd let you into every crack and cranny of my brain." She shook her head, still staring at the ceiling. "Though I'm not sure even a man as scarred as you could stomach what you'd see. What they did to me," she said, hyperventilating and shaking now.

"Hush child," November whispered. "It will all be alright."

The lights seemed to glow brighter, the shadows themselves almost seemed to retreat into the walls. For a brief moment, even the birds flying over the RV fell silent. Annie continued, whispering, "No, no it's fine. I can tell him. Leon, the nightmares aren't nightmares, they're memories. Since I was six, Leonidas, they tortured me. I was let out two years ago. Do you understand me? I wasn't the only one. Hundreds of us were brought. Candidates they called us. Shadowlings. Their cursed projects. No souls were nearly so horribly fated as us,

Leon. Not even the once-prince." Her shoulders began to shake, and she closed her eyes, breathing in slow whimpers now, her body contorting as if she wanted to curl up, to wrap herself in a ball.

Images flashed through my mind—memories of what I'd seen. Annie, as a child, in a dark room. The sound of slithering, of screaming. A man in a hat, then a howl of pain.

"For two decades they broke me, Leon," Annie murmured, her voice soft, but her shoulders continued to shake, seemingly completely out of rhythm with her words. She spoke firmly, but her body trembled like an invalid's. Spittle flecked across her lips, and tears now traced from her eyes in wet streaks, dampening the fluffy white pillow. "For two decades they exacted misery... Five hundred of us," she said, her voice straining now, as thin and sweet as strands of cotton candy. "Five hundred brought through... Most dead now. Some made cordial. Twelve of us saboteur... Replacing the others in the order when they fell to angel or demon or god..."

I wasn't sure what to say, if I ought to speak or not. Something seemed sacred in that moment; my own pity tugged at my thoughts, but also my fury at her deception.

"But even twenty years of torment, I could forgive," she murmured, softly. "Really, Leon, I could." She twisted, looking at me now, blinking. Her eyes flicked about for a moment, beneath the lights. "Where... where am I?" She swallowed. "Oh. Yes... I remember now."

My voice came husky and defeated. My fingers felt like lead bearings on my hands, dangling my arms uselessly at the ground. "Twenty years..." I said. "That's a long time."

"Isn't it? But I don't lie. Not now. I could have forgiven them pain. I've befriended pain," she whispered.

My next question lodged in my gullet, and I hesitated, clearing my throat and feeling, all of a sudden, the glowing heat of the light behind me. "If you could forgive them... then why have you been hunting them?"

Annie's sad eyes softened. "They're like me, really. All the saboteurs—they endured the same, many worse... The Shademaker does as she pleases. I wouldn't have tried to get revenge for the tiny offense of agony..." She shook her head. "But Leon..." Her gray gaze burrowed into my skull, fixing me to the floor like a butterfly pierced to a page. "They took someone from me. Killed someone, while I watched..."

"A friend?" I murmured, suddenly parched.

"No... More than a friend. And no, not that either, I see what you're thinking. Not a lover. My angel, Leon." Annie sobbed, glancing up and over her shoulder now, staring gray-eyed at empty space. "They killed her. Murdered her as I watched. Said the protectors of humanity couldn't consort with the celestial."

November rounded on me now, eyes blazing. Shadows tried to rise from crevice and corner. "They killed my guardian angel, Leonidas, and so they will all die. We told them we'd hunt them if they did it. They didn't listen. They killed her as I watched, and so now, we kill them, one at a time... February is next..."

Annie winced, her cheeks softening, her chin less rigid, her eyes wide and tear-stained. "Leon, don't look at me like that. I'm not crazed. I'm determined. I know what I'm saying. And I know what I'm doing. You're right; your brother was only a tool to leverage your aid. I knew I couldn't reach February without you. I knew it. And so I lied to you. But what I said was true. I was only released from the Twilight Citadel two years ago. I thought you were dead. The night of the Grimmest Jest even reached my ears, bound in the pocket realm though I was. I thought my only remaining friend had died..." She gasped a sob. "When I found you alive... I... You won't believe how my spirit rejoiced; it was the first cup of refreshment to my soul in nearly a decade. But I also needed to fulfill my oath... My angel... she was so kind, so caring. She tended my wounds, comforted me. She didn't deserve to die like that, Leon. She wept only for me as they took her. For me..."

To my astonishment, I found I believed Annie... My powers were fleeing, I couldn't reach her mind, and yet... I believed her words. Which only made it worse. In a faint voice, I whispered, "You need me to break in so you can kill February.... Truly? Napoleon had nothing to do with this..."

"It was the only way I knew to-to get your help. And for that, I'm really sorry. I should have told you the truth. But I'm not experienced at breaking into prisons, Leon. I made a promise to my angel. And if I was caught..." Annie swallowed, shaking her head. "February would not treat me kindly."

"What would happen if February caught you?" I scowled at my old friend.

Annie returned the frown from where she remained tied to the bed, her gaze just as reproachful. "She'll sequester me, first. Taking me to a room with a sealed door. Lights everywhere so I have no access to shadows."

"Then what?"

"She'll contact January to send the cordials to bring me back to the Twilight Citadel."

"How long will that take?"

"Why does it matter?"

"I want to know what you put me on the line for."

"I didn't put you on the line."

"How long!"

Annie sighed, a weary sound. "Hours, days, I don't know. And in the meantime, Leon, she'll torture me. After she contacts Regent January, after the lights have beat on me for an hour or so, sapping my strength completely, isolated from any help or ally. After, then she'll torture me. You don't understand what these people are like..."

I wanted to cry, I truly did. I even held the cold back, allowing it to slip like sand through fingers. But I gave a slow, sad shake. "I'm not the murdering sort anymore," I whispered. As I said it, the words crested over me like heat, coming down and resting on my shoulders. *What about Napoleon?* A small, sad voice whispered in my ear. *What about your brother?*

I bit my lip. Vyle's teeth—I'd come so far. It was the only way...

As if sensing my thoughts, Preacher reached out, patting my shoulder with his free hand.

I leaned in, pressing my head against my friend's massive shoulder and he wrapped an arm around me, drawing me near and letting me close my eyes for a moment as my powers continued to seep and bleed away.

Annie was murdering saboteurs.

I couldn't help her in that.

She'd betrayed me, she'd lied, and she'd brought my brother's name into it.

I closed my eyes, sighing once, then, my head still resting against Preacher's shoulder, I murmured, "Annie, I'm sorry, but I don't trust you. I can't have you conscious for what comes next. And as my powers are sapping..." I winced, feeling the emptiness in my mind, the lethargy, the muddiness. My eyes opened, and I straightened. "We have to do this the hard way. Preacher?"

My tall friend stepped past me in one quick motion. Annie blinked—no time to cry out as Preacher's giant form extended over her small frame. The backwoods boxer drove the butt of the gun into the side of her temple with practiced precision.

Her head snapped back, her eyes rolled, fluttered, then shut.

My heart tore with grief even as my fist closed in grim resolve. She'd murdered two saboteurs; she'd intended to murder another. I was no ally of the wereblade-wielding death machines. But I knew what I had to do next.

I still had to find Napoleon. Still had to enter the Hollow and put an end to this.

Chapter 46

Preacher and I marched along the trail towards the Hollow's gates. They were exactly as I recollected. A towering threshold of steel, stippled with fragments of reflective glass and ridged with rivets and plates of soldered metal.

Preacher wore his cattleman crease hat, the wide brim tipped over his eyes, his gaze fixed on the gates themselves. Over his shoulder, Annie's unconscious form dangled, her hands bound behind her. We'd left her helmet back in the RV, and Preacher had stashed her wereblade in his belt.

I tried not to look at my unconscious childhood friend. I couldn't afford to hesitate, not now. Already, my breath came in hesitant puffs and my eyes flickered along the doors. I couldn't read his mind anymore, but I knew both Preacher and I were occupied by a single thought...

Saboteur February.

The lieutenant of the deadly order holed up in the Hollow. Would she kill us on sight? I'd never met February before, didn't know what she looked like. And still, each step closer along the road brought a new and more interesting collection of chills shooting up my spine.

I moved towards the reflective lights shining from the mirrors in the door. As we drew nearer, I spotted *movement* in the glass. White eyes stared out at us, flashing teeth as pale as snow.

I shivered.

"Banes," I muttered, staring at my feet. "Cursed djinn—don't look at them."

My words in Annie's dream had been true. If the reflections spotted us, or the eyes in the mirror fragments noted our approach, the alarm would raise.

But we weren't here to skulk or sneak. We'd come to barter.

"Greetings!" I called, raising my voice now and stepping *firmly* into the reflection from one of the mirrors. I winced against the glare of sunlight, and raised a hand to veil my eyes, swallowing my nerves. "We're here to speak with February!"

Though I stood in the reflection, the motion in the glass fragments continued, eyes and faces like wraiths beneath a pond. Hair like ghostly string fluttered on hidden waters.

"We come with gifts suiting your station as is only apt!" I called, louder now. "November the saboteur—intent on assassinating February!"

I refused to look in my childhood friend's direction now. My mind was made up, like a slowly closing trap finally snapping into place. It had taken me a while to reach the conclusion, but now that I'd arrived, I refused to recant.

"February! Open!" I called, louder now. I passed through another reflection of glass, but again, no sound. The gates remained sealed. No movement, no yelling, no gunfire, no shouts.

I shared a look with Preacher and shrugged, rubbing at my chin.

"February," I tried again, raising my voice until I screeched. "We wish to barter!"

Again, only silence...

I shivered now, glancing to the trees. Grendel had known we were coming to the Hollow—he'd said as much. Had he arrived first, warning February against us?

I shivered. "February!" I tried again. "We—"

Preacher jammed his six shooter at the sky and fired twice.

The two blasts peeled out over the Hollow, carried on the wind. Then a passing second, and the gate cracked. Dust dislodged, trailing in sheets to the ground, stones skittering across the old road. Above us, the walls of thorn and vine arose to the clouds like the incline of some volcano.

Preacher lowered his smoking pistol, jamming it back in the leather holster, glaring out from beneath his brimmed hat, waiting quietly with Annie still flung over one shoulder.

The doors groaned. Chains rattled from within, and the gates slowly opened.

Five or six pale people stood fidgeting restlessly in the threshold, but I couldn't quite make out their features or forms in the dark entryway.

Someone else stepped from behind the twitching pale forms, and all my attention zeroed in.

Despite myself, I felt my heart skip a beat, and my feet crunched against the ground, shifting ever so hesitantly back.

My fingertips trembled, and my eyes fixed on the nearing figure.

A woman approached...

Though to call her a woman was to call Odin a man.

Every motion, every hint of movement about her, came with a regality born of pain. No hitch to her step, no hesitation. No pause to clear her throat, nor waving of her fingers against a sudden glare of sun or puff of dust. The million and one momentary distractions most succumbed to seemed insignificant to her. As a child, I'd once watched a fly buzz around a pile of droppings only to come and land on a cow's open eye. The cattle hadn't even blinked as the tiny insect prodded along its glazed eyeball...

This was a woman without distraction, and in the same way, she looked at me the way the cow had beheld the fly. So small a nuisance, I didn't even deserve the courtesy of a blink.

She came clad from head to toe in red armor covered in black hooks. She wore no helmet, but her wereblade displayed proudly on one hip. The woman had middle-aged features, perhaps no older than fifty; pale hair extended past her face in ribbons. She stared out at us, her eyes narrowed, her skin wrinkled in few places, suggesting perhaps she'd never cracked a smile in her life.

"November?" called the proud, angle-featured woman. Even her voice didn't have time for hesitations or tone. It was a crude iron block of a word. A weighty, powerful voice with no space for nuance or humor.

The barbs on her armor resembled a thousand little fish hooks, all protruding in different directions. They twisted about her in a thorny, ragged embrace.

By now, my powers had nearly completely faded. I could still discern smaller minds—a chipmunk in the trees above us, a few ants crawling on the ground before me. I even managed to track a bumblebee flit from a wild lilac and venture in swooping slow patterns towards the open gate. I watched its progress, morbidly curious as it hovered over February.

The moment it crossed the threshold of the doorway, though, I spotted a small, nearly indeterminable flash of red light.

The mind of the bumblebee died and the thing fell to the ground.

"The Seal is in place," I murmured to Preacher, keeping my voice as low as possible. "Invitation, trade, or death."

Preacher nodded once, hefting Annie on his shoulder, but he also had his gaze fixed on the single, solitary point of attention standing in the gateway.

The woman in the hooked armor pressed a hand to her wereblade, every motion intentional, not a moment of physical effort wasted. Her booted feet had come *just* shy of the threshold where the bumblebee had tumbled.

"You're February?" I said, venturing to keep the quaver from my words. Even still, my voice cracked, and I swallowed after the simple inflection, wetting my suddenly dry throat.

The woman's shadow extended around her now, like a swirling cape. A second later, I realized my mistake. The entire Hollow was one *giant* shadow. I detected no lights extending from within, only darkness and shade.

My fingers reached back, surreptitiously, but urgently, trying to guide Preacher to take a few steps back. Before we could retreat, though, Lieutenant February's steely voice probed out from the dark, her white hair framing her noble features, her eyes flashing with black as she stared at Annie draped over Preacher's shoulder.

Her voice carried a faint Eastern accent. "You have brought her to me?"

Preacher hefted Annie, sending her tumbling to the ground. My old friend rested quiet and still in the shadows of the giant prison walls.

"Yes," I croaked, "If you'd just come out here and speak—we wish to negotiate."

February's eyes flashed, and she crossed her arms over her armored chest, resting her limbs on carefully placed hooks with practiced ease.

"Blue-eyed fox with golden words," she said. "You bring me a gift. And who are you both?"

"Friends," I managed to eke out. "This prisoner of ours killed July, by her own admission. Killed April too. Assassins in your order, yes, my lady?" I added this last part with a forced, toothy smile. Station must recognize station—another one of my father's little lessons.

The pale-haired woman's lips rolled back, revealing a grimace. I wanted to reach out, to test her boundaries, but my powers had nearly completely depleted at this point. So I stayed still, watching from beneath my flat cap.

"You know of the murders?" February's voice demanded, echoing from the shadows, from the trees behind us. A million whispers itched in my ears.

"Everyone does, my lady! The Ardent Gazette announced it three days ago. I hadn't heard about April—but Ann—umm, November admitted it herself."

A soft tongue, the color of soot extended from February's mouth and tested the confines of her lower lip. She went still, half twisted, her hips facing one way, but her torso the other, like a poised snake.

"And you bring her to me? What do you wish in exchange?"

I coughed, clearing my throat. "Napoleon Rex! A prisoner of yours. Number five-thousand-thirty-eight."

Lieutenant February shifted a bit. The five pale forms behind her, still not quite determinable amidst the shadows, began to giggle among themselves, flashing jewelry visible on their persons.

February ignored them. "What do you wish with the child Rex?"

I didn't blink; my chest felt on the verge of exploding under the sheer pressure of it all. But I'd come too far to turn back now, speaking even as I was with a devil in the flesh. Only one path remained before me, and so I took it. "A fair trade, your eminence! November came here to kill you."

February tapped gauntleted fingers against her armored forearms. The shadows were still strangely stiff and still around her. The pale beings at her back continued to giggle and chuckle like children in the back of a classroom.

Sweat prickled my brow. Maybe we'd overplayed our hand. I hadn't considered our position perfectly. In any other barter, the trade offered would have seemed generous even. A murderer of demi-gods, a murderer intent on February's own neck, in exchange for what? A young, fourteen-year-old child. The son of Maximus, yes, but not the first heir, not even the third.

And yet, I wondered now if I'd been rash.

"I pray your patience, my lady. But we're not here for trouble. We'll pay for Napoleon, if so needed."

Preacher was standing still, but one hand moved, ever so surreptitiously to his belt, shifting the wereblade, just a bit, out of sight behind his back.

February, though, only had eyes for Annie and for me.

"Little blue fox," she murmured, standing in the darkness, amidst a wealth of shadow. "I'll trade November in exchange for *your* lives," she said simply.

"Our lives?"

Shadows almost seemed to harden about her, and her voice boomed now, "You think to come here, unannounced, without protection, and to barter with *me*? What do you take me for, boy? Some Stormer serf? Some Endeavor whore?" Her voice rose in volume as she spoke.

Now, Preacher didn't need my advice to start stepping back, rapidly, retreating further from the doors.

February screamed.

Suddenly, the shadows around her burst forward like soldiers, flying towards us. Ten arms of sheer black sped from the doorway, spreading across the ground and encasing the land in darkness. One of the tentacles ripped Annie from Preacher's grip. Another slammed into me, sending me flying backwards with a yelp of pain. I hit the dirt and groaned, blinking and watching Preacher avoid the blow from a third, but then three more crushed him down. A final arm of shadow slammed into his chest, sending him tumbling back and skidding along the dust and dirt.

For a moment, I sat in the road, massaging my head and blinking against stars over my vision. Preacher landed a few feet behind me, also gasping and trying desperately to push back to his feet. The arms of shadow had spread to encapsulate the sky itself and February remained where she was, motionless.

Annie, though, dangled from the arm of one of the shadows.

"Search her!" snapped February, her voice carrying the military bearing of one accustomed to authority.

The arms of shadow lifted Annie in the air. Darkness extended into her clothing, into her shoes, searching, seeking.

"Weapons, potions, tricks and mischief!" shouted February. "Anything!"

The shadowy arms searched for any hidden tool, any hidden weapon, across her person, through pockets. Annie remained unconscious, motionless. Helpless. And I'd been the one to throw her to the wolves.

The arms of shade finished their search, then lowered Annie, dangling her upside down in front of February's face.

The dead-eyed lieutenant leaned in, her lips pulling back in another canine grimace. "Yes..." she murmured at last. "It is *her*." She looked surprised and glanced past Annie towards me and Preacher, where we were still struggling to our feet in the dirt.

I spat grime from my tongue and croaked out, "Wait a moment! My brother—a fair trade. At least invite us in! Let us negotiate."

But February chuckled now, shaking her head, stroking her fingers across one of the hooks jutting from a gauntlet. "I don't think so. I accept the prize and offer your lives in return. Good day, gentlemen. November and I have things to discuss..."

I stood in the middle of the road, breathing heavily, desperately looking around as the doors began to grind and twist, echoing with the sound of rattling chains. Laughter peeled out from the five pale forms behind February. The ruby-armored saboteur clicked her fingers, and the massive tentacles of shade dragged back into the door, melding into the darkness itself. The doors continued to shut and, faintly, I heard a quiet, crisp command. "November may enter the Hollow."

I yelled in frustration, watching a flash of red sparks as the Threshold Seal allowed a shadowed limb to drag Annie's unconscious form into the belly of the old prison.

The doors slammed shut.

A growl in my throat burst out as a frustrated scream flung at the metal gates. No answer. No Napoleon. Annie gone. Trading for Napoleon would have made it all so easy... But of course, when had my life ever been easy?

Preacher and I stood motionless on the dusty road, both of us breathing heavily at the ground. I cursed and shook my head. We shared a look, dusting ourselves off and adjusting our hats. Preacher prodded the wereblade at his back, making sure it was still there.

"Think we just got her killed?" I murmured.

Preacher looked pointedly at me.

"I know," I snapped. "I know... I thought it might go better than that."

Preacher kept his gaze fixed on me.

"I know!" I said, insistently. "Tomb's trove, alright. Here, help me sit down. If I go unconscious, make sure to wake me."

Preacher paused before reaching out a hand. He pointed firmly at me.

I waved away his protest. "I know what I'm doing. I know what I'm doing. Come on. My talent is almost fully retreated. There's no more time. Help me."

Preacher rolled his eyes emphatically, but then approached, helping me lower into a sitting position, my legs crossed. I glared at the metal doors, glared at the Hollow's walls. Grit my teeth in focus and then, wincing as I did, I extended my mind.

Sensing the thoughts of humans was out of the question. Already, my powers had nearly completely vanished in that regard. Sensing the thoughts of the genies within? Again, an impossibility. I likely would have instantly gone unconscious if I'd tried. I certainly wasn't going read the mind of February, either.

But while my powers were fleeing, while dishonesty had cost me...

I could still sense the minds of things creepy and crawly...

Could still sense the minds of something small.

In fact, I was quite practiced where such things were concerned. My own surveillance system, back in my RV after all, was discernible at enormous distances. The smaller the mind, especially if the thing had no soul, the easier it was to connect over miles.

But we weren't miles away.

No. Annie was still just within the walls of the Hollow, carried away for the moment.

Preacher clapped a hand on my shoulder, squeezing tight.

"I'm ready," I murmured. "Remember, wake me if I go out. If we don't do this part perfectly, she's dead. Simple as that."

Preacher patted me again and put both hands on my shoulders, holding me firm. We still sat in the dusty road, facing the sealed doors of the Hollow. I was done running.

We needed an invitation into the prison. Which meant, we needed leverage.

Nothing living could cross the threshold seal.

Not a single living thing could cross without an invitation from February herself.

Annie had an invitation, but she was bound by shadows, unconscious, and her mind was far too large for me to control or read or puppet in my diminished state.

No...

Using Annie was out of the question.

Which was why I'd planned for exigent circumstances. I winced, thinking about my friend's reaction. It hadn't been a pretty plan. She'd likely hate me for it. But it had seemed the only thing at the time.

My eyes sealed shut completely, my dwindling talent probing out, flinching tentatively like someone sunburned trying to find a comfortable seat.

With extending tendrils of thought, I skipped over madness, skipped past beings and beasts alike. Each time my mind tried to land on one of these, I could feel the nausea building. I knew if I attached, I'd fall unconscious. No, my target was something much smaller.

Something I had killed...

I winced at the thought of it, grimacing.

"I really hope she's in a forgiving mood," I muttered. And then, my thoughts connected with the small, dead mind. "Hello there," I whispered.

Chapter 47

"And what would happen if February caught you?" I said, scowling at my old friend.

Annie glared up from where she remained tied to the bed, her gaze just as reproachful. "She'll sequester me, first. Taking me to a room with a sealed door. Lights everywhere so I have no access to shadows."

"Then what?"

"She'll contact January to send the cordials to bring me back to the Twilight Citadel."

"How long will that take?"

"Why does it matter?"

"I want to know what you put me on the line for."

"I didn't put you on the line."

"How long!"

Annie growled. "Hours, days, I don't know. And in the meantime, Leon, she'll torture me. After she contacts January, after the lights have beat on me for an hour or so, sapping my strength completely, isolated from any help or ally. After, then she'll torture me. You don't understand what these people are like..."

The memory played as I watched through the black and white gaze of my hidden, dead ally. Just like Annie had warned, I watched as February dragged her to a cold and clean room. I watched as lights were brought in: flashlights, high-beams, even—what looked like—a headlight ripped from a car.

I continued watching as Annie was chained to the wall her hands yanked and bound over her head against the deluge of illumination. I winced, even through the small, beady, black and white gaze. Then, I watched as February stood in the door, leering at my old friend.

"Little sister... What a pleasure it is to host you. I'll be back, darling. Very soon. Then we'll talk."

With a snarl, February slammed the door. Her voice echoed out, indeterminable words to the mind I possessed, but translated into my own thoughts.

"Don't go near her! Don't enter that room or I'll gut you and salt your intestines like slugs. Now get back!"

Then I'd heard the stomping of booted feet.

Annie was left dangling, her hands chained above, her head lolled to the side. I waited, cautious, watching through my perch and at last, certain the coast was clear, I animated the dead tarantula I'd buried in my old friend's ear canal.

One of the smaller tarantulas for certain, but you'd be amazed just how much can fit into a human being's ear, even as two of the legs were crushed beyond use—I hoped they didn't fall off.

Buried deep enough even February's shadows had missed it. And if they'd found it, what was a dead spider, anyway? Gross—certainly, but a weapon?

Not in their minds.

I could feel, despite my cast mind, Preacher's hands still gripping my shoulders, holding me upright where I sat cross-legged on the road just outside the prison gates.

Animating a dead spider was more difficult at long range. But it was the same trick I'd shown the genie Grace back on Mr. Gallows' farm. The thing remained dead, but I had control of its legs, of its movement.

The tarantula crawled out of Annie's ear, and my gaze flitted in black and white, my many controlled eyes reflecting back the beams of flashlights and headlights. The spider alone wouldn't have been much use...

Which was why I'd also covered him in alchemical thermite—the very powder Kay had given me for half-off. I hadn't known if I'd use the thing on an electrical box, or a door lock... Now, though, another target came into focus.

One must improvise in situations such as these.

The dead spider, with its six working legs, crawled its way up Annie's extended arms, over her head. I could feel, tensed through the decaying body, the dusting of metallic powder clinging to the thing's fury abdomen.

I paused on Annie's knuckles.

Her chains were thick. For a moment, I wished I'd added more alchemical thermite. But there was no going back now.... I felt a flicker of unease.

This would simply have to do. I remembered Kay's admonishment. *"Completely harmless to skin. Can even drink the stuff, and it won't hurt you. But the moment it touches metal. Boom."*

I completed the climb, dragging the dead spider off Annie's knuckle and pressing its body suddenly against the metal lock.

Boom indeed.

I glimpsed all of it for a faint second, catching a final image through a flying eye sac. The spider exploded, little bits and pieces scattering as the thermite attacked the metal chains. Annie rocked back and forth, swaying with the sudden motion above her hands—the chain snapped, and she fell with a thud to the floor.

Then my connection died.

My mind swam, my breath coming in ragged gasps. Such a minor trick normally would have been as easy as snapping my fingers, but now it rocked me. It had been a long while since I'd told an intentional lie, and I could feel the effects rising and squeezing at my chest like a fist.

I wasn't done, though. Annie's chains were broken, but the next part required improvisation too.

I huffed a breath a few times. "This is it. Hold tight," I said sharply.

Preacher squeezed my shoulders reassuringly, and I kept my eyes sealed.

The spider had served as a sort of marker, and I snapped back my attention to this dark, sequestered section of the prison. I found my thoughts grazing Annie's. I couldn't see, nor could I hear. I simply sensed her presence.

Wincing, I drew as near as I could before placing six words in her mind. *"Get up, get out, then run!"*

But then, my stomach twisted, my head exploded in pain. I'd overextended. Touching a human mind while in such a weakened state proved costly.

I coughed, gagging on my own vomit, doubling over. "Do it," I gasped to Preacher with my last throws of thought. "Do it now!"

My friend reacted even as my skull split. I heard gunshots, again, Preacher trying to get the attention of the Hollow. The blasts subsided, my own ears continued ringing, my stomach threatening to empty.

Then again, in the distance, I heard the creak of chains, the grinding of gears as the doors to the prison began to open once more. What luck.

My life in a nutshell. So, so lucky. Perhaps sarcasm wasn't worthy of a gentleman, but sometimes it was all a man had left. My eyes swam, and then, twitching and writhing in agony, with zaps of pain shooting from my skull, throughout my nervous system, I fell mercifully unconscious in Preacher's steady embrace, a final *bang* of his revolver reverberating in the air above.

***

When I regained consciousness, I found myself staring up at an armored form surrounded by swirling shadows. My ankle twitched, tugged by one such shadow, my leg scraping against the dirt before the tentacle of shade lifted, leaving me in the dust at the feet of its master.

I blinked, my mouth sour, shaking my head as I did. As my eyes adjusted once more, I looked up and squeaked.

My gaze traced thick, armored boots, along greaves and hooked armor, up further to a proud, sharp-featured face and white hair fluttering on the breeze.

Saboteur February stared down at me, her wereblade gripped in her right gauntlet.

"Explain yourself," she murmured. "Why are you still *here*, mortal!"

I coughed, dislodging dust from my throat and sat up, still wincing against my pounding headache. My gift had completely deserted me now. I could feel the conspicuous absence in my mind. I frowned, shaking my head as if to clear a water-logged ear. It felt like something had been amputated. I leaned back, hands against the dirt, then, slowly, pushed myself up, patting at my arms and legs and dusting myself off.

Lies muddy the mind. I felt a jolt of fear. Had I lost my powers for good?

I could feel an empty, twisting sensation in my stomach. My chest prickled with nerves and grief, but at the same time, a far greater, more immediate threat loomed, still standing in the threshold of the Hollow, framed by the two purple and glass doors.

Behind her, the pale figures I'd seen before were once more hidden in shadow, still watching and moving and shifting about with mad motions.

"A-apologies," I stammered, blinking back a headache, then—wincing—meeting February's imperious gaze. Her eyes were even scarier up close. At least I didn't swallow *too* loudly. I forced the next words, quailing beneath the lieutenant's horrible stare. "You've made a terrible error."

February's long fingernails clacked against one of the hooks on her opposite arm's protection. "Pray tell?"

I exhaled slowly, calming myself, allowing my emotions to settle like weighty stones in my gut. "November—Why did you let her free in the Hollow? It's a labyrinth down there, full of shade and shadow."

February didn't twitch. She didn't reach to scratch an ear, she didn't blink, her head didn't even move. Her lips barely parted to allow the freezing words. "What I do with my prisoners is of my concern, little blue fox. You have wasted my time. A grievous crime." She waved a hand dismissively. "Kill him!" she called, waving towards the white forms in the darkness.

The giggling, cackling figures began to step forward, odd, dangling jewelry glinting from their forms.

Fear jolted through me and reached out to suppress it...

But couldn't.

No powers, no diminishing fear. I was defenseless. I'd never felt so naked before, now facing the execution order of the lieutenant of the saboteurs. I winced, trying to face the assassin without trembling.

"Wait," I said. "You're not listening. November escaped. She's gone!"

February watched me for a moment, but then held up a single finger. The pale forms, still not quite discernible in the murk, went still. Or, at least, they stopped moving forward. Two of them, it seemed, now hooked arms and were dancing around and around, doing the do-si-do. One of them giggled so loudly that another began making clicking sounds in rhythm with the laughter like some sort of deranged beat-box.

"What do you mean?" February snapped, her eyes fixed on me. The thick shadows around her swirled and shifted, reaching out towards me and probing at my cheeks as if to open my eyes even wider.

My eyeballs watered at the intrusion, but I didn't back away, risking only a half glance over my shoulder and a soft exhalation. Behind me, I briefly spotted Preacher standing off the side of the road, a far enough distance from the doors so he couldn't be so easily snared. It had taken some convincing for my friend to go along with this portion of the plan.

But I couldn't afford to put him in harm's way. And without my powers, I wouldn't be able to protect him for what came next.

I'd simply told him one of us needed to be outside, in case everything went hellbound. But in reality, if February lost her temper, if things shifted an inch to the left, or the right, then having a lookout would matter only as a witness to a murder.

Still, though he'd protested, Preacher had finally relented. At the very least, he still held Annie's wereblade. And I'd be lying if I said it didn't provide some relief knowing my old companion remained safe. At least for the moment.

I returned my attention to February.

"Annie escaped. I sensed her. I'm a Wit."

"A Wit."

"Yes. An eternal talent."

"I know what a Wit is, little fox."

"Annie escaped."

February continued frowning. By her annoyed look of normally stagnant features, I surmised she didn't believe me. Her hand rose again, gesturing once more towards the white forms. But I raised my voice, cutting off any motion with sheer, piercing volume. "You took her to a small room! Locked the door. Placed lights all around. You chained her to the ceiling, yes? How would I know any of that if I wasn't a Wit?"

February had gone very still now, her nostrils the only part of her moving as she took in a slow, shaky breath. I could detect the rage simmering in her eyes, and she fixed me with her darkened glare. The red, ruby wereblade at her side began to twist and form, the dagger extending into a wicked sickle, gleaming and razor sharp. The perfect size for cutting my head from my shoulders.

"How do you know this?" she whispered.

The shadows around her began to thicken, to extend around me now, like demon claws, threatening to rip at my flesh. But I'd said too much to back out now. Besides, abandoning Annie in the Hollow had never been part of the plan.

If she died, it would be on my head. Not to mention, I still had Napoleon to deal with. For the sake of us all, I had to go through with it.

Another small reason to leave Preacher behind.

I didn't want him to see what came next. I wasn't sure I could bear the look in his eyes. He believed in me. Secretly, I think, he'd always assumed I wouldn't go through with the execution. He'd been right the first time. He thought he knew me, thought he saw a gradual change reforming me.

But even men of God could be wrong at times. Though it cursed my very soul, I had to finish this. Which meant I needed to survive these next few moments. Needed to think. No powers, no Wit—just me and a legendary assassin.

A legendary assassin, though, who'd hidden herself inside a prison, creating a bastion of defense. A legendary assassin who followed protocol, sequestering Annie while she contacted her higher-ups. An assassin, who, at her core, *feared* my old friend.

Even without the Wit, fear could be used. Exploited.

At least, so I hoped.

The giant purple and glass doors loomed above me, like the threshold to Hades itself. The mountain and the walls of the Hollow prickled with thorn, and vines extended up like some looming, horrible skyscraper, threatening to defile the horizon itself. A tremor pulsed down my back in frigid prickles. But even if I couldn't suppress my fear unnaturally, I could pretend... Fake courage was nearly as good as the real thing.

"I know this," I said, speaking with far more confidence than I felt, "because I am a Wit, like I said. November is now free, your eminence. She's loose in the Hollow. I saw it happen. I didn't mean to bother you, but I knew you hadn't spotted the escape yet. So, with much haste, I returned, hoping to warn you. She's still coming for you, my lady. She still hunts you."

February's eyes flickered, widening only a fraction. For me, though, this was as good as a gasp of horror.

Fear. The cancer of the mind. And a familiar ally.

I didn't blink. I didn't twitch. I just watched, waiting on tenterhooks.

"She escaped?" February said, snarling. "She..." The saboteur whirled around, screaming. "She escaped?"

The pale figures all scattered back, as if shoved by a wave of shadow. They scrambled in the dark, like worms wiggling beneath an upturned rock. The figures spun around, and I heard the retreating sound of thumping footsteps.

February rounded back on me, teeth bared. "If you're lying to me, little fox..."

"I'm not."

Her eyes flooded with rage and she screamed, "Did I say you could interrupt me!"

A fist of black shadow burst from within the doorway, gripping my jaw, and squeezing *hard*. A tooth cracked; my jaw ached and I winced, lips squished awkwardly, my tongue lolling. No place for pride now. If she wanted, she could crush me like a... well, like a spider.

"If you're lying to me, mortal, I will exact such torment, the likes of which will cow far greater forms than you. I'll start with your tongue, then your eyes, then each of your lovely little teeth. Do you understand me? No. Don't answer. I'm speaking, little fox. I'll go to your toes, then any fingers or other parts you might value. Do you understand me? I'll keep you a living, soulless, flesh husk. Do I make myself clear?"

I blinked, about the only gesture I could do without wetting myself. The shadow fist still gripped my head in its vice.

"You may answer now," February hissed.

"I understand," I squeaked.

At least no gunshots resounded. Preacher was sticking to the plan, for now. I knew, though, if he thought me in mortal peril, he'd throw caution to the wind and come running. As much as I loved him for that, I also knew it would cost everything. I only had a slim chance—the faintest of possibilities. Anything might ruin it now. Anything unplanned, anything unexpected...

As if in answer to the thought itself, a soft voice cleared and then a figure emerged behind Saboteur February, stepping forward and coughing delicately. He stood just inside the Hollow, quiet and smug.

My heart sunk.

The figure wore a Sunday suit and a top hat, his golden eyes flashing beneath the dirt and mud-stained brim of his hat. "Ah, my lady," he said, in a sing-song cadence. "This is the vagabond I mentioned. I told you he'd come. And I must advise you, don't believe a word he says."

Horror welled in my stomach, starting as a churning, twisting sensation, like a dagger driven deep, but then rising in butterflies up to my throat, tickling and scratching until I swallowed the forming lump.

He'd beat us to the Hollow after all. She'd allowed him entrance. How long? An hour? Three? What had he been telling her?

From the shadows, and coming to a halt next to February, Grendel emerged, flashing a wicked grin beneath golden eyes.

Chapter 48

Sometimes, things that go bump in the night stake claim to sunlight as well, if only to better see the terror in their victim's eyes. This particular night terror crossed his arms over his Sunday best, fingernails stained with blood pressed into the folds of his mud-streaked suit.

Grendel clicked his tongue and shook his head in mock severity. "Not a pretty thing," he murmured, "to see a savant struggle so."

My heart was now somewhere in the vicinity of my big toe, likely trying to burrow into the earth and escape. The rest of me, however, remained standing in the dust, beneath the enormous tentacles of shadow hovering on the air, spreading out from within the mouth of the gaping Hollow. Grendel didn't come *too* near February, remaining at a respectful—and *safer*—distance. But I could hear the purr in his words, the soft, pleasurable delight as his eyes darted over me, likely searching for the softest, tastiest cuts of meat.

"What are you doing here," I said through clenched teeth, staring at the Endeavor bounty hunter.

"Ah, Ex-Prince," he murmured. "You should have known I'd reach her first." He winked. "Some of us move faster in the woods."

I shivered. My luck had run its course, smashed to pieces against a wall of misfortune. I was dead. Annie was dead. It was over. Somehow, this horrible realization brought with it equal parts despair and a weighty exhaustion that clung to me like wet tissue. For a moment, I just held Grendel's glare at a complete loss for words. I could hear the sudden sound of thumping footsteps behind me.

"Don't!" I shouted, my voice creaking in the air. "Don't come a step nearer!"

The footsteps only picked up their pace.

"Corker's breath, Preacher, get the hell back!" I screamed, turning and staring wide-eyed and gasping at where my friend had broken into a sprint, covering the distance from the road to the gates in record time.

His own eyes stared out from his handsome, dark features, fixated on where Grendel continued to purr in the doorway. Preacher paused at the tone of my voice; his chest heaved as he breathed desperately, shaking his head in small, tiny jerks, his features crooked with panic.

"Don't," I repeated, still loud.

His eyes swam, searching, fixated on me. He tapped his forehead desperately, one foot still in front of the other, caught in motion, uncertain. One part of him stuck in his loyalty and fierce desire to save me, the other part gripped by his trust—I'd never led us astray. Not yet.

I tried to keep a brave face, nodding once, my neck hairs prickling where they'd turned towards Grendel for the faintest moment. Putting one's back to a feral beast wasn't a comfortable proposition, though Annie

311

seemed to manage it easy enough. But in that moment, I was defenseless anyway.

If Preacher could have read my thoughts, he never would have hesitated. None of this was part of the plan. None of this was going to end well. I hadn't considered Grendel arriving so soon. I'd known he'd head to the Hollow, but I'd thought we might have a snowball's chance in a volcano of making it out before he arrived.

And now...

I'd failed.

A profound emptiness filled me. Not just in my mind, but in my chest. My heart faded and shriveled on itself. Nothing left before me. No tricks, no deceit, nothing.

And yet, I refused to let the despair paint across my features. I forced a smile, summoning it from deep within. If I hadn't already lied to Annie, this small curving of my lips would have been an even deeper deception.

But this lie was meant to protect, to save, to communicate. *It's all going to be okay. It's fine. I'm going to be alright.*

I smiled and nodded once, hoping the expression was reassuring.

I was as good as dead. Annie, too. My brother would live to see another day, until someone else came along, discovering what had happened all those years ago.

But there were others who needed Preacher. I thought of Mr. Gallows and his wife. I thought of little Sussanah and the Gallows orphans. I thought of Preacher, tears streaking through his blush as he applied the makeup in bold, stroking patterns as if applied by the excited fingers of a child.

No.

Preacher couldn't die with me.

I couldn't allow it...

And so I lied with a smile. I lied with a nod.

Preacher remained motionless, one foot in front of the other, frozen on the dirt path, facing the purple and glass gates. His eyes bugged beneath the brim of his hat.

"It's okay," I called, loudly, my neck hairs still standing on end, betraying my horror.

Preacher desperately tapped at his forehead again.

But I couldn't reach out... my powers were gone. My mute friend was well and truly voiceless now, even to me. I held out a hand, soft and steady. A halting hand. I hoped Preacher couldn't see my fingers trembling at this distance.

And then, my attention was ripped back to the demons in the doorway. A fist of shadow yanked at my head, turning my gaze to fix on February.

Now, all five of the pale figures who'd been sent to investigate Annie's cell had returned. I could see them fidgeting and twisting nervously in the deeper, darker portions of the Hollow. I heard the way they cackled with nervous jolting bellows, the volume inappropriate, the cadence sending more shivers along my spine.

"She's gone?" February asked, her voice cold and cruel and...

A faint note of fear?

The wan faces wagged in the dark. Pale forms swayed and twisted like beams of moonlight draped in the heart of the ocean.

February's cruel gaze fixated on me, the fist of shadow clenching my skull. "You knew she would escape?" The assassin lieutenant demanded.

I kept one hand raised behind my back, a calming, placating gesture. *Stay still,* I thought desperately, though, without my gift, he wouldn't know. *Get off the road.* I didn't hear Preacher's retreating steps, but, at least for the moment, he didn't draw nearer. I knew it would rip the backyard boxer to pieces if anything happened to me. I knew he'd blame himself.

But the measure of guilt would be worth his life. It had to be.

Little else could be salvaged from this titanic debacle.

"I knew," I said, gasping. "I did, like I said, I'm a Wit."

February glanced at Grendel. "Is this true?"

"You cannot trust him."

February returned her glare to me. "Did you free her?"

I shrugged helplessly. "How is that possible, my lady? I was out here. You never gave permission for me to enter. I only detected the escape."

February's eyes narrowed, studying my face, thinking. But even demigod assassins weren't well versed in the old tarantula-in-the-ear canal trick. I could almost sense her thoughts behind her deadly gaze, probing through every possibility. Then, at last, she sneered. "Kindred, there is a saboteur released in the prison. She's here to kill me. I need you to find her."

Grendel's golden gaze shifted from me to February. "To kill *you*, my lady?"

"Yes. A foolish, insane child. She doesn't know what she's doing. I need you to find her."

"And you, mistress?"

"I'll be," February coughed, "making certain the prison is safe."

More fear. I didn't smile, I couldn't. But there was something about the fright in such a powerful killer's voice that made me want to chuckle. Annie had her scared. Little orphan Annie had big bad February quaking in her boots. She hid it well. But not *so* well. She glanced sharply around, her movements nervous now, suggesting she'd finally decided to believe me. Annie was on the loose. Annie was coming for her.

The immortals were often fearless... Fearless because they thought they were untouchable. But one poke— one hard jab in the eye... And suddenly even the gods quivered.

I coughed, hiding a chuckle as out of place as the giggles of the pale forms in the shadow beyond.

"And *you*," she said, pointing at me and giving a stiff little bow, her hooked armor clinking. "You die painlessly as an expression of my gratitude!"

"Um, wait!" I said, quickly.

"No more waiting."

"No, please," I said. "You're in danger. I came here to warn you, to help you!"

"How could one like *you* help *me*?"

"I'm a savant," I said quickly. "Ask the Kindred. He'll tell you. I've been here before, to your Hollow. I know the labyrinths. I know the prisons. I also know November. I'm the one who brought her to you," I said, urgently. The only weapons remaining to me were my words and desperation. A final kick of twitching legs beneath a taut noose. The only hope I had. "I'm a savant," I repeated, more insistently. "I know these prisons. I know the Banes. I know November. I can find her before..." I trailed off for nothing short of shameless dramatic effect... "Before she finds you," I said, with a helpless little shrug.

February had now turned fully, her back to me, the shadows circling and whirling around her like a tornado. A defensive protection against all comers. Her eyes flit to the darkness, moving around the interior of the Hollow, seeing things in the bleak black that I couldn't make out with my human gaze.

"Is this true, Kindred," she snapped.

Grendel stared at me, searching, his tongue tracing his bottom lip in a slow, predatory motion. When he spoke, his voice came more like a growl than words. "Let me kill him, mistress. End this nuisance. For you."

February, though, raised her voice. "I didn't ask you that, beast! Is he a prison breaker? Well? Tell me the truth!"

Grendel continued to stare at me. In that moment, I was struck at how my fate hung in the balance on the simple say so of my enemy. The Endeavor were as ruthless as Imperium, especially towards those like me. A simple lie, and she'd likely let him rip me to shreds.

The truth... though...

The beast man watched me. I wasn't sure where Caliban was. Or where his children had gotten to. Perhaps Grendel had come ahead. Or perhaps the rest of them were somewhere deeper in the Hollow, waiting, watching, hoping to get a bite of me.

"What are you playing at Leonidas?" Grendel murmured.

I looked him straight in the eyes, unblinking. "Lie," I said, "And you'll never find out."

"Well?" February snapped. "Beast? Is he a savant, can he help you find the crazed infant?"

Grendel's eyes flashed. Then, in a grumbling purr, he murmured, "Yes... Leonidas is telling the truth, mistress... He is a savant."

My stomach fell again. Relief welled inside me, and I released a breath I hadn't realized I'd been holding. Had he told the truth to save his own skin, or out of fear what might happen if he lied to a saboteur? Had he done it for some noble purpose? Kindred didn't think of themselves as *evil*. Few did. They were predators and the rest of us prey.

But then his words came complete. "In fact, mistress, perhaps Leonidas and I can *both* go searching through this cursed prison. You take care of yourself, my lady. Guard yourself. We'll find this saboteur for you. We'll kill her. Only, just, make him offer his word."

"Fine," February snapped, waving a hand. She was already moving, clearly distracted as she hurried away from the gaping doors and strode back into the darkness. The pale figures around her fell into step behind her like ghosts in mist. "Savant, you have my permission to enter!" she called. She paused, twisting, staring at me over the hooks on her shoulder, eyes fierce. "Give me your word you'll do everything in your power to find and kill November."

The nape of my neck itched, and I stared at Grendel purring in the doorway.

A flash of luck. A terrible, wonderful stroke of chance.

Grendel thought he'd trapped me, thought he'd tricked me. The cat wasn't being honest for honesty's sake. He was simply playing with his food, enjoying the torment before downing the morsel.

But I'd already lied. My powers were already gone. He thought it would be an agonizing decision. He thought, like him, everyone valued—above all things—their own power.

He thought wrong.

And so I lied again.

"I'll do whatever it takes to find and kill her," I declared, my voice resonating in the dark, and flitting past Grendel with barbs of sound.

The Kindred jolted, staring, confusion etching across his face. "Wait a moment," he said swiftly.

But February overrode him. "Fine, then, savant, you may enter. You have my permission. The Seal will allow it! Hurry, and don't hesitate!"

Then she twisted again and began moving rapidly, carried by a wave of shadows and disappearing into the deeper gullet of the old prison. Fear trailed behind her, the scent of it lingering on the air. Annie had her scared; Annie had her on the run.

I'd survived another moment, and I'd earned my invitation in.

The Threshold Seal sparked and sputtered, nearly invisible until I stepped forward, crossing it. My skin tingled as I passed through, raw power zapping across my body. I shivered at the sensation, but at the same time, I pressed on and in, moving towards where Grendel awaited in the darkness.

One step closer to doom...

Grendel bared his teeth at me. Around me the doors began to shake and shudder, sending tremors through my feet, up my legs. The chains rattled. I heard Preacher loose a growl of frustration from the open road. But then, the doors scraped inwards, closing like the lid to a coffin, sealing me in my tomb of choice.

Chapter 49

The doors sealed shut behind me with a final groan, leaving me standing in the darkness. I trembled in the atrium of the Hollow, my ears tickling with the sound of Grendel's soft breathing, my eyes useless in the sheer black. The sealed doors prevented even the smallest glimmer of light from slipping through their blockade.

I swallowed softly, blind, my ears perked.

"Leonidas Rex..." murmured Grendel's voice, in that same, creepy sing-song way of his. "What shall I do with you, hmm?"

For a moment, I considered not answering. No sense in giving him a better target... But, then again, he could probably already see me. The eyes of beasts were often better suited to dim light. And so, just to keep him talking—instead of biting—I replied in a shaky tone, "You wouldn't want to kill me... Not now."

"Oh? Wouldn't I?"

I heard the faintest scrape of movement to my right and took quick steps to the left. My hands probed to my jacket pocket, hunting for something, anything. I still hadn't replaced the knife I'd lost outside the Endeavor bar. The Wit had left me, without so much as an adieu or promise of return.

I was alone in the dark, unable to see the monster in front of me.

My fingers closed on the dwindled pouch of tiger's eye. Three left. I also felt my fingertips graze the cold, cylindrical containers of the gold dust tubes. Also three of these. I could feel the heft of the silver Lancelot watch in my right pocket...

Three tiger's eye, three sticks of gold dust, and a cursed watch...

Not exactly an awe-inspiring arsenal. Still, I tried to think. I was locked in a pitch-black room with a hungry Kindred... But I did have one advantage. Most eternals avoided the prisons, refusing to see what could become of them if they too crossed the wrong person or lost the wrong skirmish.

Eternals, even old ones like Grendel, avoided the Hollow and its like. But as for me, I studied these places. I knew the prisons; I'd been to this one before, had spoken to one of the old architects, even, before she'd died. I knew the tunnels, knew the guardians...

Now, all that stood between me and the source of my knowledge was a wild bounty hunter with a taste for man flesh.

"I'll make it quick, Leonidas," Grendel whispered in the dark, his voice like the first crackle of fire. "You've been a worthy adversary."

"I wouldn't do that if I were you," I said, my voice barely a murmur. "You heard February. She wants us to find November."

"Ah, yes... well... I think I'm through taking orders from saboteurs. It doesn't sit well with my constitution."

"Care for an amendment?"

"Hmm. Oh?" Grendel's voice chuckled in the dark. "Funny. Stop moving, Leonidas. I can see you there, pressed against that wall."

I shuddered, my head darting about, but my eyes as useless as if I'd sealed and blindfolded them.

"Right then..." I murmured. "Here I am..."

I heard the soft steps before I heard his growl. He picked up pace, closing the distance, footsteps pattering.

"I smell wet dog," I said, louder.

Grendel sneered; then, tracking his sound alone, I knew he'd lunged. With a yelp, I threw the first remaining tiger's eye, launching it and ducking at the same time. Grendel's arms swished through the air above me. A knee collided with my chest, sending me tumbling. With a snarl, Grendel reoriented, flinging himself at my fallen form. I could hear the swipe of his arms, the snap of his teeth.

And then, my stomach twisted, a hook in my belly—I was ripped fifteen feet over Grendel's head, teleporting towards where the tiger's eye had smashed against stone. I knew the layout of the atrium; I'd rehearsed two years before.

Six tunnels. Three on the left would lead up towards more guardians, lighter cells. Three led down, beneath the earth, beneath the Hollow. Down to where Napoleon was being kept. Two of the three were also pitch black. One, though, I knew from experience, had veins of moonore illuminating the walls. Without the Wit, I needed the use of my eyes. So, desperately, scrambling along the walls, poking and prodding at the tunnels and feeling my way, I searched for the rightmost tunnel.

"Leonidas!" Grendel screamed.

My fingers struck a wall, fell through a gap... The first tunnel leading down.

"Come back here!" he screamed. And then, I heard snarling and grunting, the sound of straining, popping muscles, of ripping and tearing and pain. Grendel was shifting.

I yelped, moving faster in the dark, groping blindly. My fingers moved along another portion of wall, then fell through a second gap. The middle downwards tunnel.

This time, Grendel didn't shout with words, but loosed a horrible *yowl*! Clawed feet slammed to the ground, ripping against stone.

My fingers scraped along a final dusty pillar, and my hand fell through a final tunnel.

The third one. The rightmost tunnel. I yelped and flung myself through, just as something sharp swiped above my hair, ripping a chunk out of an ear. I winced, feeling warm liquid trickling along my neck like the cold prickles heading up my spine.

"Bad kitty!" I shouted, if only to goad him further as I sprinted, racing blind down this tunnel, desperately hoping I'd chosen the right one.

I heard a howl, the sound of a large, muscular body squeezing through the tunnel behind me; the ragged, putrid breaths of a monster in pursuit came like mist. I picked up the pace, sprinting breakneck, forcing down my premonitions of pain, of sudden death.

Hotfooting in a straight line, I heard feet thumping beneath me in the sheer dark. I needed to reach Napoleon. I needed to put an end to this.

Grendel came after me, like a chugging train—me a helpless passenger having fallen on the tracks. No way out.

And then, up ahead, I glimpsed glimmers of light.

A flood of relief. I'd chosen the correct tunnel. I hounded forward, angling to avoid a narrower portion of the passage. As I moved, claws ripped at my jacket. My shoulders jerked with the sudden motion, and I tumbled, ricocheting painfully off the coarse tunnel wall. With a yell, I tore my second tiger's eye from my pocket and threw it. Another sucking sensation, another furious screech behind me, but I was sent tumbling twenty feet ahead.

Now, the moonore shone around me.

Jagged glass sections hung from the walls, seemingly embedded into the dust and stone. Moonstone traced the sections of broken mirrors, the twisting, pearlescent ore glowing soft in the dark. As I passed along the tunnel, beneath the broken sections of glass, I saw *things*—pale things—staring out at me from within the mirrors themselves.

I shivered as I ran, my breath coming in worn gasps now, my feet pounding in rhythm with my wild heart.

I heard a yowl and a smashing sound behind me. A backwards glance caught a glimpse of Grendel knocking three of the mirrors loose, sending them smashing to the ground as the beast's massive form tore through the tunnel. I glimpsed whiskers and scything teeth, fangs and sharp claws. A bloodied snout indicated where Grendel had slammed into the wall.

But minor pain from a bumped nose only further propelled the enraged bounty hunter into a ferocious burst of speed. He leapt off one of the walls, bounding at a ninety degree angle off the floor before slamming back to the tunnel with a calamitous *thud*.

I yelled, trying to push faster, but Grendel's beast form was gaining. I was running out of time. The tunnel ahead dipped down, burrowing into the earth. The further we went, the thicker the glass sections became. Soon, portions of the wall were entirely plastered in shattered and broken sections of mirrors, leaving little dust or rock or moonstone visible around it.

The illumination from *within* the mirrors seemed brighter here.

As I ran, and as Grendel gained, cutting the gap between us again, I heard soft giggling, and playful, maniacal laughter.

I cursed, racing even further and then coming to a small alcove. I pulled up short, stumbling beneath mirrors on the ground, mirrors on the walls, mirrors on the ceiling.

But worse still...

Nowhere left to run.

Chapter 50

I yelled in frustration, whirling around, unable to find much in the way of protest due to my pounding heart and tattered breath. I'd chased myself down a tunnel into a dead end.

My back pressed to the smooth glass, my fingers probing at the reflective material behind me. "Where is it," I muttered, desperately, fingers probing at the wall behind my back. "Where is it!"

Grendel now stood fully illuminated in his beast form. The black and gold-furred creature seemed a cross between a grizzly bear and a demon, twice as tall as me, with a body as thick as a small SUV. In this form, Grendel had to weigh at least five thousand pounds, and his teeth bared over lips scabbed with strange red scales. The teeth themselves were vicious and curved, like ice picks flashing in the glow from the moonore buried behind the mirrors.

Grendel was huffing, breathing heavily, his head low, rocking back and forth as he stalked towards me now, savoring his cornered prey.

"Come on... one second!" I yelped, desperate, my fingers still probing at different gaps beneath the glass behind me. Pushing rocks, twisting pebbles in their berth, sending trickles of dust scattering to the ground. Some of the dust landed in the heel of my shoe and I grimaced, resisting the urge to itch.

But Grendel was no longer in the talking mood. His legs were like a bear's, but also covered in the strange, red scales. Portions of his black-furred body were streaked with this scaly flesh as if the fur itself were poking out from beneath armor.

The scales glinted like a dragon's beneath the flashing mirrors; the thick, steel trap of the beast's muzzle opened in a roar, and Grendel came pounding forward.

The time for talk was over.

I hadn't found it. I pushed and probed, but couldn't find the stone... Had I taken a wrong turn?

I yelled in horror, lifting the only object left to me from my pocket.

Lancelot's shield.

I raised it high, clicking the button on the side and letting the thing spring open. The bear's claws slammed into the shield like scythes, crushing the barrier down on my shoulder. I bent and contorted, nearly broken under the first blow. I yelled in pain, my ankle twisting beneath me from the sheer weight of the attack.

Grendel snarled and struck again, another slamming paw the size and weight of a sledgehammer. Again, I yelled, keeping Lancelot's shield aloft. The blue sparks were already dancing across my wrist. I could feel the curse tingling through my hand, my fingers, up my arm.

Now wasn't the time for the shield's hex. I couldn't keep this up for long, or I'd kill myself with inane romance.

No... I needed another way out...

I gritted my teeth against another batting paw, the claws sparking where they struck metal, gouging against the reinforced, magical shield. Over the demon bear's shoulder, I stared at the cracked glass in the ceiling, the fragments of mirror along the walls...

Was it worth it?

I had one last trick. But was it worth bringing *them* out to play? Those strange, pale beings who'd hidden in shadow behind February. Did I really want them joining the party?

Grendel lunged now, teeth worrying at the shield, threatening to rip it away completely. He tore and shook, and my arm nearly snapped from the effort.

No choice. Tomb's trove.

I ripped one of the gold dust cylinders from my pocket, cracked it with my free hand like a glow stick and then tossed it behind Grendel. Gold dust glinted, the contents scattering across the ground.

And then...

Laughter.

Maniacal, echoing laughter began to vibrate through the deeper parts of the walls, echoing around us.

Grendel slammed his claws again, this time aiming for my exposed legs. He ripped through a shin, and I howled—his claw catching bone. My leg swept from under me and I fell, slamming to the dust. My head jolted, my chin ricocheting off hard stone. My shield slammed into my temple, and stars danced across my vision.

Grendel roared in victory, pulling himself to his full height in the small alcove of the tunnel. The bear's monstrous head, streaked with red, demon scales scraped the mirror behind him. Nearly thirteen feet tall, Grendel's eyes blazed gold and indigo as he opened his mouth in a roar, preparing to lunge for the finishing blow.

The gold dust had settled now, behind the bear, falling soft like silt on stone. And then... the laughter shook the walls.

Grendel froze, the beast suddenly pausing, sniffing at the air, still pulled to his full, horrifying height.

More laughter, more giggling. And then... I saw it first.

A corpse-pale hand pushed through the glass directly above Grendel. A head followed the hand. More hands, more feet emerged from the glass surrounding us. Laughter now swelled, filling the alcove, trembling in the dark, gloomy cave.

Grendel whirled around now, growling at this new threat.

Then, genies crawled from fragments and fractions of mirror and glass, pulling their pale, pallid bodies from the dark.

Banes—every last one.

A clan of genies gone insane. Given to their gold lust, given to their insanity. A clan of genies who had made a home of the Hollow, and who didn't take kindly to intruders.

The Banes moved towards the gold first, ignoring me and Grendel for the moment, investigating the glinting dust. A few of them dropped to their knees suddenly, scraping with fingers and jamming dirt and gold alike into their mouths. Giggling and laughing and swallowing and choking.

More Banes emerged, rising like a tide from within the mirrors and spilling out into the now cramped tunnel. Like a pack of vultures, they descended on the glinting dust. Grendel roared again, and swatted, sending one of the Banes flying who'd gotten too close.

Even a Kindred, in such tight, claustrophobic spaces, could be intimidated by an insane clan of wishmakers.

These genies, though, were far too disturbed to spend much time in the realm of wishes, like their kin...

No. Banes preferred nightmares.

One of the Banes in particular took a handful of the gold dust, shoveling the feast past his colorless lips, and then turned, slowly, head cocking. But it wasn't a human gesture; rather, it seemed as if his head were on hinges and suddenly fell, an ear pressed to his shoulder as he examined the two non-Banes who'd wandered into the lair.

The fellow in question was larger than a human, but not by much. His face was pale, and he had no hair—in fact, none of the Banes did—his flesh was the color of water beneath moonlight. His veins stood out against his nearly translucent skin. I detected the usual twisting, swirling tattoos embedded in genie-flesh. He also had earrings and a nose ring. In fact, his face was covered with piercings. Hoops through his eyebrows, studs through both nostrils, jagged teeth through the very center of his ears. Even parts of his neck had been pierced.

The jewelry in question all glinted with silver and emerald, platinum and sapphire. Not a stitch of gold on him. This genie had a small crown circling his bald head, pressed skin-tight to his pallid flesh.

He grinned now, flashing pure white teeth the same hue as the moonore, as if, perhaps, he'd ripped out his own teeth and replaced them with filed and smoothed clumps of the precious metal.

"Oh dear, dear..." he said, giggling. "What sees Mr. Me? What sees Mr. Me?" He began clapping his hands together in delight, still crunching and chewing on his mouthful of dust and gold.

Grendel bared his teeth, snarling, his fuzzy rump facing me for the moment as he sniffed out this new threat.

"The eyes of night, sheer delight," said the pale genie. "The heart of treasure, fondest pleasure. Sing, sing, sing!"

"Again and again and again!" crowed many of the other genies, clapping in rhythm with the strangely crowned Mr. Me.

The genie with the crown whistled some more, clicking his fingers and making kissing noises, as if he were trying to attract a puppy to heel. He giggled some more, waving his fingers beneath Grendel's slobbering fangs.

"And can it see?" the genie said, softly at first. His tone began to increase in volume though. Even Grendel seemed confused how to respond. "Can it see?" Mr. Me asked, louder now. His face began to contort, his eyes widening, pale moons for eyeballs staring out, wild and truly mad. "Can it see? Can it see!? CAN IT SEE!?"

And then he lunged towards Grendel, fingers scrambling at the demon bear's eyes.

At the same time, more of the genies began to straighten, rising from the dust, turning at the commotion. Their eyes also glowed like tiny pale moons.

Grendel sent Mr. Me rocking back, slashing the genie across the chest.

The wishmaker didn't bleed. His flesh ripped and gouged, but more like torn pastry than skin. Mr. Me glanced down, cocking his head the other way, in the same sort of flopping, unhinged motion. He pulled a piece of his chest off, holding it up to the moonstone light and squinting now. He examined it for a moment, curious.

One of the other Banes darted forward, snatching the chest flesh from Mr. Me's hands, and laughing, he tossed the strand of ripped flesh towards another genie. This genie grabbed the flesh strip and whirled it around her head like a lasso, cackling louder and louder.

"Can it see?" some of the others were chanting.

I looked up and around, all too aware now that more faces, more eyes, more pale skin was pressing to the mirrors on the other side. Hundreds of the Banes were gathering, coming to examine the commotion, hundreds of lunar eyes staring through the glass, into the tunnel, unblinking, watching.

Grendel had backed up now, one clawed foot treading on my already slashed ankle.

I yelped in pain, but quickly stifled the noise lest I regain anyone's attention. I'd already stowed my shield, refusing to let the curse settle too deeply; I'd been eyeing Grendel's fuzzy, demon-scaled buttocks with a bit too much interest.

Mr. Me reached a hand into his chest, through the flap of skin now. He pulled out a small, hovering sphere of black smoke.

The smoke itself was the size of a golf ball, and he didn't so much hold it as allow it to float an inch off the tip of his fingers.

My eyes widened in horror.

A dreader.

Where genies dealt in wishes and secret desires, the Banes had long deserted their first love. Now, they fed on fears and horrors. They played in the night with horrofiends and wishrot. And instead of wishes, they granted nightmares.

A dreader was the substance of someone's secret fears and terrified thoughts.

Mr. Me swirled the ball of shadow over his hand for a moment. Then, with his other hand, he rolled his fingers until they shaped a finger gun. He pointed it at Grendel and murmured, "Bang." Then he pursed his horribly pale lips and blew.

The ball of smoke flew forward and slammed into Grendel's beast chest.

Instantly, the bounty hunter went rigid. He stood stock still for a moment, his enormous form motionless beneath the crowds of Banes gathering in the mirrors above and around.

Then... the thousand-year-old killer, the eternal of unknown origin began to whimper...

It started like a pitiable leaking sound and grew louder... Then louder still. Soon, Grendel was howling in pain at some unseen nemesis. Grendel began slashing at the air, slashing claws and gouging his teeth at phantoms. The demon bear toppled on his side, legs kicking, jaws snapping helplessly, whimpering like a scorned pup, kicking wildly about.

Mr. Me and the other genies laughed louder now, some of them dancing, others darting forward to poke at the whimpering Kindred, then darting back before they could be struck.

For my part, my fingers still groped the wall behind me, my chest pounding wildly. For now, I'd gone unnoticed. Hardly a threat...

"Do you see?" a voice said suddenly.

I nearly leapt out of my skin, jerking around sharply. A pale head with two moon eyes was pushed through the mirror next to me. My cheek grazed against flesh as cold as ice. The disembodied head suddenly grinned, flashing teeth.

"Do you see?" it whispered.

"Hush," I gasped, quickly, renewing my efforts, pushing my fingers beneath mirrors, behind fragments of glass. Pushing and prodding, twisting stones, gouging granite. Nothing. No movement. Tomb's trove, where was that skinting button!

"Do you see?" said the head, chuckling now.

"Quiet," I murmured. "Please, be quiet."

"Do you see!?" it said, louder now.

I didn't reply, deciding that my answers only seemed to alarm the Bane.

Grendel was still whimpering, but no longer thrashing, rather having curled up in a fuzzy ball, twitching and yelping every couple of seconds and flinching at some unseen aggressor as his nightmares were made reality for him and him alone. I wasn't safe yet, though. The Bane inside the mirror next to me grew irritated by my chosen path of silence.

Louder, it began to say, "Do you see?"

My fingers scraped along a ridge of dusty stone... This felt familiar... It had to be right... Was that... no—just a nub. This! Yes! No. A stone fell loose, tumbling to the ground. I cursed again, turning fully and scrutinizing the wall.

"DO YOU SEE!?" the Bane screeched in my ear so loudly it hurt.

Other Banes were now joining the chant. Hundreds of pale, moon eyes all twisted now, focusing on me. I glanced over my shoulder, shivering. And then, the Bane with the small circlet of silver and ruby cocked his head again, standing beneath the largest stretch of mirror on the ceiling. Mr. Me stared at me, his pale, pupilless eyes fixated. And then, he giggled softly.

"Want to hear a joke?" He asked.

I shook my head, but didn't dare respond, feverishly scrubbing stone with now bloodied fingers.

Mr. Me reached into his ripped chest again, pulling out another small sphere of black smoke. Again, it hovered over his fingers.

Deadman's teeth... I renewed my frenzied scraping along the small bar of stone beneath two cracked mirrors. My fingers ripped along the edge of a particularly jagged section of glass. Warm blood spilled down my ear, down my ankle, and now down my fingers, but I kept searching.

"Come on!" I said desperately.

I glanced frantically back. Mr. Me had formed a small finger gun out of his free hand, pointing it in my direction.

He grinned, flashing moonore teeth. Then he pursed his lips to blow on the dreader.

My fingers suddenly pushed a protrusion of stone and it *clicked*...

Clicked?

Stones didn't click.

Mr. Me blew, and at the same time, the portion of stone I'd been standing on suddenly twisted, spinning like a foosball player on a metal stick. The floor fell out and I tumbled through, dropping out of sight and falling into a dark chute with a loud shout.

Chapter 51

My back skimmed against the smooth stone chute and a scream lodged in my throat, held back by the breakneck motion through dark rock. I picked up speed, faster, faster, deeper, darker. At last, I felt the stone give out beneath me, and—briefly—I flailed on open air. A quick jagged yelp followed a plummet.

Head over heels, yelling, then a loud *splash!*

I kicked, desperate, water in my ears, my mouth; gagging and coughing, I propelled myself back up, something bumping my foot as I kicked. Gasping for air, I broke the surface, looking desperately around and blinking water from my stinging eyes.

Above, I spotted an open tunnel in the ceiling gaping down at me. A warm glow of moonore light spotlighted through this gap, illuminating the deep fountain bowl I'd landed in.

I kicked over to a marble edge of the basin, dragging myself up and rolling onto dry ground. For a moment, I just lay there, stunned, aching, cut and bruised.

I groaned, gasping at the ceiling. Around me, I could hear the steady churn of tumbling water. I smelled moisture on the air, but unlike the Loophole, the water here seemed fresh.

Grendel hadn't followed—likely still under the influence of the horrible dreader. I'd seen lesser beings rip their own skin off, or eat their own lips while entrapped in one of those packaged nightmares. Shivering, I grimaced, slowly pushing to my feet.

Behind me, a waterfall poured into a frothing basin; steam rose above the rippling blue, intermingling with the moonore spotlight beaming from the tunnel above. As I blinked, adjusting to the more spacious cavern, I spotted more of these skylights. More spotlights of moonore light flooded into the cavern, illuminating other small fountain basins. Additional miniature waterfalls tumbled from the walls themselves—blue waters, crystal clear, pouring into the makeshift ponds.

I stood dripping, shivering and trying to catch my bearings...

I'd been worried I'd taken a wrong turn in the dark.

Now, I knew I had.

This wasn't the under level to the Hollow.

I didn't know where I was.

The combination of the many waterfalls, many marble-ringed ponds, and the moonore spotlights shining through the ceiling created a strange, eerie sort of aura. Wafting vapors of steam arose from the water behind me, speckling my cheeks with froth and caressing me with warmth.

For a moment, all I wanted was to lie down, to sleep, to float into one of the fountains, allowing the water to carry my weight.

I glanced back towards the deep fountain behind me, my injured ankle nudging against the smooth marble and sandstone wall. My feet slipped, though, and that's when I realized I was standing on a large sheet of glass.

For a moment, my heart jolted, but then I breathed more lightly.

Not reflective glass—not the mirrors Banes liked to sleep in. No, this glass was opaque, but see-through. It seemed stained with steam and spread across the entire cavernous room. Beneath my feet, I saw more water, sloshing and splashing. The giant sheet of glass seemed like a glaze of ice covering an ocean. The waterfalls all spilled into the ponds and the ponds deposited into this greater body of liquid beneath the opaque surface. The skylights above illuminated sections of the translucent material, reflecting in the milky glass.

That's when I spotted *things* in the liquid.

I yelped, stumbling back, my shoes squeaking against the wet ground, droplets flickering around me in the low light as I steadied myself.

Large things hung suspended *deep* down in the water. Some the size of whales...

Others the size of entire city blocks.

Far, far, far, down—deeper than I could see, the things remained frozen, rigid, as if encased in ice. The steam continued to rise from the surrounding ponds, the moonstone beams of light seemed even more intense.

I leaned in, my gaze fixed on a beautiful face directly beneath my toes. A celestial countenance, with pristine, porcelain features. A sleeping face the size of a small mountain.

I retreated with more squeaking steps.

I'd definitely taken a wrong turn. I could only guess, but it seemed I'd stumbled on one of the deepest chambers, a hiding place for the most dangerous of captives... A jail, frozen in time and ice and water for the dominions and the archangels... for those birthed before space and memory itself.

I found my eyes darting back towards the colossal face beneath me, strangely drawn to the horrible beauty. Was it my imagination, or did the sleeping face's eyelids flutter?

"Step away from there!" a voice called behind me.

I whirled around, my heart in my throat, my feet slipping on the slick glass once more. I stiffened, now, gaze fixed on a large dais made of sandstone. I hadn't seen it behind one of the waterfalls at first, but now, heart-pounding as I rounded one of the ponds, I spotted a ruby-red throne centering the sandstone dais.

And sitting on the throne...

I swallowed. Vyle's teeth.

I'd definitely taken a wrong turn.

Saboteur February now wore her helmet. Like Annie's, it completely covered her face, with no visible eye-slits, or mouth openings. A crude, blunt metal helm, shaped like the severed head of an eagle, with swirling, magma scrawl spelling out words in a language I didn't know.

Beneath this demonic helm, she sat clad in full, ruby-red armor with hooked spikes. Unlike Annie's, February's helmet also boasted streaks of the same substance as her wereblade—pristine red crystal. The molten scrawl on this helmet moved slower, cautiously, deep red flames gouged into the surface, rotating and spinning in soft orbiting circles.

The three prongs pointed up at the ceiling, beneath a section of the chasm absent of moonore light.

As I rounded the fountain and fell still, I realized just how large this chasm was. As far as the eye could see, in every direction, beams of moonore spilled through tunnels in the ceiling while waterfalls tumbled from stone walls or cracks in the chasm roof. Also, a sheet of slick, opaque glass covered steaming ponds, where sleeping silhouettes were suspended in the water.

"Well?" February said, one arm against the cold crystal of her throne. "My guards left... Someone called them away—was it you?" Her voice came cold and cruel. With her helmet on, her words echoed from the shadows and from deeper corners of darkness throughout the room, resounding from the portions least touched by the moonore light as if from a million little hidden speakers.

I could feel a lump in my throat... I'd escaped Grendel only to now fall into the clutches of February again. What ill-fated, hex-cursed luck.

"Banes are notoriously distracted guardians," I murmured, softly. "I could have told you that."

"And you have. Well?" February tapped her fingers against the throne arm. "Did you find November? Where is the beast?"

"Ah... Grendel... Yes, about him. He's taking a nap, unfortunately."

"A what?"

"Disrespectful, I know. But he's sleepy right now." I gave an apologetic wince, standing my ground and refusing to take another step in the lieutenant's direction.

February growled, shaking her helmed head. "No matter... Useless, the lot of you eternals. My own sisters will be here soon enough. Then we'll hunt that traitor like the maggot she is!"

I nodded, slowly. "Never heard of maggot-hunting. No matter. If you won't be needing me... then... Maybe I could just be going."

"No!" she said sharply. A single, gauntleted hand lifted, held out towards me. She pushed slowly from her throne, standing tall at the top of the dais. The ruby armor cast vibrant patterns of light throughout the area.

"Yes?" I asked through gritted teeth. "How can I be of service?"

February took one lazy step down from the dais, followed by another, moving gracefully in her horrible, hooked armor. The molten scrawl on her eyeless helmet continued to spin, spin, spin.

"I permitted you to live in exchange for bringing the traitor to me. If you can't do that, I see little use for you now. Perhaps you'd like to sleep with our friends below..."

She pointed towards the murky figures in the water beneath the glass.

I took a shaky step back, eyes darting just past February. "What happened to your saboteur creed; ought you not defend mortalkind?"

Her eyes narrowed. "You're an eternal talent. Not mortalkind."

She had me there. I coughed delicately. "Well, perhaps I can help anyway. No need to be rash."

"Help me? How might you help? You've failed, savant. Come here, taste my sting."

"I can help," I said, my voice rising a bit, and I coughed. "Because I know where November is."

A small corner of February's lips were just visible in one of the veins of crystal. Beneath the mask, they curved into a foggy smile. "Oh... the things your kind will say to cling to life for a second longer. No—no more words. Come here."

"I mean it!" I called, no longer backpedaling. Instead, I pointed over February's shoulder. "See, she's behind you. She's standing right there."

February chuckled, shaking her head now. She would have continued laughing, I imagined, if at that moment she hadn't been slammed from behind by a giant fly swatter made of pure shadow. February, in her pretty armor, was sent skittering off her dais, skipping down the sandstone steps and skidding a good fifteen feet across the glass, face down. She came to a halt by bumping head-first into one of the marble walls circling the pools. Her helmet clinked against the divider, and she turned around sharply, shadows helping to twist and lift her to her feet like a marionette on strings.

Just as quickly, she was now standing on the wall, her back to the tumbling waterfall, glaring through a beam of moonore light.

November stood with one foot on the sandstone dais, her eyes narrowed in fury. A single length of chain dangled from one of her wrists, attached to a half-melted cuff. Her face was streaked with ash and her eyes blazed.

February flinched, briefly, still balanced on the wall of marble, half held aloft by shadows, her ruby and metal boots planted firmly.

"November," February said, her voice low, cautious. "My dear... what are you doing here? I've missed you, Annie. It's good to see you again."

"Don't listen to her!" I yelled. "She wants to kill you, Annie!"

February snarled, turning towards me and flicking one of her fingers. A shadow lashed out, slamming into my chest and sending me tumbling *through* one of the waterfalls and out the other side. I skipped across the glassy ground, groaning as I rolled to a halt just beneath the ruby throne. So much pain. My shoe now felt slick with blood inside and out. Groaning, I looked up, blearily, eyes on Annie's outline.

My old friend glanced down at me for a moment, shaking her head. "You tricked me," she murmured.

I winced. "You lied."

She looked back through the moonore beam to the edge of the pool. "You never intended to let them hurt me, did you?" she asked, softly. "I heard your voice... It woke me. My chains had broken."

I rubbed ruefully at my elbow, glancing nervously to where February stood in front of the waterfall. "I had to improvise. Didn't know I could trust you." I frowned, the scowl deepening. "Still don't."

Annie spared me a full glance now, taking her eyes off the threat of February for a brief moment. Her expression softened, and she shook her head. "Truly, Leon, I am sorry. I shouldn't..." She swallowed. "I shouldn't have used you."

I thought I could hear a low, whistling tune somewhere in the back of my mind, a song stuck in my head. It took me a second, but then I recognized one of the small ditties Annie and I used to sing when skipping along the palace gardens.

I stared at my friend, wondering if she could hear the song too. Some people were just born to be friends... I'd tricked her, used her to open the Hollow gates. She'd demanded entry, and so I'd provided it. But I'd also known the risk. I'd played the odds, played with uncertainty and danger... I'd lashed out in my anger at her betrayal, using her as a pawn...

Using her as my father might have done.

I shivered in horror at the thought.

"I'm sorry too," I murmured, my voice cracking.

Annie looked ready to say more, but then her eyes widened in horror and she screamed, "Look out!"

Chapter 52

Annie jumped, propelled by a gust of shadow at her feet, and she slammed into my crouched form, sending me stumbling down the dais and out of the way of a flash of red.

A ruby chain swept overhead, slamming into the sandstone steps and sending chunks of the substance flying through the air.

February howled and spun the chain around again. A scythe attached to thick links of crystal whirled once, twice and she whipped it forward, this time aiming for Annie.

Confident I was safe, Annie dove the opposite direction this time, rolling behind the throne. Chains struck the red dais in a shower of sparks.

"November!" February called, her voice rising. "You shouldn't have done this, girl! We all know! The Shademaker knows! Regent January knows! There's nowhere for you *Annie*—come, let me bring you peace!"

November snarled, rolling over the top of the throne and slipping down the front on a surfboard of shadow. She sent a fist of shade rising from the recesses circling the wall, lifting the circlet of darkness and trying to lasso February where she stood.

The shadows tightened, like a suddenly released rubber band, and wrapped around February's ruby armor, tangling in the hooks and tightening even further. The lieutenant cried out in fury, and shadows of her own arose, scything towards November, but my old friend saw it coming. She flung February, still tied by the band of darkness, tossing her into the water and shoving down, trying to hold her beneath the churning blue liquid.

I stared in awe and horror as the lieutenant of the saboteurs was bent over the edge of the small pond, a noose of shadow around her neck, dragging her into the water.

For a moment, I thought it was all over.

But then, with desperate, clawing motions, February rotated, still drowning, but sliding her body painfully *around* the circle of the pond. After a moment, she pulled herself beneath the moonore beam above. The shadow around her became fuzzy, then loosened, then faded completely beneath the spotlight from the ceiling. From what little I knew of saboteurs, this made sense. Their powers manifested in darkness. The darker the setting, the more powerful their magic. Annie had faced off with Preacher under the cover of night. Her shadow had grown restless in the shade of the Loophole's trees. The mountain top fight with Grendel's brood had occurred beneath a thick cloud cover and obscuring mist.

Now, though, *pure* unadulterated light seemed to greatly weaken the abilities of the saboteurs.

February leapt to her feet spitting and spluttering beneath her helmet. Annie didn't have a wereblade. She didn't have armor, nor did she have her helmet.

But her eyes blazed with wrath, and she didn't back off as February came charging forward, jumping from a disc of shade to another, crossing the gap between them through the air itself.

They met in the sky with twin screams of fury, wereblade whirling, scythe flashing, shadows rising, colliding.

They disengaged, both panting, neither dead yet. I could barely track the rapid movement. This time, February turned, and began skating through the air, dancing around the beams of moonore light, weaving in and out of the spotlights. Annie's attacks of shade disintegrated where they hit the light beams.

"November!" February called, taunting as she ducked under another shard of black. "You never could control that temper of yours!"

"Silence, demon!" November screamed. She sprinted up the dais, up the throne, leaping off the top of the headrest and somersaulting through a waterfall to tackle February from a shelf of shade.

The two of them tumbled, slamming into the glassy ground with dull, damp *thuds*. I stood frozen, wondering if I should help... if I could. But what could I do? I was down to two vials of gold dust and one tiger's eye. My shield? Perhaps...

I began inching closer, trying to intervene without being seen. If I wasn't careful, February would rip me to pieces.

The wereblade in the shape of a scythe cut down, slashing towards November's unarmored neck. But my friend rolled away and the weapon scored a glancing blow against the thick glass beneath them. Jagged white marks stained the glass, but February kept coming, lashing out with another burst of chain extending from the wereblade. At the same time, she sent a wall of shadow up, trying to flatten November.

"You killed her!" Annie screamed. "You murdered her! You heartless, soulless—" Annie grunted as she was sent flying, kicked in the chest, stumbling and crashing into the backrest of the raised ruby throne.

February stood for a moment, breathing heavily, wereblade gripped tight, hooked armor gleaming beneath moonore light.

"Don't be such a baby," she snarled. "We all had to do it. Don't you think we wanted to keep our angels too? You don't understand, November. None of them are allies."

"She was! She was my friend!" Annie screamed, scrambling back to her feet, hands balled into fists.

"No, she tricked you! That's what they do! They're not human. They're not like us." February spat. "What's the point. Reasoning with you is like reasoning with a child about their pet rabbit. All emotion, all misplaced affection. You don't have what it takes. I should have seen it before approving. I should have listened to July!"

For a moment, the two women glared murderous rage across the glassy ground, one beneath an encasing of ruby and iron, the other wet and slick from the waterfalls. A beam of moonore light stretched between them.

"July is dead," November whispered. "So is April. I'll bring you all to Hades. Even January. You'll never kill another angel. Not again."

"Oh? And you'll stop us?" February snorted. "If I remember correctly, last time you tried, you wept in a corner while we strangled your little spirit friend. Do you remember how she wailed? Begging? Pleading for us to stop?"

"She was begging for you to stop hurting *me*!" November roared. "You witch!"

She leapt forward again, but too fast, this time...

I spotted the trap a second before she did. February had been baiting, waiting. Now, as Annie plummeted down, so did February's sickle. Instead of slicing with it at Annie, though, which would have been blocked, she slammed it into the glass floor.

A calamitous crack. The glass splintered. A hole smashed through, like a bullet in a windshield, and Annie yelled, trying to catch herself.

Annie scrambled, slipping into the water. Her fingers scraped against glass. I spotted a jet of blood as she ripped a hand on the shards.

February wasn't done though. As Annie tried to kick and rise from the hole in the floor, February raised her hands and yelled, "Fool!" Suddenly, discs of darkness sped towards the pools and ponds, covering them like lids.

The sound of the tumbling waterfalls became a pounding. The water was blocked by the shadow lids and suddenly began to spread, flooding the ground, pouring into the room itself, glazing the glass.

Annie dragged herself from the hole in the ground only to be met by a wave of steaming water. It caught her in the chest, sending her tumbling and like driftwood carried to sea, skidding across the ground.

I had my own problems, though.

Water slammed into my legs from behind, knocking them out. I yelped when I felt the steaming liquid singe Grendel's cut on my ankle.

I kicked, trying to catch myself, but more water spilled into the throne room. The waterfalls continued pouring; the moonore light illuminated the clear blue. Steam rose around me, and soon, I was treading water, spluttering, trying to find somewhere to land.

The throne... I had to reach the throne. It was the highest point.

I splashed, kicking, whirling around and then spotted the jutting ruby seat. With a yell, I began swimming, water turbulent behind me, steam wafting in front as I cut through the liquid. More waves rocked me, sending me slipping and spinning. Ahead, I spotted February, skipping from one shadow step to another, climbing towards one of the tunnels in the ceiling.

Annie yelled, and I watched her rise from the water, giving chase.

February whirled about, a sickle at the end of a chain flashing down and ripping towards my old friend. The trick with the lids on the pools seemed to have cost her though; February was breathing heavily.

As her chain ripped forward, though, this time, mid-air, Annie—or was it November, I was no longer sure— was a step too slow. The curving scimitar of ruby slashed across my friend's belly, and she yelled in pain. One hand clapped to her ribs, but she still kept coming, chasing the tiring February.

For a moment, the lieutenant of the saboteurs had paused, standing on a shadow shelf; I could practically imagine the grin on her face where I tread water. She raised a hand, a thick spear of darkness gripped in clenched fingers. Annie's injured form had lagged, briefly, giving February an opening.

I stared in horror, gasping, looking desperately around for something... But finding nothing, nothing, then *there!* A piece of glass from where February had smashed the floor. It rested against the dais of the throne. The fragment of glass twitched and fluttered beneath the water, but I lunged, snaring it.

Not much I could do from here. Not much at all.

Still, gasping, splashing, swimming, I jutted my hand beneath the glowing beam of moonore light, holding the jagged shard of glass, my fingers bleeding.

I directed the light now, reflecting off the glass, aiming it straight at February.

The bright beam shot like a laser, cutting through February's spear. Cutting through the shelf she stood on. Annie, still gasping, had barely avoided the spear thrust, and now panting, was being beaten from her own purchase in the air.

But as the aimed beam of pure light caught February, she shrieked, slipping, one foot falling. Her spear of shadow vanished. I felt a flutter of vindictive satisfaction.

November yelled incoherently, her rage swelling up like the water.

February stumbled back with a surprised gasp as a wave of shadows in the shape of needles spewed towards her from Annie, trying to pin her to the wall.

I aimed the beam of light again, but this time, February turned tail, cursing and moving rapidly, far, far faster than any human. She fled towards the tunnel in the ceiling, ducking through moonore light which caught the spears. November still chased, jumping from one disk of shade to another. She was gaining, getting closer... I lowered the mirror, fearful of hitting my friend's conjurations now.

Annie reached out a hand. February continued to flee. Was it my imagination, or was she getting slower? Even more tired?

November only seemed to be gaining energy.

Then... a horrible misstep for February, as if she were distracted by anticipating my reflected beam of light. She stepped into a beam of her own, trying to leap off another shelf of shadow to finally reach the tunnel in the ceiling.

But the light melted the shadow, and February tumbled. She yelled, one hand thrown out, and I spotted her wereblade glint and arch, falling from her hand and dropping into the rising tide of water. February cursed, but caught herself with another materialized ledge.

Annie, though, kept coming, like a truck up a highway.

Chapter 53

February rounded now, her movements slower for certain. She was tiring; I could tell even from here. Water lapped against my chin, my cheeks. Steam wafted up, covering my vision.

I heard February give a horrible shout. "No! Listen to me. Girl, listen!"

Annie howled, and, through the steam, I watched her tackle February.

Again, February just managed to escape, but now moving like a limping doe, hind leg scored by a wolf. November just kept coming. They both ascended towards the tunnel. Again, February began to lag... Annie was going to catch her. She was going to—

Something grabbed my foot.

Something large.

Very large.

And it pulled, yanking me beneath the water.

I tried to scream, but my mouth filled with liquid. I choked, even as I was dragged down. I kicked desperately, again and again. Whatever had grabbed me loosened, and I bolted back towards the surface. Not before, though, turning, my eyes open in the warm, blue water, staring down.

I was directly over the hole in the glass February had caused.

A hand was reaching up.

A hand made of pure light.

A hand with fingers larger than my legs, a palm wider than my body. The enormous, hill-sized head I'd seen, the twitching eyelashes were now moving. Both eyes were open, staring directly up at me. The hand darted through the hole in the glass once more as the colossal thing tried to grab me. Bubbles burst from my lips as my head broke the surface.

Again, I only had a second to draw breath as the monstrous hand wrapped around my ankle and yanked me down again.

More bubbles, more swallowed water, more gagging. I thrashed about, screaming soundless in the liquid, air pockets swarming past my cheeks. I kicked with my heel, pounding down once, twice, a third time. I tried to slip my foot free, but the grip was so strong.

My only saving grace was that whatever lay dormant beneath me was still only waking, still only just rising from slumber. Blood streaked my heel, courtesy of Grendel's gouging claws. This, it turned out, was perhaps the greatest mercy. The slick blood allowed me to slip my shoe with ease. I kicked once more with my other foot, drowning now, lungs gasping.

I managed to kick free a second time, my head breaking the surface of the water again. This time, I didn't waste my time drawing breath. Rather, I screamed.

"Annie! Help!"

In a brief moment, in an image that burned into my mind, I spotted my friend pause, one hand practically touching February's hooked armor. February herself was clearly spent, exhausted, missing her wereblade, put to task by the battering of the enraged younger woman and her ally's beam of light. Fear was the cancer of the mind, and Annie had scared February. I'd seen it the first moment I'd reached the Hollow. February was halfway into the tunnel above, Annie just below her.

Still, at my shout, Annie glanced back.

I tried to swallow air. No more energy to scream.

Annie's eyes landed on me, and she stood stuck. One hand reaching towards February, who continued to wriggle up and away, helped by hands of shadow, pushing her along the tunnel in the ceiling, pushing her to freedom.

November screamed in frustration, glancing at me once more, then looking back at her sworn enemy. On one hand, an old friend, but a friend who'd used her, lied to her, betrayed her. On the other, an old enemy, finally in her grasp after years of planning, of careful thought. Years of work had gone into tracing February, chasing her down, getting this chance. She was tired now, weakened, her guards called away, her sisters still absent.

November might never get another chance like this.

"Hel—" I tried to shout again, but was yanked back beneath the water once more, this time, the hand had a very firm grip. It wasn't fitting for a prince to beg for aid... But then again, much of my legacy didn't suit me.

Bubbles didn't squeak past my cheeks because I had no air left to lose. Dark spots danced across my gaze as fingers longer than my legs wrapped around me, squeezing tight. The grip went higher, wrapping *both* my legs this time.

I couldn't kick. It felt like I'd been encased in cement.

My lungs screamed in pain. The black spots only worsened but did nothing to diminish the agony of drowning.

My mouth opened, swallowing water, choking more. Down, I was dragged further down. Now, the hand was pulling me *beneath* the glass. I knew if that happened, there'd be no escape.

Already, though, I was out of options. I couldn't even reach my pocket with the shield—not that it would be much use here—the hand was too tight, the top of the pointer finger, as thick as a small tree, pressing my pocket against my thigh, effectively sealing it from use.

I hadn't thought I'd die this way... Drowning. Nothing noble in it.

I'd often had the chance to consider the way I'd perish. I'd assumed the Endeavor might catch up with me, or one of my Imperial enemies. Maybe even Percy. I'd thought it possible I'd die on a field of battle, finally having given in to my lesser nature, joining my father's army. Another more fanciful part of me had thought I might march into battle against my own brothers, under the indigo eye of the Endeavor. Who would have seen that coming?

The rest of me... though... The small piece of hope Nimue had managed to salvage from the wreckage of my soul had longed for something quieter... A cabin in the woods. Maybe even a friend or two. I'd never much pictured myself with a family. My only experiences with families ended in ruin. But to die old, with a couple of dogs, and a couple of friends, and certainly one cat...

That wouldn't have been so bad...

I didn't think, though, it would end like this.

Especially with Napoleon so close. Now, though, I felt a flicker of relief. No one expects a drowning man to save the world. I wouldn't have to kill my brother after all. I found, despite the pain in my lungs, despite the scraping of the glass against my belly as my legs were pulled through, I smiled...

My elbow ripped on the hole in the glass, blood fluttering up and past me, wafting on the water as the hand tried to pull me through without scraping its own knuckles too badly. It had paused, briefly, to navigate the glass. For a moment, we were caught in the largest version of a monkey's paw I'd ever seen. Still gripping me, it made it difficult to pull back through the opening in the glass.

The giant face beneath the opaque surface burned bright, staring and then its lips opened and it began to swallow. Water began to churn, swirling, swirling, drawn in through the glass, towards the sucking lips of the colossal thing beneath.

And then...

Something dark slammed into the finger next to me. A dagger of shadow. Another dagger slammed into the finger, again, again. Bright light burst from each wound, instead of blood. The water around me suddenly rumbled as if an underwater volcano had erupted.

An instant later, Annie was at my side, prying desperately at the fingers gripping me, kicking in the water.

She beat ferociously at the hand, indifferent to its size, indifferent to the effort. She screamed silently beneath the water, bubbles fleeing her lips, intermingling with the dark spots casting over my vision.

And then, with a herculean shove, aided by a jagged blade, the first finger loosened its grip. My left leg fell free.

I was weak, though... too weak...

I felt a flash of regret. I'd been looking forward to my death. Looking forward to the chance to abandon this burden of expectation.

Annie, though, continued fighting ferociously, slashing and gouging and kicking and screaming without words beneath the waves. There's nothing like unearned acts of selflessness to trick someone into valuing their own life...

My eyes still stung, my lungs felt like bursting, but with desperate, pitifully weak kicks, I tried to extricate my second leg.

Alone, I never would have managed.

But Annie dove, now, using a jagged shadow to saw at the fingers. More bright light burst, more rumbling from the deep, and then...

The hand lost its grip.

My legs yanked free, scraping against more glass. Annie lifted me with her, swimming, fast, propelled forward by some unnatural force. The two of us cut through the water, up, up, and we burst forth. She lifted me, carrying with a heave through the liquid.

I gasped greedily, sucking air and feeling my lips sting from the sheer effort of it.

Splashing, thrashing, avoiding any more hands in the murk, Annie dragged me onto the sandstone dais, pulling me up the steps.

I couldn't walk. I could barely move. But I allowed myself to be yanked forward. I blinked, dark spots still shooting across my gaze like comets.

Annie pulled me, desperately, whispering in my ear, "Hang on, Leon. Hang on... It's going to be okay. Just hang on."

The saboteur pulled the savant from the blue water, through the rising cloud of steam and then collapsed—me on top of her—onto the only portion of the chasm still above water... The ruby throne.

I leaned back, my head resting against the cold red crystal, Annie breathing heavily as she shifted onto the arm-rest, trying to give me space, still whispering fiercely in my ear. "It's going to be okay... It's going to be okay."

It's going to be okay... For a moment, I thought back to when we were children. She'd said the same thing then too, hadn't she? In the gardens on that sunlit morning...

My gaze flickered, my eyes scanned the water... No more glowing hands. No more groping fingers. Even the rumbling seemed to have subsided for the moment. My eyes traced the walls, up, up, flitting towards the tunnel in the ceiling.

No sign of February.

Annie had come back for me.

I breathed a sigh of relief and closed my eyes, feeling the warm water lap against my fingertips where they dangled over the edge of the gemstone arm rest.

Chapter 54

"There... through here. I'm certain this time," I said, my voice labored.

Water dripped around me, falling in rivulets down my skin, tracing towards the stony ground and dappling gray with dark spots.

Annie leaned against me, also breathing heavily, the two of us limping through one of the tunnels in the back of the throne room built into the side of the chasm wall itself. Every so often, I glanced over my shoulder, but no one followed. The edge of the waves could just be seen lapping against the mouth of the tunnel, but going no further as the floor seemed to slant up, angling away from the throne room.

"You're sure?" Annie murmured, still leaning against me, her head pressed to my shoulder.

"Positive," I whispered. I hissed suddenly through clenched teeth as I pressed too firmly on my ankle. Another shoe missing—I just couldn't seem to hang on to those. Blood streaked down my bare foot, mixing with the water in a weak, red stain. My right foot left bloody prints each time I stepped forward.

Annie hadn't fared much better. I remembered the slashing sickle, the scream of pain. Now, her hands pressed to her ribs, tight. I tried not to look, but my curiosity couldn't help but notice the color of Annie's blood...

Black as shadow, spilling past her fingers, coating her arm. Where the blood struck the ground, it hissed like steam and sent up a faint puff of white light. I shook my head, deciding some mysteries were best left unsolved... Especially given the circumstances.

Annie gripped her ribs, the two of us moving together, pressed against each other through the dark tunnel, up, up. Some people are just meant to be friends, I suppose.

Even after they betray, lie and use each other... especially if they follow it all by saving each other's lives.

"I'm sorry," Annie whispered, her voice echoing in the dark. "I'm truly sorry, Leon." She sobbed. "I know... I know you don't believe me. You never want to see me again. I know that. But please... I couldn't bear to think you didn't know how sorry I was. For..." She gasped... "For lying to you. For using you..."

I breathed slowly, feeling the wet prickle of Annie's buzzed head against my cheek. I rested my head against hers and continued my limping effort up the dark tunnel, moving side by side with my old friend.

"I'm sorry, too," I said. "I should have told you the plan. Shouldn't have gone behind your back. I—I was angry with you."

"I know..." She paused, then, with a tiny hint of humor, she added, "I saved your life, you know."

"Thank you," I said. What else was there to say?

"Leon?" she asked, softly.

"Annie?"

"I saved your life..." I could definitely detect a smile behind her words now.

I growled. "Are you going to bring that up forever?"

"Probably. Does that mean you'll still be my friend?"

It was such an odd question, given our circumstances, our surroundings, given the way I'd seen her hunt February, battling like a warrior of old. And yet, every part of Annie seemed to mean it. Like a child again, scared of being alone.

I closed my eyes, feeling her warmth against me. Remembering the songs we would sing, remembering the way we would laugh, chasing each other around the fruit trees outside the kitchens. They weren't good times... They were moments of sunlight in a dark night. Sometimes, that's all you were given.

"I'll still be your friend," I said. "You did save my life after all."

She giggled, but then winced and coughed, clutching her ribs. "Don't you forget it," she murmured.

Ahead, I thought I glimpsed a flicker of flames... Torchlight. No more moonstone, no more mirrors... An honest to goodness torch.

"We're getting closer," I said urgently, feeling the excitement in my voice. "Just up ahead. See that?"

She turned, staring and nodded once.

I didn't dare pick up the pace, given the state of us, so I continued to limp, eyes on the light now, feeling a burgeoning hope rising in me.

"Annie?" I said, soft.

"Leon?"

"Did February escape?"

Silence. A weighty one, thick and complete.

Then, "Yes, Leon. She did."

"Did you leave her to reach me?"

She nodded again, and her voice caught in her throat. "Mhmm." For a moment, it seemed like she didn't want to speak, but then, quietly, she sighed. "I can't pretend I won't try again. But I know I can beat her, Leon... I wasn't sure. For decades, I wasn't sure. I trained against *them*. While they trained to kill celestials, the gods, the monsters and creatures... But I trained to kill them. Still, I didn't know if it would be enough. Now, though..." She breathed a quiet, sad sound. "Now I know. Perhaps that's enough. I've always known my chosen path would take years... I'm patient, Leon. One thing about being locked in a shadow realm for twenty years... It makes you patient."

I coughed, feeling a lump form in my throat. "Thank you," I said, my voice husky.

"You're very welcome... Leon?"

"Annie?"

"I don't think Preacher likes me very much." I could tell she was intentionally changing the subject, and I wondered if she could tell I was letting her.

"Oh, you'll grow on him. He just takes some time. He tried to beat me up the first time I met him."

"Really? Did he succeed?"

I cleared my throat. "It's really cold down here, isn't it?"

"He did, didn't he? He beat you up. Preacher beat you up."

"You don't have to repeat it that many times. Besides, he sucker punched me. Ask anyone."

"I will."

I snorted. "Fat good it'll do you if you don't know sign language."

She grinned and her cheeks dimpled like they so often did. Our steps were dragging and slow, having covered the distance to the torch light. We came out of the intersection into another tunnel, this one curving into a flat-stone, spiral staircase.

My eyes flashed, fixed on the ground, and I swallowed.

"What is it?" Annie asked, leaning back and pushing lightly away from me now to watch my expression.

"I... this is it," I said quietly. "I knew this was the right path."

Memories fluttered across my vision... A pistol in the dark... a finger on the trigger. *Do it. Do it!*

I couldn't.

I let out a slow groan, like a creaking hinge on an ancient door. I felt very old all of a sudden, staring towards the top of the stairwell.

"What is it?" Annie asked. "More guardians?"

I shook my head. "None this deep. The only things down here are under lock and key.

"Oh? You look ill."

"I... I'm not a good man, Annie." I turned, looking at her now. The poorly set break of her gently sloped nose cast jagged shadows across her smooth skin. The torchlight in the bracket centering the wall flickered, the orange and reds illuminating us with warmth as water continued to fall, slower now, still speckling the floor.

I shifted uncomfortably, feeling the rough grain of the stone ground beneath my bare foot, wincing against the gash in my ankle.

"What do you mean?" Annie asked.

"I mean... I..."

"You're here for your brother, yes?" she said. "I know I tricked you. I'm sorry. Like I said, I shouldn't—"

"It's not that," I said quickly. I wanted to hold her gaze, to meet her green eyes, but I couldn't. I glanced off to the side, swallowing back a desire to scream.

"What is it, Leon?" Annie murmured. "You look like you've seen a ghost."

"No. Not yet. Down there though..."

"What?"

"A ghost." I looked up now, stepping back again and allowing Annie to lean against the wall for support. My shoulders faced the mouth of the descending stairwell. I could feel a sudden cold, and I set my teeth. A quiet dread had entered my chest the moment I'd set foot in the Hollow. I'd rationalized, I'd promised myself... But now none of that mattered.

For a moment, I was glad I'd lost my powers. If I could hear what Annie thought of me... if she ever knew...

"A ghost?" she said softly, tilting her head in curiosity. "Whatever do you mean?"

"Napoleon was a kind-hearted child..." I murmured, collapsing shoulder-first against the jagged cavern wall, using the support of unyielding stone to keep me upright. "Only four years old at the night of the Grimmest Jest, only a toddler. He didn't deserve... He didn't..."

I stared over Annie's shoulder for a moment. Beneath the torch, I spotted a flash of blue eyes. A parted hairdo and a suddenly leering face. My poltergeist stared past Annie, chuckling now, laughing silently, pointing at me and bending over in mirth. He slapped his little knees, laughing and pointing and laughing and—

"Get out of here!" I screamed, jabbing a hand past Annie's cheek. "Get out! Go!"

She jolted back, staring at me, stunned. "Leon..." she said, her voice trembling. "I—I..."

I quickly shook my head, gasping. "No, Annie, sorry, not you. Just *him*..."

Annie whirled around, but the poltergeist vanished the moment she turned. It struck me as odd Annie never seemed to see my tormenting spirit. If anyone could, I imagined it might be her. Then again, I was no expert where fractured souls and poltergeists were concerned.

Annie frowned, turning back now, extending a hand towards my head. "Are you feverish? Poison... It must be. Your cut is—"

"Not poison!" I pushed her hand away.

She winced, leaning against the wall, her elbow tucked against her wound, stained with the strange black blood. She paused for a moment, exhaling sharply, then the shadows along her skin began to shimmer. A thin fold of shadow, pure black, like a strip of cloth slid from the crevices of her clothing, covering the wound like a bandage. I stared at the strip of shadow in quiet awe, grateful for the momentary distraction. But it didn't last long. Annie checked her makeshift bandage of shade, then murmured. "What then? Leon, what has you so scared?"

I slid down the wall now, my arms draping over my jutting knees. I shook my head slowly. "I have to kill him, Annie. I have to do it now. He's only fourteen. He's been here for ten years... I should have done it before, but... I couldn't. How could I? Napoleon Rex was the least like our father."

"Wait, hold on. Kill him? Wow—that's a lot... Why Leon? Why would you kill him?"

"Because of what I did," I said, my voice creaking again. I felt like I'd aged a million years in that moment, staring down the barrel of my own choices. I could see the writing on the wall, could see the horrible inevitability.

I knew what I had to do.

Chapter 55

"Leon, you're scaring me. What did he do?"

"Nothing." I laughed, a humorless, dark, echoing sound. "Absolutely nothing. He was chosen is all. My father chose him. I should have said no. I should have resisted. I was eighteen at the time, fourteen years his senior. I should have been better."

Annie just watched, still clutching her wounds. She slid down the wall now too, slowly, sitting cross-legged on the ground, wincing, but fixing her eyes on me. "Tell me," she said.

They weren't comforting words, but they weren't accusing either. Tell me. A demand. But also an offer.

I'd never told anyone before. Not Preacher. Not even Nimue. I couldn't. How could I tell them? How could I tell them the single greatest secret of the Imperium? No one else knew. Not Augustus. Not even Napoleon. Not Head instructor Nico. Not any of the field marshals in hiding. Not Grendel. Not the saboteurs. Not even the gods.

Only I knew...

... and so did *he*.

"The night of the Grimmest Jest..." I said, my voice wobbly, my fingers shaking so bad I had to press them against my belly. "I... The rebels came. In the dark, in the night, on my father's birthday."

"The night they killed your father, yes?" said Annie. "When they killed the Imperium generals. That's when the Endeavor finally shattered the Imperium."

I nodded stiffly. "That's what they believe, yes."

"I don't understand."

I looked at her now, from beneath a deep brow. I reached out, one finger tracing her cheek. "My father hated death, Annie. It scared him more than anything. He cursed Augustus to avoid it. And... and my father always had a plan."

My own mind leapt back, picturing that rainy night. Picturing the soldiers break into the palace. I could once again hear the crash of thunder, the patter of rain, the cool wind suddenly whipping through the third floor from the balcony as killers came, descending on us like locusts.

"I knew what I had to do," I said.

Tell me. She wanted to know. What did it matter anymore? It would end tonight. No more guardians between me and what waited the floor below at the bottom of those twisting stairs. Napoleon was helpless, defenseless, trapped like a rat in a cage. Trapped where I'd put him. All my fault.

"My father had me practice for this. It was one of the reasons he trained me the hardest. I was his escape plan."

"His what?"

"I was his escape plan. He'd suspected treachery—thought the Endeavor might try something. And so..." I swallowed. "So he told me what to do."

"What did you do, Leon?"

"My little brother," I said, desperately wishing I could sob, wishing I could cry, wishing I could scream. But emotions long foreign to me wouldn't allow themselves to be summoned, not even to appease my conscience. And so I sat there, dry-eyed, aching everywhere, and spilling the filth I'd long kept buried in my throat.

"Napoleon was with us. All of us had to be at my father's birthday. All of us. Augustus was late, as usual—probably dallying with his new sweetheart. They thought they were in love. They were late, but the rest of us weren't. Napoleon was the youngest, of course. Only four, like I said. But the thing about young minds, Annie—they're pliable. They're easy to control. They also don't take up much space—not at that age. They're still learning, growing."

"What did you do, Leonidas?"

"I did what my father told me—what we'd trained for. I saw the guns; I saw the bullets. My father's eyes fixed on mine. Do it now, he said. Now. How could I disobey? He was a tyrant, a cruel, murderous tyrant, but he was also my father, Annie. I was eighteen—not that it gives me any excuse..."

I paused for a moment, trailing off, my mind jolting. I pictured my father, pictured his smile. His birthday was always a particularly cruel event for those so unfortunate as to have been born without a talent or a penchant.

Some of the things I'd seen. The things he'd made them do, while his children and his generals and his friends watched, laughing. Those poor wretches lining the gardens, set on fire, used as human torches to illuminate the path. They were the ones shown mercy compared to the others.

I shivered, closing my eyes for a moment, trying to dislodge the picture. In a shaking voice, I continued.

"And so I ripped my father's mind from his very skull. Yes, I did that. I ripped his mind, like plucking an eyeball from a socket. Of course, that wasn't the full plan. The Endeavor started killing. The bullets that hit my father roused a cheer. They didn't know they were shooting an empty husk.

"Already, I had his mind in my grasp, already I carried it and... and... I placed it in the safest place possible. The one person my father knew they wouldn't kill."

Annie breathed slowly. "Your brother?"

"Napoleon, exactly. Annie, he's not alone down there. My father is in his mind. The tyrant of the Imperium, Grand Imperial Maximus Rex still lives. The Mutilator, some called him. The Merchant of Death, others said. He's in my brother's mind, where I put him. Where I hid him."

I shook my head, my voice trembling now, shaking along with my fingers as I stared at the ground between my legs, eyes gaping, tracing the patterns of torchlight cast along my knees.

"No one else knows," I murmured. "No one. My secret. My father's secret. If anyone knew, if the Imperium found out, they'd free my brother. They'd resurrect my father into another, more able body. It was the plan all along. Secrecy was vital, though. He told me to tell his generals, especially Augustus, once things settled. But I never did. After placing my father's mind, I leapt from the balcony, saving my own skin. I knew they wouldn't kill Napoleon. He was only four. Even the Endeavor have to worry about optics sometimes. The Ardent Gazette wasn't as influential then, but still active. Fat good it would do to their claim of a new rule if they baptized it in the blood of a child."

I scoffed. "And so they dragged him, little Napoleon Rex. They brought him here, buried him deep, then threw away the key. Not a threat. They plan to kill him anyway, when he comes of age at sixteen.

"Little did they know, my father's mind is dormant, hidden in Napoleon, waiting to be brought back, to be given its own, unoccupied body. My father didn't want to be stuck in the shell of a four-year-old. He didn't envision being kept for a decade, locked away..."

"But you didn't tell anyone?" Annie whispered.

"No. I didn't. How could I? He was my father. But he was also a murderer. A psychopath. But if I freed my brother, then it would become apparent. All it would take is one Wit, Annie. A single mind reader to pick up on what lurked beneath his thoughts."

"Maybe... maybe it didn't work?" Annie said. "Maybe your father died."

I shook my head firmly. "I was young, but powerful. I knew what I was doing. I'm certain of it."

"How certain? Maybe your father died. I've never heard anything like this before. Two minds in one body... How is that possible?"

"Very possible. Only one active mind... The second one dormant, hidden, safe, protected as long as the host lives. Like a virus, incubating, waiting to break out and take control."

"But he hasn't? Napoleon is still there?"

"Last I came, yes... My brother is in full control. My father's mind is still stuck, somewhere hidden, buried where I left it, like a skeleton beneath floorboards. But now don't you see, Annie? I have to kill him. I can't let Napoleon out. Not now. If I don't kill him, Maximus Rex will walk free. The Imperium will rise again. Thousands more will die. He always wanted to take control of the unknowings too. The mortal realms. The world itself would be in jeopardy under his rule. He'd use them like cattle, like slaves, like sport."

"Stop, stop..." Annie said, holding up a hand and shivering. "It's all so horrible."

I nodded, shaking my head softly. "It's exactly that. Horrible. But what other choice is there, Annie. I can't leave him down here. Someone will eventually find out. And I can't free him—my father will escape. He'll find a way. He always does."

"Leon. You can't kill your baby brother."

"I can't avoid it."

Annie stared at me, lips pressed together. "I... I came here to kill February... I wish I had... But she deserved it. She's like your father. She deserved it. But Leon, listen to me..." Her eyes were hard. "I was taken from the palace about the same age as your brother. I know what it is to sleep in darkness for years. You did wrong by Napoleon. Now you have to make it right."

"How?" I said desperately. "My father has had a decade to leech into every crevice of my brother's mind. He's linked now. Napoleon's life is as much my father's as it is my brother's."

"You can't kill him."

"I have to."

"Well, then go alone. I'll stay here, waiting for you. But I won't be party, Leon. No. You just can't."

I puffed a breath, blowing air and watching the torch flicker above. Annie didn't understand. She'd been locked up at the age of five, before she'd even seen exactly what my father was capable of. I thought of those faces, those accusing eyes on the corkboards in the bars of Picker's Lake. Of other small towns. Entire family lines hunted down to the third generation, grandmothers, children, fathers, uncles, brothers, aunts, sisters, friends, favorite teachers—anyone who would challenge his rule. He wouldn't just kill upstarts, but everyone they ever knew; their immediate families first, while they watched, then others soon after. Many of them taken as slaves or worse. The lucky ones died quickly.

Never Forget.

I never would.

Annie didn't understand. Now wasn't the time for cowardice. It had already cost me, two years ago. Now was the time for action. I had no gun, this time. But I did have the shield. I remembered how it sprang open like a guillotine.

I ground my teeth together, pressing hard. The more I thought about it, the worse it got. Best not to think. Best to simply do.

I pushed back up, angrily stomping away from Annie, towards the curling stairs and stepping into the dark, circling down to the deeper levels, to the lower dungeons of the Hollow.

Chapter 56

I left a bloody footprint on the final step of the curling staircase as I exited onto a familiar platform. I shivered as I stared across the walkway over the abyss. The room before me was round, and wide, as long as some football stadiums.

Except instead of grass and painted white lines, the surface of the circle fell away. I found myself staring into an endless abyss, as dark as tar, gouged into the floor of the entire room.

I swallowed, nervously shifting as I stared off the edge of the chasm. I kicked a stone, watching it tumble and disappear. I waited, counting, listening for the quiet tap from below.

It never came.

I didn't know how far the abyss went. When I'd first researched the Hollow, I'd been told this particular room had once been the vineyard for genie treasure. The abyss, it was said, descended all the way to the Earth's core, from where the living gemstones leeched their sustenance.

But now, there were no gemstones. No genie plants. Only dark walls and a sheer drop.

And a single wooden walkway, like a dock over dark waters.

This walkway extended from one end of the chasm to the other, a thin, wooden-planked affair, with no railing to speak of. Memories surfaced of my first sojourn across the bridge, sprinting, trying to outrun pursuers, to outrun my own choices...

Now, though, no one chased me.

Annie stayed upstairs, waiting...

She refused to be party to what I had to do... But her refusal didn't change anything.

I swallowed, stepping onto the creaking walkway above the chasm. Little more than a rope bridge minus the ropes. The boards creaked and swayed with each hesitant step. My bare foot scraped against the rough wood. As I walked, though, I did my best not to glance to my right or left into the endless fall. My remaining shoe squished and squelched from the water damage in the rubber that soaked through my sock and squished between my toes.

At the other end of the walkway, I spotted the single, solitary cell.

The sons of Maximus Rex even had private accommodations in captivity.

They'd put Napoleon in a spiked cage, wide enough so he could exercise. The cage centered a small wooden platform built into the chasm wall on the opposite end. The walkway led up to it, so guards, on occasion, or, more often, some of the lesser prisoners, could shuttle food and supplies down when needed.

Otherwise, Napoleon had little in the way of conversation. Though he did have a single bookshelf, visible in the dark.

As I strolled across the bridge, my eyes fixed on the chasm ceiling far above... This was no way to live, down in the dark like this, with only strained sunlight coming through cracks in the ceiling on cloudless days.

I found my breathing labored as I stalked across the walkway. My foot hurt, and I winced... maybe it was best I take a break.

"No..." I growled to myself. "No more stalling. Man up."

I cursed and ground my teeth, closing my hands into fists and moving with renewed energy across the swaying, creaking bridge, ignoring the chasm drop on either side, my eyes fixed on the cage.

As I drew nearer, though, the memories returned again...

"Leonidas," my brother's voice had probed the dark. "Is that you?"

The sheer hope in his tone, the desperate, desperate hope still cut me deeper than any scar I'd been given. I wondered what he'd thought in that moment, when I'd turned and ran. He'd recognized me and I'd fled. He'd pleaded after me, and I'd left him in the dark.

And now...

Now I'd returned for worse.

I paused, unable to simply will myself forward, one foot in front of the other, my bloody footprint seeping into the plank behind me. I stared at the bars of my little brother's prison, my eyes probing the dark, trying to seek out his huddled form.

"Nap?" I called, my voice croaking. "Nap, are you there?"

No answer came...

"Napoleon Rex!" I called, louder now, taking another tentative step forward. The floorboards creaked and swayed beneath me. Two of them had molded through, giving me a glimpse of an infinite plummet beneath the precarious wood. I shivered, staring for a moment into the sheer dark.

I glanced over my shoulder. The stairway was still empty. Annie was upstairs. No one else had followed. It was just me and some bars and my brother.

"Napoleon," I tried again.

For a faint moment, I spotted a shadow shift in the far corner of the cell. My throat went suddenly dry. I stared at the spot. "Napoleon?" I said softly.

Stop calling his name! A voice screamed in my mind. Was I trying to make this harder on myself than it needed be?

I had to do it...

I had to.

The Greater Good.

I ground my teeth together, stomping the rest of the way across the bridge and stepping off onto the larger platform holding the cage.

I froze, though, frowning now.

The cell door was open.

I stared at the gap in the metal and took a tentative step forward.

The door to my brother's cell had been left ajar, about three inches. I peered through the bars now, but it was dark out, and no sunlight came through the cracks above; only bits and streaks of moon and stars glimpsed through slits in the mountain top.

I winced, peering towards the shadow I'd seen.

"Napoleon?" I murmured softly.

I reached out a trembling hand, my fingers touching the cool of the metal. Something wet against my thumb. I pulled my hand away, staring.

Blood.

I reached higher up the frame, avoiding the crimson stain, and pushed the door open completely. Then I stepped into my brother's decade old cell.

Napoleon was there, his eyes closed, his small chest rising slowly up and down. He had the same sandy-blonde hair I remembered from his youth. His cheeks were paler than my olive complexion and his nose upturned. Small-framed glasses perched on his nose which was thin like the rest of him. He was also missing his left arm, a birth defect. Perhaps one of the reasons our father hadn't pushed him as hard as the rest of us. What good was a one-armed soldier?

Napoleon wasn't alone.

I went stiff, staring into the dark, catching the glimmer of gold above my brother's head.

Grendel stared back at me from where he had his arms wrapped around my brother. He sat with his back to the cage, my brother reclining against his chest. Grendel embraced my brother in his lap, leering over his head.

"We've been awaiting you," Grendel said quietly. He held a half-gloved finger to his lips and shushed. "Careful. Don't wake the boy. He's only just drifted off."

My back prickled, and I stood frozen in the caged doorway. Horror and fury competed for dominance, but fizzled out in a whimper to a far greater emotion: guilt. I'd never wanted anyone to see... to know. Telling Annie was costly enough, but an enemy of mine? An enemy so close to the bleached bone skeletons in my darkest closest. I shivered in horror. All of this, though, I pushed aside, refusing to let my emotions spark. With the likes of Grendel, I should have known there'd be no victory. There's no winning against someone trying to make the world a worse place; such interactions are measured only by degree of loss on both sides. "Grendel," I said in a would-be casual tone, my voice croaking. "Nice to see you made it."

I hated the way his hands gripped my little brother's shoulders. Hated the way his eyes flashed above his head. Hated how defenseless I felt in that moment to do anything...

Do what, though? Grendel was threatening the very thing I'd come to destroy...

I began to shake my head in sheer disbelief.

"Now, now, Leonidas. I've outplayed you. Admit it." Grendel chuckled, bobbing his head up and down. "One as like of I must often consider the moves of an opponent in degrees. Why, I ask myself, involve yourself with the assassin. Why go to the Hollow at all?" He leered and whispered, as if into my little brother's ear. "For Napoleon Rex, of course... It didn't take me long to find out. Your brother... Such a wee little boy." He gave Napoleon a soft shake. My brother's head shifted to the side, his eyes still closed behind his glasses, his chest still rising and falling, very slowly.

"Grendel," I growled.

"No, no, don't wake him," the bounty hunter said, shaking his head quickly. "Here's what I'd like you to do... You want your little brother. I understand. Truly. I once cared for others myself. I know the feelings..." He paused, but then nodded, doubling down. "At least, I remember them."

"Grendel, you're two steps behind on this one, friend."

"Silence!" he screamed, jabbing a finger at me. Nap's eyelids fluttered for a moment, his head lifted. His eyes seemed to flit, and he murmured, "Leonidas?" But then he closed his eyes again, leaning back against Grendel's shoulder.

My brother's voice. Very much his voice. Even in just that word, I remembered it. It had haunted me for two years...

No. A lie.

For ten.

"Leonidas, here's what I want. See that lovely little abyss behind you? That big old tumble and fall?"

I glanced back if only to humor him. "Hard to miss," I replied through tight teeth.

"Yes, well... I'd like you to be so kind as to take a dive." Grendel wagged his head as if agreeing with his own words. "It's the only way your brother gets out of this, see." He gave a little wiggle of his finger over the left side of my brother's chest. "Cross my heart and all. I give you my word, Leonidas, as a Kindred, give you my oath on Caliban that if you throw yourself, then I will guarantee his safety. I will deliver him myself, personally, to wherever it is you'd like me to take him."

Grendel smiled now, nodding as if he'd presented a particularly nice construction paper project for a parent's fridge.

I stared. "And if I don't jump?"

"Well, I would have thought the answer was obvious. I'll kill your brother, and I'll hunt you down anyway."

"It seems like you're not so confident on that hunting part."

Grendel glared. "You're a slippery customer, Leonidas. What can I say? Take this hostage situation as a compliment."

I shook my head, rubbing my jaw. "You're funny, you know that," I said. "Your offer only makes my life easier."

Grendel frowned, but just watched me, waiting.

I leaned against the cage now, my eyes slipping from Grendel to my brother's sleeping, bespectacled face then back.

The Kindred had offered me a way out. I only had to refuse now... a simple refusal and he'd do the dirty work for me. I might not be able to outrun him, but if I brought him to Annie, I was sure the two of us together, even with our injuries, might be able to give Grendel a run for his money. Especially seeing as he was alone, and, judging by the blood-slicked door, injured as well.

Grendel had offered me a kingly gift and he didn't even know it.

I shook my head in disbelief...

So why... then... wasn't I saying anything? I should have refused. I should have turned and ran. All it would take was a quick slice of his claws. My brother was sleeping. What could be more merciful than that?

Leonidas?

I winced against the single recollected word from my brother's sleepy voice.

"Well?" Grendel snapped. "Take the tumble, heir. I never took you for a coward."

At these words, I couldn't help myself, I began to laugh. A deep, aching bellow bursting suddenly from my lips and shaking through the air. I clapped a hand against the metal bars and laughed some more.

I wagged a blood-stained finger now, pointing it towards the Kindred. "You're funny, you know that?" I said. "You don't know how funny you are."

Grendel growled. "I'll kill him, Leonidas. I've killed younger for less."

"I know you will. That's what makes it all so ridiculous!" Now I was shouting, my arms spread as if to embrace the cage itself. A single, hard cot lay wedged in one corner. A small bookshelf in the other, the bindings, even from here, seeming well worn. "These things can never be easy, can they? Hmm? I'd made my mind up before seeing you. Really, I had..."

"Leonidas..."

"No, I'm being serious. I'd made a choice. I'd come here to fulfill it and there I see you; your stupid, stained suit and your ugly little hat with your greasy, dirty paws wrapped around my skinting brother!" I shouted now, spittle frothing from my lips with a rising rage. "That's my baby brother! That's my brother! Don't you understand! I won't let you hurt him! I should have refused you the first time! I won't—not for you, not for anyone, not again!"

Grendel blinked, seemingly taken aback. "I... Again? What are you talking about?"

I shook my head, my breathing softening for a moment. "I... I don't know... I don't know, Grendel."

Leonidas? Is that you?

I closed my eyes against the memory. Such small, simple words. Words full to the brim, though, topped with hope. How could such a small child, in this deepest pit of despair, with no one for company, no family, no friends, no love... how could he afford the cost of hope?

He'd seen me. And the hope had come springing up like mountain water from some sudden stream...

Hope.

How dare he hope?

How dare any of us?

How dare I kill it?

I stared at my brother now. He slept so peacefully, so quietly. My father's mind was somewhere in there, buried. A stark contrast to the slumbering child if ever there was one.

But why did every skinting thing have to be about daddy dearest? Wasn't there anything he didn't touch? Anything he didn't ruin?

Grendel growled. "Leonidas?"

"You see," I said, voicing my thoughts loudly now. "I can't... I'm lying to myself if I pretend I can. I can't. You know it. I do. I'm not like you!" I screamed. "I want nothing to do with you. You made us like this. You turned us on each other. You broke us. I don't want you. I don't want to be like you... Greater good!" I spat. "Forget the greater good. Maybe if people stopped caring so much about the bloody greater good, they might accidentally stumble upon doing the right thing."

"Leonidas, what are you talking about? I will cut his little neck."

"I suppose you might. And... I suppose..." I glanced back towards the stairwell, towards where Annie had remained behind, refusing to come with me. And yet staying upstairs... Staying because she didn't want to see the dirty work? Or staying because she thought I might not?

Just another little glimmer of hope.

Hope that Leonidas Rex wasn't the monster everyone thought he was—wasn't the monster he was made to be.

Leonidas? Is that you?

"I suppose..." I said at last, scowling. "I suppose I can't let you hurt him."

Grendel looked completely confused at this point. His frown deepened and he gave a little flourishing wave of his fingers now, as if ushering me out the door.

"Are you mad? Have those genies rubbed off on you, savant? Enough time wasting." He growled, now gripping my brother's throat in dusty, dirty fingers. "Jump from the ledge. Jump or he dies. Do it now. Now!"

I held my hands up, shrugging.

"You win," I murmured. "I can't do it. I was never as strong as him. I wasn't built to lead armies and nations, I suppose. Let him live. That's your promise?"

Grendel's golden eyes strained over my brother's shoulder where their heads pressed against the bars above the cot. He nodded, once, both golden eyes bobbing like buoys in the ocean.

"My word," he said, in a strained voice.

"Fine," I replied. "Look. See. I jump."

I turned with a light step... In fact, I don't remember the last time I moved so unencumbered. I smiled as I did, facing the dark abyss, the inevitable plummet. I wondered would the rocks hurt more after the final crash, or would, eventually, a body find magma in the center of the earth, flesh stripped from bone by searing heat...

Such lovely options before me.

I glanced back.

Perhaps what lay before wasn't as important as what was behind.

Or maybe I was just overthinking it.

Grendel rose cautiously to his feet and dragged my brother along with him. He kept a grip around Napoleon's neck, carrying him as if he were little more than a rag doll. He must have given my brother something, or struck him, because Napoleon continued to slumber, his small chest rising and falling in shallow gasps.

"Your word," I repeated, eyes hard now. "No more hunting my friends. You leave the boy unharmed."

Grendel wagged his head, hungrily now. "Yes, yes. Get on with it. No tricks, Leonidas. Jump. If you don't, if you run, if you charge me, any of it—I will crush his windpipe and throw him into the abyss."

As if to prove the point, Grendel took a step out of the cage onto the walkway, angling my brother over the drop off and gripping his wrist tight. Grendel's eyebrows rose to meet the brim of his top hat. "Go, little dove. Dive for me."

I put a finger to my forehead in a mock salute. "I love you, little brother," I said softly. "I should have realized that sooner." My voice felt stuck in my throat. "Goodbye," I whispered.

Then I jumped off the edge into the abyss.

Chapter 57

Three things happened. Two of them predictable, one of them less so. One must improvise in situations such as these.

Even as I jumped, my fingers had probed towards the final solitary tiger's eye left in my pocket. This time, if Kay had given me a bad batch, I was dead.

But what's life without a little bit of luck.

I dove over the wooden platform, twisting as I did and launching the tiger's eye up, hard!

At the same time, Grendel pulled my brother back, leaning forward himself, golden eyes glinting at the top of the chasm as if he couldn't quite believe I'd actually done it. I could even see his teeth flashing into a grin, watching me plummet, down, down...

Then...

The tiger's eye smashed on the platform behind Grendel.

I felt a hook in my stomach, a sinking sensation and then I teleported up and back towards where the tiger's eye had landed.

Now, I was behind Grendel. He continued to stare, and I could hear him chuckling as he leaned over the edge, peering into the chasm.

I took two skipping steps behind my nemesis, the shield sprouting from my wrist as I did. And then I swung the Lancelot shield like a guillotine at Grendel's wrist, bringing it down hard where his fingers still held my little brother's only working arm.

Grendel screamed, whirling about but losing his grip on my brother.

I wasn't done. I brought the shield around, spinning, and this time slammed it into Grendel's face. He howled, arms flailing, and then he toppled, falling. Even as he plummeted, I watched him transform, his figure shifting, fur sprouting, a muzzle with many teeth protruding. He twisted about, trying to reshape, reform as he fell... fell... fell.

Soon, I could no longer hear him scream.

And then, exhaling so loudly I thought my chest might give out, I collapsed to my knees, staring down at my little brother's sleeping face. I reached out, stroking his cheek, and murmuring, "I'm sorry... I'm sorry... I'm sorry."

The words kept coming, and I couldn't seem to stop. The ashen black, skeletal pendant dangling from the chain around my neck slipped from my collar as I bent, waving towards my brother's sleeping face. I snarled, jamming the cursed thing back into my shirt. Then, my shoulders began to shake. "I'm sorry," I said, gasping. "So sorry." I sobbed...

My eyes were...

Wet.

I blinked, stunned. Tears fell from my eyelids, falling down and tapping like dewdrops against my baby brother's chin.

"I'm sorry... I'm sorry..." I continued, gasping for air, and then suddenly like a dam being burst, I bent over my little brother's form, leaning across him like a mother sheltering her young on that fragile wooden bridge.

And I wept.

I'd never cried before... I wasn't sure what it might feel like.

And in that moment, I wasn't sure my feelings mattered at all.

I just cried, and I cried, holding my little brother, lifting him and holding him tight. I could feel his chest still rising softly and then... in my ear, I heard a soft whisper of a voice. "Leonidas. Brother? Is that you?" Napoleon said, his voice frail. Then his head lolled again, and he drifted off.

I wept all the more.

That's where Annie eventually came and found me, bent over my brother, covering him in my tears. Tears too late, perhaps. Tears impotent, unable to restore what had been lost. What I had cost him.

Annie whispered softly, shushing me, stroking my shoulder. With tender motions, she helped me to my feet, balancing my brother between the two of us. Careful, like holding all the treasure in the world, we escorted my brother back and up the cut stone steps, up the torch-illuminated halls.

I knew the way out from there... The same route through the sewers I'd taken before. Threshold Seals only prevented entry. They didn't prevent exit.

And so, at my instructions, limping, carrying my unconscious little brother, Annie and I navigated through the dusty halls.

We reached what looked to be a vault door with steel a foot thick. Swallowing, I reached into my shirt, pulling out the cold, iron key around the leather thong we'd recovered from back in the Librarian's mansion. I handed the key to Annie, watching as she turned it in the giant door which led to the sewers. The door clicked open and groaned on rusted hinges, allowing us down. Even the smells didn't shake me from my tears.

They kept coming, streaking my cheeks. A lifetime of tears, a lifetime of burden.

I carried my little brother with the help of Annie.

I wasn't a man meant to lead a nation. An heir though I was, the only burden I was suited for was this. Carrying my brother. And even in that, I needed help.

We moved through the dark sewers, beneath the Hollow, following the trail out... out... Through the old bolt hole I'd left in the grate the last time I'd been through. Out into the small clearing of woods.

"Preacher," I said softly... "Preacher, over here!"

My tall, musclebound companion was leaning against one of the trees, his eyes fixed on the trapdoor in the forest floor. As it rose, he hurried over, gesturing for us to hand Napoleon to him. Preacher lifted the boy, gently, carrying him in his arms with a surprising amount of care and caution.

Preacher glanced down at my brother, smiling and then looking at me, quirking an eyebrow. I couldn't help but notice my old friend didn't seem at all surprised to see the boy alive.

I winced, pushing up the last rung of the rusted metal ladder in the forest floor. I reached back, helping Annie out as well. My two friends and I stood in the forest outside the Hollow, each of us glancing from one to the other.

Preacher kept watching me, his eyes searching.

"I didn't solve it," I murmured, answering his unspoken question.

Preacher raised his eyebrows.

I shrugged. "I don't know. I'll have to keep an eye on him."

"I'll help," Annie murmured. She froze, glancing at me and adding, "If... if you let me." She winced then said, "I... I know you might not trust me. I get it. But I promise not to lie anymore. I promise."

Preacher was frowning now, but I glanced at him. "She saved my life," I murmured. "She gave up February to save my life." I turned back to my old friend. "It isn't easy out there on your own. Maybe you should come with us for a week or two. Just to recover or something... If you want, that is."

I glanced off, clearing my throat. When I looked back, though, Annie had tears in her eyes. She nodded quickly. "I'd like that," she said brusquely. "It's been a long time since... yes, well, yes, I'd like that."

We both, almost in unison, turned to look at my tall, musclebound friend.

We watched, waiting.

"She really did save my life," I murmured.

Preacher sighed, looking more at me than Annie, but at last, he shrugged then nodded once.

My chest exploded with joy and it took everything not to burst into song. Once a man with no human friends to speak of... now I had two.

Preacher cradled my little brother's head against his large arm, rocking him slowly back and forth. The scent of the trees lingered on the air, the warm nighttime breeze moving down through the branches, witnessed by the watchful moon.

"RV?" I asked.

Preacher nodded, careful not to jolt my brother too much.

He gestured with his shoulder, and then, the four of us, my brother in Preacher's arms, moved through the forest, heading towards the old trail. I just glimpsed the roof of my RV through the branches and undergrowth, along the path Preacher had already cleared.

"So," Annie murmured as we moved through the forest, our footsteps soft, our movements shallow. "About that druid friend of mine..."

I glanced at her, ruefully rubbing at the back of my head. "I mean... That was then." I glanced towards where Preacher carried my brother. "He's small and helpless. I'm going to need help keeping an eye on him," I said. "Also on Napoleon, too."

Preacher grunted, rolling his eyes up ahead. Annie's gaze twinkled.

I shrugged. "That druid... She can change my face, my identity?"

"All of it."

"But I couldn't see anyone again? Not Preacher? Not you? Not Paul? Or the Gallows children?"

She patted me affectionately on the arm. "Not any of them. It would be too easy to trace back to you. Still want me to set it up?"

I frowned, watching as Preacher reached the door to my RV first. He pushed it open gently, still cradling my brother in his large arms. He stepped into the cabin and moved towards the bedrooms. I paused, one hand braced against the frame of the RV, one foot still out in the dirt and the leaves.

"I... you kept saying something," I murmured. "Bound by none..."

"Bound to none," Annie said. "I remember."

I rolled my eyes. "A bit heavy handed, but point taken. I get it. I need people. We all need people." I shook my head.

Annie, though, gave a good-natured laugh, staring at me for a moment, her twinkling eyes illuminated by a rising moon. She shook her head mirthfully, patting me on the shoulder. "Oh, Leon. No... Not that you need people, though perhaps that's true too, but that people need you. The distinction is crucial."

Then, she stepped past me into the RV, shaking her head as she did. She whisked away towards the front of the RV, leaving me confused and strangely happy.

I supposed the identity changing druid would have to wait after all. Maybe in a few years... Once Napoleon was steady and once I found a way to extricate the poison I'd put in his mind. My father was still dormant, trapped. My brother would have to be watched, protected, guarded. I'd have to make sure no Wits got near him, no Imperium. Then, I'd have to figure out how to remove Maximus... permanently. Was there a way? If my powers came back... Perhaps. Even then, I'd have to find a method, practice it like a surgeon acclimating to a scalpel.

But I'd made my choice. We were all endangered by my decision. But Napoleon, at least for now, was safe.

That would have to be enough.

***

Preacher took the first shift driving. I sat in the passenger side, peering out the window, watching the mountains and trees and dipping valleys along the old roads. Annie sat on the floor next to my seat, leaning back, her head resting against my thigh, her eyes closed as she slept.

Preacher kept one hand on the wheel, but the other held up a small clam-shell mirror as he examined his face, closed the mirror, and applied a streak of pink blush beneath his eyes. As always, he used quick, sloppy motions as if applying the makeup with the hands of a child.

I glanced into the rearview mirror, peering at the second reflector we'd placed in the hall, angled so it could share the reflection of my bed. Nap slept against my pillows, his eyes closed, a dash of his blond hair fluttering with the breeze whipping through the old room.

A faint whisper of a smile crossed my lips as Preacher closed his mirror a second time, steadied the RV on the old roads, then reached for some lipstick, humming softly as he did.

I looked over, sharply. "You're humming!"

Preacher frowned, shook his head, continuing to apply his lipstick.

"Yes! You were. I heard you! Your vow of silence is over!"

Preacher rolled his eyes.

I smirked. "It counts."

Preacher shook his head.

"Does too."

He shook his head more adamantly now.

"Fine... but it counts."

He reached out, smearing lipstick along the side of my face, down my ear and into my beard. Now it was his turn to smirk, placing the tube back in his makeup bag, stowing it in the glove compartment and returning his attention to the old mountain roads.

I glared at the side of my friend's face as I rubbed the lipstick off my cheek and wiped it on the back of Annie's head. Perhaps not the most dignified of scenes, but sometimes I forget my manners. Forget the expectations.

Preacher glanced between the two of us, his lips straining out a delighted, mischievous smile. He pointed at me, then made a slitting motion across his neck.

I winced, my finger hovering where I'd wiped the lipstick. "You're right. She might kill me. I'll blame you."

He scowled.

"She doesn't know sign language. Yes, I'll blame you. Serves you right."

Annie shifted a bit, snuggling against my leg, her head resting on my thigh. I glanced again in the mirror and for the faintest moment I thought I glimpsed a smile on my baby brother's face where he lay on my bed, his round glasses glinting in the moonlight through the window.

Preacher was humming again, softly—a song I knew well. I smiled, the lyrics echoing in my mind along with the faint tune. *Country roads... Take me home... To the place...*

It bothers me that even without speaking my mute friend wins most our arguments.

But other times, like tonight, I just lean back, staring out the window, watching the mountains and forests and swishing rivers pass us by, humming along with my friend. I roll down the window, just a bit, and I inhale the fresh air beneath the watchful moon.

In the distance, though, echoing in the mountains, there reverberates a soft, almost inaudible sound I ignore. It starts as a whisper through the trees, then a rattle of branches and a whir of wheels on dusty roads.

But the call, the invitation extends through the dark, under the cover of night.

An invitation to all the knowing. An invitation to a bloody celebration.

The whisper of wind, rattle of branches almost seems to morph, to move, to rearrange.

A chant of voices, vibrating through the wilderness, the forests and the lost places of the world.

You can't kill bloody death. It comes for you all.

I almost detected the skeletal leer of ebony skulls in the shadows of the trees.

You can't kill bloody death. It comes for you all.

I shivered, pulling my hat low over my eyes.

Ares' birthday tournament would be the spectacle of the century. I'd just have to make sure to give it a wide berth, avoiding it entirely.

After all, I'd be an imbecile to tangle with a god of war.

The End

The story continues with Book 2 – available now!

Augustus Rex is on the hunt for his brother. Illusionist, Leonidas Rex knows he can't escape capture for much longer. He plans one final job before getting out of Dodge.

A prison break to rival all others.

Leonidas Rex, the once-prince, sets out to save a genie from Ares' gladiatorial birthday tournament. Facing monsters aplenty, in the heart of a thrice-cursed battle arena, Leonidas Rex hopes the aid of the marksman Preacher and the assassin November will be enough to outwit a god of war.

Other books by Joseph Daniel

The currents sweep east, but the dead float south. This corpse laden tide carries with it the destinies of a tomb raider, a knight turned captain, and an empire fraying at the seams.

A grave robber who dabbles in the alchemical arts, Edmond Mondego has spent the last seven years in search of a God Grave. He hopes to find magic within to relinquish his murdered wife's soul to the land of the living. What he finds instead is an imprisoned goddess stripped of her power but in full possession of divine secrets, including a rumor: every five years, one living soul is returned to the Emperor of the Gilded Islands.

Meanwhile, the Lord Captain Augustin Mora, newly appointed commander of His Imperial Majesty's Ship Intrepid, guards the forbidden waters for his Emperor. Edmond's profane plundering of a God Grave and the machinations of the admiralty send Augustin on a quest to capture the tomb robber. But an enemy from his past muddies the waters, and Augustin is forced to reunite his old knight's guild and put hand to hilt once again.

And so, Edmond sets every ounce of cunning and guile to raise himself through the ranks of nobility, evading Augustin Mora and all manner of assassins; he has only one goal—to convince the Emperor to use the magical boon for his wife's soul, and, failing that, to take the throne for himself.

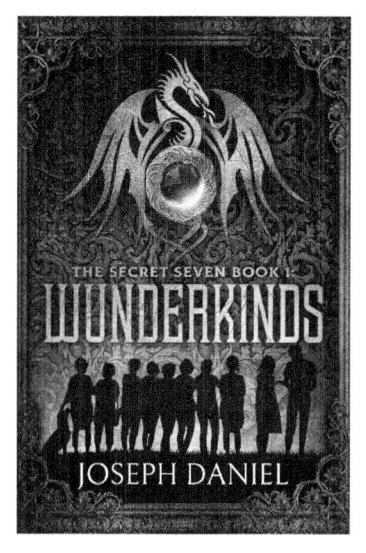

All the best parts of Percy Jackson, Artemis Fowl, and Harry Potter in one series of Books!

Complete series

Ten children taught themselves the ancient arts, unknowingly surpassing the greatest mages in the land. Then the wizards from the Academy came to town, but not on a recruitment mission. They were there to hunt rogue mages.

In a world filled with magic, practiced only by those authorised to do so, ten children have chosen to teach themselves the ancient arts just to see if they can. It's harmless, right?

Wrong.

Their use of magic has been detected. Official inquisitors, wizards by training and name, descend on their quiet community hunting for rogue mages.

The children don't know it, but their innocent tinkering has set in motion a series of events that will change the whole world, and they are standing on the brink of war.

Printed in Great Britain
by Amazon